10|11

BY C. E. MURPHY

THE WORLDWALKER DUOLOGY

Truthseeker

Wayfinder

THE INHERITORS' CYCLE

The Queen's Bastard

The Pretender's Crown

THE WALKER PAPERS

Urban Shaman

Thunderbird Falls

Coyote Dreams

Walking Dead

Demon Hunts

Spirit Dances

THE OLD RACES UNIVERSE:

The Negotiator Trilogy:

Heart of Stone

House of Cards

Hands of Flame

THE STRONGBOX CHRONICLES:
written as Cate Dermody

The Cardinal Rule

The Firebird Deception

The Phoenix Law

WITH MERCEDES LACKEY AND TANITH LEE

Winter Moon

Wayfinder

Wayfinder

C. E. MURPHY

BALLANTINE BOOKS ❧ NEW YORK

A Del Rey Books Trade Paperback Original

Copyright © 2011 by C. E. Murphy

Published in the United States by Del Rey, an imprint of The Random House Publishing Group, a division of Random House, Inc., New York.

DEL REY is a registered trademark and the Del Rey colophon is a trademark of Random House, Inc.

ISBN 978-0-345-51607-7
eISBN 978-0-345-52926-8

Printed in the United States of America

www.delreybooks.com

9 8 7 6 5 4 3 2 1

Book design by Caroline Cunningham

For Silkie

Once upon a time . . .

In the city of Boston, there was a tailor who could not be told a lie. Even the most honest of men couldn't offer Lara Ann Jansen so much as an insincere compliment without her knowing the truth of it. It was the bane of her existence—until a handsome weatherman recognized it for the gift it was, and named Lara a Truthseeker.

He had searched a hundred years to find her, a truth that no one else would believe. His name was Dafydd ap Caerwyn, and he was a prince of the Seelie courts: an elf. He needed Lara's help to find the man who had murdered his brother Merrick ap Annwn.

Both reluctant and eager, Lara agreed to join him in the Barrowlands, the world from which Dafydd came. No sooner did they arrive than they were attacked by nightwings, the night sky itself made into demonic creatures given life by magic. Together Lara and Dafydd fought the nightwings off, only to face a far greater threat: the anger of Dafydd's father, Emyr.

Emyr was resentful of a human's interference in his realm and more than eager to remind Dafydd that it had been his very own arrow that struck Merrick down. Afraid, and angry that Dafydd had misled her—oh, he had not *lied*; he was more careful than that, but neither had he told the whole truth—Lara fled the shining citadel that housed the Seelie people, and in the surrounding wood, found a blind poet.

Like Lara, the poet Oisín was mortal, though he had been within the Barrow-lands a very long time indeed. He shared a prophecy with her:

> *Truth will seek the hardest path*
> *measures that must mend the past.*
> *Spoken in a child's word*
> *changes that will break the world.*
> *Finder learns the only way*
> *worlds come changed at end of day.*

Armed with the prophecy, Lara faced Emyr again and forced a discovery none of them wanted: that Emyr's older son, Ioan, who had been for many years hostage to Emyr's oldest enemy Hafgan, had embraced his adopted father's way of life and now rode against the Seelie people at the head of an army. It seemed Ioan was the likely culprit behind the magic that had forced Dafydd to murder Merrick.

At dawn, Lara, who had been just a tailor only the day before, rode with Dafydd's army to face their common enemy.

Cruel magic ripped them apart, sending Dafydd back to Boston and leaving Ioan the opportunity to kidnap Lara and her gifts for his own people, the Unseelie. But once within his domain, Lara forced the truth from Ioan: he had ruled in his adopted father Hafgan's name for aeons, and now sought a powerful staff called Worldbreaker, in hopes of regaining the Barrow-lands for the Unseelie.

Thanks to Oisín's prophecy, Lara knew the staff was meant for her hands. Determined that no Unseelie should wield it, she returned to Boston through use of a true path, a magic her growing power could now command.

To her horror, months had passed in her world. Worse, Dafydd ap Caerwyn, the last person to be seen with her, had been jailed for kidnapping and possible murder, charges he had not denied. As were all the Seelie, Dafydd was allergic to iron, and was very ill when Lara rescued him from prison. Only a link to the Barrow-lands, such as the worldbreaking staff, would return him to health. Lara, whose love for the Seelie prince had grown strong, was ever-more determined to find the staff and heal Dafydd.

Just as hope seemed at hand, the nightwing monsters from the Barrow-lands attacked in Lara's world, binding themselves together to become a many-headed hydra. Dafydd and Lara fought them off, but at great cost: Dafydd's strength was drained utterly, and Lara was forced to turn to Ioan for help in returning Dafydd to the Barrow-lands, where he might yet survive.

Angry and afraid again—but this time afraid of losing Dafydd forever—Lara hunted down the man who had brought the nightwings to her world. To her shock, it was Merrick, Dafydd's brother, who had staged his own death as part of a power play within the Barrow-lands. He retreated to his own world, and Lara Jansen, resolved to uncover all the hidden truths, follows him. . . .

Wayfinder

One

Music tore the world apart.

There was no rhythm to it, no melody to find, no predictable rise or fall in the thundering notes. Instead it was the sound of instruments at war with one another, screeching and bellowing as they strove to be heard. Lara Jansen stumbled under the cacophony, battered by it from all sides, and wondered what had gone wrong. She had traveled between worlds twice before—once under her own power, which should have been impossible. Even then, though, the pathway between her home and the elfin world called the Barrow-lands hadn't been fraught with agonizing, aggressive music.

But the worldwalking spell distorted the very weft of the universe. It was a magic not meant to be: her world and the Barrow-lands were barely meant to touch, much less to be traversed regularly. That was a truth she knew in her bones, in the same way she'd always known whether she was being lied to. Falsehood had rung sour notes in her mind as far back as she could remember, and that gift now said that the magic which thrust her between worlds was dangerously wrong.

Worse, the staff she carried reverberated in her hands, its ivory carvings bright with power that could break worlds. Its presence clearly distorted the spell further, as if the Barrow-lands, a world of magic, struggled to keep the weapon's destructive ability away.

The music surrounding her surged, stringed instruments breaking with groaning snaps, keyboards playing flat and sharp with desperation. A vocalist joined the music in Lara's mind, searching for a harmony until her voice turned to an unholy shriek. It finally shattered, and Lara fell between worlds to land hard in the Barrow-lands.

Music turned to the sounds of battle: to cries of pain and anger, to the metallic clash of blades, and to the incessant rumble of hooves against packed earth. A singular, voluble curse shot out above the rest of the uproar. Lara cowered as hooves flashed over her head, a horse's belly looking broad and endless above her. There was no time for panic, just for a single terrified lurch of her heart that twisted into unexpected awe. She'd seen animals leap cameras in film, but the effect paled beside actually having a thousand pounds of horseflesh sail overhead.

No one, she thought, no one in her right mind would take time out from being nearly trampled to think how poorly cinema compared to reality in such situations. And because truth was her gift, and lies came hard to her, it seemed likely that in that moment, she was very probably *not* in her right mind.

Nothing else would explain why she scrambled to her feet, using the staff as leverage, and whipped to face an oncoming army. A rear vanguard, given the sounds of fighting that came from behind her, but still enough to be called an army. They rode across ruined earth, meadow flattened into green-streaked dirt, fresh clods ripping free to offer a loamy scent that counteracted the tang of blood in the air. The riders wore armor of moonlight silver, sculpted and patterned so delicately it looked like it couldn't possibly withstand a single blow, much less the height of war. Lara knew better: she had worn a suit of the armor once, and for all its lightweight beauty, it was improbably strong as well. There was magic in its forging, as there seemed to be magic in every aspect of the Barrow-lands.

Cries of surprise rose up as the battle host swept to either side of her, leaving Lara a fixed point in a thundering wave of riders. Pale hues shot by: white, golden, strawberry blond hair streaming from beneath silver helmets; blue and green and yellow gazes glancing her way as the riders rushed past. Seelie warriors, so close that she felt horseflesh and body heat against her skin. Her heartbeat soared, fear so acute it became a kind of excitement.

The staff reacted to the emotion with an upsurge of its own, as if it had life and personality. She grasped it more firmly, half-formed thoughts rushing through her mind. It had sent tremors through her own world. She was certain that in this one, where it had come from, it was a force to be reckoned with.

Without fully considering her actions, Lara lifted the staff in both hands and slammed it end-down into the torn ground.

It groaned, waves rippling away from the epicenter she'd made. Discordant music erupted around her again, though this time she heard a thin true note buried in the sour tune. There was no time to follow it: keeping her feet took all her concentration, and the riders surging around her had no less trouble with their mounts. The sky boiled with a spiral of clouds, the staff's magic reaching as high as it did low. It urged destruction, eager to lash out with pain and, it seemed to Lara, vengeance. She tightened her hands, feeling the carvings press into her palms, and whispered to the cool ivory. "A truthseeker of legend could make things come true by force of will alone. You will not destroy the Barrow-lands while I wield you. I will temper your magic and guide it, and you will bend to my will. This is *true!*"

The words built to a crescendo in her mind, then released with a flood of pure song that roared across the staff's more static will. Strength surged from Lara so quickly that only her grip on the rod kept her upright, but the earth's rumbling ceased, and the skies stopped boiling. She put her forehead against the stave, feeling its objection to the limits she'd enforced, but certain her desire to do no harm had mitigated the staff's passion for destruction.

A fleeting thought crossed her mind: that the weapon was humoring her, and would only behave so long as doing so suited it. For anyone else, it would be a fanciful idea, but there was no inherent dissonance, suggesting there was truth to it.

That was a problem to be considered later. A voice broke through the other sounds of battle, and Lara lifted her gaze to find the man who bellowed *"Truthseeker!"* with such fury.

Emyr, king of the Seelie court, bore down on Lara with his sword bared and hatred raging in his cold blue gaze.

The part of her that had become bold in the past few weeks felt the impulse to stand her ground, to see if the Seelie king would swerve at the last moment. Pragmatism prevailed, though, and she ducked to the side, trusting Emyr's guards not to trample her. They scattered, avoiding her and giving him room to wheel his horse. Dirt flew from beneath its hooves as it charged her a second time. This time the guards scattered to avoid Emyr, and Lara found herself abruptly alone on broken earth, awaiting a fate she had no way to avoid.

Then another rider was between her and the king, so sudden, so close, that a collision between them should be impossible to avoid. Lara saw a glimpse of fresh anger cross Emyr's face before his horse gathered itself and leapt over the intrusive rider and Lara alike. Not effortlessly: it couldn't be effortlessly, not with the scant feet the beast had to prepare itself, not with the height it had to clear. But to Lara's eye it looked as though Emyr's mount had suddenly, carelessly, decided to ignore gravity, and by so choosing had ceased being in its thrall.

The crash with which it came down on her far side belied their apparent weightlessness. Soft earth gave way, the horse sinking to its ankles. Lara gasped in concern for the animal's well-being, but it barely stumbled as it continued forward, then came around again under Emyr's guidance.

"He'll ride you down." A gauntleted hand thrust itself into Lara's vision, fingers grasping in invitation. Lara heard the truth in the words and seized the offered hand, then shouted with surprise as the rider hauled her bodily upward. She caught a glimpse of white hair and green eyes, and then she was seated behind the rider and gasping with astonishment. Her savior, Aerin, owed her nothing, much less a lifesaving gesture—especially since the last time they'd seen one another, Lara had broken the Seelie woman's elegant nose.

"What audacity is this!" Emyr *did* ride them down, broadsiding Aerin's horse with his own. Lara shrieked and slammed one arm around Aerin's waist, holding on desperately while trying not to drop the staff. She had been horseback a countable number of times in her life. A second impact would dislodge her.

And Emyr knew it. He pulled his horse around, blade leveled at Lara, though his words were for Aerin. "The mortal is mine!"

"The mortal," Aerin replied with remarkable calm for a woman bellowing to be heard over the battle, "is our only chance at learning what's happened to your son and heir, my lord."

Dismay turned to a cold weight in Lara's stomach, beating back the heat of the day. Her whole purpose in returning to the Barrowlands was to make certain of Dafydd's safety. She hadn't even considered the possibility that something had gone wrong with the magic meant to bring him home. "Dafydd didn't make it back?"

Aerin half-turned in the saddle, giving Lara a cool look. "Dafydd ap Caerwyn disappeared on the battlefield this half-year ago, moments before you joined forces with the Unseelie heir."

"Joi—" Lara thunked her head forward, not caring that it met Aerin's cold silver armor. "You mean before he seized me. Or kidnapped me, more accurately. Not that it was actually Ioan..." She trailed off as the difficulty of explaining her adventures washed over her.

"Half a year," she said much more quietly. She had been torn from her own timeline when she'd traveled from the Barrow-lands back to Earth, but had hoped this journey might not have thrown time so badly askew. "Aerin, I have a lot—"

She broke off again, realizing it wasn't the Seelie warrior with whom she needed to speak. She straightened her spine and called for an unfamiliar form of address, putting as much deference into it as she could: "Your majesty, the last I knew, Dafydd was alive."

Not *well*: she couldn't go so far as to intimate that, not with her talent for truth-telling. But alive, and she hoped that would offer some reassurance. It had been enough for her, until Aerin's grim announcement that they hadn't seen him in months. Still, it was all she had, and she thrust burgeoning worry out of mind.

"I understand I have a lot of explaining to do. This obviously isn't the place to do it." She gestured at the battlefield, feeling a thrum of eagerness from the ivory staff she carried. It saw the potential for destruction in the surrounding war, and was willing to help express that potential to its fullest. Fingers tightening, she quelled it and turned her attention back to Emyr. "If I might beg clemency until the day's fighting is through, your majesty, so I can tell you what's happened under quieter circumstances..."

It wasn't cold. Six months may have passed, but the weather was as it had been when Lara left: clear, hot, beautiful. She'd passed from winter to late summer when she'd traveled to Earth under her own power, but what little she knew of the Barrow-lands made it seem possible that there was no winter season, only endless summer.

Summer or not, though, a cold front rolled over her as Emyr grew ever-more frigid. The king's element was ice. It imbued him even when he was at rest, his skin so pale its shadows were cool blue, and his hair silvered with it. She'd seen ice grow around his throne and up the walls of his chambers when he was angry. It now crept across muddy grass, turning stalks to crystalline streaks in the muck. Aerin's horse lifted an impatient foot and smacked it down amid crackling earth, and blew a frosty breath into the summer afternoon.

"Call my guard back," Emyr said after long moments. "Sound the retreat. Hafgan's army will not press the advantage. They are as weary as we, and it will cause worry that we fall back. I will hear what the truthseeker has to say."

Lara lowered her gaze and murmured "Thank you," an instant too early. Emyr spat his final words as though they were knives: "And if her answers are unsatisfactory, I will see her executed before dawn."

Two

The Seelie court had changed in the months she'd been gone. Months for them: it had been only weeks for Lara, though a more complex and busy few weeks than she could otherwise remember. But in that time something darker had come over the Barrow-lands.

They did not, as she expected, retreat to the pearlescent Seelie citadel hidden in deep oak forests. Instead there were encampments at the borders of the meadow, tall silken tents bright against the treeline. Bright until Aerin rode them closer, at least: then Lara could see the stains and worn points that spoke of travel and use. Their lifted spires and swooping peaks aflutter with bright banners were magnificent, but in places the banners were threadbare, and the cords that held tent doors open were yellowing with lack of care. In the hours Lara had spent with the Seelie, their penchant for maintaining unruffled beauty had impressed her. The small signs of deterioration struck her as symbolic of deeper fraying within their society.

Despite the threat hanging over her head—and there'd been no mistruth in Emyr's voice, making it credible—Lara laughed into Aerin's shoulder. She knew almost nothing about the Seelie. Certainly not enough to read meaning into details of well-worn battle gear, but she had, at home, studied psychology. It was difficult not to apply human psychoanalysis to an alien race.

Aerin pulled her helm off, sending threads of white hair around her face as she glowered over her shoulder at Lara. "Something amuses you?"

"Only my own arrogance. Aerin—" Half a dozen topics fought for precedence, and Lara settled on an apologetic, "I'm sorry for hitting you. I completely misunderstood what was happening that day. I thought you'd driven Dafydd into the Unseelie army on purpose. That you were a traitor." An echo of the horror she'd felt then came back to her, feeding on her new concern for Dafydd. Lara clenched her teeth, fighting it down. She needed to be clearheaded now, not tangled with emotion. Struggling for something nonconfrontational to say, she blurted, "Your nose looks all right."

Aerin's mouth thinned. "I gathered that was your assumption, when you ordered me arrested. All Seelie have some talent for healing themselves. I've come away from greater injuries unscathed."

"Recently?"

A spasm crossed Aerin's face. Rather than answer, she urged their horse forward again, guiding it through the encampment until they reached what was unmistakeably Emyr's tent. No larger than the others, its fabric walls were sheened blue, as though glacier ice had touched them, and the snapping banner that flew from its peak showed the white citadel in outline. Aerin gave Lara a hand, dropping her from the horse's back as readily as she'd lifted her earlier, then swung down with a grace so far beyond Lara's capability she couldn't even envy it.

"Rub him down, if you will," the Seelie woman said to a guard who stood at attention. "He's seen no battle, but he'll go in again more readily if he feels spoiled."

"Do horses really look that far into the future?" Lara asked as the guard led the animal away.

"Any beast as wound with magic as our horses certainly can, if they wish." Aerin flipped the tent flap open, gesturing Lara in. "We keep them happy, so when we ride to battle we know it's to battle we go. You've ridden with us before."

Lara made a sound of agreement as she stepped into the tent. The Seelie horses did something inexplicable to the distance they traveled, diminishing it, as if each step they took covered six or eight paces. According to Dafydd and Aerin, the horses themselves worked the spell, so it was easy to believe a badly tended animal might decide to go elsewhere rather than take itself into the dangers of battle.

Easy to believe. She pressed the heel of her hand to one eye, partly adjusting to the dimness inside the tent, but more in weary acknowledgment of a phrase she had never used before. Her truthseeking talent had always shown her the world in terms of black and white, of true and false. Nothing was easy or difficult to believe; they simply *were*. Only in the past few days had she begun to hear and use shades of gray in the form of half-truths or vernacular phrasing.

"Are you well, Truthseeker?"

"Well enough." Lara dropped her hand, glancing around the tent's interior as Aerin let the entrance door flap fall back into place. It was markedly cool within, and she wondered if every Seelie tent was affected by the element its owner wielded. Probably not: Emyr's tent was dominated by a scrying pool and a table of maps, beyond which hung another door flap, pulled open to reveal a sumptuous bed with a deep silver tub at its foot. This was the king's tent and the king's tent alone. Lara doubted many others in the army were as singularly well-provided for, and therefore as able to leave an impression of themselves in the air itself. "Where's Emyr? I thought he wanted to talk to me."

"His majesty," Aerin said with the slightest emphasis, "is bound to no one's whim. Not even a truthseeker's."

"I didn't mean..." Lara sighed and glanced around for a chair, finding none. The tactical meetings she presumed were held in the front part of Emyr's tent must not last long, then, or his commanders would spend uncomfortable hours standing with increasingly itchy feet. Unless Seelie didn't suffer from that kind of circulation problem, which seemed probable. Lara thrust her chin out and glanced roof-ward, trying to pull her thoughts into a semblance of reason.

Half a dozen tiny globes hung in the tent's peak, offering the soft silvery light she remembered from the Seelie citadel. She had no idea what powered them. Magic, clearly, but whether it was an individual's will or if they were somehow manufactured, she couldn't imagine. Either way, the light they offered was flattering, even to the merely mortal. "I just wondered if I had time to get cleaned up. Not that I have any other clothes with me."

Aerin, as if given permission, turned a curious eye on Lara's outfit. Her dress was a classic style, boxy shoulders and a narrow waist above a full skirt, and it fitted perfectly. Or it had, before it had been torn and made filthy by climbing mountains. Lara had a sudden image of herself looking like a battered but beloved old-fashioned doll incongruously clutching the staff as though it were a weapon. She fought the impulse to twist the staff behind her back. It would only draw attention to it, especially since it stood taller than she did.

"Is this what women in your world usually wear?" Aerin asked eventually, and eyed the staff. "And how they..."

"Accessorize," Lara supplied, but shook her head. "No to both. I dress conservatively, compared to a lot of people, and the staff—"

"Is of Seelie make." Emyr flung the door flaps back and stalked in, his armor not daring to so much as rattle and spoil the entrance. He was as tall as Lara remembered, though the armor lent breadth to his slender form, and made him that much more alarming. "That weapon has not been seen in our lands in aeons, Truthseeker, and it is, should you wonder, most of the reason you still live."

Air rushed from Lara's lungs, leaving stars in her vision. "It is?"

"It tends to favor its wielder," Emyr said sourly. "Or has, since it passed from immortal hands to mortal. Where did you get it?" He put his helmet aside, and Aerin stepped forward to help him remove his shoulder-pieces and breastplate. Lara's gaze lingered on the former, searching for a name for them. They had to have one, but her expertise lay in the fine details of sewn garments, not forged. She could see the mastery in even the padded silken shirt he wore beneath the armor, and for an instant regretted that she'd had no hand in its making. Seelie clothing had awakened that faint pang in her from the first moment she'd seen it, and reminded her again that her ambitions had been those of a tailor, not a hero.

Lara brought her attention back to Emyr with a sigh, briefly silenced by the realization she had so much story to tell it was difficult to find a place to begin. She finally said, "I found it in my world," though she felt like she juggled truth and lies with her answers as she went on. "The Unseelie king had suggested I look for it there. Your majesty, the last I knew, Dafydd had been returned to the Barrowlands by his brother Ioan. Has Ioan not contacted you?"

Emyr's face turned white with anger. "Hafgan bid you search out that staff? Dafydd is captured by my traitorous son? What more ill news do you bear, Truthseeker?"

Lara groaned and sat on the floor, needing a seat more than she cared for propriety. The floor was rugs thrown over earth, somehow unmarred by their muddy feet, and she frowned at that a moment as she sorted her thoughts. "Okay. I need you to just listen for a few minutes. I'm a truthseeker, so you know I'm going to tell the truth even if sounds preposterous. Right?"

Both Aerin and Emyr nodded when she glanced up, the latter begrudgingly. Lara nodded in turn, then spread her hands. "When you fostered Ioan, made him hostage to good behavior, whatever it is you want to call it that prompted the exchange of firstborns between you and Hafgan, Ioan embraced his new family, far more than Hafgan's son Merrick ever did in the Seelie court. Ioan even changed his physicality through magic, so he's more broadly built and golden-skinned like the rest of the Unseelie."

Emyr's expression darkened further and Lara climbed to her feet again, full of nervous energy now that she was speaking. "It gets more complicated. Ioan has been ruling in Hafgan's name, literally, for a long time. Centuries, probably. Hafgan retreated ages ago, and Ioan never admitted it to you because he thought you'd see it as weakness and try to destroy the Unseelie court."

Aerin's gasp was audible over Emyr's lower growl, but Lara rushed on, as she stood and paced the width of the tent as she spoke. "Ioan believes that the Barrow-lands were once called Annwn, and were...I'm not sure. Ruled jointly, maybe, by the Seelie and Unseelie, until the Seelie called the sea to drown the Unseelie coastal lands, making them exiles in their own country. That the war between you stems back that far, so far that it's legend even to those who lived then." Lara could barely conceive of a lifetime so extended that lives became history and history legend, though she recognized that her own childhood memories were scattered and hardly complete. Lives lived over millennia instead of decades would almost necessarily fade into obscurity, but events of the magnitude Ioan had spoken of seemed like they should stand out in anyone's mind.

"He thinks this staff was the weapon that broke the world, back then. He thought it was sent to my world so it couldn't be used again. I found it there, waiting for me."

"Waiting!" Emyr burst out. "For *you?*"

"For a truthseeker," Lara said, unexpectedly steady in the face of his anger. "For someone who could see through the spell laid on it and perhaps command its power. Probably any truthseeker would do, but there aren't that many of us." Dafydd had searched her world for a hundred years, trying to find someone with her talent, and having found her, had ended up nearly dead and now disappeared for it. Lara's heart clenched, hurting her chest, and it took a few seconds before she could speak again.

"The point is, none of what Ioan said rang false to me, Emy— your majesty. It didn't exactly sound true, either, but I've never dealt with history turned legend before. And he was right about the staff being in my world." She frowned at the Seelie king, whose narrow face was drawn with anger. "Which means I've got a lot more to try to settle here than just the question of who murdered Merrick ap Annwn."

A laugh of frustration burbled up and she cast her gaze skyward again, as if the baubles lighting the tent might lend her strength. "Except he isn't dead. He framed Dafydd in hopes of starting a war between your court and the Unseelie court, so he could be the last man—elf—standing, and take the spoils. So Dafydd brought me here in the first place because of fraud. Because of a lie."

There was so much more to say, but Lara fell silent as shock created lines in Emyr's face. Age didn't mark the Seelie in the same way it did humans, but watching Emyr's pale skin turn to ash and the scouring of lines around his mouth told her how Seelie might look if they did age: still beautiful, but also terrible. Vampiric, as though whatever vitality they'd had had long since drained away, and left only a walking shell. Lara felt momentarily sorry for the Seelie king, though his arrogance didn't, as a rule, invite compassion.

"Merrick is a master of air," she said wearily. "Of illusion, shaped from air. I'm sure Dafydd did draw and nock the arrow as everyone saw, but the Merrick he shot and killed was nothing more than a phantom. A ghost of himself. I've stood face-to-face with Merrick, your majesty. I promise you he's alive."

Color flooded back into Emyr's face, the heat of rage warming his features in a way Lara had never seen before. He snapped around to his scrying basin, simply a pool on a tall slender pedestal, and ice crackled from his fingertips as he seized the basin's edge. Lara said, "Wait," and Aerin directed a warning sound at her as Emyr shot a glower her way. But he released the stoneworked pool's edge, evidently understanding he would have a great deal to look for once he began. Better to search it all out at once, than have her interrupt him time and again.

"Merrick called a nightwing attack into my world," Lara said. "I closed the breach between the Barrow-lands and Earth to stop them. It worked, but it also closed off Dafydd's source of strength. I *had* to find the staff, so he would have something of the Barrow-lands to draw on to help him stay alive."

Old anger turned Emyr's expression bleak. "That staff abhors the touch of Seelie hands. It should have destroyed him, and your world with him."

Lara stuttered, then lurched on with her story: "It tried. It threw down an earthquake in a part of my world that doesn't normally get them. It didn't seem to affect Dafydd adversely. I thought he might be getting better, but nightwings infested a human man and came after us. Dafydd fought them and almost died for it. I used the staff to reopen the break between the worlds, and Ioan came for Dafydd. To bring him back to the Barrow-lands, where he might have a chance to heal."

Anger rose up, burning through worry to create heat in Lara's chest. She had come across worlds to offer help, and had found an unexpected passion in exchange. Now that love was threatened, and she had already laid down a promise, a truthseeker's oath, on what would come to pass if that happened. Lara lifted her chin, meeting Emyr's eyes with a forthright glare. "I told Ioan if anything happened to Dafydd, his life was forfeit. So, your majesty, I really think we should go talk to your older son."

Three

"You must be mad." Aerin spoke so pleasantly it took Lara a few seconds to hear the content of her speech, though it set dissonant bells ringing in her mind. "If Ioan ap Caerwyn holds Dafydd hostage, he would have long since sued for peace, or threatened his life to gain his ends."

"Not if he sees destroying your people as the only way to save his own." Lara spoke crisply, still hot with anger. Her magic wouldn't allow her the comfort of an uncertainty: *Dafydd will be all right* only set more atonal notes chiming through her head. She wanted action, if only to burn off some of her fear.

Emyr, though, growled, "*We* are his people," and turned again to his scrying pool. This time cold steamed from his hands before he even touched it, and his grip turned the water within to crackling ice. Lara sidled toward him, hairs lifting on her arms as his chill permeated the tent. He snapped, "Stand aside, Truthseeker. Your presence causes difficulties enough."

It had in the Seelie citadel, but there had been another mortal there: Oisín, poet and prophet, whose magics were of a different kind from Lara's own. Together they had disrupted Seelie magic without meaning to, a truth that itched at the back of Lara's skull. Her world weakened the elfin people, and her magic, in conjunction with another mortal's, disrupted Seelie power even in the Barrowlands. Humans were bad for the Seelie, though what little folklore she knew suggested mortals were also tantalizing, even irresistible, to the fairy peoples.

Emyr would not, she imagined, appreciate being likened to a youth with a taste for bad girls. Lara hid a grin in her shoulder and stayed where she was, hoping her amusement wouldn't bleed over and affect the king's spell. Aerin took up a post half a step in front of Lara, further preventing her from moving forward, though she could still see the pool's surface.

She had once triggered the scrying magic herself, a talent none of the Seelie had imagined might lie within her truthseeking skills. Then, images had awakened in the depths of the ice, carrying sound and color and life. Now Emyr's power lifted ice upward, making frost-rimed sculptures across the pool's surface. An interior garden, built wholly of metal and stone rose up. The ice wicked away color, but Lara could see it in her mind's eye: marbled tree trunks with golden leaves, the vines entwining them made of emerald. They grew and sprawled around a pool, a few of the vines clambering over stone benches, though those details faded away as Emyr focused on the pebbled pathway leading into the garden. "I would speak with the Unseelie king."

It took a long time, Lara thought. A long time for a man to step into shadows which, by rights, ice should be unable to show so darkly. He was a broad-shouldered form, nothing more; the hair he wore long masked any hope of seeing his features while he stood in shadow. "Emyr." A note of curious mirth colored the other king's deep voice. "Have you called to parley?"

"I have called to look on the face of the Unseelie king. When did you last step out of shadow when we spoke?"

"When did you last give me cause to? My people are relegated to shadows; why should I not contain myself within them when we speak? Is it not appropriate?" The Unseelie king's sarcasm was unexpectedly wonderful to hear, its delivery so deliberate that even Lara, who had never been especially comfortable with irony, could enjoy the game he played with words. "You, lord of the shining citadel, stand in the glaring light, while I, master of the dark palace, remain hidden in gloom. Surely you cannot object to such figurative, if theatrical, stances."

"I would see your face." The words came out as clipped breaths of frosty air, individualized by Emyr's precision.

Silence met his outburst, and then a dramatic sigh. "I gather, then, that the Truthseeker has returned. After so long, I wasn't sure she would."

He came out of the shadows as he spoke, changing the ice sculpture's focus from the trees to himself. Even without color, he was very much as Lara remembered him: broader than Emyr or Dafydd, partly due to the cut of his clothes, but mostly thanks to a wider, slightly shorter frame. An ebony circlet set with rubies kept long black hair from his face. He was unquestionably more classically handsome than either his father or his brother, though now that he stood in proximity to Emyr, Lara could see more of the Seelie king in his eldest son than she'd remembered.

Pain twisted Emyr's expression, betrayal so clear that it might have been a knife slicing across his face. A second image sprang up in the ice, this one, Lara thought, called from his memory, rather than any new visitor within the scrying spell.

It was a young man—a boy, really—with finer, longer features than Ioan possessed. Even in ice, his hair seemed wheat-pale, not the white or silver sported by Aerin and Emyr, but touched with sunlight.

His eyes, like all Seelie's, were light-colored, but less deep-set in his face than Ioan's. The boy wore Seelie clothing: winged shoulders and light, fluting fabrics that wove in and out to make snug-fitting patterns against his torso. Despite the differences in coloration, Lara had no doubt this was Ioan as a child; Ioan as his father remembered him.

Ioan turned his attention from Emyr to the sculpture, then twisted away to gesture at the pool behind him. A third image rose from the water, as colorless and as vivid as the ice child Emyr had wrought. First the boy, and then a youth who bore a striking resemblance to Dafydd, though he wore his pale hair long and smooth, rather than the jagged rock-star cut that Dafydd favored. Still, the height of his cheekbones, the expressive mouth, and the slenderness of his frame all called Dafydd to Lara's mind.

But then he changed, the image evolving more rapidly than Lara thought possible for its living counterpart. Though it was only water, it called darkness the same way Emyr's ice scryings did, coloring hair to black and skin to a darker shade of pale. The water-Ioan lost height, shaping it to breadth, and his Seelie garb was put away for the heavier stuff worn by the Unseelie. Within moments the transformation was complete, leaving an almost-perfect echo of the Ioan whose image Emyr had called forth.

Almost perfect: the real Ioan wore the ebony circlet, where the younger version did not. The latter turned up his palms as if to say *what else did you expect?*, then fell away into the pool with a splash. The remaining image sought out Lara's gaze. Despite the diminutive size demanded by the scrying pool, she found as much presence and command in his simulacrum as she had when she'd met him in person.

"Welcome," Ioan ap Annwn said with genuine warmth. "Welcome back to Annwn, Lara Jansen."

Emyr smashed the image to pieces with his fist.

Lara flinched backward with a yelp, and even Aerin's hand went to her sword, as though the ruined vision might somehow prove a threat. Emyr's harsh panting filled the tent, then disappeared as he stalked from the scrying pool to shove Aerin aside and catch Lara's dress.

Or very nearly: his hands came together, grasping. Lara's heart-beat shot up, fear and anger rising to the fore. She lifted the staff crosswise over her chest, making it a barrier between them. Eager-ness thrummed through the ivory, as if Emyr were a recognized op-ponent. His hands splayed and his lip curled as he stilled his action. "How dare you—"

"How dare *you*," Lara said incredulously. Her hands were icy, as though Emyr had caught them in his grip and called his element into play, but they gripped the staff with conviction. She could probably manage a single blow if she needed to: neither Emyr nor Aerin would expect her to respond physically to his advance. "I don't care if you're the king of Heaven. You don't go around manhandling people." Beyond Emyr, Aerin's astonishment suggested that, as king, Emyr both could and did behave so aggressively. Offended at the idea, Lara spat air, not quite uncouth enough to draw liquid for the full effect. "You damned well don't do it to *me*."

Tension pulled at Emyr's upper lip, like he'd smelled something vile and was just polite enough not to speak of it. But he withdrew a step, giving Lara her space and autonomy. She remained where she was, staring at him and glad that her hands still refused to shake. A month earlier she might have screamed if a man had come at her the way Emyr had just done. She might not have, too: society dictated foolish amounts of discretion in response to bad behavior, especially for women. But she could hardly imagine that she would ever have stood her ground, or thought of risking brute force against a larger adversary. The Barrow-lands, Dafydd, and her own burgeoning magic had lent her confidence she knew was growing, but coming up against it directly still surprised her.

Not quite as much as it surprised Emyr, perhaps. Lara lowered the staff by degrees, neither Seelie moving until it rested butt-down against the carpets again. "With all due respect, your majesty, Ioan's probably the only one who has any idea where Dafydd is, or what kind of condition he's in. Cutting off communications," in a temper tantrum, she carefully didn't say aloud, "wasn't the most tactful thing you could have done."

"With all due respect," Emyr echoed flatly. "Truthseeker, I thought you were not given to embellishing your statements. I find that phrase difficult to believe."

Lara gave him a pointed smile. "I assure you I meant it with every bit of respect appropriate to the moment, your majesty." There were relatively few colloquial phrases she had been able to use throughout her life. *With all due respect* was one of them, because it could be invested with precisely as much respect as she felt was due.

Emyr made a sound that indicated he understood all too clearly what she meant. "Spoken in a child's word," he quoted, bitterly. "Changes that will break the world. What have you done to my people, Truthseeker?"

Guilt made a tight knot in Lara's stomach before she banished it with indignation. "As far as I'm concerned it's been barely a month since I first *came* here, Emyr. Even if you take the time that's elapsed, it's only been a year and a half." She had, once again, become a time traveler. Skipping months at once, lurching from what had been a simple, linear life into the chaos of other lives moving on without her. At home, that had distressed her badly. Her attachment to the Barrow-lands was far less profound, and as she had left and returned in the midst of battle, worrying about a handful of disarrayed months seemed useless.

Useless except in terms of how Dafydd ap Caerwyn might have fared in those long months. He'd lived out the time she'd missed at home in jail, awaiting trial on charges of her kidnapping and presumed murder. Ioan, she hoped, would have treated his brother more humanely, but she couldn't be certain of that until she saw him again. She made a fist, the staff's reassuring carvings marking her palm. "Either way, I couldn't have possibly affected Ioan's choices. He decided to become Unseelie long before I came to the Barrowlands. I may be destined to break your world, but you can't lay that fracture on my head." *That was all you,* she wanted to conclude, but had the wisdom to stop her tongue.

As a child wouldn't. The prophecy Emyr had quoted sang through her mind in its entirety: *Truth will seek the hardest path / measures that must mend the past. / Spoken in a child's word / changes that will break the world. Finder learns the only way worlds come changed at end of day.*

She was the truthseeking child, according to Oisín, the mortal poet who had first spoken the prophecy. A child by Seelie standards, who viewed her twenty-three years as inconsequential. And if she'd had doubts as to whether she might break or mend a world, the staff she now carried had clarified that: even on Earth, where its powers were muted, it had the strength to call up earthquakes and storms. Here, in the land of its making, she had every confidence it could destroy or create as its wielder desired.

God should have that kind of power, not Lara. She dragged in a steadying breath, then met Emyr's eyes. "Is Ioan right, Emyr? Did you use the staff to drown the Unseelie lands? Is that what started your territory wars?"

"Ask Hafgan, if you would know what happened." Emyr threw away the words with a sharp gesture and turned his back on her.

Exasperation flooded Lara. "I would, but he's not here. You must've been there when the sea rose. Aerin? Were you?"

The Seelie woman stiffened and cast a discomfited glance at

Emyr. "I don't remember a time when the Hundred were not drowned, Lara. They may not have been, in my childhood, but..." She passed a hand over her eyes and shrugged. "The memories I have weigh in favor of them always being drowned. I remember swimming in the high tides with Dafydd and Merrick when I was a girl. I recall Rhia—" She broke off as Emyr hissed, and when she resumed again her voice was softer. "I recall the queen watching over us, and how she loved the waters."

"Rhiannon." Lara finished the name Aerin had not, and this time Emyr's hiss was directed at her. She shook it off, more curious about the Seelie queen than concerned about the king's anger. "Oisín mentioned her once. Even Dafydd barely remembers her. What... what happened to her?"

"She died," Aerin said when it became obvious Emyr would not speak. "Saving Merrick, in truth. He swam out too far. The queen went into the water before anyone realized something was wrong. Merrick returned, but our lady..."

Lara put her fingers over her mouth, comprehension lurching through her. Ioan, so far as she could tell, had been embraced by the Unseelie king Hafgan, while Emyr had never warmed to his own adopted child Merrick. Now she understood why, and for the first time felt real sympathy for the Seelie monarch. It wouldn't be easy for even a charitable man to forgive a child for costing a wife's life, and nothing about Emyr had ever suggested he was of a lenient mind.

"Put her on a horse." Emyr's harsh voice cut across any thought of condolences Lara might have offered. "Put her on a horse, Aerin, and stick her there. We ride for my traitorous son's head."

Four

Stick her there was a literal explanation of the magic used to keep Lara on her horse. She wasn't uncoordinated, but her exposure to horses was limited. Rather than permit her to slow the Seelie riders down, she had twice now been bespelled so that she simply couldn't fall off her horse. She could climb down, slowly and carefully, but that wasn't something she wanted to try at full gallop, in spite of her reservations about their task. And it would have been far worse to be left behind. At Emyr's side she had a chance to mitigate his decisions, though the odds of the Seelie king listening to her were slim.

They rode now at the head of a host, Aerin and a dozen other guards behind them. Lara's place just to Emyr's left wasn't a position of honor so much as a location from which she could be easily watched. Guards rode behind them to ensure she wouldn't peel off and ride breakneck across the countryside alone.

Not that she would: the only two places in the Barrow-lands she knew at all were the Seelie citadel and the Unseelie palace. The one was hardly a refuge when Emyr was infuriated with her, and the other would be her destination regardless. It was the only chance she had at learning Dafydd's fate. Whatever Emyr's intentions, Lara's own were to find the amber-eyed Seelie prince. The hope of seeing him again—of seeing him healthy and fit—urged her forward even if nothing else did.

Forest surged by, the horses crossing unnatural lengths with each step as they left Emyr's war far behind. In very little time, even the forest was gone and the land sloped up toward rough mountains. In the distance a sheer rock face rose as though it had been thrust out of the earth so recently that erosion hadn't yet thought to touch it. From what she'd learned of Barrow-lands history, it seemed possible that it had in fact erupted in living memory.

The thought was a true one, filled with deep bassoon notes, as if the sound of tearing stone had been transmuted into music. That would have been enough, but the staff, which lay strapped across her back now, sang an answer as much as her truthseeking sense did. If one part of the Barrow-lands had drowned, another area had risen. The bleak gray wall ahead of them was part and parcel of that, and the staff exuded smugness over the fact. Lara bent her head over the horse's mane, discomfort crawling along her spine. Ioan hadn't intimated that the staff had personality, but she had no other word for the barrage of feelings.

The thought twinged discordance and she amended it. She had another word: *sentience*. But that was too alien to be fully considered. Oisín, who had carried it for years, might be able to explain the weapon's evident character, but the poet wasn't among the riders approaching the Unseelie court.

Emyr's curse barked across her thoughts, and her horse obeyed the command that the other riders gave their animals: it slowed, prancing to the edge of a plummeting canyon. The soaring escarpment lay on the canyon's far side, emphasizing again the impression that granite had simply been torn asunder, a ravine ripped open so the rock face could be permitted to shoot skyward. On the far wall a narrow, plunging ledge jutted down sheer rock face, its foot lost in darkness. Sparks of pain flew through Lara's skull as she stared at it.

"The crevasse looks as though it narrows to the right," Aerin called. "Perhaps there's a crossing point. Shall I ride to see?"

Below Emyr's grudging agreement, Lara asked, "Haven't you ever been to the Unseelie palace?" Her vision pounded, bolts of searing light breaking through the image of what she saw and what she knew was there. She had always had a susceptibility to migraines, but only in the past few weeks had their auras been triggered by deceiving magic.

Emyr growled. "What reason would I have to visit my enemy's stronghold?"

"To see your son?" Lara suggested, and only too late wished the words away. Emyr's lip curled, but she raised a hand, barely aware she was silencing a king. "The forest path to the Seelie citadel is glamoured. It can't be seen until you're on it, so the horses have to know the way."

"What of it?"

Lara caught her horse's reins up. It whickered in surprise, as she'd done nothing to suggest guiding it before, but it went willingly enough when she turned it away from the precipice and rode back through the gathered guards.

"Clear a path." She would never have imagined herself giving calm commands, nor for a dozen riders to make way as if she had every right to give orders. Only Emyr hesitated, and then, irritated, he, too, pulled back from the cliff's edge.

It was easier to see from a distance. The air didn't twist as badly. Lara's headache faded, allowing her to look through the disguise that had been laid upon the entrance to Unseelie territory.

The rift in the earth was unquestionably still there. But across from them was not flat rock face, but rather a black maw gouged into the cliff. She had ridden it before: she *knew*, despite what her eyes wanted to see, that the cavern hid a tongue of stone broad and solid enough for a horse to leap to, and that the plummeting pathway visible along the flat wall in truth led straight down into the canyon's depths. It was a far more difficult illusion than the one laid to hide the Seelie citadel. That one had merely surprised her, while this wrenched at her vision and had nearly cost her the contents of her stomach when she'd first ridden it. Even now, knowing its truth, it was nearly impossible to see through, though the longer she frowned at it, the clearer it became.

Its trick was in flattening the real landscape, so that the eye saw a nearly endless edifice rising behind an equally lengthy ravine. In fact, the stone rising up before them was cut into a nearly perfect squared corner, with great lengths of granite running at close to ninety degrees. One shot off to Lara's right, where Aerin rode to explore the slight narrowing of the crevasse. The other was almost straight ahead. It was down that angle that the pathway ran, still plunging as deep into the chasm as it did in the illusion. Lara blinked once and the entire glamour smoothed back into a single plane, still fighting the truth she believed in. Dafydd's glamour hadn't been so persistent. Once she'd seen through it to recognize his elfin features, it hadn't worked on her again. Whomever had cast the spell into these great stone walls had poured tremendous magic into the job. Lara wondered suddenly if the maker had survived his efforts.

And now, very likely against wit and wisdom, she was going to lead the single man whom they had probably most wanted to keep out of the hidden city into it. Lara patted her horse's shoulder and tried not to feel foolish at murmuring "Trust me" to the beast.

It snorted agreeably, and in the instant she drove her heels into its flanks, Lara wondered if it was trust, or if the magic-riddled horses could see through the glamour. It hardly mattered: it sprang forward in a run and leapt fearlessly into the chasm. Lara's stomach dropped and she had an instant to be grateful for the spell that kept her stuck to the saddle.

A heartbeat later they landed in a clatter of hooves against the broad cave tongue, glamour giving up and no longer trying to fool Lara's eye. The horse pitched down the incline leading to the Unseelie city. Behind her, Lara heard Emyr's shout of astonishment and preparations for his host to follow. Only a few seconds passed before the first of his guards hurtled across the void and gave chase.

Gave chase, as though there might be hope of escape. At best Lara's precipitous arrival would offer the Unseelie a momentary warning before Emyr burst in on them. Not that there would be many people left in the city, not if things were as they'd been the first time she had visited. It had seemed then that everyone able-bodied was already at war, and after months of battles, she didn't imagine that would have changed.

Still, Ioan was there, or Emyr's scrying spell would have called up a location other than the palace garden. He could be warned, and perhaps could tell her of Dafydd's fate before Emyr arrived. That knowledge might be enough to stop the Seelie king.

Sour notes lingered with the thought, suggesting it would take more than just news of his younger son to placate Emyr. A struggle between gratitude at her power's continuing development, and resentment that she could no longer abide in false hope for even a moment, rose up. Someday she might be able to turn her truthseeking sense *off,* a thought worth pursuing.

The plunging path before her ended, her horse's hooves slipping against stone as they reached flat ground. The roadway took a sharp curve into a carved gateway in the rock wall's face. The horse gathered itself again and they burst through the unguarded passage into a cavern so vast it defied the eye. Even on a second viewing, Lara found it all but incomprehensible.

The enormous block of granite was little more than a shell, its interior hollowed out, probably by magic. Erosion wasn't impossible: even at a full gallop Lara could hear the incessant thunder of a distant waterfall that fed the small river wending through the cavern. Not impossible, but unlikely: there were cordoned walkways along the high walls, and the town itself sheltered in the cave's dark reaches looked to her like a thing grown up from magic, not made by builders' hands.

It was in every way the opposite of the shining Seelie citadel. Where that was soaring opalescence, the Unseelie city was low rambling black mother-of-pearl. Lara tore through its streets, half fearing her horse's hooves would damage the delicate-looking stone, but no chips flew. A few astonished children, wearing brightly colored and warmly woven clothes, scattered away, and sent alarmed cries to their caretakers as the rest of Emyr's guard rushed in seconds behind her. Lara crashed through the open courtyard that joined palace to town, guiding her horse over silver-pebbled pathways and down half-remembered halls in search of the pool Ioan had met her at, and which Emyr had called up with his scrying spell.

Her horse, more sensitive to changing landscape than she, dropped into a trot that snapped Lara's teeth together with every step, then fell into a more comfortable amble as it entered the enclosed garden with nowhere left to run. Lara let it go to the pool and drink—Seelie bridles lacked the bits humans used—and examined the floor, wondering if getting down was worth the effort.

Ioan ap Annwn startled her with his greeting. "Welcome back, Truthseeker."

Lara's spine stiffened and she turned to glare at the Unseelie king, who had emerged from among the brittle trees. "'Welcome'? Welcome *back*? Is that really the appropriate phrase, when last time I was here it was as a kidnap victim, not an honored guest?" Hooves rattled against the stonework floors beyond, and she bit back her ire. "Emyr's right behind me. Ioan, where's Dafydd? What's—?"

Emyr swept in, *his* horse slowing not at all as the king stood in the stirrups and drew his sword. Ioan shot Lara one dismayed glance, then crashed into the pool, avoiding Emyr's first attack. Lara shrieked and hauled her horse's reins, trying to pull away from danger. The beast pranced sideways until it ran up against marble trees that would let it go no further. Lara, wanting a weapon, reached for her ivory staff, then left it where it was, strapped across her back. She would do more harm than good, probably to herself, if she joined the fight.

Ioan scrambled out of the pool as Emyr sent his horse crashing into it, silvery water splashing across the garden. Aerin rode into the garden's entryway, Emyr's guards behind her as she turned her horse so it blocked egress. Ioan glanced her way and she, too, bared her blade. Exasperation rushed across his features and he muttered "You were kinder as a child" before drawing a belt knife and turning his attention back to the monarch trying to kill him.

Emyr's horse surged in a circle, spraying Ioan anew, but Emyr didn't bother bringing the beast out of the pool. He had every advantage of reach and speed already; Ioan's only weapon was the small knife, and the pool was shallow enough that Emyr retained the height advantage as well. He lunged, a quick, beautiful movement that saw the air around his sword chill. Ioan skittered back, knocking the tip of Emyr's sword aside with his knife. "Your horse is your vulnerability, Emyr. Don't make me kill it."

"Will you not even call me Father?" Emyr lunged again, this time bringing the horse closer yet to the edge of the pool, and this time only narrowly missing Ioan as he darted back again.

"Would you even wish me to?" Ioan watched as Emyr lunged a third time, then darted in as Emyr's blade retreated. Lara drew in a cold breath, but neither king nor beast was Ioan's target. Instead the saddle's strap parted under his knife, and Emyr, all indignity, slid sideways into the pool as the saddle came free. The splash was rimed with ice, and he came to his feet thigh-deep in the pool, frost crackling across his armor.

Ioan slammed into him before he fully had his balance. Emyr went down with a shout, driving his horse away. It scrambled free of the pool and shook itself before turning its elegant head to stare disdainfully at the men wrestling in the water. A spike of empathy for its evident opinion ran through Lara as Emyr, looking like a drowned rat in silver armor, rose again with one gauntleted hand holding Ioan beneath the surface.

The water was too ice-lined and choppy to clearly see what happened, but Emyr shouted and his feet came forward, sending him onto his back. Ioan popped up and lifted a fist. Water rose in the same gesture, Emyr captured in its grip, and Lara remembered suddenly that the Unseelie king's element was water. Emyr was alive because Ioan wished it, but there was no reason to expect his goodwill would hold. Emyr held the Seelie people together; without him, the army might break, and the Unseelie might finally win the land they claimed was theirs.

It was a claim Lara preferred answered in ways that didn't involve regicide.

"You will *stop!*" Her voice boomed across the garden, across the palace, across the whole of the Unseelie cavern. Echoes rained back on her and both combatants froze, Ioan with a hand still uplifted, Emyr in his watery grip. Even Aerin lowered her sword, and Emyr's discontent host ceased their shuffling and muttering. Lara's horse twitched an ear, then edged forward at her urging, stopping at the pool's edge as she glowered at the men within. "Put him down, Ioan."

A spasm of protest crossed Ioan's face, but he did as he was told, opening his fist to drop Emyr gracelessly into the water. Emyr surged to his feet, water streaming from his armor. Lara made a guttural sound of warning as he turned on Ioan, and for the second time, both kings went still. Neither looked happy, Lara suddenly their common enemy.

Well, her agenda was not their own, and now she had their attention. Hands tight on her horse's reins, she frowned down at Ioan. "Where's Dafydd? Why hasn't he returned to Emyr's court?"

A second spasm, this time of regret, darkened Ioan's face. "Because he's dead, Truthseeker."

Five

Nerveless, Lara slid from her horse's back and put a hand against its shoulder so she could keep her feet. She was cold all over, her heartbeat too slow. She wanted to protest: *No, it can't be true!* but neither her power nor Ioan's flat words would allow for it. They rang on in her mind, finding notes that were true and notes that were not within what he'd said. Half-truths, the same kind she'd sensed when Dafydd ap Caerwyn had introduced himself as David Kirwen, the ordinary American translation of his name.

"You're lying," she said without conviction. He wasn't quite telling the truth, but nor was he without question telling a falsehood. "Tell me what you mean."

"I mean he's dead, Lara, or close enough as it makes no difference." Ioan, like Emyr, like all the others in the immediate area, seemed unable to move beyond where he'd been when Lara's order had broken over them. It was just as well: Emyr's expression said that if he could move freely, Ioan would be dead by now, or Emyr dead in the trying.

And Ioan had once been Emyr's favorite. The glorified older son, given away to an enemy king as a hostage for good behavior. Distance had made the heart grow very fond indeed, and Dafydd had been unable to live up to the expectations of a brother who wasn't there. Worse, Merrick had been raised under a Seelie roof by a father figure who loathed the sight of him. That status quo had held for aeons, and now was so undone that the beloved eldest would be dead if the father had his way.

Immortal elves were not so very different from mortal humans after all, it seemed. Lara closed her eyes, put her forehead against the horse's shoulder, and again said, "Tell me what that means." This time she infused it with command, bitterly confident she could force Ioan to confess all if need be.

"He returned from your world nothing more than a shell." Ioan's voice was brittle, as if the words were indeed forced. "His magic was burned out, leaving only a husk behind. I've never seen it before, not even in the oldest among us. Healers could, or would, do nothing to help."

Emyr snarled, "They refused—?"

Ioan's voice cooled further. "They refused an enemy prince, if that's what happened. Some did try, of that I'm certain, but they could do nothing. The living power in him was so ruined that I don't know how he continued to breathe. I kept him for weeks. Months, hoping the land itself would help him regain his strength. But in the end all that was keeping him alive was the healers, and their gifts were needed elsewhere."

Lara focused on her horse's shoulder. The hair there was brown and gold, shifting subtly as the animal breathed. It was a small thing, normal, and helped her move past the fear chilling her blood so she could speak. "And?"

"And so I brought him to the Drowned Lands," Ioan said softly. "To the waters that—"

Anything more he might have said was lost to the crash of metal against flesh. Something ripped loose inside Lara, as if the fabric of power she'd woven had suddenly been shredded by an unexpected force. Her chest hurt, air gone from her lungs. She barely turned her head in time to see Emyr smash a second fist at Ioan, the compulsion that had held him frozen now broken.

The broader man caught it with a grunt, trembling muscles visible beneath the wet silken fabric plastered to them. Blood welled along his cheekbone where Emyr's first blow had landed, but his voice remained calm and soft. "To the waters that my people believe to be restorative. There is the potential of a hundred steads there, all the life that might have been, had they not drowned. The waters are rich with power. I could think of no other way to save Dafydd's life. My lady Truthseeker, call off this dog before I am forced to drown it."

Lara muttered, "The dog isn't mine to call," but added, more sharply, "Emyr, leave him alone."

Tension left Emyr's arm almost instantly, his body obeying even as his mind resisted. Ioan released him and backed away, water pouring from his clothes as he left the pool. Within seconds he was dry and tidy, as though the ruckus had never happened. Lara closed her mouth with a click and looked elsewhere to keep herself from staring. It didn't work: in an instant she was gaping at the Unseelie king again, though she knew he would regard the magic he'd just called to be little more than a parlor trick. "What's the problem with having sent Dafydd to the Drowned Lands to recover?"

Aerin sighed and nudged her horse a single step forward, calling attention to herself. Lara had a sudden impression of the white-haired woman's life, always standing second to a king and his family, always there to answer the questions that needed answering but which royal pride refused to acknowledge. "They're the waters Rhiannon drowned in, Lara. They might be restorative to the Unseelie, but the Seelie regard them as deadly. Sending Dafydd there is tantamount to an execution."

"Don't be absurd. We're not separate races, one born of starlight and the other bred of earth. We're one people, divided by a schism older than memory. What heals one will heal the other." Ioan looked as though he'd had this argument a dozen times before.

"You are no part of us," Emyr snapped. "You're earth-grubbing, dank-loving fishermen and farmers, and we are—"

"You are my father," Ioan reminded him. "Or had you forgotten that, Emyr? I'm the child you engendered. An earth-grubbing, dank-loving stoneworker and king."

"And what have you done with the king before you?"

"Hafgan? Like Dafydd, he has returned to the Drowned Lands." Ioan's voice dropped. "Were his stories true, Father? Did you drown the Unseelie lands and uproot a people?"

"I owe you no answers."

"*I* want an answer." Lara stepped forward, anger rising in her again. She had lost time and now Dafydd to the Barrow-lands' bickering and politics. They had asked her to uncover hidden truths. She was not going to stand aside now, not when she had come this far.

Emyr waded out of the pool. It was a measure of him, Lara thought, that he could be as unforgiving and regal as he was even standing thigh-deep in water. "Did you drown the Unseelie lands, Emyr? Did you start this war?"

"I do not recall." The precision of his words belied their softness, making them more a threat than a confession. But the music in them rang pure, if unsettled: his voice could carry a whole orchestra of sound, perhaps as the result of age. The symphony it played was one of foreboding and distrust, directed as much inwardly as toward Lara. Emyr *didn't* recall, and from the rumbling music, loathed that inability. "It is why I said to ask Hafgan," he went on, music thick with stress. "And yet it seems his memories were failing, too. When so much time has gone by, Truthseeker, what does it matter?"

"People are still dying over it, that's what it matters. Ioan, the Drowned Lands, the healing waters . . . are you sure Hafgan's not just dead? You're not using a euphemism?" Lara doubted it; figures of speech tended to set off warning bells, and Ioan had come across as sincere.

He shook his head. "At rest, but not dead. He could be roused," he said reluctantly. "If it is necessary, he can be awakened."

As could Dafydd, Lara concluded silently. Relief swept over her as heat, making her want to turn away and hide her face until her expression was under control. But Dafydd's health, important as it was to her personally, might be the least of the concerns she faced. Clinging to the hope of his recovery, she steadied her voice to say, "Okay. So we have two old people—"

Emyr made such a violent sound of protest that Lara laughed. "Forgive me, your majesty. Ancient peers. Venerable elders. Respected monarchs. Old people," she repeated with cheerful emphasis. "Neither of whom can remember all the details. I might be able to help you remember, but I'm going to need both of you. And probably anyone else old enough to remember the drowning of the lands. Was Oisín here then?"

Aerin nodded, earning a dark look from her king. Lara, though, smiled. Oisín and she had not only mortality in common, but also love for an immortal. More usefully, though, their magic interfered with elfin power. Glamours and other misguidances might cease to function with two human magic users on hand. That would save time, as she doubted either Emyr or Hafgan would willingly reveal the secrets they half recalled.

"And what will you do if you find answers?" Ioan wondered.

Lara touched the staff she wore across her back. "Try to fix what was broken. Isn't that the whole idea?"

Ioan's gaze sharpened as if he hadn't fully seen her until then. "That—?"

"I found it in my world, like you thought I might." Lara spread one hand and let it fall, willing to let the simple explanation suffice. "I have to be sure of what's happened here before I'll be ready to use it, but it has tremendous power. If anything can help set things right here, I think it can."

"*If?* If you're willing to use it, if there's anything to be healed? How can you doubt?"

"Because none of you know the whole truth, and I'm not about to start rearranging the landscape here on anybody's say-so."

"Forgive me, Lara." The lines of Ioan's face hardened as he spoke, intimating that he had no expectation of forgiveness, but every expectation of obedience. "My people have suffered far too much to wait any longer. I will have that staff from you now."

His voice rang with command, even with truth, but Ioan's demand was so preposterous Lara had a fleeting moment of simply not believing him. Her gift had changed in the past weeks, adapting enough that she could have such moments, but the sensation of disbelief was still almost entirely new.

He wasn't *lying*. It was simply that his expectations lay so completely opposite her own as to be astonishing. Lara worked past the emotion to respond with cool certainty: "No. You won't."

"I—" Ioan, as astounded by the refusal as she was by the ultimatum, broke off, then scowled in an excellent mimicry of Emyr. "You are alone, Truthseeker, and in the heart of my city. How do you expect to stop me from taking it?"

Lara heard Emyr's guards shift, closing ranks, preparing to fight. That was answer enough, but the staff thrummed with anticipation that warmed her spine. Emyr had said it abhored a Seelie touch. Even if Lara herself couldn't stop Ioan with words, the staff itself seemed likely to reject him. "Do you really want to test me, Ioan?"

His lip curled and smoothed again very quickly, as if he'd hoped threat alone might cow her into giving up the staff, but he was wise enough not to press the matter. Lara nodded, satisfied, and went on. "I don't trust any of you with it. Not you, not Emyr, maybe not even Dafydd. You all have your own agendas. I'm the only outsider."

"My agenda," Ioan said through his teeth, "is merely the survival of my people, Truthseeker."

"By which you mean the Unseelie, despite having argued that Seelie and Unseelie are all one race not two minutes ago."

Chagrin flushed Ioan's cheeks. Lara rolled her eyes. "I'm hardly going to give you the staff so you can commit genocide. What I will do is collect every puzzle piece I can and put them together to make the clearest picture possible before doing anything."

"What gives you the right," Aerin murmured from the sidelines.

Lara splayed a hand in exasperation. "Dafydd does, by asking me to come here and solve Merrick's murder in the first place. You all do, by your word for what I am. *Truthseeker.* You can't give me that title and then not expect me to go seeking the truth. And you may have thought I would fetch and deliver this staff to you, Ioan, but you yourself named it Worldbreaker. I don't believe any neutral truthseeker with a weapon like that in her hands would be inclined to offer it to an individual with an ax to grind. What does it take to bring someone back from the . . . healing waters?" Lara chose the less ominous phrase deliberately. "Is it a spell? Can we bring Hafgan and Dafydd here like the worldwalking spell brought me here?"

Aerin, softly, said, "No one returns from the Drowned Lands," but Ioan raised a hand to silence her.

"No one returns without help," he agreed, "but that doesn't mean no one returns. There are trials to be faced, but they must be faced even when bringing someone to the healing waters. The petitioner must be found worthy."

"And if they're not?" Lara wished she hadn't asked even as the words slipped out. The pitying expressions around her answered as fully as she might need. "Well, you were trying to save Dafydd's life and you were found worthy. I'm trying to find the truth of what happened to this world, so hopefully that'll be enough to see me through. I want you to agree to a cease-fire while I'm gone."

"What makes you so certain we'll allow you to go?" This time it was Emyr with the half-made threat.

Lara's eyebrows rose. "Aside from me intending to bring back your son and heir?"

"And my old enemy," Emyr pointed out. "Perhaps the loss of one is worth the loss of the other." Aerin's face tightened, but she held her tongue as Emyr continued. "You are an outsider, Truthseeker, with an agenda of your own. You returned the staff, a dangerous weapon, to the Barrow-lands, and I have no way of knowing you won't offer it to my enemy or destroy my lands if you're allowed to run unchecked."

The staff was suddenly warm again, eager to fulfill Emyr's expectations. Lara reached for it, moving slowly because she knew the action could be seen as aggressive, and didn't speak until she had it in her hands, one end resting against the stoneworked floor. It seemed brighter, as if trying to draw attention to itself, and she wondered what kind of picture she made, bedraggled in mortal wear but holding a weapon of immortal make. She drew herself up, aware she was much shorter than the elfin folk around her, but making the best of her presence.

"I *have* the staff, Emyr, and I'll defend myself with it if my own power isn't enough. But I won't sit idly by while your two factions work to destroy one another. If rousing Hafgan, awakening Dafydd, and lifting the Drowned Lands is what it takes to end this mess, then that's what I'll do."

They couldn't stop her: the staff all but hummed in her hands, suggesting ways she could make an escape. The earth below would break with one sharp blow, a tunnel tearing through granite to offer her a pathway out. The cavernous roof could be splintered with no more than a surge of willpower. Lara had no doubt the staff could drag her skyward and send her soaring through the shattered ceiling.

And both would destroy the Unseelie city. She knotted her fingers against the staff's intricate carvings and tried to exude calm, not encouraging any of the dramatic scenarios the weapon proposed. There was a door out. She would use that, like any normal person. Not that she felt normal. She never had been, not with her odd talent, but for the first time, standing there with the staff, she felt as though she had the potential to be vastly more than she was. That she could, if she wanted to, rule this world, and perhaps her own as well.

"He won't stop you," Aerin said unexpectedly. Some of the flare left the staff. Lara breathed more easily and blinked toward Aerin, who continued, "I'll go with you so the Seelie will not be forgotten, no matter how far you travel."

"And the Unseelie?" Ioan asked.

"It's your story she looks to corroborate," Aerin muttered. "I doubt she'll forget your kind. But send a representative, if you like. Quests are always best done in threes."

"A point well made." Ioan smiled and turned to Lara. "I'll join you."

Six

"Abandon your people in the midst of war?" Emyr sounded pleased by the idea.

Ioan widened his eyes in flawless innocence. "The truthseeker has proposed amnesty, Father. Will you not lay down your sword for the little time it takes us to journey to the Drowned Lands and back?"

"Little time? It could be months. Years!"

"Which is negligible to immortals," Lara said. "Maybe you could stay here to ensure the Seelie court's good behavior."

Emyr looked down his nose at her, disdain no less effective for the water still dripping off him. "I am a *king*, Truthseeker."

"Which should make you an effective bargaining tool. More effective than your firstborn sons turned out to be. Speaking of which, have you seen Merrick, Ioan?"

Astonishment lengthened Ioan's jaw. "Merrick is dead."

Lara crushed her eyes shut, trying to remember who she had shared what information with. For a moment she wished she was at home, gossiping with her friend Kelly Richards, if for no other reason than her certainty that Kelly had been told everything. "No, he isn't. Merrick was the mastermind of his own demise. He framed Dafydd. A power play." She shrugged, eyes open again, and sympathy splashed through her as she saw Ioan struggle to fit the news against what he thought he'd known. "He controlled the nightwing hydra you fought in my world," Lara added. "I caught up with him a few hours later, and you'd hit him pretty hard. I thought he might have come looking for payback."

"That was—" Ioan broke off, held his breath, then, more steadily, began again. "That was months ago. I hadn't spared a thought for the . . . hydra . . . or you, in some time, Lara."

"It was this morning, in my timeline. So where's he been all this time? Hiding? Recovering?"

"Dead," Emyr said, and shrugged arrogantly as she looked at him. "All we have is your word that he lives at all."

Ioan, to Lara's gratitude, spluttered, "A truthseeker's word is incontrovertible! How can you—"

"Even a truthseeker can be misled, especially if young in years and power. More likely by far his resurrection is a conspired tale between the two of you to draw me here so you might execute me." Badly tuned string instruments sang through Emyr's theory, proof that even he didn't believe what he suggested.

Lara gestured toward the pool. "Use it to scry for him. Prove me wrong."

Pique thinned Emyr's lips, and Lara fought down a triumphant smile. Ioan, though, took a few quick strides back to the pool's edge and knelt by it. The unbroken surface shimmered, then deepened, water turning stormy gray. "If I can find him we may have more than one task to complete, Truthseeker. Hafgan and Dafydd's return, yes, but hunting down our cousin may be more important still."

Emyr made a sound of angry disbelief. "That spell works in ice alone!"

"What is ice," Ioan murmured, "but frozen water? The scrying spell has long since been mine to command, Father. You might have considered that, in the years we were apart. We might have been closer, had you ever thought to answer my seekings." He dismissed the comment with a wave of his fingers, though Emyr went briefly still, staring at the man his son had become. Ioan, as if ignorant of the hard look, brought his full attention back to the pool.

It showed nothing more than relentless gray whirls and white-caps, a chaotic ocean reflected in contained waters. Lara edged forward, trying to find a pattern in the breaking waves. "I thought the scrying spell could find someone anywhere." Rather like a cell phone, putting people in touch at the farthest points on the globe.

"Almost anywhere. If he's within Annwn, certainly, but if he's returned to your world . . ."

Very much like a cell phone, then, reliant on the coverage available. Lara flashed a smile, somehow reassured that magic and technology had similar limits, though her humor faded as Emyr slid her a triumphant look. "Your protestations of his survival lack teeth, Truthseeker."

Lara mumbled, "Lara. My name is Lara," though she doubted Emyr would deign to use it. The title objectified her, and it was always easier to ignore an object than a person. "I'm not going to argue about it, Emyr. Either he's dead like you're pretending to believe, or he's hiding in my world. Either way, he's a problem we don't have to deal with right now. Will you call a cease-fire?"

A thrum of determination went through her as she asked. She was almost certain she could enforce a reprieve by using the staff, but it was a solution she shied away from. Like escaping the Unseelie city, the first methods that came to mind were violent: splitting the earth between the two armies, for example, so that few, if any, could cross over and make war on the other. They weren't options she wanted to explore, regardless of the ease with which she suspected they could be done.

Once again, an image of herself as she'd been only a few weeks ago—quiet, shy, always ready to remain in the background—rose up in contrast to what she'd become. The very idea of wielding significant power, secular or magical, to get her point across would have been inconceivable. Now it was a matter for debate, even if she was determined those debates remain internal.

Caution crept into Emyr's cool gaze as he studied her, and Lara wondered what subtle change had come over *her* face to prompt discretion in the Seelie king. "Three days," he finally said. Beyond him, Aerin's head came up, surprise clear in the action. "Three days from dawn my army will strike again, and strike hard. If they find themselves battling an enemy whose leader has abandoned them, so much the better for us. If you can affect change, Truthseeker, best do so quickly." Emyr raised a hand and his horse, still soaked from its prance in the pool, came to him. He swung up onto it with consummate grace and rode for the garden entrance, guards scattering to make way.

He stopped at Aerin's side, looking down at her. "Join them. I will scry you nightly to learn what comes of this adventure. Should you not return, our vengeance will be in your name."

Aerin paled but nodded, and whispered something in the elfin high tongue, so quiet that even Lara's gathering talent couldn't decipher it. Emyr softened briefly and he put a gauntleted hand on Aerin's hair, then rode past her, his guards falling into place behind him.

Not until the hoofbeats had faded did anyone speak. Ioan said, "Well," with pleasure, and Lara, at the same moment, asked, "Why did he do that? He can't want me to succeed."

"You could not see your own face, Truthseeker," Aerin replied. "Emyr remembers when your kind were our justice. I think you may have reminded him of that time, and reminded him of powers even he doesn't want to cross."

"What? I thought he was the law. I thought there'd never been more than a few truthseekers anyway. What?" Lara bit down on further repetitions, feeling like an actor dropped into a play she didn't know the lines to.

"It only took a few," Aerin said. "And Emyr's word has been law as long as I can remember. But once upon a time—"

"Oh, no. That's how fairy tales start." Lara turned back to her horse, burying her face in the solidity of its shoulder. "I don't like fairy tales."

"They seem to have a fondness for you," Ioan murmured. "Aerin is right, Lara. Yours was not an expression to interfere with. Even I would have shied from it, and you and I aren't at such cross-purposes as you are with my father."

Lara gave him a sharp look. "Don't be sure of that. At least he didn't kidnap me."

"Can we not let that be bygones?"

"No, we can't. I'm not doing any of this for you, Ioan. I'm doing it for Dafydd. If I have to uproot your entire world to get him back, I will. That might end up being to your advantage, but this is not about you." Lara spoke with ferocity, as if doing so could quell the worry that rose in her every time she thought of Dafydd.

"I envy him," Ioan said after a moment, "to be capable of inspiring such loyalty on so brief an acquaintance. Be that as it may," he added, "Aerin is right about another thing. Our ancient histories and legends suggest truthseekers were once the law in these lands, and, not even royal blood was above them."

"What happened?"

Aerin shrugged. "Rhiannon died."

"She was one person!"

"She was the queen of Annwn." Ioan's simple phrase rang deep bells through Lara, making vibrations that bounced against each other and resonated out again. Lara shuddered, overwhelming emotion rising up to sting at her eyes and send cold bumps scattering across her arms. She cleared her throat, then did so again before gathering enough voice to speak.

"Why is that so important? That was the most...true thing... that I've heard here. One of the most true things I've ever heard. It felt like—" She broke off, lips pressed together as Ioan and Aerin gave her curious looks. "It felt the same way pure faith does in my world. Like you'd just said 'God is the king of Heaven.' It's so true that saying it is almost silly. Like..." She faltered, but the two elfin folk, fair and dark, were both smiling with wry comprehension.

"Rhiannon was our goddess, Lara. Queen of Annwn, heart of the land. Annwn was born of her, and without her cannot help but be a shadow of what it was. Emyr and Hafgan both loved her, it's said, and she danced between them as her mood took her. They were jealous of each other, and of her mortal lovers, but when she died they were devastated. That story," Ioan concluded softly, "is so beloved to our peoples that not even time has worn away its telling."

"But how can you kill God? Or a goddess, how can you—?"

"Your god, I think, doesn't walk the earth," Aerin said, as quietly as Ioan had spoken. "Ours was one of us, the first of us, the womb and magic and vision from which we and this land were born. And for all the endless years of our lives, we can die by accident or violence, and so could she. We're not like you, Lara."

"That's not a god," Lara protested. "That's— I mean, my God doesn't walk the earth, no, or not mostly, but He's eternal, and humans are mortal. You keep reminding me of that." She sent a sour look after Emyr, though he was long gone.

"Mortal flesh," Ioan said, "but immortal souls. You go on forever, in a way we do not."

Hushed truth ran through his words, more like water over stone than the symphonic song Lara was accustomed to. She finally said, "That's awful," feeling it entirely inadequate, but Ioan laughed.

"Perhaps, but then, we would consider your brief span of physical years in exchange for an eternity of disembodiment terrible, too. We follow different paths, Truthseeker, and different fates await us."

"But not for the next few days," Aerin concluded pragmatically. "Until we return from the Drowned Lands, our fates are most certainly bound together, and most particularly bound to..." She trailed off, frowning at Ioan.

"We were children together," he said after a moment. "For a little while, anyway. It may as well be Ioan, especially as I think the royal title would sit poorly on your tongue."

"Hafgan is king of the Unseelie," Aerin said, though without conviction.

"Which is why I took his name when he went to the Drowned Lands. The continuity was more important to my people than my name was to me."

"The continuity was more important to *my* king," Aerin corrected. "Had he known of Hafgan's abdication—"

Ioan's eyebrows rose fractionally, a hint of humor coming into his response. "He would have invaded. Hence its importance to my people."

Aerin thinned her mouth, clearly exasperated at the shaving of details, but she let it go to continue what she'd been saying. "We will be greatly in your power, which I acknowledge so that you're aware I understand our debt and danger. Do not abuse it, *teyrnfradwr.*"

The word echoed in Lara's mind, rendering meaning though she was certain she hadn't genuinely understood it. *Traitor,* or something close, full of bitter connotations. Ioan pursed his lips and glanced away, then met Aerin's gaze without guilt. "I mean you no harm, nor will any come to you through any inaction of my own. I believe all of Annwn needs Lara's help, Aerin. This is not done for myself alone, or even for the Unseelie people at the expense of the Seelie. It would be counter to my own purposes to lead you into harm's way."

Lara exhaled. "What's the problem, Aerin? He's telling the truth, but even if he wasn't, I've seen you fight. I'm the weak link here, not Ioan."

"You don't understand." Aerin turned a look of condescending pity on Lara. "The Drowned Lands hunger for Seelie lives. Without Ioan's presence, we will most certainly die."

Seven

But I'm human! The childish protest, made in half-offended innocence, still made Lara wince the next morning. Aerin had been scathing, and even Ioan was apologetic, making it clear that only Unseelie could pass safely into the Drowned Lands, so long as they had the strength to succeed in the trials.

They rode out together at what Ioan claimed was dawn, though there was no way for Lara to tell within the enormous Unseelie cavern. Someone had worked all night to take in a cream-colored tunic and rich, dark-red doublet so they would fit her small frame. She suspected the leggings she wore had recently belonged to a half-grown teen, as their hem had only been brought up an inch or two. There was padding in the seat and thighs, just enough to make riding slightly more comfortable, and Lara suspected her gratitude, already significant, would know no bounds before the journey was over.

She was escorted by the two elfin warriors—escorted, because she was the most likely to fall off her horse. Ioan and Aerin rode close to either side of her, even though Aerin had once again worked the magic that kept Lara stuck in the saddle. Less stuck than before, though, Aerin had said: Lara would never learn to ride properly if she trusted magic over her own talent and instinct.

Lara muttered "What instinct?" again now. They had been riding for a long time, but with only magic-born globes like those from the Seelie citadel for light, she had little idea of *how* long. Long enough to make her thighs and back ache, but at her skill level, that had only taken a few minutes. Her discomfort was worsened by the supply packs strapped across the horse's haunches. Intellect told her they were far enough back not to disturb her ride, but she kept edging forward in the saddle, trying to give them more room.

Ioan reached over to pat her horse's shoulder. It turned its head toward him agreeably, but continued forward without missing a step. Lara, though, clutched its mane when its head moved, then felt patient glances from not only Ioan and Aerin, but their horses as well. "We don't ride horses as a matter of course in my world."

"Do you not travel, then?" Ioan edged his animal further forward, so they rode abreast of one another instead of with Lara at a slight point. That made more sense: he knew the path they were taking, though for the moment there was no choice in the stone-cut road they followed. It was struck through sheer stone, a pathway tall enough that its ceiling was lost to vision, though echoes suggested there was a roof. Lara glanced up as she had dozens of times already, wondering if one of the globes of light might be sent skyward to show how tall the enclosure was, but once again dismissed the idea with a shiver. She could almost imagine it reached to sunlight if she didn't *see* that it closed above them.

"We travel," she said firmly, eager to take her thoughts away from the enclosed roadway. "Just not on horses. We use . . . self-propelled carriages called cars. There were several of them on the road when you came through to fight the hydra. The wheeled boxes in different colors?"

Ioan squinted, then grunted in surprise. "Those would keep a rider dry. How do they work?"

"With what we call an internal combustion engine. Technology, instead of magic." Lara shook her head. "I could explain a steam engine to you, but not a combustion engine. And I wouldn't anyway."

"To keep us simple?" Aerin asked archly.

Lara risked a dirty look over her shoulder. The horse ambled along, undisturbed by her motion, and triumph lanced through her before she answered. "To keep the air clean, maybe. The fuel those engines burn smells terrible and is bad for the atmosphere. But even if I understood them well enough to explain it, they're made of steel. Seelie couldn't make them anyway."

"We could use another metal, perhaps."

"I think the whole point of iron and steel is that once it's molded it can be reheated without losing its integrity. Most metal is too soft."

"Is this?" Aerin tapped her moonlit armor, and dismay splashed through Lara.

"I don't know. It's at least as strong as the plate mail my people used to use, but it's lighter, so maybe it's harder, too." Lara wrinkled her nose. "Anyway, I really can't tell you how they work, because I honestly don't know. Mostly in my world we have mechanics to take care of car problems. People don't fix them themselves, if something goes wrong."

"You must have some idea," Ioan said dubiously. "There's no one here who can't check a hoof for stones, or rub down swollen muscles if a horse comes up lame on a journey. Surely you can do the same for your 'cars'?"

"No, we have . . ." Lara put a hand over her face, suddenly embarrassed at her reliance on other people's knowledge. "We call for help if something goes wrong. With cell phones, which are sort of like your scrying spells, except everyone can use them."

"No wonder Dafydd stayed so long in your world," Aerin finally said. "It sounds very . . . interesting."

"That, and it took a hundred years to find a truthseeker," Lara muttered. "Ioan, how long are we— Oh! Is that light?"

Ioan, solemnly, said, "It is," and chuckled when Lara urged her horse forward a little more quickly.

The road bent in front of her, then abruptly opened onto daylight so bright she threw an arm up to protect her eyes. The horse, startled by her boldness, pranced a step or two to the side. Lara yelped, eyes screwed shut as she grabbed for the saddle's edge. Ioan, still chuckling, caught her horse's reins and waited for them both to settle before releasing them.

Lara mumbled thanks and patted the horse's shoulder in apology as her eyes adjusted. Water reflected in the distance, helping to explain the sudden brilliance, but it was the countryside sloping down before her that made her catch her breath.

Jewel green swept away from the mountainside, spreading to lowlands peppered by houses that looked to have grown there. Ancient stone walls sat beneath thatched and slated roofs, and tiny figures were visible through motion as they worked fields stretching nearly to the water's edge. Mountains curved around the bay protectively, only the beach offering easy access on either side. Even Aerin was speechless as she gazed over the valley, though she turned to Ioan, accusing if still silent.

"We must grow our food somewhere," he said in response. "Magics have given us many choices within our earthen hall, but we must still fish and grow seed to survive."

"This land was *drowned*."

"Most of it. The hundreds lie beyond, in the water. See, even yet? There are shadows of the spires that once rose there, shaping the sea. That's where we go now, not to these few leagues that survived the drowning."

"You thought everything was underwater?" Cold dismay sluiced through Lara, leaving her rigid on the horse. "Didn't you wonder how any of them had survived, then?"

"That's been a question of debate among my people as long as I can remember." Aerin kicked her horse forward, taking the lead into grounds where Lara thought the inhabitants might well strike first and ask questions later. Ioan, sharing the unspoken thought, cursed softly and urged his horse into a gallop after Aerin, leaving Lara behind on the mountainside.

Pervasive mist softened the valley air, holding its own against the warm afternoon sun. The fields below were wide, bordered by hills and streams and rough stone walls. Different shades of green grew up as the fields came closer to the sea, and finally walls stood between yellowed beaches and the cultivated lands. She could see the slope of the earth all the way from her mountainside vantage to the beaches: it tilted down abruptly with the mountains, then very gently into miles of farmland. At some point in the distant past, the beaches themselves must have been farmland, too, until the sea came up to drown them.

If there were shadows of the towns-that-had-been lying within the water, she didn't yet have the eyes to see them. The bay was protected, but not idle and calm: sky-colored water rolled in and out again, hiding all the secrets it could.

Secrets that she had agreed to unveil. Lara shook herself, then leaned forward to whisper "Please don't let me get killed" into the horse's ear before kicking him into motion after the other two.

The downhill ride wasn't as bad—quite—as leaping the Unseelie chasm had been. Lara held on, alternately shrieking and laughing, until their chase brought them over a cresting hill and into a scene of chaos.

She reined up, though her horse's impulse was clearly to join the fray as Aerin, shouting, charged a group of farmers and by proxy, Ioan, who forced himself in front of her, their horses crashing together. One of the farmers, a woman, jumped forward to brandish a scythe at Aerin. Aerin backed away, more because of Ioan's interference than the armed farmer, though to Lara's eye the woman had a sure hand with the instrument-turned-weapon.

The noise, for half a dozen people and two horses, was astounding. Lara could pick no words out of the uproar, though Aerin's soprano was unusually aggrieved. Ioan bellowed over the farmers, whose voices were raised together in war cries as one drew daggers and spun them in his hands. They were more than the peasants the idyllic pastoral setting suggested, Lara realized. They were very likely trained warriors, which, given the history of the land, seemed wise.

Warriors who evidently didn't recognize their king. A dagger flew, narrowly missing Ioan himself and wedging flawlessly into the armor joint at Aerin's shoulder. She screamed as much in rage as pain, and transferred her sword to the other hand as she drove her horse forward again. Ioan rushed her a second time, drawing his legs up to launch himself bodily from his horse to tackle Aerin. They crashed to earth in a rattle of armor and supplies, both horses dancing in agitation. One of the Unseelie ran forward, carrying a spade he lifted like a piston, ready to drive it down even as Ioan balled a fist and cracked it across Aerin's jaw.

She hit back and scrabbled for the blade she'd lost when he tackled her. He dropped a knee onto her forearm, shouting incomprehensibly over her yell. A flash of resolve rushed over the spade-bearing Unseelie's face, and he changed his grip to swing it like a baseball bat at the back of Ioan's head.

Lara stood in her stirrups and roared, "That is your *king!*"

Later, although her shout had been infused with truth, she

thought it wasn't her power that had stopped the brawl. The Unseelie farmers simply hadn't been aware of her presence until she yelled, and then there was no chance of mistaking her as one of them. Her humanity, not her power, ended the fight.

But not soon enough. The spade, already in motion, slammed into Ioan's head. He fell forward, arms flung out, and dropped across Aerin, whose shouts were muffled beneath his weight.

Too late, the farmers lowered their weapons to preparatory stages, horror spreading across the spade-bearing man's face. Lara, swearing vehemently, rode forward and slid from her horse's back with none of the care she had taken earlier; Aerin's spell was indeed weaker than it had been.

What little medical knowledge Lara had said the bludgeoned king shouldn't be moved. Aerin had no such knowledge or compunction, and shoved Ioan away. He flopped to the side, head lolling and blood beginning to pour from the back of his skull. Lara cried out with dismay and knelt, trying to cradle his head so the wound wouldn't sustain further damage. "Get a healer."

"Who—*what*—are you?" The woman with the scythe looked torn between obedience and curiosity. Lara curled a lip and the man with the spade dropped it and ran for the distance.

"My name is Lara Jansen. I'm a truthseeker, and this is your king you just brained. He's still breathing." She bent close, making certain that was true. *Willing* it to be true, though she didn't think a truthseeker's power stretched that far. "What the hell were you thinking?"

"We saw—" The woman faltered, eyebrows drawn down. "We saw the Seelie woman, saw the man come after her—"

"And decided to hit the one tackling her, too?" Blood filled the lines of Lara's palms and dripped from the sides of her hands to stain her borrowed leggings. Someone would never want them back, after this.

"The light," the woman said uncertainly. "I thought he was fair as well. Now I see more clearly, and see our king."

Lara cursed again, this time barely more than a gurgle of frustration. She wasn't in the habit of swearing, and under pressure, felt her vocabulary lacking. "At least the shovel wasn't edge on. He'd have taken the top of his head off entirely. Do you have any talent at all for healing others?"

The woman, stricken, shook her head. "Healing another is one of the great gifts. Like truthseeking. You're *mortal*."

"So's Ioan going to prove to be if a healer doesn't get here fast." Lara bent her head over Ioan's, holding her breath so she could hear his. She was a literal world away from her deity, but she whispered a prayer anyway, trying to infuse it with strength and song to help the Unseelie king survive.

Aerin sat up, wrapped a hand around the dagger, and yanked it free with a sick shout. Her chin fell to her chest while she gulped for air. Then she looked up with a mixture of guilt and fury. "They attacked *me*!"

"Of *course* they attacked you!" Lara looked up with tears of anger suddenly hot on her cheeks. "You're a Seelie warrior, charging full speed into the single protected land they have left! You're lucky you're not dead, but I swear if you were I wouldn't shed a tear! Thank you," she added in a snarl to the farmer woman. "For not killing her."

"Thank her armor, not us," the scythe woman said flatly. "It was no decision of our own to spare her life. I am Braith," she added with the air of someone making a reminder, not an introduction. "What is a truthseeker doing here with our king?"

"I came to learn the truth about how the lands here were drowned. If I can, I'll try to raise them again." Lara placed a hand behind her, reminded of the staff strapped across her back. It had tremendous power, though whether it could be used to heal a badly injured man, she didn't know. Dafydd had drawn strength from it, but that had been magical weariness, not physical damage, and even then it had wrought a cost in the landscape. "But it's not going to matter unless a healer gets here soon. How long will it take for one to arrive?"

Silence greeted her, and she looked up to find three sets of Unseelie eyes hungry on her. Belatedly, it struck her that speaking the raw truth—that she would try to raise the Drowned Lands—might not have been the wisest thing she could have done.

For the first time in her life, meeting those desperate gazes, Lara thought *no pressure,* and heard amusement, not censure, in the untruth's music.

Eight

"You should come to the village," Braith said very softly. "The healer will wish to bring Hafgan there, and your presence and explanations will be desired. Almost none of us have met a mortal, and none at all have seen a truthseeker in years beyond counting. We would like to speak with you."

From the undercurrents in Braith's speech, Lara thought they would *like* to swallow her whole, as if she were a vessel of hope that could be drained to sustain them. And when she was emptied, the staff would be theirs for the taking, a more cynical part of her psyche added. She glanced at Ioan's barely breathing form, then exhaled softly. "I would be honored." That was true, and gave her a moment to think before shaking her head. "But we only have three days from this morning to complete our . . . quest. There'll be time to visit when we're done, though."

"Are you mad?" Aerin's voice broke on the question. "The quest is over. We cannot go on without him!"

"Something you should have thought of before riding roughshod into hostile territory," Lara snapped. "We have to go on without him. Just because no Seelie goes into the healing waters doesn't mean it's impossible. And I'm not one of you at all. Different rules might apply."

"But if they do not." Braith's gaze fastened on Lara. "If you do not, we may forever lose our chance to regain a homeland. The Unseelie people are already weary, Truthseeker. We can't afford such a blow."

"Then don't tell them all what I'm doing, and we'll do our best to survive. Aerin, can you ride?"

"The wound heals," Aerin replied shortly. "I *can*."

Anger expanded in Lara's chest. "Let me rephrase that. Will you ride, or will I leave you here with—Hafgan—and these Unseelie while I go ahead?"

Aerin bared her teeth, but climbed to her feet. "I will manage."

"Then we're going." Lara spoke decisively, though uncertainty made a pit of discomfort in her stomach. She didn't like abandoning Ioan, and liked the prospect of riding through Unseelie lands unescorted even less. But reluctant or not, she saw no other option. It would take days in her own world for a wound like Ioan's to heal. Even if magic accelerated the process, there was no telling how quickly he might recover. The delay could be more than they could afford.

Resolved, she waved Braith over, changing places with her. "Hold him, keep the dirt out of the wound if you can. Keep pressure on it, and keep it higher so it doesn't bleed as much. I don't know if it'll help, but it won't hurt. And if you have any way to send messages, please warn everyone that we're riding to the coast and shouldn't be bothered. I don't want another incident."

The last was directed more at Aerin than Braith, but Aerin ignored her, remounting awkwardly and maintaining stony indifference as Lara fetched her own horse and climbed up. Not until they were well on the path again, leaving a protesting Braith behind, did Aerin bark, "What manner of people are these, who attack a lone traveler in farmlands, and then all but slaughter their own king? No wonder the sea rose to drown them. It must have been Rhiannon's way of keeping down numbers, the way one might drown rats."

"Aerin," Lara said half under her breath, "this would be a good time to shut up."

It was hardly possible the Seelie woman heard her, but Aerin gave her a sharp look and went quiet. Her point, though, was a good one, and Lara thought about it as they cantered over low hills with only the triple beat of their horses' hooves as their sound track. Braith had seen two fair-haired warriors, she'd said. That might have reflected Ioan as he'd once been, but no more, and not for a long time. It wasn't impossible that the four Unseelie fighters had seen Lara in the distance, but she'd been far enough behind to not constitute a threat, and Ioan had been in the midst of the fight.

Lara drew up suddenly, sick certainty lodging in her gut. "Merrick is here."

"What?" Aerin's face was white with pain as she brought her horse around. "No. These fields and mountains are within the Barrow-lands. Emyr would have scried him, if he was here."

Lara pointed toward the still-distant sea. "Not if he was taking refuge in the water. He's Unseelie, right? So they should embrace him, at least in theory. And probably block Emyr's scrying while they were at it. No, I'm right, Aerin. I mean, could you ever mistake Ioan for fair-haired?"

Reluctance shifted Aerin's features and she shook her head. Lara nodded sharply in turn. "Someone made them see him as a Seelie warrior, not Unseelie. It could have been a glamour he cast himself, but why would he do that? It'd be asking for trouble. But Merrick casts illusions, and that shovel might have removed one more obstacle between himself and ruling Annwn."

. "The Barrow-lands," Aerin muttered.

"They both sound true as names. Furthermore." Lara pounded a fist into her palm. "Furthermore, if without Ioan we really can't get to the Drowned Lands, then Merrick's down three rivals for the throne and all that's left is Emyr."

That, finally, drew Aerin's concern. "We should go back."

"No. We have to go on. Emyr's got an army surrounding him right now, but Merrick's Unseelie. He might be able to enter the Drowned Lands himself and murder Dafydd and Hafgan, who are defenseless, both. Besides," Lara added hopefully, "maybe the waters will heal your shoulder instantly."

Aerin spat the peace salve away. "Or suck my life from the wound."

"For pity's sake. If you're representative of Seelie/Unseelie relations, it won't matter if the Unseelie get their lands back. You're going to end up killing each other anyway."

Aerin's smile was not nice. "Let me fervently hope that is truth, Lara Jansen. That it is fact you intend to draw in stone."

Lara cast her gaze to the heavens, then rode again for the shore, this time in silence.

A road, silvered beneath the sand, led straight into the water. Aerin reined up so far from the ocean's edge that Lara laughed. Her horse trotted down to stand ankle-deep in the soft tide, dropped its nose to investigate the waves, then gave her a disgusted look, as if scolding her for the water's brackishness.

"There are freshwater pools here," Aerin announced stiffly. Lara, still smiling, glanced back at her, then nudged the horse back up the beach. It blew into the pool Aerin showed them, then, satisfied, drank noisily. Lara felt as though it was saying *You see?* This *is how water ought to be.* She made a sound of agreement, then slid from its back and turned to contemplate the ocean.

"Ioan's element is water. This would have been easier with him, he could have kept a bubble of water away, kept air around us, so we could follow the road."

"Or he could have let the water collapse and drown us both."

"Which would have done him no good at all," Lara said impatiently. "The first time Emyr fails to raise you with the scrying spell, he'll ride in and destroy the Unseelie city. Ioan wouldn't risk it."

"Even if he thought it might mean wielding that staff himself?"

Lara bent her arm over a shoulder to touch it, then let her hand fall, unable to argue the possibility. "Tell me again what happened to Rhiannon. She drowned saving Merrick, right? It wasn't that the sea reached up and snatched her."

Irritation flashed through Aerin's voice: "Even the Drowned Lands aren't so vindictive. Yes, she went into the water and never returned. Nor have any Seelie since her."

"How many have tried?"

Stony silence answered her. Lara glanced at the Seelie woman, whose jaw was set with resolution. "All right. Ioan said there were trials to be passed to enter the Drowned Lands. Don't you usually have to announce yourself, before a trial?" She clawed the staff off her back and stood contemplating its ivory carvings for a few seconds.

They were beautiful, but they were merely border patterns, not even the animals or mythological figures she'd seen depicted in Celtic artwork. They had no story hidden in them, a thought which she held on to until it came back as clear music, undistorted by falsehood. There were no hidden answers there.

"Who do you think you'll announce yourself to?" Aerin sounded interested despite herself.

Lara looked up from her contemplation of the staff, wobbling it in her hands. "The Drowned Lands themselves, I guess. Do you think they'll recognize this?" Without letting herself fully consider the action, she drove it deep into the sand.

Aerin's howl of alarm was drowned beneath a cry of protest that rose from the land itself. The staff flared heat, searing Lara's palm. She jerked away with a shout, and a wave of triumph erupted from the staff as it stood free for a handful of seconds.

The sand beneath her feet collapsed, a divot opening up into the earth. Water spilled in, suspending particles and grabbing at Lara's ankles with quicksand intensity. Inside a heartbeat it had risen to her knees, clinging and terrifying. Lara seized the staff again, panic making a tiny concession to bewilderment: *she* was sinking, but the staff hadn't moved an inch, remaining a solitary solid thing in a melting beach. "Knock it off! Stop it! *Stop* it!"

The staff shuddered, resisting. Lara clamped her hands around it harder, though the heated patterns already threatened to scar her palms. "God damn it, I found you and you'll do what I say! *Knock! It! Off!*"

As suddenly as it had collapsed, the sand beneath her surged upward again, water spraying out to glisten against the earth before it sank harmlessly away. The rising ground took Lara with it, as if she'd been thrown into a game of blanket toss. Her knees buckled and she fell to them, but held on to the staff. Its heat was gone, though grumbling resentment washed through it. Lara dropped her forehead against it, panting for breath. "That's better. Thank you."

"You speak to it as if it lives. What . . ." Aerin trailed off under the sound of rushing water, and Lara looked up to watch the seas part along the silvered road that stretched into them. The ocean bubbled and spat, pulling open in an utterly unnatural manner. The Red Sea might have looked as the Barrow-lands bay did, pulling apart to leave a damp, glimmering pathway into the deeps. Not even fish were left gasping in the air; fistsful of water reached out, clawed them back into their retreating walls, and sent them swimming to safety. Waves continued to roll forward, splashing the beach to either side of the watery avenue, but where the sea defied physics, the tide merely roiled and crashed against itself, fighting to connect again with the space it had been banished from.

A man, expected only because Moses had once walked a similarly empty channel, strode out of the depths.

Hysteria swept Lara, cold sweat and a high laugh both breaking. She scrambled to her feet, unwilling to face what approached while on her knees. That was a posture reserved for devotion, and she was not—*was not*, despite every picture storybook she'd read as a child—*was not* in the presence of a literal, God-sent reenactment of the Red Seas. Not here. Not in Annwn, a land of elfin immortals whose own gods were, in her faith, pagan impossibilities. There was something else, another truth to be had, another way to explain the parting waters and the man coming from their heart. Her God had not sent him.

If He had, though, He had done so with an eye for artistry.

The man approaching wasn't *in* the water; he was *of* the water. It shaped him, and each step he took left sprays behind even as they also pulled up water from the road's surface. His hair was wild and white, not so much sea foam as the tide itself, alive with motion. His skin changed as Lara gaped, shifting in shade from Caribbean blue to slate gray and all the hues of ocean in between, so looking on him was watching an endless chase of color. He might have been Poseidon, except every depiction of *that* sea god Lara had seen was of a broad-shouldered, stern-looking bearded being armed with a trident and sometimes graced with a fish tail.

This creature was elfin through and through. Narrow-hipped, slim-shouldered, with long limbs and upswept ears. He carried no weapon. He didn't need to: Lara had no doubt the ocean itself was all the armament he required.

And like the ocean, his canted eyes were filled with stormy potential, and his voice with the crash of waves. "How dare you strike at the heart of this land again? How *dare you* lift *that* weapon, and on my shores?"

"I need safe passage to the Drowned Lands." Nothing gave Lara the right to make such a preposterous demand, but it came out steadily, even calmly. "Believe me, I have no intention of using the staff as a weapon. It has its own ideas, but for the moment I can control it."

The sea man eyed her, air growing damper and cooler with his regard. " 'For the moment.' "

Lara cursed the impulse that had made her use the phrase. Cursed the truth that was her gift, in other words, and sighed as she recognized that not admitting to the caveat would have sounded a lie to her own ears. "It's powerful. It has a will of its own."

His skin, his gaze, his entire being, darkened as though a storm came over the ocean. "You have no idea what you bear in your hands, mortal woman."

Lara looked at the staff, then over her shoulder at Aerin, hoping for guidance. Instead she found Aerin on her knees, wide-eyed and pale, knuckles pressed over her mouth. A posture reserved for devotion, Lara remembered, and her heart knocked. Aerin had shown no such reverence in discussing Rhiannon, whom she'd called their goddess. Whatever the elfin sea lord was, it was evidently well beyond Aerin's expectations.

Lara turned back to the water-creature, just as glad she'd had no expectations to be shattered. "You're probably right. I probably don't. But I found it so I could heal with it, if it's possible. If it's not, I'll bring it back to my world and hide it again rather than let it be used here to do more harm."

"That staff should not be taken from Annwn or the seas," he snarled. Lara could see Emyr in him suddenly, the two of them both creatures of such elemental power and great age that arrogance was their greatest stock in trade. But the sea man relented a fraction, not precisely softer, but indulging in a clear curiosity: "I hear truth in your words, mortal female. Are you an arbiter of justice?"

"I'm a truthseeker," Lara said cautiously. "My name's Lara, Lara Jansen. I don't know if I'm an arbiter of justice. I do know that two men of royal blood are somewhere in the Drowned Lands, and without them I'm never going to find out the truth of what happened to Annwn, or have a chance at setting it right. And I know this staff is God damned dangerous." Twice. That was twice in ten minutes she'd used a phrase that almost never passed her lips. Kelly, back at home, thought Lara's reluctance to damn in God's name was quaintly amusing. In the Barrow-lands, though, Lara had learned that naming the Holy Trinity was a magic in and of itself, and the curse carried a particular weight. Lara turned a brief glower at the staff, as though it had prompted her to swear, then gave her attention back to the watery man. "I'd be just as happy to finish what I need to do with it and give it to someone with a record of being able to handle its power."

"And who would that be?" This time real interest lightened the sea elf's voice, and Lara wondered if answering would be condemnatory. She was certain, though, that *not* answering would carry a price of its own, and after a moment shrugged.

"Another mortal. A poet named Oisín."

"Mortals," the water creature growled, then, more approvingly, "Poets. There may be wisdom in that; poets cross the boundaries of age and time. But that staff is not meant to be ruled by anyone, Truthseeker. Not for long."

Lara hesitated. "Not even by one such as you?"

Something complex happened in his eyes, ancient sorrow rising to mix with chagrin and unequivocal acceptance. "I was never meant to rule it at all. I learned that long ago."

The corner of Lara's mouth curved up. "All the more reason to help me get into the Drowned Lands, so I can rescue the prince, save the world, and return it to neutral hands."

"Neutral." The sea man's eyebrows, barely noticeable until he spoke with them, rose. "This poet is neutral?"

"I think he loved her. Rhiannon, the one whose staff it had been."

The sea lord stiffened, the water coursing beneath his skin going still. Lara bit her lower lip, then rushed on. "I think he went to great lengths to protect it so no one else could use it. No one unworthy. Maybe it's not neutrality, but it's a different path from the one it seems Emyr and Hafgan took. It looks more like neutrality, and from where I'm standing, that might be close enough."

Slowly, incrementally, he relaxed again, until his was a body in motion once more, all the moods of the ocean reflected in him. "An arbiter indeed. Tell me, mortal woman, Lara Jansen, Truthseeker. The journey into the Drowned Lands is not a gentle one. Are you prepared to undertake the trials?"

"I am." A twinge of honesty struck her and she added, "I don't understand what that means, really, but I'm willing to try. This land, Annwn, it's damaged. Even I can see that, and I've only been here a little while. Oisín made a prophecy about me. He called me a truthseeker and a worldbreaker, and said I'd find the way to mend the past. The only way I can see to do that is going in there." She nodded at the sea beyond him, marveling briefly that she'd become accustomed, in a few short minutes, to the way it held itself apart from the silver road. "I want to help," she said quietly. "Please help me to help."

"And your companion?" The sea lord took apparent notice of Aerin for the first time, and Lara heard her flinch to attention.

"I will join her if you'll permit me, Lord." Aerin's soprano was ragged with emotion, and she came forward roughly to stand beside Lara when he gestured for her.

He pressed his thumbs against their foreheads, a cool watery touch. Power staggered Lara, power unlike any she'd encountered so far. The entirety of the world's oceans were in the caress, thundering, calm, corrosive, sustaining; he encompassed all of that in his fragile elfin form. Sea life in all its myriad shapes, with its cleverness and dull-wittedness, inquisitive or reclusive, light-filled and shadowed, ran through him so that he *was* their life, and they were his. Temperature spread through his touch, from the heat of sunlight on the water to the great blocky ice floes that hid black water from the light for decades on end.

"You will see the lands as they are," he said mournfully. "Not as they once were, but the ruin that they are now, for even I cannot bring them back to their glory. But you will walk among the ruins as though you walk through air, and you will touch them as if they are dry land raised from the waters. You will survive the drowning, Truthseeker, but only the Hundreds will tell whether you survive the trials. You have three days before the water takes you."

He dropped his hands. Lara nearly fell as the surge of power retreated. She was left gaping after him as he returned to the depths without another word, and not until the silver road was empty again did she dare to ask, "Who *was* he?"

"That was Llyr," Aerin whispered. "Father of the sea, and father of my people, for he is Rhiannon's father, too."

Nine

"That was..." Words fell away, leaving Lara staring down the silver-sheened road that led into the ocean. Llyr was gone, taken back by the water without a ripple, though the bay remained as it had been, stricken by a parting that went against the laws of nature. Lara's chest was overfull, awe and astonishment poured into her until she couldn't breathe. Her first impulse had been right: not Poseidon, perhaps, but surely the same elemental power by another name. She still felt his thumbprint against her forehead. The power sweeping from it heralded changes in her body, changes wrought by the will of a creature so far beyond mortal, even so far beyond immortal, that she had only one name for it.

"That was a god," she finally managed, though it was still half a question. "An actual, honest-to-God...god." Truth rang through it, expanding what she thought she knew into new spaces. She had faith in her God, singular or triumvirate, but His words came back to her: *Thou shalt have no other gods before Me.* She had always thought that meant other gods were false, and so not to be worshipped. Not once had she considered it could lend credence to their existence, and was meant to establish a hierarchy of belief.

Aerin said, "I told you ours walked the land with us," though the acerbic note Lara expected was missing. "But Llyr is one of the old gods, and it has been long on long since he's been seen. My grandmother would not remember the last time an old one spoke to us. Who are you," she added more falteringly. "What are you, Truthseeker, that you bring back our ancient gods and shake the order of our world?"

"I don't know." Half a truth: the answer, *worldbreaker*, stood out in Lara's mind, but that was more than she wanted to face, much less voice, even if she was certain of what it meant. "All I know is that I mean no harm."

"What we mean and what we do can be oceans apart." Aerin turned away, still quiet with trouble, and, one-armed, stripped the horses of their tack while Lara watched with a sense of incompetence. "Llyr didn't grant them the ability to go into the water," the Seelie woman explained as she worked. "We'll have to go alone. They'll be fine. Not even the Unseelie would harm them. They know too well the value of a good horse."

Lara glanced at the ocean, then at Aerin. "If you trust them so little, why did you agree to come when Llyr asked?"

"What would you do if your god threw down such a challenge?" Aerin collected her saddlebags with a grunt and nodded for Lara to take up her own. "I still believe the Drowned Lands are cursed for my people, but surely there's no better way to enter them than with the blessings of a god."

Without looking back, she struck down the silver road, and Lara ran to catch up.

✑

The sea fought its forced boundaries as they walked deeper into the parted waters, sloshing over to wet their feet and dripping from above as if they'd entered a network of damp caves. The air turned heavier, weighing at Lara's hair and clogging her lungs until a deep breath turned to a wracking cough. She crouched where she was, one hand wrist-deep in water to balance herself against the road, and tears spilled down her cheeks as she hacked for air. "I thought Boston could get muggy."

Aerin put a hand out, offering to draw Lara to her feet. "Llyr said we would survive the drowning. It will be worse, though, before it is better."

"Survive the—" Those had been the sea god's words, but Lara had put no real thought into them. She took Aerin's hand and stood, still struggling to breathe freely as she glanced back the way they'd come.

The path behind them was thick with water. Not just on the road, but in the air, droplets mingling to form globs that spun and shivered as they grew. Aquariums were easier to see into: Lara felt like she was underwater with her eyes open, no protection between them and the element. Primal fear thickened her lungs even more, making air harder yet to pull in. "It's filling up."

"Not even a god can part the waters forever." Aerin turned Lara away from shore, back down the path they faced. It was clearer than the road behind them, though a spike of pain shot through Lara's vision, warning that what she saw was very likely a glamour meant to distract and reassure.

She crushed her eyes shut, not at all eager to have the glamour displaced. Better to believe she walked into clean, clear air, if she could. For a rarity, she envied people for whom belief was subjective. Even with her eyes closed, music crept around her thoughts, assuring her of the truth: she walked into the ocean. That it hadn't drowned her was an oversight soon to be rectified.

"Oh, to hell with it, I'm just making this worse." Lara let go of Aerin's hand and dragged in the deepest breath she could, then put on a surge of speed and ran forward. Ten steps; twenty; then thirty before her lungs began to burn. An athlete would do better, she thought. Even Kelly, with her love of adventure sports, would do better. Lara staggered forward, tears in her eyes again as her heart beat a painful protest at the sudden lack of oxygen. Her eyes were still closed, letting the glamour trick her as best it could. Water dampened her skin, full-on humidity, but not the immersion of having splashed into the sea. The lie of it sang through her mind, but she shied away from admitting it, concentrating instead on one more step. One more. One more.

She lost count of how many she'd taken before instinct ripped away deliberation and her jaw gaped open to suck down air.

Water flooded her lungs, cold and deadly and relentless. Lara hacked it out and tried again, fingers clawing at her chest as if she could rip it open and find sustaining breath that way. Salt stung the welts that rose and she thrashed, trying to escape both the drowning and the itching pain. Gravity lost its hold on her, the silver path below no longer a road but simply a watery gravemarker. She rose up, kicking and coughing, drawing more water in with every panicked inhalation, but the surface was impossibly far away. The sun was a distant dot refracting through gray waves, parted waters long since closed above her head. They hadn't been so deep when she'd crushed her eyes shut and begun her mad rush; she was sure of it. Maybe she'd run farther than she'd thought. Maybe the glamour, once acknowledged, had swept her into the ocean more quickly, its primary mission already accomplished.

Her chest *hurt*. It weighed so much, filled with water the way it was, and its weight wanted to pull her back to the ocean floor. That was closer by far than the receding spot of sunlight up above, and seemed vastly easier to reach. She'd stopped flailing; her arms and legs, like her chest, were absurdly heavy. Waving them seemed futile, a waste of what little energy she had left. An idle thought crossed her mind: if she could kick her way down to the sandy earth below, she could curl up there and rest a while. Perhaps the pressure in her chest would ease then, and she could swim to the surface after a few minutes of relaxing.

Swimming down was much easier than struggling upward. Within a few seconds she reached the ocean floor and listlessly curled into a ball.

Sand rose up at the pressure of her descent, tiny particles floating into her nose and mouth. Lara dropped against the earth with an unexpected soft thud, the jarring thump knocking water from her lungs. She coughed, then rolled onto her hands and knees, gagging and choking on water as it came up again, emptying from her lungs as quickly as it had filled them. Floating sand collapsed into rich loamy soil, darker brown where Lara spat up mouthful after mouthful of bitter saltwater. She gasped and wheezed, tears streaming from her eyes once more, until there was nothing more to force out of her body and she collapsed in the dirt, rolling over to stare skyward.

The sun above was clear and warm now, the ocean's interference washed away. Lara drew a shuddering breath of clean fresh air and shivered as a breeze pinned cold wet clothes against her skin. Exhaustion held her in its grip, her body still too heavy to move, but the pain in her chest was fading. She was, by all rights, dead.

The thought ran sour in her mind, its bells tarnished by sea water and age. For a long time she couldn't move beyond the concept, stymied by its wrongness. Finally she croaked "By all rights bespelled?" aloud, and *that* had the ring of truth to it.

"That was the most foolish, and possibly the boldest, thing I have seen someone do in a long time." Aerin came from nowhere to sit beside her, arms looped around her knees as she, too, heaved for air in the aftermath of drowning. "I lacked your courage, Truthseeker. I came one step at a time. I'm not certain yours wasn't the wiser way. A quick drowning may be easier than a slow."

Lara wheezed, trying to find her voice, and coughed until tears came again before she could speak clearly. "On the other hand, you can talk better. Ow, oh, ow." She pressed a hand against her chest, then rolled over again to curl up with her forehead in the dirt. "I hope it won't be that bad going back."

Nonplussed, Aerin made a sound. "I don't know. There are other things to worry about first."

Lara groaned, "The trials," and Aerin, cautiously, said, "Among other things. Lift your gaze, Truthseeker. See what I see."

"That tone suggests I'd rather not." Lara coughed again, then raised her eyes to look over the Drowned Lands.

An army of ghosts marched on them.

They were men and women and children, and they bore no weapons. But neither did they need any: even from a remove they were cold, drawing warmth and life from the air. Lara hitched back, knowing the sea lay behind her and that ultimately she had to go forward, but reluctant to let the dead close the distance.

"Are they real?" Aerin's hoarse whisper barely carried to Lara's ears.

Lara, dismayed at her own conviction, said, "Oh, they're real," before wondering how they could be. She'd been told time and again that the elfin races had no afterlife, no soul to continue on after death, but each of the undead pacing toward them was an individual, loss and horror written on their faces. If they had once had color, it had been bleached from them, the way relentless sun might bleach bone to brittle white. Some carried farm tools and fishing materials; others led skeletal horses, skin tight over protruding ribs.

They left no mark on the earth as they passed, nor made any sound, but the air grew colder, and Lara, shivering in her wet Unseelie garb, thought she might freeze before they even reached her.

Beyond them, beyond the black fields they crossed, stood the remnants of a city. Broken obsidian towers jabbed at the sky, ugly where they should have been graceful. Details were lost to the distance, but a single ragged banner flew from one of the ruined towers, a testament against oblivion. Lara abruptly liked them for that, even though defiance had never been her way.

"They draw closer, Truthseeker." Aerin was on her feet, sword in hand. If her injured shoulder bothered her, Lara could see no sign of it. "What do we do?"

"We can't fight. There are hundreds of them."

"Thousands," Aerin disagreed, truth ringing in the assessment.

Lara gritted her teeth. "So maybe you should put the sword down."

"And let them come at us unhindered? We have two days and a little, Lara Jansen. We cannot stand here and wait on them if we wish to revive Dafydd or bring back the Unseelie king." Aerin's lip curled with the last words and she wove a figure with her sword, making it a threat to the oncoming ghosts.

Dafydd. Lara closed her eyes, building an image of the Seelie prince. Warm-skinned, shaggy-haired, delicately elfin even hidden behind a mortal glamour. She hadn't forgotten him, but he had fallen from the forefront of her thoughts. There had to be a way forward, because he lay somewhere beyond the ghost-ridden fields, and it was much too early to give up.

Emboldened and feeling entirely unwise, Lara repeated, "Put the sword down," and strode past Aerin to meet the approaching undead.

She met a woman first, and offered a hand as she would to a human. The woman gazed at Lara's extended hand, while behind her the masses came to a slow halt. Their stillness answered any lingering doubts of whether they lived or not: no living thing could be so eerily motionless. Only the woman before her moved, looking again from her hand into Lara's face.

"My name's Lara Jansen. I'm a truthseeker." Barely a month ago Lara had never heard the word, but describing herself that way, especially within the Barrow-lands, came naturally. They understood, here, what it meant, maybe more profoundly than she herself did.

And even the dead, it seemed, knew what to make of the word and its portents. A flush of color ran through the woman, enlivening her a little. Then her jaw dropped, gaping like a vampire's, and the woman surged forward, fingers clawed and hunger in her gaze.

Lara shrieked and fell backward, hands uplifted to block the woman's attack. But Aerin was there, unsheathed blade whispering between them. She threw Lara a look of *I told you so* disgust, worsened when Lara shouted, "No!" and dove under the blade to reach a second time for the undead woman.

This time their hands connected. Cold power rushed Lara, seeking sustenance. It dove inside her, pouring toward the sound of bells; toward the music that guided Lara in truth and falsehood. Lara steeled herself against the attack, the knowledge of *how* rising up like the tide. The skill lay in the bells: she whispered, "I'm sorry, no. The power's not for you," and it rang out from her core. Not the alto and soprano tones she usually heard in her own voice, but deep reverberations, baritone peals from church bells meant to be heard for miles.

The tolling notes shook apart the frantic power channeled by the undead woman. She released Lara and staggered back, her retreat echoed by the army massed behind her. Aerin finally lowered her sword, mouth agape as Lara crept toward the dead Unseelie and offered her hands a third time.

"Tell me who you are. I'll carry your story beyond here, back to Annwn, so you won't be forgotten. I swear it on my—" *Oath as a*

Truthseeker leapt to mind, though she'd taken no oath. Lara swallowed a breath and changed the phrase, not wanting to foreswear herself even with the best of intentions. "On my blood as a Truthseeker."

The woman whispered "Truthseeker," then seized Lara's hands in a cold grip, and told her story.

She was Glenna, a farmer, with dirt still beneath her nails. She knelt in the soil, a trowel in one hand, a sack of root vegetables rich and warm-smelling at her side. Birds, mostly raucous crows, called and shouted while she worked, the boldest ones winging toward the bag of sun-warm tubers. But suddenly they were silent, and in their place came a sound of thunder from a clear sky. Glenna looked up in time to see a wall of water crashing toward her, high and silver and full of fury. She was on her feet, running, then. A dozen steps, no more, before the ocean took her. She could swim, but not in this. Familiar panic rose in her breast, the same sensations of drowning Lara had just encountered. Only there was no sea god to promise her a chance to survive the drowning, and when the waves rolled smooth again, Glenna floated dead on their surface.

Caddoc, behind Glenna, whispered his tale, too. A warrior, fighting under hot sun: practicing bladework with other soldiers, beneath the obsidian spires of the distant city. Water surged in around the castle, coming from every direction at once; he and others like him drowned in the weight of their armor, clawing for the disappearing sky.

Smiths, weavers, scholars, artists: their stories came over Lara like the water itself, relentless waves pounding into her. Flashes of vision ran so close together they became a mosaic, a collage of a thousand lives in the moments they ended. Parents snatched up children as if they could hold them higher than the waters; students clutched manuscripts the same way. A boy ran for the highest of the towers, chased by rising water, and when it caught him in the castle's apex, he threw himself from the windows and struck out in a defiant swim. Some few turned to the inescapable tide and greeted it with elegance and grace. But they died as the others did, so quickly, leaving only drowned lands behind. Their lives poured into Lara until she had always been there, a forever monument to what had been lost.

The shock of release was as great as the power of listening. The tide of immortal lives lost pulled back, leaving her gasping on hands and knees, as shocked to have survived this as she'd been to live through the drowning. The staff, safe across her back, pulsed with power, and for a moment she wanted to draw it out to help her stand. But it had tried to split the earth back on the shores of the Drowned Lands. What it would do within their actual borders wasn't something she was eager to discover. Instead she sat back on her heels, uncertain of when she'd fallen. Aerin grabbed her elbow and pulled her to her feet, less elegant than the staff's support might have been, but equally effective.

Glenna stood before them, paler than before. Wan, fading, with a different desperation in her eyes. Lara croaked, "Rest," and put a hand over her throat; she sounded as if she hadn't spoken in weeks. Exhaustion swept over her, limbs trembling and thirst coming on her hard. She spoke slowly, making sure the words made sense: "Rest. I understand now, and I won't forget. You won't be forgotten."

Aerin hissed, "What are you speaking of?" but Lara shook her head as Glenna stepped back and began to fade.

They weren't ghosts. They were the memory of the land. Someone—Llyr, perhaps, if he was god of the sea and the things in it—had invested, or lost, so much in the drowned countryside that it survived in the water itself; in the inundated earth, and in the shards of homes and buildings and bones now hidden beneath the water.

"Oisín will help me write it down," Lara whispered to the changing land. The black earth was emptier now, not just of the visible ghosts, but even a sense of sorrow was lessened. "All your stories. All your names. You've waited long enough. Rest now. Go with..."

"Rhiannon," Aerin said in a very low voice.

Lara looked at her, then at the darkening land and finally nodded. "With Rhiannon. With Llyr. Go into history, but not legend. You won't be forgotten. I promise."

Glenna lingered the longest, and when she was gone, so was the sun. Stars in a multitude of colors thickened the sky. Lara, staring upward, entertained the idea that the drowned Unseelie had just passed into starlight, and from Aerin's discomfited expression, thought the Seelie woman imagined the same. Song wrapped around the fancy, exploring it without finding absolute truth or falsehood in it. Lara smiled and sat down in the dirt, weary but satisfied.

Aerin's acerbic voice took her good humor away: "We've stood here on this farmstead half a day and you're smiling?"

"Half..." The stars slipped into place in a more meaningful manner. Lara gaped at them, then at Aerin. "I was out half a day?"

The Seelie woman gestured impatiently at the horizon, which didn't so much as hint at sunset. "Emyr scried me these long hours ago, while you shivered and cried out and whispered stories of the dead. He was none too pleased, Truthseeker."

"You didn't tell him Ioan was injured, did you?"

Shiftiness crossed Aerin's face. Lara groaned, then leveled a finger at the other woman. "If we get back and Emyr's obliterated the Unseelie city, I'm holding you responsible."

Alarm replaced Aerin's evasiveness and Lara bit back rue. There had been some truth in her threat, enough to not sour it in her mind, but she had briefly forgotten the power her gift offered. *She* wouldn't want to be told a truthseeker held her responsible for anything... but nor was she inclined to reassure Aerin on the topic. Everything she knew about the Seelie woman suggested she was loyal to her people, commendable enough. Lara's loyalty, though, lay with Dafydd and to the truth. She would have preferred a companion whose motivations aligned more snugly with her own.

Then again, Aerin had every reason to want Dafydd back, if nothing else. Want him back not just for the Barrow-lands, but perhaps for Aerin herself. From her perspective, it had been only a few days—months, now—since he'd left the Seelie court to find a truth-seeker. She knew it had been decades for Dafydd—Lara had been there when he'd told her—but what she likely saw was her lover returning after a mere handful of days with a new, mortal interest on his arm.

Lara muttered, "Relationships are hard enough without time travel."

Aerin said, "What?" sharply, and Lara shook her head.

"Nothing. Nothing important, Aerin. Sorry. Look, I know we only have two days left and three trials to find and survive, but I'm so tired I'm shivering. I don't think we're going to be bothered again right here. Could we sleep until sunrise?"

"You may," Aerin said grudgingly. "I'll stand watch."

"Try not to kill anybody, okay?" Lara crawled to their packs and unrolled a blanket, folding it beneath herself to gain more protection from the cool earth before tugging a second one over her. From beneath the sudden warmth, she mumbled "Thank you," and in moments sleep brought dreams of elfin faces and names and stories that would never leave her.

Ten

"Do you have a plan?" Aerin's question, only slightly less welcome than the encroaching sunrise, shook off any hope Lara had of stealing another few minutes' sleep. The most she could do was refuse to move, buried in her blankets, while she struggled to turn half-sleeping thoughts into coherent words.

"We'll go into the ruined city," she finally answered. "So many people died there. Seems like a good place to hold rites of passage. I wonder if we both have to pass. Should've asked Ioan."

"The quest is yours, Truthseeker. It's the hero, not his companions, who has to prove himself."

Lara pushed up on an elbow, throwing blankets back so she could glower blearily at Aerin. "Are the Seelie completely unfamiliar with the concept of reassurance?"

"No, but you would hear the falsehood in my voice."

Lara groaned. "I never thought I'd miss the little white lies people tell each other. All right." She climbed out of bed, shaking dirt from the blankets and rolling them up again as tightly as she could. Aerin watched with professional disinterest, only nodding when Lara's attempts to repack met her approval. A brief glow of delight warmed Lara. She wasn't an outdoorsy camping type like Kelly, so successfully packing gear was an accomplishment worth taking pride in. It was the little things, Kelly often said, and Lara found herself in agreement.

Aerin tossed her a chunk of dried meat, followed by a piece of even drier bread, then swung her own pack up onto her shoulders with well-practiced ease. Lara watched, eyebrows furrowed as Aerin checked the pack's hang and shifted a canteen of water to her hip for easy access. "The city's half a day's walk if we're quick."

"I doubt I'm quick." Lara eyed Aerin's longer legs, then crouched to pull her own pack on and copy the placement of a water canteen. "Too bad we couldn't bring the horses."

"We might have ridden through the ghost fields undisturbed yesterday afternoon, had we had the horses." Aerin's tone suggested it was entirely Lara's fault they'd been deprived. She set out with long strides, quick enough that irritation spurted through Lara. She could match Aerin's pace for a little while, but would end up exhausted and slowing them down that much more if she responded to the Seelie woman's machismo. It took active determination to not run and catch up, but Lara settled into a pace she could maintain, gnawing on salty meat and chalky bread. Food that would last forever, probably, though she wouldn't want to live forever if it was all she got to eat.

The earth underfoot was unfamiliar: clots of dirt and poking stones rather than the smooth paved streets she was accustomed to at home. It smelled better, though, fresh and warming with the sunrise, without patches of gum and worse to navigate. The backpack, this early on, wasn't onerous, though a few hours of carrying its bulk would exhaust her shoulders. It would take as little time for her calves and feet to become weary from walking on soft, shiftable ground, but as long as she didn't give in to Aerin's silent challenge, she would be fine.

Within an hour Aerin slowed to an amble, waiting for Lara to catch her, and then matching Lara's gait. "You're smarter than I thought."

Lara laughed out loud. "That's what we'd call damning with faint praise, Aerin. You're half a foot taller than I am. I couldn't keep up even if you weren't trying to make me look bad. Your shoulder's not bothering you," she added awkwardly.

Tension thinned Aerin's mouth. "Not since the drowning. I inspected it while you... communed... with the dead. It appears to be healed."

Lara glanced into the sunrise at their backs, mountain shadows still lush with black this early in the morning and the meadows at their feet blue with first light. There was no hint of the sea that had risen to swallow the land, not from where they were; not with Llyr's gift of vision riding them. Lara touched her temple thoughtfully. Most glamours gave her headaches, but nothing in her perception wavered or bent the way glamours did. He couldn't, she thought, have actually changed their reality, but the perfect presentation of a drowned world without any hints to it being a lie sent a shiver down her spine. Llyr's power vastly outstripped the Seelie and Unseelie magic users she'd met. She turned back to the path they were on, subdued, and asked, "The waters?"

Aerin scoffed. "Deadly to my kind." Her certainty, though, had vanished. "A gift from Llyr, perhaps."

"Llyr, whose waters they are," Lara said quietly, but didn't press it further. Aerin grunted in relief and pulled a few steps ahead to discourage talk.

The city in front of them grew incrementally closer, clear gold sunlight picking out details invisible from the fields. There were places where the obsidian towers were shattered, though time and tide had worn their sharp edges smooth. Others had never broken, but were still dulled; what Lara's eye wanted to finish as crisp curving lines were gentle and rounded, having long since given up their architect's conceit. Low city walls grew up from the earth as they drew nearer, all of them banked with earth. Lara imagined they would be buried in sand, if she could see the city as it truly was.

A chime rang, warning, and for the first time her vision wavered. The air thickened, light filtered by gray-blue water and filled with new elements: a school of fish, and kelp brushing against her skin as it grew up from the ocean floor. Breathing became more difficult, her chest aching, and her ears popped as the pressure against them increased. The chime sounded again, louder this time, and distorted by the poor conductivity of the sea. Lara stopped where she was, eyes crushed shut, and rebuilt the image of *earth,* not sand, encroaching on the city walls. Whispered, "Llyr's vision is a gift. A truth from a long time ago. I accept it." She twisted her arm back, feeling for the staff pinned in place beneath her pack, and felt a faint electric shock as her fingers brushed against the ivory rod. "Llyr's truth is the truth of the moment. Without it we're all lost to the ocean floor. I *accept* it."

A ripple of agreement washed through the staff, strengthening her belief. Sunlight slowly warmed her back again, the air thinning and becoming easier to breathe. Her ears popped again, compression releasing, and after long seconds she dared open her eyes and drag in a ragged breath. The Drowned Lands were once more as Llyr had offered them: not resplendent in their heyday glory, but ruins that could be walked through as tourists might.

Aerin stood a few yards ahead of Lara, facing her with wide eyes. "What in Rhiannon's name was *that*?"

"That was my power trying to kill me," Lara said hoarsely. "Us. Are you all right? I never heard you swear before."

"It's not an oath one voices around the king." Aerin patted herself down, a jackrabbit pulse visible in her throat. "I am well. I thought for a moment I would drown."

"You won't." Lara forcibly put the thought out of her head and thrust a finger toward the city. "Let's go. Time's wasting."

Of all the visible city walls, the gates had come through closer to unscathed than anything else. Coral grew up over them, not in the astonishing colors of tropical waters, but in cooler yellows and grays and bleached whites that looked dead when not immersed. It prickled and reached out and up, making an imposing barrier between the farmlands and the city itself. Glimpses of shaped stone were visible beneath it, but time had long since hidden away whatever carvings might have once graced the city's entryway.

Sitting in front of the gates were a pair of young men, rattling dice cups at one another and throwing down bones against the earth. They both had the Unseelie look to them, dark hair and gold skin, though they looked sun-browned rather than as if they'd leeched color from the earth itself. Lara slowed a dozen yards away, exchanging astonished glances with Aerin. Together they edged forward until the youths—though why Lara thought they were young, given the unaging aspect of all the elfin peoples—glanced up, then scrambled to their feet in a fit of embarrassment. One cried "Halt!" as the other scooped up a spear with a gleaming metal head.

Lara murmured "Do you really use that word when you're standing guard?" to Aerin, who snorted.

"No strangers come to the Caerwyn citadel. We say very little at all when standing guard."

"I am called Evrei," the guard who'd spoken before said. "This city is guarded by my brother Evrawg and myself. Who goes there?"

Lara began, "My na—" and was cut off by Aerin's interruption: "You guard a dilapidated hunk of coral. Why should I not go over the wall?"

"Certain doom lies that way," Evrei said pompously. "Only one of the doors behind me leads safely into the city."

"There are no doors at all," Aerin protested. Evrei took one step back as the other youth—Evrawg—rolled his eyes and took a confidential step forward to murmur, "Of course not. He's lying. Can't trust him, you can't."

Lara put a hand over her face, trying not to laugh. "Aerin—"

"We have no *time* for this, Lara!" Aerin's sword was in her hand when Lara looked up again, her expression set as she advanced on the guards. "We'll pass with your leave or without it, but it's your own heads you're risking."

Evrei pressed into the coral with an elbow under the sounds of Aerin's threats. The delicate stuff crackled, dust sheeting to the earth as two arches gave way within it. The silvered path they'd been following split, each new road leading through one of the doors, city ruins visible beyond their shadows. Aerin hissed from the back of her throat, a feral sound of accomplishment.

"Evrei, which door— Aerin, *don't!*" Lara ran forward, grabbing for Aerin's backpack as she stomped through the closest door. She missed and skidded to a stop on the door's threshold. Aerin vanished between one step and the next with no footprints, no sound, no flash of color to say she'd once been there.

Lara's gut filled with bile. Never mind that Aerin had carried most of the food: more important, Emyr would scry for her at sunset, and find nothing. Nothing, or worse, the doom promised by Evrei. The Unseelie city stood in danger now, unless Lara could get her back.

Her, or the two royal scions resting somewhere in the Drowned Lands. Lara dropped her chin to her chest and cursed. Evrawg, brightly, reassuringly, said, "Ah, she'll be fine. Nothing to worry about! Go on after her, why don't you, and see for yourself?"

"Because you're the brother who always lies." Lara turned from the doorway, feeling as if her pack had grown twice as heavy in the past minute. "Evrei, which door is the safe one?"

He pointed to the door Aerin hadn't taken, a trace of sullen pout marring his mouth. "How did you know? We didn't even get to say that one of us always tells the truth."

"I'm a truthseeker. You couldn't trick me if you wanted to." Lara sighed. "But if it makes you feel better, I'll ask the question the right way. Which door would your brother tell me to take?"

Evrei pointed to the door Aerin had disappeared through, though the pout still pulled at his lips. "You're only supposed to ask one question."

"Evrei, I could have asked if the sky is blue or if grass is green. You can't lie to me." Lara hefted the pack on her shoulders, scowling at the doorways. "'Truth will seek the hardest path.' *Shit.* Aerin, when I catch up to you . . ."

The threat unfinished, Lara stalked through the door leading to certain doom.

Eleven

Murky night enclosed her as she stepped through the door. Mist crawled up, encircling her thighs as if to hold her back, and the city shifted in her vision, becoming darker, grimmer. Lara retreated a step and encountered rough sticks that cracked under the pressure of her pack. She twisted around, heart jolting, to find the doors bleak hollows overgrown with impassable coral. Evrei and Evrawg were gone, if they'd ever really been there at all. The thought wavered tunelessly and Lara put it out of mind, unwilling to explore what was true and what wasn't, especially having deliberately chosen the wrong door.

What had once been city streets sprawled before her, but she no longer saw them as Llyr had enchanted her to. Silver stone was buried beneath drifting sand, and scuttling bugs peeked out of bone shelters sunken in the moving earth. The homes and towers that had graced the Unseelie city were dank now, lightless and lifeless, and the defiant banners that had flown no longer rose above the town. Chilly wind passed through instead, lifting Lara's hair in thin dancing tendrils and holding it aloft the way water would. Coral snatched at the strands, trying to tangle it and hold her in place.

She shut those thoughts down, too, and forced herself forward. Aerin had left no footprints, or the shifting sand had already taken them. Had already taken *her*, perhaps; Lara sank ankle-deep with each step, sand clouding up to grasp at her calves and knees before wafting down again. Pressure swam against her legs and over her arms, wind carrying more weight than it usually did. She wondered what devils hid in it. Song pounded inside her skull, encouraging her to pull down the veil of Llyr's gift and *see* what accompanied her as she walked across the ocean floor.

It would be a very brief viewing. A minute or two of appreciating just what monsters and dangers roamed the drowned city. Then, without Llyr's gift at hand, she would join them, one more lost soul far beneath the sea. And if she was lost, so were all the memories she'd promised to return to Annwn. So was Dafydd, and so, maybe, was Annwn itself. She'd seen no forgiveness in Emyr's eyes. If she didn't come back with answers, he would ride on the Unseelie city and destroy it. The transformation would be complete: Annwn would be the Barrow-lands in totality, a land of the dead and dying, though it might on the surface appear to be more.

An orchestra's worth of triumphant music flooded her, pushing back the weight of heavy air. She had seen the Seelie as dying, had even seen the rival peoples as two halves of a whole, but the entire land's metamorphosis had escaped her, at least in conscious thought. Drowned Lands, Barrow-lands; together they made up a whole, and she doubted suddenly that the Barrow-lands would ever be healthy, so long as the ground she walked now still lay beneath the sea. Whatever Hafgan and Emyr had done so many millennia ago had spelled doom for both of them. Hafgan, perhaps, had realized it earlier, and fled back to the Drowned Lands. A generous soul might think it was to lend his strength to maintaining what little memory of the land was left here, but Lara suspected his intentions were darker. Harboring his power, perhaps, so that when Emyr was weak enough Hafgan could attack without compunction.

She'd become cynical since meeting Dafydd ap Caerwyn. She wasn't certain she was proud of that, but it lent her a sour strength to forge beyond the gates and enter the city itself.

Broken walls rose up cleanly, streets remaining delineated, but the ground was uneven, stone from fallen buildings making hills and toe-stubbing lumps. Lara scrambled up them, fingers dug into shallow earth, and slid down their far sides with her attention more for the grim skies than the path she took. The ebony towers shone darkly in the murky light, as opposite to the glowing Seelie citadel as could be imagined.

Her mind's eye abruptly filled in details of shattered architecture, finishing the spires and swoops of the towers. They'd echoed the Seelie citadel once, though this city was built around its soaring towers where the Seelie city was entirely contained within the palatial structure. Still, their hearts were one and the same, another reminder that the highland and lowland peoples were of a kind. Or that they had been, before they'd been torn asunder by the staff Lara now carried across her back.

The staff pulsed as she thought of it. The air flinched, then surged in, weightier than before as it pried at the ivory rod. Lara's breath clogged, her confidence slipping away as the air—*air,* she insisted, not water—took on a determination to separate her from the staff. Muck thickened, daylight fading until the only light came from the dark towers.

The air—the ocean—lit up around her in wrong colors, a flood of black light illuminating the things she hadn't been able to see before. Sea life flickered by, darting around her at the last moment. Lara was grateful, as it seemed wholly possible, in the wavering blue light, that she might register as a ghost herself, and that fish might swim through her without noticing. Bits of net wafted through the water, constantly tied and untied by the currents. But it was the city itself that came alive in unnerving pulses.

Fallen buildings were reconstructed in the changing light. From one moment to the next walls flickered into place and faded again, reminiscent of an old hand-cranked film. But no ancient film had the quality of effects the withering city showed her. Beasts swam within the broken city walls, serpents and kraken and long-toothed monsters she had no name for. Lara stood rigid on the ocean floor, heart sick in her chest, certain that any motion on her part would bring a tentacled, hard-beaked behemoth whipping down on her.

Women sauntered by, their bodies so beautifully formed that Lara's avocation as a tailor twitched to the fore, eager to measure and mark them for clothing. Their long hair streamed behind them, paragons of femininity, but the faces they turned to Lara were stretched in raging screams, like the Sirens of Greek legend. Men trailed after them, but not lovelorn sailors: these were ragged skeletal horrors, as tormented in appearance as the women whose paths they traced. Fish darted in and out of their skulls, escaping through parted teeth and eye sockets. Lara pressed knuckles against her mouth, holding back gasps.

The impotent fury of a drowning people had not left their city unmanned. Not when those who died were creatures of magic themselves. The phantasms revealed by the towers' light were *real*, as able to rend and destroy as any mundane animal. Motion would almost certainly attract them, and she had no weapon with which to fight.

Warmth pulsed from the staff again, contradicting that belief. A stillness swept through the ocean. Then as one, the city's protectors turned toward Lara. Toward the staff she carried; toward the embodiment of the city's downfall. The next breath she drew was thick with water, though the black light didn't relent. There were more magics at work here than just Llyr's, and the only question was whose were the strongest.

Lara whispered "Llyr's," investing the word, the thought, with a thread of desperate truth. She didn't dare unleash the staff, not yet, maybe not ever, but the air cleared a little. She lurched a step or two forward, sand still clouding around her feet. It settled again quickly, though, making divots like any sand dune might. Wind—*wind*, not water, she told herself fiercely—rushed over those depressions, smoothing them out again so she left no more trace of her passage than Aerin had, but the greater ease of movement was heartening. She wasn't utterly without power, even in a dark realm where her magic could be her undoing.

Laughter barked free, distorted by the thick air. Never in her life had she imagined herself to be in any way powerful. Yet in the midst of a lost land a world away from what she'd known, she was willing, even eager, to rely on a talent that mere weeks ago she'd only recognized as a sometimes-frustrating quirk.

Laughing had been a mistake. Monstrosities half-hidden in ruined buildings darted forward, drawn to the sound. It marked her as alive, and the living were unwelcome in the Drowned Lands. Lara spared a thought for Aerin, whose blade would do her no good against enemies she couldn't see, and then she was running, no longer caring that speed would attract attention.

The sea beasts were faster than she was, much faster, black light showing them in their natural element while she ran as if in a nightmare, slowed by the density of water. The back of her mind screamed panic, urging her to hurry, but every step came more slowly as mist and water clawed her back again. Something latched on to her ankle, sending her sprawling, and cold hands scampered up her leg in search of a vital place to strike.

They encountered the staff instead. Heat flashed against Lara's back, blister hot, though soothing water struck as quickly. Behind her, though, a shriek rent the air, its pitch so high and loud that black light fell apart. For brief seconds the world was as Llyr had commanded it to be: warm skies above, a silvered pathway beneath Lara's hands and knees. She scrambled forward, gaining her feet already in a run, and managed a dozen steps before the light changed again. Before the air grabbed at her again, holding her back, while the infuriated creatures following after were able to surge forward, quick with the gift of water. But they only darted around her, reaching, snapping, snarling, none of them risking the staff she carried.

The towers were abruptly before her, their black-light emissions unaccountably welcoming, as though Lara had become one of the remnants of Unseelie magic. Doors, half real, half built of shimmering light, rose three times her height, abstract blue-on-ebony carvings reminding her of the staff's design. Relief burned her eyes and tightened her chest. Within the towers lay safety, a truth that reverberated through her bones. She shoved the doors in, grateful they moved easily, though sand swirled up in a dance as they opened. Lara pushed the doors closed behind her, then hobbled a few steps beyond the sand cloud. Not one of the seaborne creatures followed her, as if the half-magic doors construed a genuine barrier to the sea. Breath sobbing in her chest, Lara glanced upward to whisper, "Thank you," with the hope that she had passed through the worst of the wrong door's dangers.

A black swatch dropped from the ceiling.

It slammed her to the ground, sand washing up around them to make the creature difficult to see. A tail whipped toward her face, a vicious barb barely missing her eyes, and it lifted a long limb and struck downward, making eddies of sand.

Lara surged sideways, out from under the worst of its weight. She rolled and the thing pounced after her, landing on her backpack and shaking it hard enough to rattle her teeth. The instinct to curl up protectively warred with the impulse to run, and in the moment of hesitation the thing collapsed on her, wrapping multitudinous legs around her ribs and hips. A clatter sounded by her ear, a chitinous warning, and she had a sudden vision of a spider severing her spinal cord.

She flung herself forward, fingers dug in the sand until she was on her feet and running for a wall. The air supported her wrongly, offering waterlike buoyancy, but she was grateful: in normal atmosphere the beast's weight would have kept her pinned. Grunting with effort, Lara spun at the last moment and slammed her back into a wall with enough force that the monster riding her squealed and released her. Black ichor popped from it, drifting through thick air. The thing slithered to the ground, then shook itself like a dog as Lara backed off.

Spider, crab, stingray; there might once have been some kind of taxonomical name for the thing, before dying Unseelie magic had corrupted it into something else. It had six legs, not eight, and a plated spine that curved over broad wings and bled down to a lashing tail. Bulging eyes were set far apart on a flat head, but its mouth protruded, pincers snapping together almost too fast to see. The sound was primitive, reaching into the back of Lara's mind and speaking of danger.

"I exorcise thee, unholy spirit." The words, whispered, were comforting, though Lara was unsurprised when the many-legged thing didn't flinch. Nightwings were made purely of magic, and in the Barrow-lands were susceptible to the rituals of Lara's faith. But this chimera contained too much of animals that had truly existed. Magic might have re-formed them into one, but an exorcism wouldn't banish a nest of spiders, either. It took more mundane means.

The chimera rippled its wings, lifting up, slower than before but still quick and graceful. Blood floated from it as it pumped its wings and gained height. She tipped her head back, hair wafting around her face the same way blood followed the chimera.

It beat its wings down in two sudden rushes and was gone, black against the black distance of the tower ceiling. Alarm spurted through Lara, hands going cold and core tight as she searched the darkness for warning of its next attack. Scraps of song ran through her mind, pieces of music she'd used as spell-magic in her own world. They could perhaps be used to tear the chimera back into its component parts by calling up the truth of what it had been: "Amazing Grace" had given her the ability to see clearly, and had ripped apart nightwings as they attacked.

But too much clarity of sight would shatter the remains of Llyr's magic, a risk she couldn't afford. She reached over her shoulder, curling her fingers around the ivory staff. It was a bad choice, of that she had no doubt. But it was also her only weapon, and the chimera was quicker than she.

"I'm not any good at this," she whispered without knowing to whom she made the protest. "I barely know which end of a sword to hold. I don't know how to fight."

The chimera fell on her again, and there was no more time to worry.

Twelve

Black light retreated under the staff's white flare as
Lara thrust it upward, catching the chimera's belly. Its
weight staggered her as the blow struck home. Lara braced herself
and flung it toward a wall as hard as she could.

The air's peculiar buoyancy worked in her favor, supporting the
chimera over a greater distance than she could have thrown it herself. It hit with more force than she expected it to, Llyr's spell doing
its part as well. Lara ran forward to strike at the sea monster again as
it slithered down the wall. Its many legs went slack with the second
hit and, heart pounding, she put a hand on one of its wings, less
eager to kill it than wisdom might dictate. Impatience and a sense of
danger surged through the staff: its bent for destruction was far
greater than hers. Lara throttled it back as she explored the chimera
through touch.

Her fingers made an impression on the wing, black softness oozing between them as though she'd put her hand into a bucket of thick
warm grease. Lara's gorge rose and she pulled back, then gritted her

teeth and slid her hand up to the creature's insectoid spine. Fragments of the exoskeleton were broken, sharp edges discharging small clouds of dark blood. Its long tail twitched, not quite threatening; she thought the thing was semiconscious and reacting on instinct. The staff hummed, a soft impression of discontent, but didn't fight her again as a louder music sang in her mind.

Deep hollow atonal howls, like sea conches turned to sour instruments; that was the chimera's song. It wasn't a true thing, in much the same way the gash between Annwn and her world wasn't true. They were things not meant to be, even when magic forced them to exist. It would be better to return the beast to what it had been than to kill it. That, after all, was what she hoped to do with the whole of Annwn. If she could bring the staff under her control to save the chimera, it boded well for the healing of the lands.

The stingray looked like the largest part of the whole, its broad wings and long tail and even its small protruding eyes dominant in a way that its scuttling legs and pincer mouth weren't. Lara pressed her hand deeper into the greasy wing, holding the idea of the conch shell's music in her mind and searching for anything within the chimera that resonated.

A hint of unadulterated music teased at the edge of her consciousness. Lara whispered encouragement, sending out a thread of her own song to guide it. Just a thread: her power could still be her undoing in the heart of the drowned realms.

The chimera's tail lashed, suddenly full of life again, and scored a blow against her cheek. Icy pain cut to the bone, shattering her focus.

The staff, though, was prepared: heat and light roared from it eagerly, smashing into the chimera. The staff itself moved, dragging Lara with it so the weight of her body was behind the blow. It—she—skewered the chimera, strength enhanced by the staff's will, and a shot of glee ricocheted from it. Blood erupted from the chimera, discolored red-purple hanging in the air as the beast screamed and thrashed, long tail whipping about in spasms of desperation and pain.

Black light exploded in the tower, fighting against the staff's corrupt white. Shards of ebony, already fragile, shook and collapsed with magic's impact, as if the strike that had brought the chimera down also recoiled through the city walls. As if the staff were trying to finish what it had begun so long ago, and latent magic in the Unseelie citadel was fighting back.

Lara yanked the staff free of the chimera, horror blinding her as much as the clashing light did. She'd meant to control the thing, not be controlled by it. Someone, in making the stave, had invested it with far too much will of its own. Rhiannon had been a goddess indeed, if she could dominate its power. For a hopeless moment Lara wondered how Oisín had managed for the long years he'd carried the thing.

Eagerness leapt in it again, sucking at Lara's flash of despair, rushing back up that emotion, trying to find lodging in Lara's mind. She yelled, raw sound that hurt her throat, and very nearly threw the ivory weapon against the wall trying to rid herself of it.

Triumph scattered through her at the idea. Her fingertips spasmed, gripping the carvings at the last instant. The staff's anger replaced its triumph: out of her hands, thrown against city walls filled with magic, it would be able to exact its will. Maybe not forever, but long enough to wreak untold destruction, until either its or the city's remaining magics were burned out. Confidence sang in Lara's mind, all the purity of tone she'd been unable to find within the chimera. The staff was too dangerous to let out of her hands, and even as her only weapon, too dangerous to *use*, either.

She clawed it back into her palms, strangling it again. Its light flickered, sullen response to her silent demand that it return to sleep. That was twice within the Drowned Lands she'd awakened it, and twice it had wrought ruin. It boded ill for the healing she hoped to accomplish, but she had learned something: without certainty, she couldn't control the weapon. The stingray had *looked* like the greatest part of the chimera, but perhaps she'd been wrong. At least now she knew not to use the staff until she had learned all the pieces of Annwn's history. She was a truthseeker: armed with the full truth, she would have the skill to wield it properly. Until then, it had the advantage.

It twisted in her hands like a living thing, patterns writhing and scratching. She whispered "No," and though the sound was soft, it was filled with determination. She could quell the staff, if not use it; that would be enough, for now. Finally it went quiet, no longer struggling against her. Lara lowered her head, shoulders slumped under the weight of its magic and the more prosaic weight of her backpack.

There were still trials to pass, trials she had no proper concept of, and the two people she'd relied on were gone. Ioan was, she hoped, safe, but Aerin was either lost in the dark side of the drowned city or dead. And Dafydd lay somewhere in the Hundreds, hopefully healing from the magic-draining experiences on Earth, but just as possibly all but dead himself.

Tendrils of miserable certainty accompanied the last thought until Lara hunched over the staff, despair greater than the weight of magic or supplies. Her hopes of having passed through the citadel's most dangerous gauntlet had been shattered with the chimera's attack. It was a matter of time before she faced something she simply couldn't escape.

Warmth crept from the staff, as subtle and encroaching as her misery. Lara laughed, sharp and bitter. The staff could see her through, and the cost would be less than her life. She had no chance of helping Annwn if she didn't survive the Drowned Lands, and so, perhaps, had no choice.

Discord chimed through the last thoughts, a familiar warning. Lara opened her eyes, staring beyond the staff at the sand-littered tower floor. "Merrick tried that on me." Her voice was hoarse and she coughed, then swallowed. "It almost worked, then. Trying to convince me that something I wanted to be true, was. Fool me once, shame on me."

The temptation to use the staff as a walking stick touched her, encouragement to plant it against the floor and push herself to her feet. Lara made another bitter sound and climbed up on her own, shoving the weapon into its straps across her back. Impotent anger rushed from it, then settled, as if it trusted there would be a better time to test her again.

Alone and weary, but blessedly free from the staff's influence, Lara tried to form a plan. She didn't know enough of elfin architecture, whether there might be a hospital or holy place that would serve as a healing center somewhere within the city boundaries. At home, important buildings were traditionally located on hills, the better to dominate and inspire, but the towers themselves were the city's highest structures.

Which meant they were the best chance she had for looking down and potentially locating any remnant sites where Dafydd and Hafgan might be resting. Not that she expected anything to be recognizable, not after so much decay, but it was a course of action, better than nothing. She left the chimera's messy remains behind, pressing her fingertips against the wall as she made her way around the tower's half-lit walls. The black light continued to glow—hard on the eyes, but it offered hints of how the tower and its passages had once looked. She ignored a hallway for a ruined door, the frame filled entirely by light. Sweeping carvings, perhaps echoes of the door that had stood there millennia before, had weight and presence. Lara put her weight against the light, moving it inward a few inches. Her imagination added the creak of ancient wood, but the sediment and fallen stone that stopped the door's movement were real enough. She could get a thigh through, but not her torso. Not with the backpack on, at any rate. She peered through the crack at ruined stairs, supported by pillars and struts of light rather than stone, then twisted to gaze upward, trying to see how far they went. Wavering black-light shadows offered visibility to a few dozen feet. Lara muttered, then tried squeezing through again, half convinced that if she removed the pack, something would appear on one side of the door or the other to snatch it away and deprive her of all supplies while she slipped through.

Given the chimera's interest in her flesh, why a hypothetical thief would steal the pack was a question worth considering. The idea that the pack would go unscathed while she was attacked was hardly reassuring, but the black humor was welcome. Lara slipped the pack off, keeping it tight in one fist as she wedged herself through the crack. The stone that had supported the stairs was hip-high on the door's far side, making room to force the door open only because of a still-sturdy ledge well above her head. Nerves jumped in her stomach and Lara turned back to tug at her pack, which compressed less easily than she had. She sat down in piles of stone, trying to shove the door a few inches further open with her legs. It grated, sounding very real for all its translucency, then gave suddenly.

"You've done well, Truthseeker, and yet you should not be here." Llyr's voice came from above her. Lara yanked her pack to her chest and jerked around to see him on the rubble above her, one hand against the door she'd been trying to move. He released it and another scrape sounded as it eased back into place. "Your companion chose foolishly. Why did you follow her, when you knew better?"

"What else could I do?" Lara asked, astonished. "I don't know how I'm going to find her or Dafydd or Hafgan, but I couldn't just let her go, could I? That wouldn't be very . . . heroic." The word came awkwardly, but she didn't have a better one, not when it had been made clear that even Aerin regarded her journey as a sort of hero's quest.

Remote humor flickered across the sea god's face. He looked hollower in the black light, less robust and powerful than he'd been, though his hand was steady and strong as he offered it to Lara. His grip was oddly soft as he pulled her to her feet, as if the water of which he was made was nothing more than that, uncontained by a wrapper of skin. "A decision worthy of a trial itself, though not one set before you. I can offer guidance now that you've passed them, though little else, I'm afraid." He turned to climb the stairs, leaving Lara at their foot, staring after him dumbfounded.

"Now that I've what?"

He tossed a mild look over his shoulder and Lara scrambled after him, swinging her pack on as she ran up the stairs. "I'm sorry, but . . . what? I didn't pass any trials."

"Compassion, cleverness, confrontation. A trial is not much of a challenge, Truthseeker, if it is announced before it proceeds. Anyone might make a wise decision when they know it is part of a test."

Lara stopped again, bewildered, and after a step or two more, so did Llyr, who lifted a hand and counted off on his fingers. "Compassion. You might have fought the armies of the dead, but instead you embraced them, learned their stories, and swore an oath to return them to the memories of the living. Not even Rhiannon's children have shown such empathy when they've traveled to the Drowned Lands. Then cleverness, for you outwitted the twins, even if you did then choose the dark door. And in confrontation you not only defeated the dread beast, but far more important, you mastered the staff."

"Those weren't— I didn't know they were trials."

"As I said, what use is a trial when you know that you face it? It is what you do when you believe yourself to be alone that truly matters."

Embarrassment flooded Lara and she looked at her feet. "Those were . . . the doors, that's an old riddle from home. It could never fool me. And the army . . ." She wanted to say *I only did what anyone might do,* but Aerin's eagerness to fight proved that untrue. "I almost lost," she finally said, instead. "With the staff. It almost had me."

"Almost. But you triumphed, and I think perhaps you have also learned from the experience. Do not use it again in these lands, Lara Jansen. I fear a third time will be your undoing."

Sweet music bubbled through his voice, tempered by something deeper and more sorrowful. Lara looked up, and he turned back from the step above, tall and alien and lovely. "And I fear it will be ours," he finished at the silent question in her eyes. "The Drowned Lands tremble with its power, but my realm is vast enough. I have no wish to see the mountains clearly, Truthseeker. To me, they are beautiful in their distance. Come. From the tower roofs I may show you the path your companion has taken, and guide you to where your lover lies at rest in the heart of my sea."

Thirteen

From above the city became an intricate piece of knotwork, streets sweeping in cross-patterned loops. Degradation had taken hold too thoroughly for Lara to pick out the image for certain, but she saw hints in the longer lines and curves that suggested a leaping fish as the city's layout. It made her wonder what forest animal the Seelie citadel might be designed after, then made her reach back to touch the staff. She hadn't noticed obvious patterns in its carvings, but she might have been looking too hard for familiar shapes instead of the abstract features knotwork favored.

Llyr made a soft sound, dissuading her from examining the staff, and she dropped her hand from it to say, "The whole city is glowing."

"Unhealthy light," he agreed. "It will poison you as it poisons the sea creatures that swim through it, if you remain here too long. I had hoped to spare you the risk."

Lara's mouth twisted with faint humor. "But I had to go chasing after Aerin. I can see—" She broke off, then breathed deeply, trying for confidence. "I can see her path, I think. That streak in the blue?" She pointed, and Llyr nodded.

Her own brief passage through the city was mired with sediment and the remnants of battle. It made a cloudy path in the . . . *air*, Lara reminded herself again, though dirt hung in it the way it would in currentless waters. The Sirens and skeletal men still darted around the door she'd escaped through. She wouldn't be able to return that way: they would have all the advantage. They were comfortable with viewing things through debris-laden water, and Lara was unable to risk her power to clear that or any road through the drowned city.

Aerin had gone a different way from the moment she stepped through the coral doors. She had struck out to the right, toward what Lara thought was the fish's head in the city's layout. Bodies littered the path she'd taken along the city wall, blood lingering in black slashes as though put there by a sword strike. But signs of her passage stopped abruptly, with no hint of whether Aerin survived or not. The lingering blood remained ichory purple-black, the same color as the chimera's, but for all Lara knew, any blood visible in black light would be the same hideous shade. If Aerin had met her death there, then—

Lara sighed and glanced skyward, though the city's dark light destroyed any chance of knowing where the sun stood. If Aerin had met her death, Lara had at most a few hours to find Dafydd and find a way to contact Emyr before Ioan's hidden city was destroyed. She could waste time in worry, or she could act.

Not so long ago, she'd have taken time to worry, but now she turned to Llyr. "What's in that direction? Why did Aerin choose to go that way?"

His silence was all that answered for long moments, complex struggle showing in his face. "Rhiannon's children do not die," he finally said. "Not often, not easily. But there are accidents, there are battles. They find comfort in a place of memories, a quiet center to speak or think of those rare handsful who have gone. It may be different for mortals, whose lives are so brief they can hardly be missed when they end."

"You're—" *You're kidding.* That was something other people said. Lara ducked her head, looking for something else to say, because the sea god was unquestionably *not* kidding. Not mortal, either, and his perspective made a certain amount of sense, from the long view. "We call them memorials. We have them, too. Our lives are as long to us as yours are to you. We don't have anything else, after all."

"You have souls," he disagreed, but left it there. "A memorial, then. It would be in that direction, and will be where your fallen lover lies. See the bend, where her trail disappears? You will continue that way along the city wall. When you see the wall curve again in front of you, blocking the way, turn left sharply. The roads will lead to the memorial gardens."

"I'll continue that way? I thought you were guiding me."

Llyr smiled, no more than a ripple over his face. "My guidance is of limited use, especially in the dark of the city. Had you passed through the other door..."

"But I didn't. Will the memorial still be there? Will I find Dafydd and Hafgan there, or did I have to go through the right door to find them?"

"The city is the same, dark or light. What is in one is in the other. But you may see and feel and face things here that you might not have had to there."

"More trials," Lara said, and Llyr tipped his head in acknowledgment. Lara nodded, then turned her attention back to the city, trying as best she could to memorize the overlapping streets and curving walls. She couldn't use a truthseeker's path, but a study of the byways now might allow her to test them as she came to them, to get a sense of their trueness or falsity with regards to her destination.

Eventually she nodded again, as confident as she could be of her bearings. "How will I get past the front door?"

"There are other entrances to the towers. That, at least, I can help you with." Llyr offered his hand, guiding Lara from the parapets back into the tumbledown towers.

Shadows flickered at the corners of her eyes as they left the towers, monsters like and unlike the chimera. None of them came for her, though, not with Llyr walking beside her. Some even swam closer, like they were curious about the watery god. Pain flooded his face time and again, suggesting he lacked the power to set the amalgamated creatures to rights.

No, not the power, Lara decided, when one monstrous fish with a jaw like a coelacanth's swam up to them. Nothing else about it resembled prehistoric fish; it was sleek-bodied, delicately finned, and of bright clashing colors worsened by the black light. Llyr lifted a hand, a slow sympathetic gesture, and almost touched the thing, but recoiled at the last instant. The fish twitched as if it had been shocked and darted away with a few quick beats of its tail.

"I tried for a very long time," Llyr murmured a few steps later. "I tried to turn them back to the things they had begun as. It worked. It was only as the new creatures became more grotesque and deformed that I realized that each new burst of power I released in healing them corrupted and twisted another beast even more profoundly. The deformities only reach as far as the shallow fishing waters that were once these lands' shores. Beyond that barrier I can correct for the things magic has done here, but very little passes through it safely. These waters were once my heart, and are long since my heartbreak. I do not come here, Lara Jansen. Not if I can help it."

"I'm sorry for the pain coming for me must have caused," Lara said carefully. "But I'm not sorry you came. Thank you."

"Perhaps something bright will finally be born of the darkness here." Llyr stopped in front of a shell-ridden wall looming before them. Arches filled with black light showed the extravagance of carved doors that had once stood in them, even giving hints of the colored windows that must have dominated the doors and hall. "The city walls are very near here. Strike out on your companion's path and you will, with luck, find your way to the . . . memorials."

"And without luck I'll die," Lara said quietly. Llyr shrugged and stepped back as she put a hand on one of the light-filled doors and pushed. It moved easily, but barely: even built of light, it had the mass of stone carved ten feet high. "Llyr?"

"Truthseeker?"

Lara looked back at him. "Do you know what happened in Annwn? Can you tell me how the lands were drowned?"

A shudder ran through the sea god, washing away the edges of his elfin shape. The wild foam that was his hair stretched, dissipating into water, and when he answered it was as if the ocean surrounding her spoke. "I was there, as was my daughter's mother Caillech, and all the old gods of the land and sky and sea. But we cannot tell you what came to pass. Rhiannon was our daughter, and her blood binds us as she is bound. Seek. Do your duty, and may worlds come changed at end of day."

Electric recognition shot down Lara's spine. She pushed off the door, snatching at Llyr's vanishing form, but there was nothing left to hold. "Wait! *Wait!* That's what Oisín said in his prophecy! Did you send it to him? Did you . . . did you . . . ?"

The questions, even if she could generate them, would get no answers. Llyr was gone, the only reminder of his presence her continuing ability to breathe. Lara clutched the straps of her pack, heartbeat hard enough to feel in the hand curled over her chest. Prophecy came from God, or the gods; she'd known that, but to hear the poet's words echoed from Llyr's lips still shocked her. She said "I'm just me" to the empty city, not meaning it as an excuse, but as an expression of astonishment.

Unexpectedly, Dafydd's voice echoed in her thoughts: *I've been searching for you for a hundred years.* Being herself was extraordinary enough, it seemed. Extraordinary enough to have truck with gods and elfin immortals, and to command a power worth prophesizing.

The staff warmed against her spine, bringing a mix of heightened conceit and rueful banality to the moment. "I'm not that impressed with myself yet. Stop trying to tempt me."

A distinct sense of churlishness rose from the staff, but it quieted again, leaving Lara with a grin as she exited the city's tower structure. Power corrupted—she had little doubt of that. Still, as long as the staff's tendency was the combination of destruction, blatant cajoling, and sulking, she thought she could withstand it. And she had a destination now, which was more than she'd expected to be granted. All she had to do was survive the city and reach that destination.

She knew it for a treacherous thought even before Aerin rose up out of the sand in a full-on attack.

The Seelie woman's white hair ran to blue, the same way it had the night Lara met her. But then it had been moonlight; now it was the city's sickly color twisting what was natural. Her eyes trailed yellow fire, their usual green distorted as well, and her elegantly boned face was pulled in a grimace of hatred. Even the armor she wore was corrupted, moonlight silver corroded and blackened as if it had been buried in the sea for decades. Only her sword still shone bright, its edge unblemished as it swung down toward Lara.

Lara ducked, knowing it wasn't enough even as she did so. A spurt of panic lent her strength and she turned the duck into a dive, flattening herself on the ocean floor. The sword passed over her head in a hail of grit and sand that matched the one floating up from Lara's dive. She slithered forward, not quite daring to get as high as hands and knees, and grabbed Aerin's ankle to yank as hard as she could.

Aerin stabbed down with the sword rather than fall over. The blade caught the thick shoulder padding of Lara's doublet and drove into the ground, pinning her, but tangling the sword as well. Its cold pressure through the shirt beneath the doublet warned her of how close Aerin had come, and how easily she might sever her own muscles by moving too much. Aerin clearly had the same idea, wrenching the sword down rather than pulling it free.

Pain splintered Lara's thoughts. Her right arm stopped responding properly, trapezius cut so deeply she feared the collarbone was in pieces as well. Blood welled up, tasting sharp and bitter in the air. Turning her head to see the damage was agony. And useless: Aerin's blade remained in the way, angled dangerously into Lara's shoulder, though it was a matter of seconds before Aerin withdrew the sword to strike again.

Without the sword's presence to block it, blood swam free, billowing into Lara's eyes. Dizziness ate her in waves, making her thoughts soft and unfocused. She could turn her head. That probably meant that despite sharp deep pain, the muscle wasn't cut as badly as she feared. But there was a significant vein somewhere in there, one that fed from the jugular; she was almost certain of it. Terror pulsed through her, vivid fear that it was a vein large enough to bleed her out in seconds, unable to save herself.

She grated, "No," in a voice so low she didn't recognize it as her own. The pain lessened not at all, but some of her light-headedness faded, and her next heartbeat didn't seem to blur the air with more blood. She put more force behind the next "No," willing a difficult thing to be true: that was a truthseeker's gift, to make something that was not, be.

Staunching the blood flow did nothing to stop Aerin, though. Lara flung her left hand up, wishing against reason she held the staff in it so she might at least parry, and put all the strength she had into her voice: "Stop!"

Aerin's sword trembled to a halt an inch above Lara's heart. Distortion wracked the Seelie warrior's features as she fought the coercion, trying equally to drive the sword down and drag it up again. Lara clenched her teeth and dug her heels into the ground, shoving herself along the city street. That was her stomach Aerin would skewer if she broke the compulsion; now her pelvis; now her thigh, each push bringing a different body part into danger. But bad as gut wounds were supposed to be, dangerous as severed thigh muscles might be, she had a chance of surviving them. Her truthseeker's power would be of no use at all if her heart were pierced.

Aerin roared as Lara inched to a less deadly position, and the compulsion failed: she slammed the sword down again. Lara jerked her legs apart, the blade scraping her inner thigh with another bright flare of pain. She had cut herself with a knife a time or two. Those accidental slices had nothing on the white-hot anguish of a sword blade parting skin and muscle. The pain was so great there was a purity to it: nothing else could possibly exist within its realm.

Except, perhaps, a thready, panicked desire to survive. The only thing greater than pain was wanting to outlive it. And possibly a growing ambition to visit the same anguish on the one who'd hurt her.

That was how wars were fought, Lara thought in a burst of clarity. It had to be, and that was a revelation she'd never wanted. She laughed, knowing the sound to be almost a sob, and inched back a little farther, taking herself out of the blade's way. Aerin had driven it down too hard: it was mired in the stone beneath drifting sand.

Sitting up was difficult. Not impossible, though even the discolored blood floating around her went gray as her vision dimmed with the effort. But being able to sit, like turning her head, was probably good: it probably meant the muscle wasn't as badly damaged as she'd initially imagined. And there wasn't nearly as much blood as she was sure there should be. Aerin had broken one compulsion, perhaps, but the one Lara had laid on herself still held true.

Aerin gave up on the blade and whirled around with a kick aimed at Lara's jaw. Dizziness, not reflexes, saved her; she was already sagging when the warrior woman threw the kick, and Aerin misjudged the distance. Lara kicked her in the other knee with just enough strength in it to knock Aerin's footing askew. Aerin fell and Lara surged forward, drawing on reserves she hadn't known existed in order to pounce on Aerin's torso.

She landed with her knees on Aerin's upper arms, knowing the pin would only hold her for a few seconds. Knowing, too, that she couldn't keep Aerin down any other way, not with her arm only half responding. Not with Aerin's fighting skills and Lara's utter lack of them.

Something malfeasant crawled under Aerin's skin, as though her blood itself had been corrupted and fought to be free. Scales rippled on her skin and faded again, replaced by sharp rows of teeth bursting from her gums. Her eyes were losing their color, sickly yellow replaced by a dead black that reflected the city's dark light. Like a shark's, Lara thought, and pieces fell into place.

Aerin had lost a fight on her way to the memorial gardens. Maybe against an unaltered animal, but more likely against some creature whose largest part had been a shark. And given this new predator, this Seelie warrior woman, to meld with, it was taking the city's bleak magic and re-forming her into a deadly, undead monster.

Llyr had pulled chimeras apart, returned them to their native state. He'd paid the price for it in seeing new, more dreadful monsters born of his efforts, but it didn't matter. If the magic Lara released backfired, made monsters of greater horror and scope than before, at least she had *tried,* and there might still be a chance for redemption ahead.

"I don't even like you very much, and I don't think I know you well enough to be sure of making this work. But I can't just leave you like this. I *won't* leave you like this." Not for the first time, Lara wished she had an instrument, something to guide music with. She promised herself once more that she would learn one, when the fight for Annwn was over.

But for the moment she reached for the only weapon she had, and began to sing.

Fourteen

"Eternal Father, strong to save." It had been years
since Lara had sung the Navy Hymn, but its lyrics and
her location fit together. She wished the tune were more sprightly
than stately, but that might be for the best: easier to pull back her
God's power if it came in slower waves than if it rolled over Aerin in-
exorably.

It was condemning enough as it was. Aerin screamed, raw sound
that tore through Lara's memory, shattering half-forgotten words
into fragments. The tune, though, remained. Breathless with fear
Lara hummed a snatch or two of the music, falling back as it ripped
into Aerin and changed what she had become. Heat poured off the
Seelie woman, distorting the air as it distorted her skin. She collapsed, silence worse than her screams as ripples rolled over her skin,
Unseelie magic at war with the hymn's power. Lara scrabbled for
words, certain only of the verse's beseeching final lines, though she
dared a tiny change to them: "Oh, hear us when we cry to Thee, for
those in peril *in* the sea!"

For an instant, Aerin was illuminated, her form a shadow within a greater writhing mass that struggled for survival and domination. Her intellect was desirable, Lara thought, but her too-human shape was impractical for a sea-based predator. At least the thing struggling to envelope Aerin hadn't thought that it could evolve beyond the sea: a twisted magic from a dead land could spell ruin for all the Barrow-lands, should it reach shore. The next lyric was strengthened by Lara's horror, voice more confident as she used music as a weapon: "Oh Christ! Whose voice the waters heard, and hushed their raging at Thy word."

Aerin's shape became the predominant one again, but her skin was reddening like she'd stood in the sun too long. There was hope, Lara thought. The only question was whether the hymnal would burn Aerin away before the deviltry was purged from her body. So easy to think in those terms, though the "devil" was no more than another creature fighting to survive in waters tainted by magic gone wrong. Witchcraft: that was probably how her church would see everything in and about the Barrow-lands. Lara had never thought of witches or their magics as beautiful, though, and even under the strain of Lara's own power, Aerin was beautiful.

Selfish, shallow, childish thought; it was good to save something beautiful. It was good to save *any* life; *that* was the idea she should hold on to. Her voice strengthened again, though the contortions beneath Aerin's skin, the heat of her body, said there was almost no time left. Dafydd had flinched at the name of the Holy Trinity, and Aerin was being exposed to so much more.

A clawed hand suddenly came up and caught Lara's throat. Song squeaked into nothing, but for an instant all the black, all the discolored yellow, fled from Aerin's eyes. She rasped "Keep. *Singing!*" before collapsing again, and clarity rang in Lara's mind.

The Seelie woman would rather be immolated by God's word than live the half-life of black magic. A shaking note of laughter went through Lara's voice, and between lines she took enough breath to whisper, "Not if I can help it."

It should have made no sense to Aerin, but gratitude flashed through still-yellow eyes and she nodded once, sharply. Her hair was burning, shriveling from the ends toward her scalp, but the heat within her was purifying her as well. The shifting scales were gone now, only flushed red skin visible where they'd been. Sharp teeth still erupted through her gums, pushing away the old ones and giving her the look of an evolving gargoyle. Lara, aware it wasn't wise, shoved her fingers into Aerin's mouth and grabbed her jaw from the inside, using the feel of ivory and flesh to remind herself of what was *true* and meant to be.

The last words of the third verse broke free, pleading that God hear her call, and vertiginous power roared from Lara, *truth* as she envisioned it: Aerin whole and uncorrupted again before her. For an astonishing few seconds the black light of the city retreated under a burst of starlight.

Heat exploded from Aerin. She screamed and bucked, scrambling backward to escape Lara's grip. Her skin blistered and her hair, once hip-length, was now burned so short the upswept tips of her ears were exposed. But her eyes were her own, green with fear and fury and gratitude, and she sat where she was, gasping and fumbling at her own body, making sure it was still hers.

Lara whispered, "Holy Mary, Mother of God, thank you," smiled weakly, and tipped over sideways, unconscious before she hit the seabed floor.

She woke again because of the pain. Her shoulder sent flashes of white heat through her vision, worse than a migraine. A gurgle caught at the back of her throat, injury too offensive to even give it full voice as a shriek.

Aerin, grimly, said, "Good. Try not to scream, if you can help it. The sound will attract predators. This will hurt."

Lara wanted to ask *It* will *hurt? Like it doesn't already?*, but Aerin pulled something tight around her shoulder, and Lara's entire right side cramped and spasmed with agony. Another gagging sound caught in her throat and she clutched sand with her free hand, trying to squeeze the pain away. It in no way helped, but Aerin sat back, glowering with satisfaction. "That should hold until we return to the Barrow-lands. I'm sorry, but I have almost no talent for healing others, and even if I did, working enchantments here . . ." She shook her head.

Lara blinked, trying to focus. Trying to *think*, while her shoulder settled into a dull throb. Her doublet was gone, or rather, torn to pieces, with its padding drifting around them on eddies of wind or current. Its fabric had been bound around her shoulder and upper arm, with a bulky lump over the deep cut. Staunching blood, Lara imagined, though browning stains already discolored half her shirt.

"You should have lost more blood," Aerin said. "As it is, the muscle won't heal properly without magic. It's too badly damaged."

Lara suggested, "Stitches," light-headedly, and had a vision of stitching up her shoulder herself, a tailor's needle bright in her fingertips. Anatomy was no doubt more difficult to sew than fabric; it was warm and bled, for one thing, never mind the near impossibility of sewing herself together almost under her own chin.

Aerin frowned, uncomprehending, and the idea that the elfin peoples never needed stitches or surgery the way mortals did fluttered through Lara's mind. "Nothing. Thank you for tying me up." She winced, knowing she'd phrased that badly but unable to gather drifting thoughts enough to change it. She'd never been badly hurt before, or lost more than a knife cut's worth of blood. Aside from the thudding ache that came with each heartbeat, it made her feel uncomfortably detached, as if nothing was of particular importance.

Humor twitched Aerin's mouth before turning grim again. "You're welcome. And my thanks to you as well. I would have been lost, worse than dead, had you not done what you did. Binding your shoulder was the least I could do in recompense, especially when the fault of the damage was mine."

Lara leaned forward until her forehead almost touched Aerin's, as if proximity would help her communicate. "The doors were a test. A trial. It's an old riddle in my world. One brother always tells the truth. One brother always lies. If you had *waited*...!" Scolding delivered, she sat back again, then turned her head carefully to study the blue-lit walls of the drowned city.

They had changed, though she couldn't place how; her thoughts weren't yet clear enough. They were taller, perhaps, more like the rooms within the towers: less damage had come to them, though they were by no means whole. Still, the lichen that grew over them looked healthier, taking some of the black-light glow and turning it to growing green. That was probably more how Llyr had intended she see the city. Maybe his spell had grown in strength while she was unconscious. "Llyr said we'll find Dafydd and Hafgan in the memorial gardens. I just don't know how we're going to get there without being eaten."

Aerin's face tensed and gentled all at once. "We are already there, Truthseeker. I carried you while you...slept." She spread a hand in half-defensive response to Lara's goggle-eyed stare. "The shifting magic lingered in me, perhaps. I saw innumerable monsters, but they chose not to come near me. Perhaps they recognized that I had been one of them." The tension slipped through her eyes again. "Or perhaps it was the taint of your world's god that kept them away. Either way, we were allowed to move unscathed, and I thought these gardens might be welcoming. The Caerwyn citadel has a similar place, and it is often comforting."

"Lucky choice. It could have been haunted, too." Lara bit her tongue, ashamed at belittling Aerin's decision. "Sorry."

Aerin shrugged one shoulder. "It might have been, but then, so is the rest of this city. I searched the grounds, Truthseeker. I saw nowhere for a bier."

"Did you look underground?" The question came unbidden and Lara bit her tongue a second time, this time in surprise. Aerin looked askance at her, and Lara got cautiously to her feet. The change in elevation made her head swim again, and renewed blood flow hammered pulses of dizzying agony through her shoulder. She took a few deep breaths, trying to steady herself, then focused on speaking. "You came up at me from under the street. There must be some kind of underground structure in the city. We bury our dead. You must, too, right? Why else would they be the Barrow-lands?"

"Because it was the hills of the dead that most often lent us access to your world, and so to come from yours to ours was to enter the Barrow-lands."

"Oh."

Aerin laughed, bright and unexpected as she, too, climbed to her feet. "But we do bury our dead. Forgive me, Truthseeker. I suppose I shouldn't tease you."

Lara wrinkled her nose and smiled. "It's all right. Most people can't. It's hard to tell the absolute truth and still be teasing."

"Perhaps some of your magic lingers in me still." Aerin brushed fingertips over her short, burnt hair and flicked an eyebrow upward. "Perhaps it always will."

"I hope not. I don't think that would be good for you." Lara edged in a circle, studying the garden walls around her. She could imagine them as such, now: where lichen and coral grew, ivy and moss might have, in years long past. Stone archways, still picked out in now-softened black light, glimmered here and there beneath the coral, but they led to paths and other gardens, not into the ground. Aerin had seen nothing like that, exploring the space. "On Earth wc had kings who hid the entrances to their tombs to keep graverobbers from disturbing them. Do you do that?"

Disgust struck deep lines around Aerin's mouth. "*Graverobbers?* Who would do such a thing?"

Lara laughed. It jarred her shoulder and sent another wave of dizzy pain over her, but it helped somehow, too. "The poor. The greedy. The ambitious. Ceremonial entrances, then? Do you do something like that?"

Reluctant, still visibly horrified, Aerin nodded. "But there are none here, Truthseeker. I would have seen them."

Conviction sang in her voice, but Lara shook her head. "Not if time had changed them enough, and not if it was hidden. I understand you don't hide entrances as a matter of course, but if you were building more than a tomb, you might. If you were making a sanctuary to preserve the living, or to heal the dying, especially somewhere already poisoned by trouble, wouldn't you want to keep it secret?"

A thread of certainty wove into the words, delicate as Lara could make it. Llyr hadn't lied when he said she would find Dafydd and Hafgan in the gardens, nor had Aerin lied in saying she could find no biers. Something lay between the two truths, subtle and cautious. There was a path to be followed, one only Lara's power could bring to light, but like all magic in the Drowned Lands, it took a careful approach. Lara's eyes drifted shut, single notes touching against her skin like fireflies. They became tiny spots of light in her inner vision, slowly dancing together to shape a path.

Hushed awe came into Aerin's voice: "Truthseeker...?"

"Follow me." Lara put her hand out for Aerin's blindly, trusting the Seelie woman to take it. "I can see a pathway."

"So can I!"

Lara's eyes popped open. The tremulous filament of light remained visible, darting forward and coming close again, reluctant to stray too far from its maker. Astonished, she whispered, "I thought it was in my head. I didn't know other people could see it." It would have been vastly easier in the Catskill mountains, she thought sourly, if she'd realized Kelly might be able to see the light-built pathway that had led them to Merrick ap Annwn. But then, Annwn, drowned or not, was friendlier to magic than her world. The light and song that showed her a true path might well be invisible on Earth. "Can you *hear* it?"

Aerin shook her head and disappointment flashed through Lara before she remembered Kelly's dismay at her brief exposure to the world as Lara heard it. For Kelly, truth's song had been a terrible thing, tearing away at boundaries and driving her into herself. Aerin might well fare no better, especially so soon after Lara had ripped into her with music and faith from another world. "It doesn't matter. Come on, let's—" She broke off in a gasp, one or two quick steps more than enough to send her injured shoulder into spasms again.

"Perhaps at a moderate pace," Aerin suggested straight-faced, and fell into step with Lara's hobble.

The firefly thread sparked forward and back, dashing down side paths and around clumps of sandy earth. Where it alighted, the city's dark glow faded, though it returned as soon as the path-seeking brightness fled. Lara, following slowly indeed, watched with bemusement. Every true path she'd opened before had been a blazed trail, leading without correction to her goal. "I guess I hadn't looked for anything hidden before."

Aerin picked up on her meaning with a casual gesture around the drowned gardens. "Nor in a place so laden with its own corrupt magic. A seeking spell that works for its answer is safer than one that demands it, here. I've felt the power you can command firsthand now, Truthseeker. I think your little questing light is wiser by far."

She hesitated, then admitted, "And I fear for my own existence, should you need to call on greater magics than these a second time."

"It would defeat the point of having saved you." The firepoint light ahead of them darted between twists of coral and disappeared. Lara stopped with a wobble, staring at the darkness their guide had been swallowed by. "Something has to be there. Come on. Let there be light."

Coral shivered and melted, not into the fine dust Lara imagined it would naturally degrade to, but into nothingness. Llyr had disappeared the same way, becoming part of the water—or air— surrounding them. Lara shook herself, hissing as the motion sent fresh pain through her shoulder. "I'm not good at being hurt."

"But you're very good at finding hidden things." Aerin's voice was low with respect again. She stepped forward, brushing her fingers over the door revealed by the dissolving coral.

Unlike everything else in the drowned city, the door looked fresh and new, its carvings still sharp-edged and the glass set within it brilliant with color. Even the city's black light couldn't tarnish the image of a kind-faced man set against a bed of greenery and knotwork. "Llyr's brother," Aerin whispered. "Kerne, god of renewal. He gave seasons to the land, so Rhiannon's children could watch in wonder as their world changed around them. It was from her uncle that Rhiannon learned the gift of healing that every Seelie carries in their blood. This will be the place, Truthseeker. If there is any hope for Dafydd, this is where he will lie."

Fifteen

A flush of excitement pushed Lara through the door. It had only been days since she'd seen Dafydd, but they had been exhaustive days. Whatever lay ahead, it would be easier with him at her side.

If he had survived the Drowned Lands. Nervousness squelched her excitement, and as if in response, the firefly light and its accompanying single-note song abandoned her. For a moment she was blind, but phosphorescent light rose, replacing not only her candle spark but the black glow of the city. Aerin breathed a sound of astonishment, surprising Lara into soft laughter.

"I thought the lights in the citadel could be phosphorous. But they're just magic?" *Just,* she teased herself, when a month ago she hadn't believed in magic at all. But her world had grown beyond that, and now like so much else she encountered, the gifts of magic were as easy to accept as the air she breathed.

Given their sea-floor location, she pulled a face at herself and the very air around them as Aerin touched the green-glowing walls. "The light is a small magic from Rhiannon's mother."

"Caillech," Lara remembered, garnering a startled look from the Seelie woman with her. "Llyr told me. I don't understand your pantheon very well. Mine's—" She broke off, thinking of angels and archangels, demons and devils, saints and even the most famous sinners, and cleared her throat. "Not simpler. Different," she decided. "Mine's different."

"The old gods existed in the sea and the sky and the wind, immortal and untouchable as the sun." Aerin dropped her fingers from the wall and tested the sloping floor in front of them, then began picking her way down as she spoke. "When Llyr and Caillech came together to make Rhiannon, daughter of the sky and sea, she could live in neither and so made the land her own. All her family gave gifts so she might make a people of her own body and not be alone. We came from her, and in giving us life she lost a spark of her eternal being, so that, like us, she could die. How are your gods different?"

"I only have one." The steps were long and shallow, taking a stride and a half to cover two. Missteps made Lara's shoulder ache, and she slowed, creeping down them as she struggled to find the vital differences between her faith and Aerin's. Finally she shook her head, smiling crookedly at her half-shadowed feet. "Maybe they're not so different after all, except in number. My God made the sun and the earth and the sea, too, and made Man in His own image."

"Not so different," Aerin agreed softly. "Halt, Truthseeker. Something comes this way."

A wind blew over them as she spoke, air so cold it turned to crystals on Lara's skin. Fog came with the cold, and brought with it a world of images. A world opened up in front of her, lush and green, a forgotten paradise in which slender long-limbed elfin youths ran and laughed as they played. Dafydd was among them, bright with life in a way she'd never seen him before. Vitality poured from him as though he had to run it off or risk being burned away. His golden hair was wild, the warm tones of his skin drinking down sunlight as he played in it. That was anathema to how Lara had seen the Seelie: they were a moonlight people, pale and delicate, uncomfortable in the light. Their Unseelie counterparts, driven beneath the earth or not, had the richer colors of people meant for the sun. The idea came to her once again that they were two halves of a whole, but it faded as the images in front of her unfolded further.

A girl as beautiful—more beautiful—than Dafydd struck out after him. Her hair bounced in a white braid falling past her hips, mark enough to say it was Aerin. She and Dafydd raced through thigh-high grass, laughter shouted with the exuberance of youth. Aerin was the taller and the faster: Lara saw the inevitable long before Dafydd gave in to it, and counted down the seconds until the young Seelie woman tackled Dafydd into the earth.

The rest, Lara would have preferred not to watch, though every time she looked away their entwined bodies came to focus in front of her again. Sunset came and they walked naked back through the meadows, fairy-tale creatures brought to life.

Years shifted, not through any obvious change of season but by a tightening of the cold fog binding Lara. Aerin and Dafydd, overlooked by a broad-shouldered, black-haired youth, bent their heads over a game very like chess. The third youth—Merrick ap Annwn—reached between them with an impatient gesture, finishing the game with two or three quick moves. Aerin's features darkened, but Dafydd, tolerant, reached up to grab his adopted brother and hauled him into an affectionate wrestling match. Lara saw what she believed Aerin did: how hard Merrick tried to defeat his slightly taller brother, and his bitterness when Dafydd, victorious, went away with Aerin on his arm.

And more years: Aerin grew into her beauty, becoming austere with it. Dafydd lost much of his playfulness, though compared to the sword-bearing woman always at his side, he still seemed open-hearted and ready to laugh. Their opposites suited them everywhere from political arenas to the bedchamber, and through time marked in the citadel architecture and growth of trees rather than the mere counting of years.

Oisín, glimpsed now and then, went from a young man to an old one, and then to the ancient blind sage she had met, and he, Lara recalled, had claimed to have been old for eight hundred years, but young a very long time before that. Like Oisín, the Seelie lost vitality as they aged, though it showed in different ways. Aerin's beauty became ever more remote; Dafydd's warm golden skin became moon-touched as the endless scenes turned more and more to night instead of day. But through it all, Aerin walked with Dafydd, even up to the last minutes when he nocked and pulled the arrow meant to take Merrick ap Annwn's life. Even when, disgraced, he worked the worldwalking spell, and left the Seelie court behind.

Chilly fog released her with a shock. Lara's breath steamed on the air, but warmed immediately. Aerin turned to her, green gaze discomfited, and Lara shrugged despite the pain.

"Llyr said this path would lead safely to the healing chambers. He also said it would show me things I probably wouldn't want to see. I wish you hadn't gone through the wrong door, Aerin. I'm tired of battles I didn't really have to fight, and I don't know what more we've got to face."

"Perhaps you would find consolation in knowing that I, too, have seen things I would have prefered not to." Aerin turned away, fog thinning with her motion. "But this is the end of our journey, Lara Jansen. Look."

A small chamber lay before them, littered with exquisitely carved tombs. Almost a dozen bodies lay atop them like stone effigies, resting in silent repose for eternity.

Closest to the entrance, closest to where they stood, Dafydd ap Caerwyn lay like the others, waiting patiently for a breaking of the world.

Aerin breathed, "Dafydd," but remained still, as if ice still held her. Lara jolted forward, relief hammering in her chest so hard it dwarfed the pain of her injury. There was nothing visibly wrong with him, but then, there hadn't been when Ioan had taken him from her, either. He had only—only!—burned up the power that sustained him in Lara's world, leaving him a paper shell. Fragile, yes, but not physically damaged.

Some of the frailty had gone from him. His skin looked healthier, no longer dried and ready to crack. There was luster to his hair instead of the golden strands being strawlike and dull. But beyond that, he might have been dead, with no sign of breath in his body, no flicker of movement behind his eyelids. Nor did his Unseelie garb lend him any hint of life: black and silver were too harsh for his coloring, even when the chamber's soft green light was accounted for.

"How do we wake him up? *Them* up?" There were others in the room, after all, though she'd barely looked beyond Dafydd. One of the others had to be Hafgan, the Unseelie king, and by all rights he was the more important of the two. Annwn's fate rested with him; Dafydd's survival bore no such burden.

No, Lara thought. Only her own fate lay with the elfin prince. Much less important, and yet.

Aerin made a small, nonplussed sound. "I would not know, Truthseeker. The invocations to awaken someone from a healer's sleep are known only to the healers. No one else can work them."

Lara barked a tiny laugh. "We don't have invocations like that at all, unless you want to count people in movies yelling, 'Nooo!' and 'Live, damn you! Live!' "

"Does it work?"

"Only in stories that end happily ever after." Tightness caught her throat. "And I don't know if this one ends that way. Besides, in the movies those scenes usually follow something violent or tragic. Nobody just comes across a body and starts shouting for it to live." She fell silent, realization creeping up before she whispered, "I'm wrong. We do have a magic spell to awaken the dead who've been resting peacefully. Except it only works in fairy tales."

"And what, Lara Jansen, do you imagine this to be?"

"You people keep saying that." Lara pressed her eyes shut, trying to reduce pique. "Which doesn't even make sense, since you don't call yourselves fairies."

"No, but your folk do. It may have been long since your world and ours collided, but stories linger on. What is this spell?"

"Love. The greatest power known to man. True love's kiss," she clarified, and backed away from Dafydd to gesture Aerin at him.

The Seelie woman stared at her without comprehension. Lara set her teeth together and repeated the motion, sharp and small. "I saw you two when we crossed into the chamber. You've been together for hundreds of years." Mistruth jangled and she said, "Thousands," through her teeth, settling the sour music in her mind.

"And what," Aerin asked after a bitter silence, "do you think *I* saw, Truthseeker?"

Confoundment rose in Lara before understanding came. "... me?"

"And Dafydd, with all the vitality and joy in life I remember in him restored. Perhaps I'm wrong, but my ego will be far more salved by coming second than by acting first and being found wanting." Aerin turned away, slender body held rigid enough that her armor, so well-fitted, suddenly looked uncomfortable.

An awkward sting of empathy pricked at Lara. She wanted to be proven wrong no more than Aerin did, but if she was, it was only weeks, not aeons, lost to her. It seemed a fair trade, somehow, for the chance of embarrassment. Graceless, she lurched forward to press her lips against Dafydd's before her own ego reasserted itself.

After a lifetime of immersion in it, she more than half expected truth's song to rise up in a crescendo: a dramatic, moving sound track to accompany the scene. Instead its silence coiled around her, carrying darkness instead of the light she had recently become accustomed to. There was nothing, *nothing*, on the far side of sleep's deadly veil. Not for him, at least. There were no dreams, no hopes of new life or old friends revisited, only an emptiness that went on forever. And for all its stillness, for all that the music had died, it was *true*. Annihilation lay beyond death for the elfin peoples, an utter ceasement of being.

Lara flinched back, breaking the kiss to gaze at Dafydd with bewildered regret. Regret for herself: neither Aerin nor Ioan had shown concern over the potential ends of their immortal lives, nor did she think Dafydd would. They had forever, or near enough to it, in the days they walked the earth. It was only Lara and her kind who left mortal bodies behind after a few short decades, and she had always found reassurance in the thought of seeing missing friends again. But her brief span of years—even if they could be elongated by staying in the Barrow-lands, as Oisín had done—would be all she ever had with Dafydd. There would be no eternal reunion in a spiritual homeland.

"So you better wake up," she heard herself whispering. "Because if this is a limited-time offer, I don't want to lose out on it. Live," she added, now smiling. "Live, damn you. *Live.*"

Dafydd ap Caerwyn drew breath, and with that first breath, laughed.

Aerin gasped, a short sharp sound mixed with relief and sorrow, but only Lara heard it. Dafydd was still chortling, gaze coming into focus as he smiled at Lara. "You've been watching too many movies. 'Live, damn you, live'? Was I—" His attention went beyond Lara, not so far as to Aerin, but simply up to the phosphorescent glow of the curved ceiling. "Lara, there are things I would like to say to you, but I suddenly think now is not the time. Sunrise," he added in a measured voice, "seems to have taken on an unlikely tint."

Lara lowered her head over his chest, biting back a tiny sob. "There are things I might like to hear. This has been . . ." She inhaled deeply and shook herself. There would be opportunities for talking later, when Aerin wasn't in such close earshot, and until then there were innumerable things Dafydd needed to hear. She told herself that fiercely, then steadied her voice.

"You're back in the Barrow-lands. In the Drowned Lands. You nearly died fighting the nightwings, Dafydd. Ioan opened the world-walking spell and brought you back here to heal. That was . . ." Time's broken passage left her at a loss for words, but she tried again after a few seconds: "Two mornings or six months ago, depending. Two mornings, for me."

Dafydd went motionless, eyes still fixed on the ceiling. When he spoke, it was with careful neutrality. "And six months for the Barrow-lands? Does my home still exist in any meaningful manner, then, or have Emyr and Hafgan—*Ioan*—destroyed it in battle?"

"We have about a day to get back to Emyr before he obliterates the Unseelie." Lara reconsidered her phrasing too late: Dafydd lurched to sitting, and finally saw Aerin standing in the chamber's entrance. Delight swept his features and he surged off the bier to pull her into a hug. The words he spoke into her armored shoulder were unclear, but their sentiment was not: his gratitude for her presence knew no bounds.

Lara, lips pursed, glanced away, and was overly pleased when Aerin, wryly, said, "Not that I've lost faith, Dafydd, but I'm here at

Emyr's behest. And were it not for your truthseeker, he would ride on the Unseelie city tonight; my life is in her hands."

"And your hair?" Dafydd touched Aerin's burned locks. "What happened?"

"We fought a chimera," Lara said into Aerin's uncomfortable silence. "The only way I could think to defeat it was with a hymnal. It was hard on Aerin."

Astonished gratitude lit the Seelie woman's eyes as Dafydd spun to face Lara again. "A chimera? Lara, you must tell me everything. The nightwing battle, what happened? I remember—" Chagrin slipped into his words, slowing him, and he stood arms akimbo. "I seem to remember you throwing a crowbar at me."

"A bar of crows?" Aerin's eyebrows shot up, garnering a laugh from the two familiar with the mortal realm.

"A length of iron with one clawed end." Dafydd made claws with two fingers. "Hence its name, I presume. You might have killed me, Lara," he said with a bit more seriousness.

"You were already killing yourself. I was just trying to stop you from working any more magic. And it worked. Ioan came through a world-door and killed the nightwing. One two, one two, and through and through," Lara said more softly, recalling the ease and speed Ioan had moved with. "He brought you back to Annwn, then to the Drowned Lands and their healing waters, because you weren't recovering on your own."

"You said that. And you came here how? Not through Ioan's spell, if time is yesterday and half a year since." Dafydd strode the chamber as he spoke, leaving Lara and Aerin to watch in bemusement. He paused at each tomb, examining the sleeper atop it, then moved on until Lara's answer brought him to a full stop:

"I followed Merrick, Dafydd. He's alive."

Sixteen

"That is not possible." Dafydd lifted a hand even as he spoke, barring any protest of truthfulness Lara might have made. She hadn't planned to; Dafydd's confidence in her power was sufficient that she recognized his denial as both necessary and perfunctory. People often disbelieved reality, even when the so-called impossible had taken place before their eyes. To be told the man he'd murdered was alive, without seeing it himself . . . it took Dafydd less time to recover than Lara thought it might. He gave a minute nod, freeing Lara to speak.

"He was your brother in all ways that mattered. You know what element he commanded?"

"Air."

"And with the right glamours, air becomes illusion." Lara counted loud heartbeats, waiting for Dafydd's second nod. Waiting for him to work through what he'd been told, and waiting for the argument she knew he'd make:

"The compulsion that drove me more than once was no illusion."

"Dafydd, I can lay compulsions." Lara made her hands into fists, hating the confession. "It's what I'm doing when I make people believe me, or when I stop them from acting as they might want to. And I'm only human. A truthseeker, maybe, but still only human. If I can do it, I'd think anyone with enough will and power could do it."

"Someone of royal blood," Aerin said. "Someone of Rhiannon's line."

Lara, taken aback, blinked at Aerin. "I thought Rhiannon was Emyr's wife. And I thought you were all of her line. I thought that was the point."

"We are, but some are closer to her than others. Your faith is full of contradictions itself, Lara," Dafydd murmured. "Do you believe all mankind to be descended from Adam and Eve? Or from Noah, after the Flood?"

High chimes of discomfort sent cold crawling up Lara's nape. It was a question she'd struggled with as a child, until religion and science had come to a truce: she had no concept of how long God might think a day was, nor any reason to be utterly convinced that making Man in His image had not taken generations of evolution. There had been Adams, of that she was certain; there had been Eves. Men and women who were the first of their kind whose children, through the ages, bred true. "Point taken. But does that mean Rhiannon was both your mother and grandmother?"

Dismay twisted the words, and the staff, quiet for so long, gave a sentiment very like chuckling. Lara resisted elbowing it as if it were an annoying person only because its location across her back made the action impossible. She twitched toward it, though, and her shoulder shrieked an objection, providing another reason not to react to the object's teasing.

Aerin said, "Yes," without seeming unduly disturbed by it. "Emyr and Hafgan are the oldest of Rhiannon's blood. Their sons are her children and grandchildren both, while we others are farther removed, and less exalted."

Contradictory truth ran through it, jarring Lara's skull bones. She put a palm forward, stopping Aerin. "All right. Okay. Faith is simple. That's what's complicated about it. And truthseekers probably shouldn't try dissecting it. What's relevant is that the magic is there, Dafydd. Compulsions can be laid against your will. Everyone saw you draw and fire on Merrick, and saw him die, but none of it was *real*." The language, she thought grumpily, wasn't well suited to determine between things that had happened under coercion and things that were voluntary. "He was trying to sow the seeds of civil war," she finished. "And he's succeeded. If he can get the rest of the royals to kill one another . . ."

Dafydd hadn't moved from in front of the tomb he'd stopped at, though he finally looked back toward Aerin and Lara. "Here lies Hafgan, king of the Unseelie court. Now we are four, we royals, and Merrick only one. The warmongering will end, and Merrick pay the price. This I swear."

Resolution rolled through his words, deep and comforting. Aerin, though, snorted with humor. "A worthy oath, my prince, but there is one flaw. We have no one to waken Hafgan with love's kiss, and without him your truthseeker's quest will fail."

"Love's kiss." Dafydd turned a slow smile on Lara. "Is that what wakened me?"

A blush began below Lara's collarbones and rushed upward, so her shoulder ached anew and her face blazed with heat. Dafydd's smile grew larger still, wicked delight dancing in his eyes. "I was right. There are things I would like to say to you, Lara Jansen." Say, and, from his bright, lascivious examination, do. Lara blushed harder, blood stinging her cheeks to painful prickles and making her shoulder throb so hard she whimpered and put a hand over it. Outside pressure made the pain flee inward, twisting her stomach, but at least it was different.

Dafydd's smile fell away, concern replacing it as he truly saw her for the first time. His gaze lingered on her shirt's bloody stains before coming up to meet hers. "You're hurt."

"I'll live." Lara tested the phrase for veracity, then shrugged her shoulders. *Close enough for government work,* Kelly would say.

"These are healing chambers—"

"And if we'd come in the right way I might be willing to ask for help." Lara shook her head carefully, trying not to jolt the renewed discomfort in her shoulder. "But we came in through the back door, magically speaking, and I'm afraid calling any more power than we absolutely need to will have consequences."

"I've missed rather a lot, haven't I," Dafydd said after a few heartbeats of silence. "I'll want to hear it all."

"Let's wake Hafgan up and get out of here first. I want to get away from the Drowned Lands before Emyr contacts Aerin."

"I'm sorry, Truthseeker." Aerin sounded as though she spoke from a great distance. Lara turned on a heel, dread sickening her belly. Aerin stood rimed with ice, more invasive than the cold that had gripped them on entering the chamber. This seeped out from her, freezing the air into thin crackling lines, a reminder that only Llyr's power allowed them to breathe.

Emyr. His icy scrying spell was meant for a recipient who was surrounded by air, not water. Here, in the heart of the Drowned Lands, the magic was bound to go wrong, freezing what it touched. Hoarfrost crackled and fell, new stuff forming as Aerin turned her head to glance at Lara and Dafydd. "I'm sorry," she repeated. "I fear it's already too late."

∽

Lara jolted forward a step, stopped by Dafydd's hand on her elbow as he murmured, "This isn't right. Scrying shouldn't ice the air."

"It's not *air*," Lara hissed, but bit back the rest, still uncertain of how the pressing sea might respond if she voiced truth aloud. "If it keeps up it'll freeze us all, Dafydd."

"No. Only me. I can do that, I think." Shards of ice buckled and folded in as Aerin spoke, digging against her armor. Frost patterns appeared where they touched, cold spreading inhumanly fast. Her sword's hilt went dull with layered cold, icicles forming on her gloves when she reached for the weapon. "The magic is not right," she agreed hoarsely. "It grips me, struggles to hold me. It is not the window it's meant to be."

Lara, shrill, cried, "Then why doesn't he *stop*?" and Aerin gave her a hard smile.

"Because he must press on until he's certain I'm dead. He'll have no excuse to invade otherwise."

"He'd kill you for the chance to invade?" Lara whispered, suddenly numb. She had simply not considered the possibility, but Aerin showed no surprise as she looked to Dafydd.

"Pass me quickly, Dafydd. Go now."

Dafydd gave one grim nod and caught Lara's right arm. Pain staggered her, a guttural cry tormenting the air, and he released her again. Lara dropped to her knees, catching herself with her left hand, but jarring her body hard enough to shoot sickness through her. Her elbow collapsed, bones and muscles useless as water, and she put her forehead against the floor, unable to move further.

"I thought you said you were all right!"

"I said I'd live." The tiniest whisper of humor went through the correction, though it did nothing to push back waves of pain. Concentrating on a different worry helped: "Dafydd, what's Aerin's element? How can she stop the ice?"

"Stone." Worry flattened his voice. "Stone endures. Cold can be drawn into its center."

Lara lifted her head the few inches she could manage, face tight with horror. "Stone cracks, Dafydd."

"Hence the necessity for your escape to come sooner rather than later." Aerin managed a degree of amusement, though the edges of her voice broke apart. The air around her was thick with slush now, swirling against her in grasping patterns. Ice built up around her feet, working to encase her shins, but even as she worked to draw it in, it pooled out, encroaching on the chamber floor. Every breath Lara drew was colder, a welcome relief in subduing her throbbing shoulder, but increasingly dangerous in terms of their survival. "You saved my life, Truthseeker. Let me save yours."

"I didn't save it so you could kill yourself an hour later!" Lara made it back to her knees, though she cradled her right arm. Letting it dangle hurt too much. She'd thought when she faced the nightwings that she was becoming a warrior, but a warrior would have to face pain better than she could.

"I told you." Aerin smiled again, ice cracking around her mouth. "The Drowned Lands are deadly to the Seelie. I think it was never my fate to leave them."

"*Enough.*" Warmth rushed the chamber. More than warmth: genuine heat swept from behind Lara toward the entrance. It splashed against Aerin in a visible wave, steam hissing and the sharp scent of warmed metal billowing off her. Ice turned to drizzles, and in seconds she stood in a pool of water. Violent pops echoed around the room, like glaciers calving, and Aerin shuddered from the bone outward. Her armor shattered, blackened fragments falling to the stone floor in a rain of metallic music. She stood among them, not daring to move for long moments before she, like Dafydd and Lara, looked at their savior.

A second man had risen from the biers, Emyr's twin in everything but coloring. His sharp features were the same, dark gold skin lying so taut over bone that Lara was reminded, uncharitably, of face-lifts gone wrong. But there was more expression in this man's face than surgery would allow. His thin lips curled with contempt, nostrils flaring as if the air he breathed wasn't quite good enough for him. His gaze flickered across all three of them, distaste finally settling in fine lines around his eyes and mouth as he reached up to tie long straight dark hair back in a knot. "Emyr's whelp, a mortal trinket, and a tainted warrior. What have I bothered to save, and at what cost? You." He snapped at Dafydd, then pointed at the floor in front of him, commanding Dafydd forward. "Tell me what has come to pass."

Dafydd, to Lara's private horror, looked at her. Hafgan—because she had no doubt that of the dozen sleepers in the chamber, the arrogant Unseelie who had awakened was indeed their king—made his expression long with incredulity. Obviously he'd concluded Dafydd was the only one capable of relating a tale, or possibly was the only one worthy of a king's attention.

Lara had never been especially contrary, but Hafgan's readiness to dismiss her awakened enough affronted amusement to drown her burst of horror. She put her left hand in Dafydd's and let him help her to her feet, not caring that it took several seconds to steady herself from her shoulder's pounding. "I'm the reason you're awake, not Dafydd."

She might have said a hamster or a goldfish had roused him, from the Unseelie king's disbelieving sneer. "Emyr and no other is responsible. There are no healers here, and passion is the only other tool that can waken a sleeper. Where is he?"

Lara looked over her shoulder at Aerin, who hadn't yet moved from the circle of fragmented metal. She shook her head at Lara's querying eyebrow, and Lara turned back to Hafgan. "Probably preparing to destroy your hidden city."

Hafgan took such a quick step forward Lara didn't realize he was within striking range until Dafydd inserted himself between them. "Hear her out, majesty. She is a truthseeker."

And mortal, Lara wanted to add, *and easily annoyed by elfin high-handedness.* She'd worked at a bespoke tailoring shop in Boston, where suits were made without patterns, custom-fit to those men and women who could afford them. Many of them had been as autocratic as the elfin kings were, but none of them irritated her so much. Maybe it was the power she wielded in the Barrow-lands; maybe, despite its unfamiliarity, she felt it garnered her some respect.

Mostly, though, at home, she was paid to deal politely with the powerful and pompous. She was in the Barrow-lands as a favor to Dafydd, and had vastly less reason to ignore bad manners. They'd wanted her help, not the other way around. "That was Emyr's scrying spell you just melted. He was trying to talk to Aerin to make sure we were all still alive, but it went wrong. We all owe you our thanks for stopping it."

"Mine especially," Aerin muttered. Lara swallowed laughter, unreasonably pleased that Aerin was as ungracious as she.

Hafgan looked between them and at Dafydd before settling on Lara again. She had the impression he'd chosen his battle by saying, "I have never heard of a scrying spell 'going wrong.'"

"Have you ever tried working one underwater?" Lara winced at even asking, but there was no corresponding flex in the air, no loosening of the spell that let them breathe and speak.

Hafgan glowered at her. "I have never worked one at all, not such as Emyr does. It is not in my element."

"Then trust me: it went wrong. The Drowned Lands corrupt

magic, maybe even incoming magic." Lara liked that idea more than the thought that Emyr might sacrifice Aerin to his war, but there was equal truth in both possibilities. "And—"

And the staff she carried was probably making it worse. Lara caught those words behind her teeth, looking for something else to say instead. "And that's why I'm here. Ioan, your successor, asked me to find out the truth of Annwn's past. Emyr's memory is unreliable, even when he tries to remember. I need both of you to reconstruct the histories."

"Why?"

"Because if Ioan's right, if the Seelie did choose to drown these lands, then your people have been treated appallingly, and I want to try to set it right."

"And if we brought it on ourselves, arbiter? What then? Will you leave us in our drowned home without another care?" Hafgan focused beyond her. On Aerin, Lara thought for an instant, but he said, "Will you use that staff to finish what was begun, if it is all our own fault?"

"The thought hadn't even occurred to me. No. Trying to fix what's wrong isn't contingent on one side being evil and the other being heroes. The Barrow-lands are dying, and maybe I can help. That's enough by itself."

"Then what does the history matter?"

Lara quirked an eyebrow. "I just want to know the truth."

Hafgan gave Dafydd a sour look. "There, whelp. There's the reason we killed them all."

Seventeen

Lara's gut clenched, breath gone like she'd taken a hit. Her shoulder throbbed once, but even that damage seemed limited compared to the shock bubbling through her mind. "*Killed* them?"

"And every line that carried the blood. It took time." Hafgan smiled, narrow and sharp. "But we never thought to trace the talent in mortal lives. Perhaps I'll rectify the error."

"We?" Lara whispered, then shook her head, shock melting to angry confidence. "You wouldn't stand a chance, hunting in my world. It's too full of iron and weapons you wouldn't recognize. Don't threaten me, Hafgan. I already have the worldbreaking staff."

Dafydd shifted, a small action that spoke of surprise, and only then did Lara hear her words as the threat they were. Hafgan's face twitched, subtle admiration and acknowledgment of her challenge visible in the change. "The old ones were not like you. They would not dream of threatening, nor would they act on the threat if it were made. It would lack..."—he shifted his head forward, offering a reptilian intimacy—"sophistication."

Prickles ran over Lara's neck, a chill that wanted her to respond. To continue baiting the Unseelie king until something erupted, something dangerous and unstoppable. That was the staff again, eager for destruction, and Lara gritted her teeth against the impulse. "You seem to remember the old days a lot more clearly than anyone else."

Hafgan waved idle fingers toward his bier. "The long sleep clears the mind. But I will not answer your questions, Truthseeker. Not here, not now. Let me rejoin the world and see my people, see my brother king, before we take that journey."

Certainty pounded through Lara. She could force the issue, compel the king to answer; her power would stretch that far. But it would also make an enemy of one inclined that way already, and that wasn't, as of yet, necessary. She glanced at Dafydd, who nodded almost invisibly. Then, trying to loosen her jaw, she looked back at Hafgan and offered a short bow, the best she was able to do. "Of course. Your majesty, you're the only one of Unseelie blood among us. My understanding is that the Drowned Lands will welcome you more readily than it has us. We would be grateful if you would lead us out safely."

"Grateful," Hafgan murmured. "Not indebted? You choose your words wisely, Truthseeker."

"I always have." A flash of memory came to her: her first date with Dafydd, when she'd pedantically and thoroughly dissected his word choices for accuracy. Kelly called her a walking dictionary for the game, but Lara enjoyed it. Carefully selecting words had lent her a small sense of control over truth that was difficult to otherwise achieve, in a world of white lies and polite fictions. Smiling, she put the memory aside to focus on the Unseelie monarch again. "Will you lead us out?"

He said, "I will," with unexpected grace, leaving Lara feeling as though she'd participated in a ritual without realizing it. Beside her, Dafydd relaxed incrementally, and she resisted the impulse to see if Aerin had done the same.

A moment later, as Lara fell into step behind Hafgan, it was obvious the Seelie woman had *not*. She waited for both royals and Lara to pass and took up the rear, despite the destruction of her sword and armor. Her shoulders were high and tension-ridden, and the look she gave Lara was full of warning. Discomfited, Lara nodded without being certain of what she was agreeing to. Caution, at the very least, though there'd been no lie in Hafgan's voice.

Moreover, the city's black glow had faded when they exited the healing chambers. It was once again as Llyr had granted Lara the ability to see it: in ruins, but no longer buried in sand, no longer worn by tide and saltwater. Brilliant color ran through the garden's coral-covered walls, and the ceaseless sound of wind and sea rushed through the crevasses, gentle and relaxing.

Creating, perhaps, a false sense of security. Even without Aerin's obvious stress, Hafgan's blunt words hung in Lara's mind: *There's the reason we killed them all.* Emyr, Aerin, and others who had spoken of it had said the truthseeking talent, always rare, had died out. Assassination was certainly a way of dying out, though not usually what was implied by the phrase. For a moment Lara felt like the last dodo, only with the cognitive capability of understanding what had happened to her brethren. It made her want to run, to draw a protective shell around herself, but there was nowhere to run, not in the heart of the drowned city. Not when she was, for all intents and purposes, entirely at Hafgan's mercy. Llyr had come to her twice. She didn't expect him a third time.

The thought lost its tunefulness, unexpected sour notes crawling in. Glad for a mental occupation beyond worrying about assassination, Lara chased the falsehood down, breaking the idea into com-

ponent parts. Llyr had come to her twice: truth. She didn't expect
him a third time: wavering truth. She didn't expect him to *rescue* her
a third time: truth. Curious, she pushed the concepts forward, looking for the boundaries of her truth-knowing ability. She expected to
see him again: true. When this was over? *True,* the music of it startling with its strength. She slowed, trying to refine it further. When
she was successful? Indifferent song, not well-played, not passionate
in either direction, true or false. When she failed? The same unopin-
ionated music, unable to offer assurance either way.

A low worried laugh broke loose. At least she would survive what
was coming, if she could expect to see Llyr when it was over.

The ill-made music came again, promising nothing.

Leaving the sea wrenched water from Lara's lungs the same way entering it had. Aerin, too, collapsed to hands and knees, choking and
spitting up saltwater, until they lay curled next to one another, trembling with exhaustion. Water dripped over Lara's face when she
moved, her clothes and hair laden with it, and Aerin had fared no
better. Dafydd, though, was dry and comfortable as he crouched
over them, hands spread wide in useless distress. Hafgan, as unscathed by the ocean as Dafydd, stalked up the beach, ignoring them
in favor of looking over the sheltered cove.

The sun had long since set, judging from the beach's coldness and
the dark of the horizon. Stars and a crescent moon's light glimmered
overhead, just enough to cast faint shadows of dark on dark. Hafgan
became a sculpted piece of night when he stopped at the beach's
edge, the wind barely enough to stir his hair.

He could hear them; could almost certainly hear them, but Lara
fumbled for Dafydd anyway, weariness making her clumsy. "'Why
we killed them all'?"

He caught her hand, his grip strong and certain. Faint moonlight was far kinder to him than to Hafgan: he still looked vivacious, gold threads in his hair glinting silver under the night sky. "I don't even know who 'we' are, Lara, much less if it's—" He broke off, dismay creasing his eyes. "Much less if it's true. But it is." At her nod, his shoulders dropped. "I know nothing of it. Maybe it was an Unseelie vendetta, for the arbiters of justice allowing their lands to drown."

"You believe that's what happened?"

Dafydd shrugged. "All I know is the seas rose, Lara. A displaced people might find anyone to release their anger on."

That was true enough in her own world, too. Lara released Dafydd's hand, coiling up on herself again. Her chest ached, heavy with water, and a deep breath produced rattling coughs that took her breath. When she could move again, she sat on her heels and wheezed, "Can you work a scrying spell? We need to talk to your father."

He turned his palms up, lightning dancing in them and casting sharp shadows against his face. "My element isn't one for scrying with. I might call down a bolt from the clear night sky to distract him with, if I concentrated."

Aerin chuckled, a low rough sound as she rolled onto her back. She coughed more delicately than Lara had, then pushed up on her elbows. Even with her hair a burned ruin and wearing nothing but the wet padded tunic and breeches that fit beneath her armor, in the moonlight she was beautiful. It liked her even better than it did Dafydd, her singed locks turning muted blue and her green eyes touched with yellow. "You would have to strike him with it to keep him from riding on the Unseelie, Dafydd, and then his guard would call it an attack, and ride in his name."

"Your wisdom tempers my impulse, as always." Dafydd dropped his head heavily between his shoulders, pale hair falling around his cheeks. "I suppose we ride hard for the battlegrounds, then."

"It would be faster to find Ioan." Lara twisted her hair over her shoulder, squeezing water out. Aerin and Dafydd both blinked at her, Aerin's mouth slowly curving in a foolish smile.

"I suppose it would be. But now we're four, and only one among us Unseelie."

"But that one is their king. Not just the heir apparent playing the role to keep peace, but Hafgan himself. Will they know him?"

Dafydd raised a hand, begging patience with the gesture. "My brother is here?"

Lara exchanged looks with Aerin before speaking. "We had some trouble coming into the valley. Ioan was hurt and they took him to the village to be seen to by healers."

"You had some trouble coming in," Dafydd echoed. "Truthseeker, are you lying to me?"

"No!" Despite the vehemence of her protest, Lara dipped her head guiltily. "I'm not! But that . . . might be the edited version."

"I didn't know you could offer such a thing." Dafydd's smile was teasing.

Lara hunched her shoulders, grinning sheepishly at the sand. "I never used to. It's just so much has happened."

"Even the most honest among us might be tempted to edit," Dafydd agreed.

Lara looked up again to find him still smiling, and to find Aerin's gaze gone hard on her. Her impulse to return the banter retreated into discomfort. "What?"

"Does your shoulder no longer pain you?"

Lara clapped her hand against it, sodden padding releasing a wash of water down her chest from the impact. The flesh below, though, protested not at all. Astonished, Lara tugged at the wrappings, then thrust her arm out in a silent, childlike plea for help. Aerin leaned in to unwrap the bindings she'd put in place. Lara caught her breath with every pull, waiting for pain, but it never came. In moments, bare flesh was exposed, no hint of injury visible.

"The healing waters," Aerin said slowly. "I would not have dreamed they would welcome me, much less a mortal, and yet . . ."

"We're both better." Lara prodded her shoulder, exploring undamaged skin. She hadn't so much as noticed the pain evaporating. Being pain-free was normal, not remarkable, though now she remembered everything she'd done since reaching the beach: catching herself as she collapsed, reaching for Dafydd, pushing up to sit on her heels. Ordinary actions, except in light of having been dizzy with injury and blood loss not so very long before. "Who, um. Is it Llyr? Is he a god of healing as well as the sea? I feel like I should . . . thank someone, and my God doesn't seem exactly appropriate here," she said awkwardly. "I'm not sure He'd even hear me."

"Oh, he would." Dafydd pulled a moue. "Faith crosses boundaries. If not, your exorcism would have no power."

"Nor your songs." Aerin touched her hair, then let her hand fall. "Llyr is not our god of healing, but the waters are his. Thanks to him would not go unappreciated."

Lara bowed her head, narrowly avoiding making the sign of the cross as she murmured thanks not only for her recovery, but for the help the sea god had offered her. Both Dafydd and Aerin were looking at her curiously when she lifted her gaze again, but neither spoke. "Ioan," she said firmly. "If he can't scry Emyr in time I'm afraid the Unseelie city will be wiped out by morning. I don't know where the village they brought him to is, but I think I can find it focusing on him. Like I did with the staff back in Massachusetts," she said to Dafydd, which earned her a faintly puzzled nod.

"I remember," he said after a moment. "Just not . . . clearly."

"You were sick." *Dying,* truth's music wanted her to say, but for once Lara quenched it, happier with chicanery. "Anyway, I can do it, but I don't think we'll be fast enough on foot. Aerin, do you have any idea how far we are from the horses?"

Aerin shook her head. "No, but they'll come at my call."

"All right, good. If you'll call them..." Lara turned back to the dunes Hafgan had climbed, drawing breath to call him as well.

Only grass and shadows moved on the low beach hills. Hafgan was gone.

Eighteen

Aerin pierced the air with a long whistle, higher than a seagull's call. Lara flinched, then caught Dafydd's hand briefly, drawing his attention to Hafgar's disappearance before climbing the dunes herself. Dafydd followed after, leaving Aerin to make a sound of disgruntlement that deepened into concern as she realized who they sought. She scrambled up the hill behind them, coming to stand so that Lara was dwarfed between the two Seelie. They all focused on the distance before glancing at one another. Dafydd and Aerin's gazes sailed over Lara's head and she straightened her spine, adding the last possible fraction of an inch to her height. Dafydd, looking like he was trying not to, cracked a smile.

"Little mortal," Aerin said with such solemnity it became amusement. Her vantage point was a few inches higher than Lara's, making her that much taller still, and she laughed when Lara bared her teeth. "You stand as tall as Oisín. Are you a giant among your people?"

"Oisín's short, for a man in my era. I'm not a giant. I'm not short, either." The last came out defensively. Even the smallest of the elfin adults Lara had seen stood four inches taller than she, and there was no obvious disparity between men and women in height.

Aerin grinned, holding a hand up for peace, then turned her attention back to the landscape. Humor draining away, she said, "The stones say nothing of his passage, Truthseeker. He may be lost to us."

"Why would he do that?" Answers came unbidden before either Seelie had time to respond, and Lara lifted her own hand in turn, stopping whatever they would say. "Because Emyr's out there and Hafgan's got issues with him, if nothing else. Because he doesn't owe us anything. Because—"

"He owes you his wakening," Aerin disagreed, but shrugged in general acknowledgment. "Still, his element is heat, not air. I should be able to track him through the earth."

Lara blinked at the taller woman, suddenly appreciating the breadth of possibilities granted by an affinity for stone. "You must be a fantastic hunter."

Aerin fixed her gaze on the distant mountains, enough strain in her neck to suggest she deliberately avoided Dafydd's eyes. "I have always captured what I sought, yes. But Hafgan is connected with this land. He can, perhaps, persuade it to show no signs of his passing."

"Then we forget about him for a while." Lara's voice hardened. "The truth is, we know where he's likely to end up. Right now Emyr probably thinks you're dead and has no warning that Hafgan's on the way. Finding Ioan and scrying Emyr is our best chance to avoid a catastrophic battle. We'll worry about Hafgan later. Aerin, the—"

The sound of surf, soft enough before to have been unnoticeable, intensified abruptly, the earth rattling with it. Lara reached for the staff, making certain it hadn't come unstrapped from her back, then turned to the beach, still afraid the weapon had somehow triggered a tsunami. They couldn't run: there was no ground high enough within reach, even if they were as fast as the Seelie horses.

It was those horses that pounded down the shore, their striking hooves making the rumble under Lara's feet. They slipped between moonlit shadows from one step to the next, only half existent in the world as Lara saw it, and were at the dunes in impossibly little time. One came to a full halt, the other dancing around it. Each touch of its hoof to earth sent another jolt deep into the ground, shaking Lara where she stood. She had never seen them run when she wasn't astride, but that they struck the earth hard when they returned from their shift through space rang true with her. The Seelie army must have nearly shaken trees from their root beds as it rode. Impressed, she nodded toward them, then shot an abashed smile at Aerin. "The horses, I was going to ask."

Aerin made a fluid gesture as though she'd conjured them, then slipped gracefully down the hill to catch and calm the prancing beasts. Their tack was gone, left somewhere else along the beach, but the Seelie woman leapt onto her horse so easily it was clear she didn't feel the lack. Lara, alarmed, watched Dafydd do the same, and followed him down the hill muttering, "Remember that I'd never ridden a horse before coming here?"

He gave her a hand and pulled her onto the horse's back with enough finesse that for a moment even she thought it was her own agility making the move. Wisdom caught up, though, and she blurted, "Aerin?"

"Feel the earth," Aerin said smoothly. "Feel it rise through the horse's legs, feel it embody you, feel the connection between you and the beast and the land. You cannot fall, when you are one with the horse." It was the enchantment she'd used before to stick Lara in place. This time, though, Lara felt a hint of what she meant, a tenuous bond between herself and the horse and the ground below. The *how* of the spell suddenly came clear to her, Aerin's stoneworking talent making that union between three separate things, and Lara's confidence in it increased tremendously. Aerin gave a satisfied nod, then *hi-yah*'d! the horses up the dunes as Lara, clinging to Dafydd, closed her eyes to search for a true path to Ioan.

It was easier each time she did it, even considering the delicacy that had been necessary to create the path to the tomb in the Drowned Lands. Ioan was a vital figure in her thoughts, details of what she knew about him tumbling into place. Passionate in protecting his people, even in protecting those who weren't quite his anymore, like Dafydd. Willing to go to immoral lengths to find help. Lara's own kidnapping was proof enough of that. A skilled warrior with no evident fear. A man dedicated enough to the life he'd been given to undergo physiological changes that would make him truly one of his chosen people.

There was far more, certainly, that she didn't know, but that was enough. Each element she remembered added a piece to the symphony: the warrior, drums; the protective nature, a lonely note from a trumpet. They came together, weaving a ball of music and light that hung in Lara's mind as it gathered strength, then ricocheted across the countryside in a blaze. "Roadways," she said aloud. "Please follow the roadways."

Song gurgled as it twisted around, returning to Lara and seeking another path. She said, "Back down the beach, back to where we left the horses," into Dafydd's shoulder, and heard a trill of impatience enter the symphony as the riders wheeled and drove their animals back the way they'd come. "Does your lightning have a personality?"

"Short-tempered but easily assuaged," Dafydd replied without a hint of seeming to think the question strange. "Impatient, impulsive, callous. There's no softness in it. Why do you ask?"

"Because the truthseeking music is starting to make commentary. And the staff has all along," Lara added more softly. "It wants to be used. It wants to destroy."

"Your will is stronger than its." Determination, if not strict accuracy, filled Dafydd's voice. "Lara..."

She pushed her nose against his shoulder and said, ruefully, "This still isn't the time."

"Perhaps not, but I've greeted Aerin more enthusiastically than you, and that was hardly my intention. I feel...rushed. As though I daren't stop moving, for fear events will overwhelm us. And I barely know what's happened this past season or more!"

Something popped in Lara's chest, making breathing easier. "I feel the same way. And you're forgiven. I got a kiss, and she didn't." It was petty, but his acknowledgment in how he'd received Aerin made all the difference.

"You kissed me," Dafydd said firmly. "A favor I intend to make up for later. Now, Lara...can you tell me what I've missed?"

She said, "Turn left where the road forks," instead, as the pathway behind her eyelids veered that way. For a moment she dared open her eyes, glimpsing the roadway. Texture and color set it apart from the fields alongside it, even in the moon's scant light. A thrust of bright music lay over the road itself, not illuminating it in any real-world way. The combination made her dizzy. She closed her eyes again, grateful that she rode with Dafydd and had no need to guide the horse herself.

"I don't know most of what's happened here," she said then. She sketched out the details of Dafydd's rescue by Ioan and Merrick's reappearance, the latter of which made the Seelie prince's posture tense so much their horse whickered in agitation. "I followed him back to the Barrow-lands, through his worldwalking spell, but I got thrown out of time again. He's here somewhere, Dafydd, I'm sure of it. Hiding in the waters, maybe, although I thought he might come after us while we were in the city and he didn't. Thank God," she added with feeling, then exhaled and brought her attention back to the matter at hand. "The farmers who attacked us saw two Seelie warriors, and Ioan's no longer fair."

"Can you seek him the way we seek Ioan now?" Dafydd relaxed a little, though there was still strain in his body.

Lara shook her head. "Maybe once we stop moving. I'd need to concentrate more than I can when we're jolting."

"Jolting?" Dafydd sounded offended and Lara laughed.

"I'm not used to horses, Dafydd. Right, turn right up ahead. We're almost there." The streaking light in her mind was resolving, becoming a steady bright point. "Can you see a town?"

"Village lights. There've been one or two others along the way. You're certain this is the right one?" The question was more impressed than suspicious; Dafydd had never doubted her, not since he'd recognized her gift.

Lara pressed a smile into his shoulder, then peeked over it to catch a glimpse of torches glowing in the near distance. "If it's not, my power has gone horribly awry. That looks like real fire."

"It is," Aerin called. Lara startled, having not realized the Seelie woman could hear them over the horses' hooves. Aerin dropped her horse into a walk to make conversation easier as she nodded toward the village. "Our light spheres are easy to maintain, but they're a constant slow draw on magics. They must use fire for most light in this valley, or one of us would have discovered them long since."

"You hunt down magic use? You can do that?" Whether they *should* was another topic entirely, one Lara wasn't prepared to broach.

Aerin shrugged. "Not as a matter of course, but it can be done. It's why we hide our citadels behind glamours, to make them less vulnerable. So if there had been a long constant draw of power here, in a valley near the Drowned Hundred . . . yes. Someone would have investigated, and Emyr would have—"

"Taken action," Lara volunteered as a shiver spread over her skin. Emyr was not a nice man. Neither had Hafgan been nice, and it was easy enough to see how two leaders of such arrogance could drag their people down paths of unthinking cruelty. Ioan at least seemed less dedicated to the concept of his own superiority, and Dafydd was entirely diffident by comparison to his father. Maybe it was their relative youth, but it seemed to Lara the Barrow-lands would be better governed by the sons than the fathers.

"Yes." Aerin sounded pleased by the phrase *taken action*, and Lara cast a helpless glance toward the heavens before leaning around Dafydd to better see the nearing village.

Not only the torches danced in her vision. Even with the truth-seeker's path guiding her, the whole of the little town flickered in and out of her sight like Brigadoon. Heat banded her skull, warning of an oncoming headache. "I hate glamours."

Dafydd blinked over his shoulder at her and Lara made a face. "They give me migraines. I think the town is glamoured. Probably makes it harder for murderous Seelie to stumble across it."

Injury entered Dafydd's eyes and Lara pulled another face. "Sorry. That wasn't fair."

"I should think it was." A woman's voice came out of the darkness ahead of them and both Seelie reined up as the voice was followed by shadows releasing a familiar face: Braith, still bearing the scythe she'd threatened Ioan with earlier. Her red hair was almost black in the scant moonlight, and she looked older, grimmer, than she had by day. "That's exactly why the town is glamoured. It's one of our few means of defense, Truthseeker. We will not change that for your comfort."

"No." Lara pinched the bridge of her nose, ineffectively willing her headache to retreat. "I wouldn't expect you to. But may we enter the village? It might be less distressing from the inside."

"Who is your companion?" Braith obviously meant Dafydd; Aerin, she recognized and disdained with a single glance.

"Dafydd ap Caerwyn," he said, unwisely in Lara's opinion. In Aerin's, too: she stiffened and moved her horse a step closer, for all that she no longer had either armor or weapon.

Braith's grip on the scythe became more aggressive. "Emyr's second-born."

"The same. I bear you no ill will, and put myself in your power for the duration of our visit."

A hostage to good behavior, in other words, though doubt spiked through Lara. The Unseelie in this valley had no reason at all to keep their enemy's son alive, not when a degree of vengeance could be enacted with no one the wiser. She and Aerin stood as the only two witnesses, and aside from the staff, were unarmed. It would be the work of moments to rid the world of all three of them.

The staff rumbled anticipation through her. Whether it was for her potential demise or the possibility of battle, Lara neither knew nor cared. She slipped down from the horse to face Braith. "He means it. The truth is, he'd probably stay here forever just to keep things more settled between your two people, but that won't accomplish any of the things you and I both want. Emyr would never accept Dafydd being left here, and I can't learn what happened to Annwn without Emyr's help." Or without finding Hafgan again, but that was more than Braith needed to know, even if the lie of omission rang warning bells in Lara's mind. "We're running out of time, Braith. I need you to decide now if you'll help us or not."

Braith's gaze slipped from Lara to the two mounted Seelie behind her. Lara checked the impulse to turn and investigate them herself, feeling that doing so would undermine her own authority. Authority she'd taken on herself and, for that reason most particularly, couldn't afford to erode. Aerin had seen her take up that mantle earlier and was likely to heed it, but Dafydd, a prince in his own right, might well choose to act outside the boundaries Lara outlined.

But he said nothing, and Braith, studying him, evidently saw no threat or disregard for Lara's demands. After a long while she nodded, attention back on Lara. "All right. I'll bring you to the healers."

Nineteen

Even within the village borders, Lara's vision flickered and danced uncomfortably. She accepted Dafydd's hand up to horseback again, more comfortable riding with her eyes closed than struggling against the glamour that winked small houses and streets in and out of visibility. Neither of the citadels had affected her so badly, but neither of the citadels, she imagined, had such cause to hide. Truth jangled through that thought, wearying even in itself.

What glimpses she got when she dared peek through tangled lashes were of a comfortable little township, homes close together with fields surrounding them. The streets were cobbled, instead of the hard-packed earth that made up the roadways they'd followed through the valley. Their horses clopped over the changed texture with no concern, their footing as sure as ever. Lara, headache throbbing with every hoofbeat, wondered if anything at all disturbed the pace of beasts capable of traversing a half-dozen steps with each stride.

More than a few curious people looked out of windows or came out of doors to watch the little processional. Curious and often bitter, though Lara had the sense that it was the elders whose countenances bore the latter emotion. Others looked as though they'd never seen anything like Lara and the two Seelie, and whether their gazes lingered longest on her, or on their eternal enemies, she couldn't say. They weren't friendly, though. Hostility and caution burned in their stances, and after a minute or two Lara was happier to close her eyes against their stares, and ride unrecognizing of silent assault.

"The healer's hall." Braith spoke with portence, though the hall, when Lara opened her eyes, looked very much like the other small tidy homes she'd caught sight of. Neither it nor its immediate surrounds bobbed and weaved the way most of the village did, though the torches hung outside its door developed auras, sign of a worsening headache. Still, the stability of the house itself was gratifying, and Lara trusted her feet as she slid off the horse to the ground.

Dafydd put an arm around her waist a moment later, his voice low with concern. "Are you well?"

"Not really." Lara managed a wan smile that turned to an actual quiet laugh at Dafydd's dismay. "I'll manage. These magic-induced migraines seem to go as fast as they come. I'll be okay once we're out of here."

He nodded and released her as they fell in behind Braith, who tapped twice on the hall's wooden door, then opened the door, gesturing Lara's party to follow her.

It *was* a hall, or at least a long single room warmed by a small hearth-bound fire. An apothecary's table, littered with pestles and vials, sat fully on the other side of the room, directly across from the fire. Empty basins littered with drying rags stood at the far end, and half a dozen fur-covered beds, all with backless chairs beside them, were distributed down the room's length. Only one was occupied.

Ioan sat on its edge rather than ensconced under covers. He glanced up and came to his feet in one motion. "Lara. You made it. You— *Dafydd.*"

The second name was laden with complicated emotion. Regret, Lara thought: regret and relief and surprise. Ioan swayed where he stood, watching Dafydd down the length of the room until Lara felt as if she should retreat, leaving the brothers to their first meeting for the first time in more years than she could name. "You look well," Ioan finally scraped out, and Dafydd gave a short hard laugh.

"I'm not sure I can say the same about you. You look... different. Lara told me what you'd done, but..."

But it was no doubt too little preparation for seeing a brother, once a near mirror image, changed into someone else entirely. It would be possible to do at home, Lara thought, with hair and skin dye, and with careful weight management, though Ioan ap Annwn was actually shorter than he'd once been, height transformed to Unseelie breadth. On Earth, that would be impossible, an illusion if managed at all. Here it was all truth, willpower manifesting over physicality in ways only magic could explain.

Ioan clenched his fists, gaze dropping before he forced it up again. "It's easier for me," he said after a moment. "The Seelie court changes less than I have. You are... much as I remember you. And Lara has succeeded. In all things?"

The question intimated something none of them wanted to say in front of Braith: that Ioan was not Hafgan, though he was king of the Unseelie people. Unexpectedly, Dafydd looked to Lara for a response. Her eyebrows crawled upward and she narrowly avoided passing the question on to Aerin. Braith's silent presence stopped her: Lara was the nominal leader of their little group, and answers should fall to her. "In all things. I can tell you more later, but if you're well enough, we need you to scry Emyr immediately. There were... complications, and Aerin wasn't able to report to him tonight. I'm concerned about the ramifications, if he thinks she's injured or dead."

Ioan's chin lifted. He looked *well*: there were no signs of his injuries, not even a paleness that spoke to blood loss. The Unseelie healers had done a good job, and Lara wished she'd been able to watch that magic. It might have had a true song to it, the putting right of things broken.

It had, though, left residual marks around him: like so much in the Unseelie village, there were flutters of hard-to-see magics that sparked migraine pulses when he moved. Normal healing of severe injuries took weeks, even months. It was possible forcing rapidity on that healing made it a little less *true* than letting time do its job would. Lara pressed a hand to her shoulder, testing it for pain, then glanced at it and at Aerin, looking for similar marks that bespoke fast healing had been performed on them.

No new auras or waves rolled over her, but the injuries had been comparatively minor next to Ioan's, and it had been hours or longer since both healings had been accomplished. She would know next time to look promptly, curiosity driving her more than anything else.

She'd been silent barely the length of a breath, considering all those things, but Ioan took her silence as an excuse to speak. "Braith, will you bring water? I have duties to administer to, and a thirst upon me."

Braith cast him a dubious look, but nodded and slipped out. Ioan sat again, a wry cant coming over suddenly tired features. "Healers always say not to exert yourself."

"And patients rarely listen." Lara smiled, but it faded as she broke away from the others to sit on a bed across from the Unseelie prince. "Ioan, we did bring Hafgan out of the Drowned Lands, but he disappeared as soon as we got to shore. I don't know if Emyr should be told—"

"It's trouble either way." Dafydd joined her, Aerin following more reluctantly. "If he's told, he'll see a threat. If he's not . . ."

"We're traitors all," Aerin said dourly. "Tell him. He already sees the threat and no doubt rides on your city as we speak. Hafgan's return may heighten his eagerness, but it'll change nothing else. And if we don't tell him, it's our own necks beneath the sword."

Ioan nodded, features darkening with each argument. "But would he expect me to offer such information," he began, and Aerin again interrupted.

"Better if I speak to him, or Dafydd does. He'll want to hear nothing from you at all. Just work the scrying spell. That will be enough."

Like Dafydd had, Ioan glanced to Lara for confirmation, but nodded before she responded. "You were wise as a youth, Aerin. I see that hasn't changed."

Aerin huffed dismissively, unwilling to accept the compliment. Lara hid a smile in her shoulder, though like the earlier one, it faded quickly. Old enmities would die hard, even if she succeeded in righting Annwn's physical structure and returning land to the Unseelie peoples. Barren land, at that, in all likelihood: aeons under the sea would presumably render it lifeless, unable to be used as farmland for decades.

That was a bridge to cross when they came to it. Lara felt a silly surge of pride at the vernacular phrase, not one she could commonly use without her power twinging. But it, and she, was growing more comfortable with metaphorical language. In time she might well be able to simply turn the magic on and off.

Braith returned with a stoneworked pitcher of water and four cups, the latter of which Lara thought unexpectedly generous. Ioan, after all, had requested the water, and none of the other visitors were of her people. She might well have slighted them, and not one would be easily able to claim the insult was deliberate.

Maybe there was hope for Annwn's future after all. Lara smiled her thanks as the Unseelie woman put the stoneware on the table. Braith frowned at her, at the others, and back at her. "The healer will never let me hear the end of it if he wears himself out. Make sure he drinks, and get him back to rest."

Lara, bemused, watched her go, grateful she didn't have to respond. Only when the door closed did she say, "I doubt casting spells is what she meant by resting."

"I'm sure that neither is leaving by morning," Ioan said, "but I intend to ride with you when you go."

"One bridge at a time." Lara carried the pitcher to him, eyeing its cool contents. "Do you need this poured in a basin?"

"The smaller the surface, the less magic is needed to draw an image. And the less ability the scried have to see the scrier's surroundings. That may be advantageous. Aerin, you'll be our voice?"

"I will." Aerin took the jug from Lara and knelt before Ioan, pitcher uplifted in both hands. Lara fell back a step, wondering how long the Seelie warrior could hold a gallon or more of weight in such a fashion, but certain it was longer than she herself could. Ioan put his fingertips into the jug's mouth, then drew his hand upward, a fountain of water following.

Lara's headache spiked and she dropped onto the nearest bed, one hand splayed over her face. Ioan shot her a concerned look, but she shook her head, half watching him through her fingers. Dafydd sat beside her, concerned fingers light against her temple, and she murmured, "Migraine. My vision likes magic less and less. Maybe it's not *true* enough."

"Perhaps not." Dafydd tugged her closer, giving her his chest to rest against, and she let her eyes close for a few moments as Ioan whispered words of enchantment. She could barely hear them, much less make out their meaning, but water splashed again and she risked a squint across the beds.

A tiny, fine figure of Emyr, riding horseback, rode above the jug.

It was beautiful, like three-dimensional film caught in a loop: the horse never moved forward, only ran hard in place, silver king crouched low over its back. The faintest shadows suggested other riders nearby, but none of them resolved, the water too little to create more intricate images.

Emyr reined up and the picture shifted, no longer distant enough to see him as a rider. Only his head and shoulders appeared, barely taller than a hand span. His features were more pinched than usual, narrow mouth tight and darkness in colorless water's eyes.

Only when he saw Aerin did he show a trace of relief. "So you live after all."

Relief flushed Aerin's face as well: she hadn't liked the idea that Emyr would sacrifice her any more than Lara had. "We were in the Drowned Lands when you scried me, majesty," she said. "Your magic and its...reacted badly. That no longer matters. We succeeded. Dafydd is with us, strong and well. The truthseeker would have you hold off any strike against the Unseelie city for another full day, as was agreed."

Emyr's familiar sneer stretched the scrying. "Would she. But what of Hafgan? Has he been released from the killing sea as well?"

"He has." Aerin kept her voice steady, though her hands tensed around the jug. "And has gone his separate way from us. You may well see him before we do."

A knife-sharp smile cut across Emyr's mouth. "I most sincerely hope I do."

Chills shattered down Lara's spine, discomfort born, for once, from the honesty in the Seelie king's voice. "Destroying Hafgan won't help your cause, Emyr."

His attention shifted her way, though Lara wasn't at all certain he could see her. "You have very little understanding of my cause, Truthseeker. Do not presume to judge." He nodded once, sharply—

at Aerin, Lara thought, not at herself—and then the watery simulacrum dropped back into the jug with a splash.

Ioan flinched, visibly not expecting the magic to be cut off from the other end, but Aerin's steady grip never wavered. She unfolded from the floor, carrying the jug to the table, and filled the cups Braith had brought. Only when they were delivered and half drunk did she say, "I think any hope of his hand remaining stayed is past, Truthseeker. We would be best off leaving now."

"Ioan's supposed to take it easy," Lara protested, though even she thought it sounded weak. "I don't know what happens if a healing is pushed too far. Can it just unravel?"

"No. I'll be well enough." Ioan stood, a little pale with his boldness, and looked to Dafydd. "We're his sons. If anyone can make him see reason, it should be us." Dissonance clamored through the claim, as if his desire was less strong than his certainty in being correct. "We ride tonight."

Twenty

Soldiers of old, Lara had read, learned to sleep anywhere they could, even in the saddle. No one would
mistake her for a soldier, but between Aerin's enchantment to keep
her on horseback and the long hours since her last rest, she found
herself in camaraderie with those old warriors. Her head bounced
against Dafydd's shoulder, disturbing her occasionally, but not
nearly enough to fully waken her until Dafydd murmured, "We're
here."

Her head snapped up, physical reaction quicker than her mind.
"Where's here? Oh." The granite-ensconced Unseelie citadel spread
out before them. Never bustling, it seemed emptier than ever now,
their horses' hooves cracking loud against the stone floors and the
echoes rising unhindered toward the distant ceiling. Lara massaged
the back of her neck and let her forehead drop against Dafydd's
shoulder again. "That was fast."

"Hopefully fast enough. It was almost dawn when we entered the
passageway. I'd have thought Emyr would be here by now."

"He'll be on the crevasse banks," Lara said absently. "The Unseelie army will have followed him from the plains they were fighting on, to keep the fight outside the city. Taking the city is like fighting at Thermopylae. As long as they can keep the bulk of the army occupied, the city entrance can be guarded by a handful of people." She blinked up before she was finished, astonished at herself, and Dafydd turned to give her a look of surprised admiration.

"A few days in the Barrow-lands and you're a master tactician."

Lara shook her head. "It's just that I've ridden into the city twice now. Unless there's a back way in, and a way past that crevasse, Emyr's going to be stuck fighting out there. He should have gone to pitched battle on the fields," she added thoughtfully. "Here he's got nowhere to run. They'll be backed up against the canyon. The Unseelie just have to push them over."

Ioan came closer. "You mean it's possible his army could be utterly routed. That the Seelie could be all but destroyed, if they've brought the fight this close to the citadel."

"We have to stop them." Lara clicked at the horse, trying to urge it forward even from her backseat position, but Aerin, a few yards ahead of them, raised a hand for patience.

"Whether it's here or further out, we go to face battle, Truthseeker, and not one of us is armed for it. Outfitting ourselves now may lose a few minutes, but better that than to die for lack of arms. Ioan, can you take us to the armory?"

The Unseelie king—prince, Lara corrected herself; Hafgan, no doubt, still thought of himself as king—looked discomfited. "It's not a place I often go."

Aerin's lip curled in derision. "Then I'll find it myself." She wheeled her horse around, even its footsteps managing to sound contemptuous.

"Wait. I should be able to find it." Lara lifted her voice and Aerin's shoulders tensed, though she didn't urge her horse into a run. Lara crushed her eyes closed, bringing to mind the finely worked black-bladed swords carried by Unseelie warriors. A thrum of enthusiasm sprang up from the worldbreaking staff, as if it recognized her intention of finding other weaponry.

A path sliced through her cut-off vision, brighter and more certain than any she'd followed before. Her magic had learned: it no longer pointed to the most direct route, but instead shot through the city streets, finding a route accessible to all. The staff sang urgency, encouraging her, and Dafydd made a small sound of incredulity. It was Aerin, though, who said "Well done, Truthseeker."

She was in motion before Lara opened her eyes, hoof-steps clattering across the city. Lara blinked after her, then drew up in astonishment herself. The path, still seared in her mind, was as bright and vivid along the citadel roads as it was in her thoughts. She said "You can see that?" unnecessarily as Dafydd put his heels to their horse and followed Aerin with Ioan a few steps behind them.

"We can. Your power is growing, Lara." Dafydd sounded delighted.

Caution roiled through Lara as the staff exuded smugness. She curled a hand back, not quite touching it. "Power corrupts."

Dafydd, unexpectedly, said, "And absolute power is kind of neat," making Lara laugh and release the near-hold she had on the staff. The glaring path through the city wavered, then stabilized as she focused, determined not to lose the ease of everyone being able to see it. The staff had lent her strength: she had very little doubt of that. But it wasn't the staff's magic that created the true paths, a fact that rang with strong, pleased music. It was a tool at best, and one she would not come to rely on. A sense of resentment washed up from it before settling again, and Lara had a few seconds to look over the city before the pathway led them into the armory.

No one was left within the city boundaries. Nowhere visible, at least: the glittering black streets were empty in every direction, no hints of life peeping from the pathways that crossed the walls. Lara wondered if Hafgan had returned and taken his people away, as the unbroken walls and buildings didn't suggest the city had already been sacked. And if he had, she wondered if there would be anything in the armory for them to arm themselves with, or if it would prove a useless detour.

Not too much of a detour, though: it lay closer to the city's entrance than she'd expected, the pathway jutting down into the granite. Unlatched doors stood open and inviting, easily large enough for two riders on horseback to pass through shoulder to shoulder. A pathway wove through an enormous, globe-lit room, and Aerin made a pleased sound at the back of her throat.

Even at a glimpse, Lara could see why. Padded tunics and leggings came first on the pathway, then soft shoes, then every piece of armor a warrior could need, all in what she presumed was the most efficient order of donning them. Weapons were farther along, closer to an exit rising back to the surface. If the city came under attack, it could be protected by men and women snatching up armor and weaponry on the way to the easily defended approach. Indeed, given the size of the room and the relatively few suits and sets left, that had almost certainly happened already.

Aerin slid off her horse and stripped down, collecting new clothing as she left the old on the floor. Her bared skin was pinker than Lara thought it should be, aftereffect of the infestation Lara had sung out of her.

Dafydd, in indiscreet agreement, said, "I haven't seen her that color since the day my mother drowned. We don't often stay in the sun long enough to burn. Our small healing magics make it take a long time, even as pale as we are."

"That was more than I needed to know" was a common phrase Lara got more use from than many, but using it made Dafydd laugh anyway.

"I'm sure it was. My apologies. Here." He offered her a hand down, and together, trailed by Ioan, they sorted through trousers and tops. Lara found a padded shirt to replace the one she wore, glad to be rid of the bloodstains, but shook her head as Dafydd began offering her pieces of midnight armor.

"I'm too short."

"And we're too narrow." Aerin shrugged on a chestplate irritably, demonstrating with a flick of her fingers how the shoulders sat too widely. "But ill-fitted or not, it's better than going unarmored. Oh, phaugh, Ioan, that it fits you is not a favor."

Ioan did a poor job of hiding a smile as he drew on armor that fit him well. "Will it make amends if I ride in front?"

Aerin's avid agreement was almost lost beneath Lara's stern, "That doesn't mean you get to shoot him in the back, Aerin."

The Seelie woman spread her hands. "I've nothing to shoot him with. And why would I, when he'll be riding into the heart of battle with the enemy? Where he leads will be danger enough to a traitor."

"A detail that might be more comforting were we all not in Unseelie garb and wearing their armor," Dafydd pointed out. Pleasure leached out of Aerin and she stomped away, searching through the remaining weapons for one that suited her.

"You could go without helmets." Lara waved off Dafydd's offer of a sword, gesturing toward the staff. "This is awkward enough, and I can't use a sword. Without helmets your coloring would give you away as Seelie."

"Except Ioan."

"Ioan," Lara muttered, "has made his own bed." Sour music ran through the phrase and she scowled, having anticipated it. Ioan, after all, was accustomed to servants and had probably never made a bed at all, but she was growing used to using the vernacular. It grated that her own expectations now got in the way of her doing so.

"I suppose he has. Lara . . ." Dafydd had said her name that way repeatedly now, as if it was only the beginning of what he wanted to say. They both glanced around the armory, watching Aerin curse and discard weapons as Ioan finished cinching himself into armor that fit beautifully indeed. It was as close to privacy as they'd had since Dafydd's awakening, and he let go a quiet rush of laughter before drawing Lara into his arms. Not comfortably: he wore an armored breastplate and thigh-coverings, but his hands were un-gauntleted as he brushed fingertips over Lara's cheek and touched his mouth to her forehead.

"You are mad," he said quite solemnly. "Facing Merrick. Crossing back to the Barrow-lands without me. Challenging my father, and risking the Drowned Lands. Lara, forgive me if you think I lie, but I cannot imagine that I am worthy of such hazards. I owe you every-thing."

Lara smiled, relaxing into his touch. Armor made it less intimate than clinging to him as they rode, but that had been practicality, not sensuality. This was deliberate, and all the more comforting for it. "You're right."

He tensed, surprised, and she looked up with her smile blossom-ing into a grin. "I think I must be mad," she agreed. "There's no other explanation for following a strange man—even a handsome one, even the only one who's ever recognized my talent without being bothered by it—back and forth across two worlds. No other reason that a mouse of a woman would throw caution away and chase a fairy-tale dream presented to her on a rainy winter after-noon. Passion is a kind of madness," she said much more softly. "I've never met anyone else I really imagined building a life with, Dafydd. What else could I do, but come for you?"

His tension faded away, replaced by a hopeful smile of his own. "You imagine a life with me? Isn't that a little dramatic, Truthseeker? You've known me—"

"A month," Lara supplied. "Or two years, depending on which way you count it. But for me, a month."

"A month," he echoed. "So little time. Where's the thoughtful regard, the considerations of positives and negatives?"

"Almost the first thing I thought when I met you was that I could make a life with you," Lara replied. "And it was true, Dafydd. It was true. If you wanted it, it could be true."

He pulled her close again, both warm and awkward, and long moments passed before he murmured a response into her hair. "There tends to be a price exacted when mortals mingle with immortals, Lara. The fairy tales are full of warnings. And you've met Oisín yourself."

"There are prices for not mingling, too. Isn't it just a matter of which ones you're willing to pay?" Lara's heart lurched and she tried stepping back, but Dafydd held her. Not too tightly: she could escape if she wanted, but it was clear he hoped she wouldn't. "Unless you're not willing to pay them," she began in a whisper.

Dafydd laughed, a rough quiet sound. "I beg you, think more highly of me than that. I sought a truthseeker, Lara, never knowing I would find a woman of extraordinary strength and beauty. I would have died for you, fighting the nightwings, and counted it well worth the cost. Don't think so badly of me as to imagine I wouldn't far rather live for you. With you," he amended. "I have no idea what lies beyond these halls. I don't know if we'll succeed or fail or even survive. I do know I would rather face whatever there is with you at my side than with any other."

Lara glanced sideways, catching Aerin watching them surreptitiously. A blush built in Aerin's cheeks, echoed in Lara's, and her heart trebled in speed as she whispered, "*Any* other?"

Dafydd looked toward the Seelie woman, too, then back at Lara with solemnity in his eyes. "Aerin is my oldest friend and most trusted adviser, and we've been lovers on and off since I can remember. But she is a warrior, Lara, and I find that perhaps that's not what I want. Perhaps not what I need. She will never be less than part of my life, but nor will she ever be all of it." He traced her jaw again with a fingertip-light touch. "Is that difference enough?"

"It's very convincing," Lara admitted. "Especially to someone who can hear the truth in every word you say."

Understanding flooded her as she spoke. It had never been like her to fall hard or fast for a man; that was her friend Kelly's purview, and Lara had always gotten sufficient amusement and enjoyment out of Kelly's travails. But neither had she ever met a man who was as relentlessly honest with her as Dafydd had been. Significant as the one deception he'd laid before her had been, she couldn't argue that it had been well-intended, nor did she doubt that his regret over the choice was genuine. She had questioned her own depth of feeling, her own willingness to accept Dafydd and dream of a life with him, but it suddenly no longer seemed strange. Almost no one, perhaps no one mortal at all, had the capacity to accept her, to accept the magic that was part of who she was, the way Dafydd ap Caerwyn could.

Lara ducked her head, indulging in laughter, then looked up again. "I thought I might've lost my mind a little," she admitted. "Coming with you, coming after you, the way I did. I don't think so anymore, Dafydd. I think it's just that my power is wiser than I am. It knew what it had, when it found you. I've trusted my truthseeking my whole life. There's no reason to stop trusting it now."

His smile broadened until it looked as though he struggled not to laugh with delight. As if, Lara thought, he was afraid too much emotion would chase her away, despite what she'd just said. She stood on her toes, unencumbered by armor herself, and slid her fingers into his hair to hold him for a kiss. A smiling kiss on both parts, more joyous than arousing, but when it broke warmth stung Lara's eyes with pinpricks of happiness. "I guess the thing to do now is go survive whatever is outside the city?"

Dafydd whispered, "An excellent plan, as we can do nothing beyond that until that hurdle is met. Ioan?" He raised his voice, and Ioan came to attention with a clatter of armament, which suggested he'd been deliberately keeping himself busy while they talked. "Ioan, if you would lead us out . . . ?"

Ioan nodded, the four of them gathering at the horses. They were a ragtag bunch, Lara thought: she seemed fragile compared to the half-armored Seelie. Aerin swung onto her horse, all the more remote with obsidian armor contrasting against her pale skin and burned white hair. Even she appeared breakable, though, as Ioan took to his own saddle on the horse beside hers. The aftereffects of the healing still lingered on him, distorting and stretching his presence when Lara looked at him too long, but beneath that he looked competent and calm. "You'll ride together again?" he asked Dafydd, who nodded as he mounted, then offered Lara a hand up.

"We'll ride for Emyr first, if the Seelie army awaits us as the truth-seeker expects. If not, we'll decide our route once we're above-ground. Agreed?" There were nods all around, and Ioan kicked his horse into motion. Dafydd fell in behind him with Lara, and Aerin rode behind them. Offering protection to her vulnerable back, Lara was aware, but had no impulse to argue. The idea that Aerin could catch her if she fell when they leapt the canyon made her stomach flutter, but then they were thundering up the ridge, glamour pulling and stretching her vision, and there was very little time to think.

Ioan's horse broke free from the cavern maw and soared across the crevasse easily. Ioan bellowed something incomprehensible but sounding full of satisfaction as he landed on the chasm's far side, and Lara's fears fell away as their horse gathered itself for the leap.

A golden door ripped open in the air before them, and they crashed through it onto the Boston Common.

Twenty-one

Sunlight, ferocious and bright, was accompanied by shrieks of human astonishment. Summer colors flashed in Lara's vision as the horse stumbled to a halt, obviously bewildered. Well-kept emerald grass spread out around them, littered with goggle-eyed picnickers sprawling on blankets beneath droopy-branched trees. Low chain links made barriers between greenery and paved pathways, and a familiar cityscape rose beyond the park's boundaries.

Aerin's horse leaped through the gap a handful of seconds behind them, making people scramble aside, though the more enterprising among them snatched up cell phones and cameras even as they gawked. Aerin reined up hard, and for the first time Lara heard her words as a distinctly different language, though the sentiment was clear enough: "What the *hell*?!"

"Glamours!" Lara gave Dafydd's ribs a desperate hug, hoping he would feel it through the armor. "Dafydd, tell Aerin to work a human glamour, now!"

He barely missed a beat before his dumbfounded voice lifted in command. Liquid language, full of wet sounds, entirely incomprehensible, though Lara still caught their meaning. She had heard the Seelie tongue as English in the Barrow-lands; it made a certain perverse sense that in her own world it would revert to its own sound. That would be a difficulty later, but in the moment Lara reached past Dafydd and caught the horse's reins, pulling it around to watch Aerin.

The worldwalking door shriveled behind her, shimmering gold effect barely visible in full daylight. Aerin's countenance shifted, sending sparks of a headache through the back of Lara's skull, but she ground her teeth and kept her gaze fixed on the Seelie woman, willing herself to see the glamour as it settled into place. The changes were subtle, Aerin's upswept ears dulling to a more human roundness, her elegant long features broadening until her cheekbones and chin were less dramatically sharp, and her new-leaf green eyes faded to a darker shade. With her shorn white hair, she was still remarkable, but not-quite-inhuman. She gave Lara a panicked look, clearly seeking approval.

Relief knotted Lara's gut and she nodded once as the horse came around in a full circle. Half the people who'd seen their entrance were on their feet now, cameras and cell phones recording, and more people were running their way, voices lifted in curious excitement. For the first time since they'd recovered Dafydd, Lara wished she was in the saddle, so she could stand in the stirrups. Instead she whispered, "For God's sake, keep the horse still," and drew her legs up.

Any untrained mortal horse would, she was sure, react badly to her shifting weight, and to the pressure of her feet against its backside as she slowly came to standing, one hand on Dafydd's shoulder for balance. The Seelie animal, though, simply settled into his stance, becoming solid and comfortable as she stood. Lara had a moment of shrill amusement as she remembered the enchantment sticking her to the horse, and it was with more confidence than she'd thought she could command that she raised her voice.

"Good people of Boston! You see before you the prowess and dignity of a prince! I would like to invite you to Pennsic, a war of the kingdoms to be held in the great state of Pennsylvania! And with this invitation delivered, we must bid you adieu!" She slid down to sitting and wrapped her arms around Dafydd's middle, trying to fight down hysterical giggles. "Go! Go go go! Go! Glamour us out of their vision if you can, but for heaven's sake, ride!"

Astonished cheers erupted behind them as they charged across the Common and into invisibility.

"What," Dafydd asked, mystified, "is Pennsic?" His glamour was at full strength, ripping at the world, and sending sour music through Lara's bones, but it did disguise them. Of that, at least, she was confident. She'd felt it come over them, twisting her stomach and making her sick, but the fade-out had probably been as dramatic to viewers as their arrival had been. Lara imagined there were dozens of people searching for mirrors and other effects to explain their theatrical performance. Part of her wanted to search the Internet to see what stories people were already concocting. But once out of sight thanks to the glamour, they had merely ducked into one of a multitude of secluded areas in the fifty-acre park. Summer green meant heavily leafed low-hanging branches, which made excellent screens even without magic's aid.

Lara slid off the horse all the way to sitting on the ground, knocking the staff loose from its bindings with the impact. She let it lie where it fell, looping her arms around her knees and dropping her head instead of rescuing it. Her heart and breath came hard, like she'd been running, not riding, and she gulped air before responding.

"I really don't know. It's something where people dress up in armor and participate in a mock war. A cabdriver told me about it a few weeks ago, when I opened a worldwalking window myself. It was the only story I could think of. Could you . . . let most of the glamour go? Maybe keep enough to make people glance past us, but being inside one . . ." She shuddered, head still pressed against her knees. "It feels like the world is shredding. It keeps screaming at me. Nails on chalkboards and steam whistles and teakettles and—"

The cacophony faded abruptly, leaving comparatively mild dissonance in its place. Lara sagged and swallowed against bile, finally daring to look up. Dafydd retained his headache-inducing glamour, humanity a facade over his elfin features, but the improvement as a whole was indescribable. "Thanks."

"You're welcome. I should have thought to do it before." Dafydd dismounted and nodded for Aerin to do so as well. "It was a well-told story, Lara. Four sentences, not one of them a lie, but together creating a context that wasn't true, either."

Lara smiled tightly. "I hate it when people do that, but I hate telling lies even more. Aerin, can you understand me?"

The Seelie woman flinched, then nodded as she took to the ground. "Well enough. Your words sound strange to my ears. I cannot understand Dafydd at all, though I can hear that he speaks the same language you do."

Lara's shoulders dropped in relief. Aerin's speech still sounded more liquid than usual, but she was comprehensible now. "You sound strange, too, but a minute ago I couldn't understand you at all. Did you have to learn English when you got here, Dafydd?"

His eyebrows rose. "I did. The worldwalking spell doesn't offer translation services. I thought, though, that your magic did."

"It does. It just took a minute to start. Maybe it was the shock of transition? Anyway, good job, both of you, on the glamours," Lara said. "People will probably have photos of you before they set in, but more will be of you looking human. I don't know what else to do about that."

Aerin, carefully and in English, said, "'Photos'?"

Lara cast a helpless glance at Dafydd. "Instant artistic renditions. Perfect ones, so looking at them is like being in front of us. I'll show you later, if there is a later. Dafydd, what *happened*?"

"I hoped you would tell me. I worked no worldwalking spell." He repeated himself in the Seelie language, earning an exasperated look from Aerin.

"Of course you didn't. It was Ioan, eager to separate us."

"While he rode into the back side of the Seelie army?" Lara asked dubiously. "Dafydd, can you get us back?"

"Yes, but not immediately. The magic..." He sighed and sat down beside Lara, gesturing for Aerin to do the same. "The spell takes some time to prepare, Lara. Hours with very little other distraction."

"As Ioan had while we rode," Aerin said.

"Yes," Lara said, aggravated, "but Emyr's already upset with him, and he *looks* like an Unseelie. He'd have to be suicidal to go in there without our support, and I don't think he's spent this many centuries playing the role of Hafgan just to get himself killed now. There must be another explanation." Determination, if not absolute truth, sang through it, and she subsided grumpily.

"I had the spell prepared the first time we traveled to the Barrowlands," Dafydd said mildly, as if there'd been no disagreement. "All that was required to trigger it was the will to do so. Any of us coming to your world would have that ready, so in times of great danger we could escape easily."

"Unless you got arrested and thrown in a human jail full of iron and steel," Lara muttered.

A smile flickered over Dafydd's mouth. "Indeed. The point, I fear, is that having been unprepared to come here, neither am I prepared to take us back. We need somewhere that we can be certain of privacy so I can gather my power and return us to the Barrow-lands."

"Kelly's apartment. We can go there for privacy, and you can get us all home from the . . ."

Home. She heard the word choice just as Dafydd did, though it garnered a slow hopeful smile from him and a gut-wrenching sense of displacement for her. "Back to the Barrow-lands," Lara whispered. "You can bring us back to the Barrow-lands from there."

"I believe so." Dafydd's voice remained steady despite the bright light of hope. "Lara, is the glamour still bothering you? You look pale."

It was an excuse, and she knew it: a way for her to move beyond the astonishing reference to the Barrow-lands as home. Lara took it, grateful. "It's not as bad as it was, but I wouldn't mind getting away from it. I don't know what to do about the horses, Dafydd. I can call Kelly—well, we can turn up on her doorstep, since I don't have a phone or any money on me—but we can't put two horses in her apartment."

"I believe that will be unnecessary." Aerin reached up to pat her horse's nose. "They're intelligent enough to remain hidden if we explain the need, but I can encourage them to, as well. The same sort of enchantment that keeps you in the saddle," she explained. "A staying spell. A glamour cast over their presence should keep them comfortably out of sight until we return for them, and will allow you to escape the magic's discomfort. Is there water nearby?"

"Nowhere as secluded as this, but there's plenty of it. The frog pond is . . ." Lara glanced through the leaves like she could see the city and orient herself, then waved a hand. "That way, I think. Should we bring them there?"

"They'll do well enough on their own, with glamours keeping

them from prying eyes." Aerin stood, dusting grass from her armor, and caught the horses' bridles to draw the animals close and murmur to them. Lara watched a moment, then dropped her shoulders with a sigh.

"I wish I knew how much time has passed. You said it could easily be ten years here for a day there, if there was no spell worked to keep time in approximate alignment. I'd been there three days, Dafydd. My mother could be dead."

He took her hand, fingers gentle around hers. "I don't think so. The skyline is still familiar, isn't it? In thirty years it would change. Even if it was still distinguishable, it would change. I think it's been less time than that."

"I hope so." It didn't matter that she'd been aware that following Merrick between worlds meant she might never return to the time and home she'd known. It was still a trepidatious thought. "You and Aerin should probably leave your armor here, too. Or glamour it into looking like normal clothes, anyway." She winced at the idea, preparing for another headache, but Dafydd, chuckling, began to strip the metal garb away.

"I've been arrested once while wearing Seelie armor. I'd rather not risk it again."

"Perhaps I should remain behind." Aerin stood between the horses, hands on their bridles and increasing discomfort on her face. "I know nothing of your world, Truthseeker. I might be more hindrance than help."

"And someone might accidentally stumble on you here, or get stupid out on the green and pick a fight you felt you had to stop," Lara said. "Glamours or not, new world or not, I'd rather you were with us. Strength in numbers."

"I would have no cause to interfere with mortal battles," Aerin said in confusion. "Why should I do such a thing?"

"Imagine a man choosing to attack a defenseless woman, Aerin," Dafydd said after a moment. "Would you stand aside and watch it happen?"

"Of course not, but who would do that? What woman wouldn't fight back? Surely even mortals have some ability to defe..." Aerin let the words fade away as she tried not to scowl too obviously at Lara. "Perhaps they don't, then. Very well. I will accompany you, but I will not leave my sword behind."

"Well, it's not a concealed weapon," Lara said uncertainly. "But I'm not sure what the police would think of it. Maybe you should glamour it to look like a purse."

"A purse."

"A handbag. Like some of the women on the green were carrying." Dizziness crept over Lara as Aerin begrudgingly worked the magic, sword blinking and twisting in Lara's vision as it tried to convince her it was a leather purse, and not a weapon at all. "That's better. As long as I don't look at it." She picked up her own staff and got to her feet, dismayed. "I don't know what to do about this. I think carrying it glamoured would make me sick."

"We'll tell them we're on the way to Pennsic," Dafydd said with a grin. "Come, then. Let us find Kelly, and refuge."

The Barrow-lands were easier to adapt to than Lara's own world. Pastoral, forested magic and slender alien warriors were less of a shock than mid-afternoon Boston traffic, or the myriad people in all sizes and colors. Aerin, usually so confident, wedged herself between Lara and Dafydd without seeming to realize she'd done it. Her eyes were round with alarm, mouth pinched tight as people swept past them by the hundreds, and she held her purse with a white-knuckled grip on a strap that Lara knew full well was the sword's hilt.

Dafydd was murmuring to her in their native language, narrating the brash world she was encountering: that man in the twisted hat is from a land called *India*, that smell is a human favorite named *pizza*, these noisy boxes are *cars*.

"I know that one," Aerin said in a harsh voice. "Lara told Ioan of them. She did not say they were so loud. How can you live like this?" She turned accusing eyes on Lara. "So many people, so much sound."

"I grew up around here. I'd never been anywhere as quiet as the citadel until I came to the Barrow-lands with Dafydd. It is too loud," Lara agreed, then caught Dafydd's arm behind Aerin's back and pointed up the street with her free hand. "Newspaper vendor. I don't have any money, but at least I can see what day it is before he chases me off. Don't let Aerin panic."

"I do *not* panic!"

Lara flashed a smile at the glamoured pair and darted ahead of them, stopping beneath the vendor's canopy. He shared a stall with a hot dog seller, and her stomach rumbled as she peered at magazine covers and newspaper dates.

It was reassuringly, unexpectedly familiar. Only four days had passed in both worlds. Lara picked up one of the papers with a shaking laugh and turned it over, glancing over the lead stories while the vendor gave her a warning look. Guilty, she started to put it down, but a headline caught her eye: *Extreme Surgery Troubles Doctors*.

Below it was a photograph of Ioan ap Annwn.

Twenty-two

Glamours worked even on photography: the camera's
eye didn't see what Dafydd's magic hid, or his career
as a television weatherman would have been short-lived indeed. But
Ioan was in no way glamoured. He was lying down in the photograph, eyes closed, but that did nothing to disguise their elfin slant,
or the inhumanly high cheekbones that added to the angled effect.
Nothing about his bone structure was human: even the comparative
breadth of Unseelie jaw and cheekbone was far too delicate for even
the most gracile human males. And his ears were exposed, inky hair
falling back from the sharp, upswept points that marked the elfin
races. For an instant she imagined the mental space that would have
prompted the headline: extreme surgery, indeed. Not just extreme,
but of such a quality as to be almost inconceivable. He looked
sculpted, not natural, and as such was both utterly beautiful and
tremendously alien.

He was also, according to the scant handful of sentences she was able to comprehend, suffering from a profound head wound. Students had found him on the Common two days earlier, and had rushed him to the hospital. Doctors were still uncertain whether he would survive.

"Lady, are you all right?" The news vendor lost his hostility, edging past a stack of papers to come into Lara's line of sight, face now crinkled with concern.

"No." Her abrupt response alarmed the vendor, who went so far as to put a hand on her arm in cautious support. Lara lifted the paper, shaking it slightly to emphasize the story. "I know him."

"Jesus, they've been looking for somebody who does for days. Where've you been, with your head in the sand? Who did all that surgery on him?"

"He did it himself." It was technically true, if physiologically impossible in human terms. Lara wet her lips, trying to pull her thoughts together enough to hold some sort of normal conversation. "I'm sorry. I just got back into town and I literally have no cash on me, no bank card, nothing. May I have this paper? I'll come back and repay you, I promise, but I have friends I need to show this to, and..." Her voice was shaking by the time she finished. Ioan couldn't, by any comprehensible measure, be in Boston, much less in a hospital. She'd seen him only minutes ago, whole and well.

Outrageous dissension rang through the thought. They couldn't both be true: either he was here and hadn't been in the Barrowlands, or the photo was some kind of glamour. Lara crumpled the paper, eyes crushed shut against the sour musics vying for dominance.

Worry crept into the vendor's voice. "I guess I lose enough off stolen papers that letting one go on purpose this once won't hurt. Go ahead and take it, lady. I hope your friend will be okay."

"Thank you." Lara managed a weak smile for the man as she

backed away. "I promise, I really will pay you. I just can't right now.
I'm really sorry." Then she turned and fled, meeting Dafydd and
Aerin where she'd abandoned them on the street. The prospect of
explaining what she couldn't understand overwhelmed her and she
simply thrust the paper into Dafydd's hands with a feeble attempt to
smooth the wrinkles she'd put in its surface.

Even Aerin, unable to read the words, understood in seconds.
"This is a 'photo,'" she half-asked, and then with more certainty if
no more comprehension, "A photo of Ioan. The likeness is very
good."

"That's what photographs do," Lara whispered. "A nearly perfect
replica. But it doesn't make any sense." Her head throbbed, Dafydd
and Aerin's glamours playing havoc with her vision and only made
worse by the incomprehensibility of Ioan's presence in her world.
Her head had hurt for *days*, it seemed like: almost since they'd left
the Drowned Lands themselves. A lack of sleep no doubt exacer-
bated the pain, and certainly clouded her thoughts against any real
hope of figuring out what had happened. "He can't be in two places
at once."

"Then either this is not Ioan," Dafydd said slowly, "or the man we
journeyed with in the Barrow-lands was not."

A pure clear chime rang through Lara's migraine, sweet vibrations breaking it away at Dafydd's last words, and the impossible fell
into place: "Merrick."

The willpower necessary to cast an illusion of the depth Merrick had
commanded staggered Lara. Almost literally: she had a hard time
putting one foot in front of the other as Dafydd guided her through
the streets toward Kelly's apartment. It had begun—*had* to have
begun—with Braith's village in the valley. It hadn't just been a

glamour hiding the town that had triggered her headache. The town itself had been an illusion, and her truthseeking sense had tried desperately to correct what it knew to be wrong. But it was more than that: in the Catskill mountains Merrick had only built an illusion to fool Lara. Kelly had seen through it, rescuing Lara from her own folly. This one, like the spell Merrick had created to mastermind his own apparent murder, had fooled more than one person into believing the same story.

"The magic would be easier to control and maintain in the Barrow-lands," Dafydd explained. "In your world, tricking a single person with an in-depth illusion might take all of Merrick's talent. I fooled everyone with my glamour, but it's so very minor that the effort necessary to maintain it is almost negligible. Making you, a truthseeker, believe I had rejoined you in your world... that requires—"

"It requires my willing acceptance and belief in the scenario. And I think it required the same thing in Annwn. Maybe the real village was a little farther down the same road, and he created the illusion on the path I saw in order to waylay us. And we just delivered him into the heart of the Seelie army, Dafydd. Your father could be dead because of us."

"As you said, riding into their midst could well be his undoing. I wouldn't think, though, that it's Merrick or even Ioan they'll be seeing. I'd think it would be—"

"You," Aerin finished grimly. "The son and heir returned, perhaps with a tale of vanquished enemies. There is no one left in the Barrow-lands to protect the Unseelie city now, Dafydd."

"I'm surprised you care," Lara said with more honesty than wisdom.

Aerin's human countenance did nothing to spoil the cool arrogance in her gaze. "I dislike being made a fool of, Truthseeker."

"Hafgan remains," Dafydd said with the air of a man trying hard to defuse a fight. "He might yet be the Unseelie peoples' savior. What I want to know is how he worked the scrying spell."

"He didn't." They stopped at a crosswalk, Lara so grateful to stop moving that she didn't look to see if they could jaywalk the section. It was a Bostonian pastime, striking out into traffic with the air of one indestructible. The trick was never making eye contact with the enemy: it lent jaywalkers the moral right of way, obliging drivers to hit the brakes. It was infuriating, but everyone participated while on foot, even if they'd only minutes earlier been in a car, swearing violently at jaywalkers themselves.

Dafydd, obviously as familiar with the game as she was, *did* walk out into traffic, eliciting a gasp of horror from Aerin. As if reminded of the danger, he skipped back—scoring one for the vehicles, Lara supposed—and settled in place to hear Lara's explanation while they waited for the light.

"The scrying spell is one of ice and water. Merrick doesn't command those elements. He just created an illusion, and we probably made it easier by giving him that tiny jug of water instead of a pool or a basin like Ioan and Emyr use. He must have been being so careful." Lara closed her eyes, trying to recall exactly the words and phrases "Ioan" had used. "A direct lie would have triggered my truthsensing no matter how good his illusion was. He never said he was Ioan. He didn't even say he'd use the scrying power. He said he had duties to attend to, and was thirsty. It was all *true*. It just wasn't—"

"Connected," Dafydd said. "In the same way you intimated we were from Pennsic. My adopted brother is canny," he added in a mutter. "I always thought him more honest than that."

"You were always more willing to forgive him his birth than the rest of us," Aerin said. The light changed and she strode into the street, boldness an illusion Lara could see through.

Dafydd's jaw tightened and he moved swiftly to keep up, leaving

Lara a few steps behind. "Had the rest of you been more forgiving, perhaps we wouldn't have come to this."

"Would we not have? Would you have always been content to be the prince, Dafydd, and never the king?"

"Your ambitions were always greater than mine." Dafydd fell back again abruptly, rejoining Lara in not so much a retreat as a strategic commentary. Aerin's fists clenched, but she said nothing else, and let Dafydd and Lara take the lead again as they cut down another street toward Kelly's apartment complex.

"Does it work that way?" Lara wondered aloud. "I thought maybe there was no real inheritance, not when you all live so long. Heirs in name only, for all intents and purposes."

"For all intents," Dafydd agreed. "Even royalty dies, as my mother did, but Emyr was never likely to set aside his crown from grief, even if Ioan and I hadn't been children by our standards. Even almost by human standards," he added. "We were very young. Ioan was only nine or ten when I was born and he and Merrick were exchanged as hostages to good behavior."

"I thought you didn't have very many children. I'd think two children in ten years would be unheard of."

"It was. And perhaps Rhiannon paid the price for breeding at such a mortal rate, as I was only a child myself when she died."

"I'm sorry. Oh, good, here we are." Lara ran forward, suddenly eager to get out of the street as she buzzed Kelly's apartment. Aerin scowled at the sharp sound, hand tightening on her "purse" again, and Lara shot her a sympathetic smile. "It'll be quieter insi— Hello? Hi, Kelly? It's Lara!"

Momentary silence followed Kelly's initial "hello?," which had been half-drowned under Lara's reassurance to Aerin. Then Kelly gave a short incredulous laugh. "Oh my God. Come on up, I'm buzzing you in."

She met them in the hallway outside her apartment, eyes wide above a cheek swollen with medical staples. Lara made a dismayed sound, but Kelly charged forward to grab her in an astonished, breathless hug. "When you said 'see you later' I thought you meant in about ten years. Oh my God, Lara, you're home already? You're okay? What's going on? And David!" She nearly yelled his name, releasing Lara to haul the slender Seelie man into a hug. "You're not dead! And—oooh." Her voice dropped as she took in Aerin, then put a hand out to shake. "I didn't get your name, but you're obviously the other wom— Uh, I mean, you're Dafydd's frie— I mean, aw, shit, I mean, hi, I'm Kelly."

Aerin looked dubiously at Kelly's hand, then carefully took it in her own. "I am Aerin." She glanced at Dafydd, curiosity raising her white eyebrows. "Her injury appears profound. Why has she not healed it?"

Kelly shot Lara a look of bewilderment and Lara groaned. "She only speaks Seelie and my magic's not enough to make you understand her. Or her understand you. This is Aerin. She wanted to know why you haven't healed your cheek yet."

"Are you kidding? The best doctors in Boston say it's healing up really well. I won't even need plastic surgery, probably, to hide the scar, it should be that unnoticeable." Kelly grabbed Lara's shoulders. "Speaking of plastic surgery—"

"I saw the newspaper story. Have you—?"

"I've been trying for two days to get in to see him. There are mooks in black suits and Ray-Bans lurking around the hospital. I can't believe they haven't taken him out of Boston yet."

"How bad is he?"

"His brains are leaking out the back of his head," Kelly said with an unfortunate degree of truthfulness. "I've got a girlfriend on the nursing staff, but even she can't get me in to see him. All she can tell me is he hasn't woken up and half of the medical community on the

Eastern seaboard has come in to look at him. The papers are sticking with the extreme surgery story, but people are talking about alien invasions." She herded everyone into her apartment as she spoke, Dafydd translating her tumble of words for Aerin.

Four days was enough to have turned Kelly's apartment from relatively tidy into a minor disaster area. She darted around the living room, scooping up empty pint cartons of ice cream and blankets and socks and dumping them into trash cans and closets. Lara counted seven ice cream cartons before they were swept away, and caught Kelly's hand to stop her whirlwind cleaning.

There was no diamond on her ring finger. Lara said "Oh, no, Kel," and Kelly went still, eyes cast downward.

"He's been at the hospital all week," she mumbled. "Sitting by Reg's bedside when he can, sleeping in the lobby when he's not allowed to. The only time he's left, pretty much, was to come see me in the ER when I came in bleeding like a stuck pig. He made sure I was more or less okay, and then he broke up with me. Said he didn't know who I was anymore, that maybe he never did. I blew it, Lara. I mean I really, really blew it."

"No." Unexpectedly, it was Dafydd who interrupted, voice low but confident. "No, Kelly, if anyone is to blame, it's me. Dickon was my cameraman and close friend for years, and he had no reason to suspect I was anything other than human. Though in most ways I neither would nor could change that, I should have found a way to tell him the truth immediately after I returned from the Barrowlands without Lara. He deserved better than the friendship I offered him, and you deserved far better than the disaster I imparted upon your relationship."

"I could have picked him," Kelly whispered. Tears trembled down her cheeks and she pressed a finger above the cut on her face, giving the saltwater another path to travel than into the wound. "I could've done something else instead of turning into a criminal mastermind and spiriting us all away from a crime scene."

Lara slipped an arm around Kelly's waist, offering her a tentative smile. "Will it make you feel any better if I say no, you really couldn't have?"

Kelly sniffled. "Couldn't I?"

"Not from what I hear in your voice," Lara said. "The truth is, helping Dafydd get away was the only thing you were ever going to do that day, Kelly. You weren't going to let him die on a lab table, no matter how high the cost somewhere else might be. If Dickon can't appreciate the strength of character that shows, then he doesn't deserve you."

Kelly laughed, a shaky wet sound. "That's not fair. I have to believe it when you say it, Lara. I don't have to believe *me* when I say it, but I have to believe you." She wiped her eyes again, then hugged Lara hard. "Thank you. You might have to tell me five thousand times so I remember I have to believe you, but thanks."

"You're welcome." Lara hugged her back, then sighed. "How's Detective Washington doing, anyway?"

Kelly sank down into an armchair. "He's not out of the woods yet. We got stupid lucky with that mess at the courthouse garage, Lara. I mean, Dickon doesn't care, because he was there and he knows we left Reg behind, but David's lightning fried the whole security system. All the digital backups for the whole week got wiped out. There's no footage anywhere that proves who was in the garage, and the only one who could identify us is Reg. He's still unconscious, which is probably why I'm not in jail right now. They've got him at the same hospital Ioan's at. If we could get in there, could you help him?" Her gaze went to Dafydd and Aerin, beseeching, and Dafydd once more translated before spreading his hands uncertainly.

"Neither of us has a talent for healing, Kelly. If Reginald Washington is indeed still in danger, if they're still uncertain as to his recovery, the truth is we might best help him by bringing him to the Barrow-lands where he can be tended to by the other side of the magic that did him harm."

Kelly flashed a sharp, bright smile. "Fantastic. I've always wanted to visit fairyland. Let's go."

Twenty-three

"There is too much iron in this world." Aerin spoke through her teeth, a grimace pulling her striking features out of line. "The glamour is almost impossible to hold."

Dafydd touched the small of her back, a small soothing gesture that had little visible effect. Lara made an apologetic face, but had to look away again: the glamours dancing in place around all of them jangled her nerves. Managing forward motion was enough of a task without trying to offer sympathy to an ill-tempered elf.

Of the four, only Kelly was clearly enjoying herself as they hurried through hospital corridors. Then again, of the four, she was the only one virtually undisguised. A costume shop had provided high-quality lab coats for all of them, and Kelly had found green hospital scrubs with a V-neck that displayed her considerable assets to good advantage. Half a week's diet of ice cream and potato chips hadn't visibly damaged her waistline and the shirt's tucked-in waist emphasizer her curvaceous figure. The only glamour Dafydd had worked on her was transforming a driver's license into a hospital ID, and the result was a soap opera–style nurse, all curves and quick smiles.

Lara, much more recognizable as a recent news-story kidnap victim, was hidden behind a glamour she couldn't even see without making herself sick. A glimpse had suggested she was taller and more physically imposing than usual, with less delicacy in her heart-shaped face and drab lowlights in her blond hair. Dafydd swore the long white lab coat she wore made the illusion more effective and easier to maintain, and she only hoped the quick job would hold.

Aerin was almost as lightly glamoured as Kelly. She looked slightly more human than Ioan, but their fine bone structure and pointed ears were of a kind. A calculated risk, Dafydd called it, and swept into the secured corridor Ioan's room was in as if he had every right to be there. Unlike any of the women, he'd added breadth to his own glamour, giving himself a far more intimidating air, though none of the suit-clad security looked even slightly intimidated.

"Doctor Aerin Cragen?" he said impatiently to one of the guards. "She's flown all the way from— Don't tell me the paperwork didn't come through. If you could impress upon these gentlemen—?" He gestured to Lara, who stepped forward already hating what she had to do.

"The patient is from Ms. Cragen's ethnic group, as I'm sure you can see. She's come a long way to provide the help he needs. We must be allowed to see him." Each statement was true enough. Aerin, sullenly, as though confessing something private, had allowed that her mother's name was Cragen, and the closest thing she had to a last name was the matronym. Lara put strain into the words, making them impossible to disbelieve. It hurt her throat, hurt her *skin* to make truth heard, the task no easier than it had been in a human courtroom when it had been Dafydd's freedom she was trying to achieve. It was easier by far in the Barrow-lands, so much more receptive to magic.

One of the guards, a tall man whose width of shoulder made him seem twice Lara's size, removed his sunglasses to look first at her, then for a long time at Aerin, and finally back to Lara. "Sorry, miss. We can't. Not without the appropriate paperwork." He did, though, jerk his chin at Aerin to say, "I've never seen anybody who looks like you two. Where're you from?"

Aerin looked without comprehension at Dafydd, who translated. Exasperation slid across Aerin's face and she answered abruptly, cool expression locked on the guard. "An isolated area in Wales," Dafydd said blithely.

Chills ran down Lara's spine, not quite outraged protest at the lie, but not happy with the half-truth, either. The guard didn't look any happier, an eyebrow cocked at Aerin. "I thought the Welsh spoke English."

"I doubt your guest in there has spoken any," Dafydd said. "This group has long since eschewed any but their native tongue. It's a matter of cultural support and propagation."

The guards exchanged looks again before the self-appointed spokesman sighed. "I can call it in for permission. It's going to take a while. There's a lot of paperwork to go through, and if you," he pointed at Aerin, "weren't obviously like *him*," a thumb over the shoulder, indicating down the corridor, "I'd never bother trying. What kind of doctor are you, anyway? They've had the best brain surgeons in the country in there and they're all afraid to even give it a shot because his physiology's so bizarre." He took out a phone, not waiting for an answer from Aerin, and after a few seconds said, "Yeah, we've got a doctor from the patient's ethnic group down here, I thought you might want to come down and have a talk with her."

Warning tones shot over Lara's skin. She stepped forward and put

out a hand, trying to imbue the gesture with some of Emyr's impe-
rious expectation. The guard snorted and she drew a sharp breath,
driving it into sharper words: "You *will* give me the phone."

Anger slid over the guard's face as he handed her the phone, his
own free will clearly countermanded by her order. Lara, trying not
to tremble, kept her eyes on the guard. A truthseeker at the height
of her power could say a thing and make it true. Determined, sick to
her stomach, desperate, she said into the phone, "You will give permission to let us through to see the patient, and you will do it now."

Hesitation came down the line, an inhalation that went nowhere.
"Who is this?" a woman finally asked.

Lara clenched her fingers around the phone, headache spiking.
Magic use could wear even the Seelie out, and humans were far less
built for it than the elfin race was. For a painful moment she sympa-
thized with Emyr, unable to work his magics smoothly with mortal
interference in the area. Her own truthseeking was easier to manage
if she wasn't already hidden behind the veil of power that kept them
all from easy recognition. "This is the only person who can keep
your patient alive. I assume your interest in his autopsy is secondary
to the possibility of speaking with him."

"Perhaps," the woman on the other end said cautiously. "We can
learn a great deal from an autopsy."

"I have no doubt that your patient's return to health now would
impinge upon a convenient autopsy later," Lara said bitterly. "You
will give us permission to see him."

"Who *is* this?" the woman demanded again.

Lara shut her eyes briefly. "Someone who answers to a much
higher power than you do. Now let us through." She handed the
phone back. The guard listened for a moment, nodded, nodded a
second time, then stepped out of the way as he snapped the phone
shut. Lara stalked by with a scant nod of thanks, aware that the
others fell in line behind her. Not until they'd reached the safety of

Ioan's room and Dafydd had authoritatively ordered the nurses out did Lara sag against the wall, hands buried in her hair.

Sour music faded as Dafydd released the glamour hiding her true features. Despite Ioan's prone form on the bed a few feet away, he crouched by Lara, a hand light on her shoulder. "Are you all right?"

"The only reason they let us through is because Aerin's so much like Ioan. I could hear it in the guard's voice, the way he said she was like him." Lara's voice felt rough, as if her magic had torn her throat up. "Believe me, Dafydd, they're not letting us in, they're trapping us. Or they're trying to."

"Well, we can get out of here, right?" Kelly demanded. "Except it's just your guy here, not Reg. We've got to get him, too."

"We have to sneak out," Dafydd said cheerfully. Lara gave him a dire look from behind her arms, and he chuckled, though his humor faded away under the weight of her glare. "Even at my weakest I've been able to hold a glamour that makes us effectively invisible, Lara, and we rode out of plain sight on the Common not three hours ago. The task of getting Ioan out of this ward is hardly insurmountable."

"What have they done to him?" Aerin's horror broke over their conversation. Lara dropped her hands to look at Ioan, who was riddled with IVs and monitor patches. His skin was scaly and blackening where the needles slipped into his arms, the veins spreading beneath his skin in a dangerous fiery red.

Sick dismay crashed over Lara. "It's stainless steel. It's all steel. They're killing him!"

"Aerin!" Dafydd leapt to his feet and caught her wrist just before she bodily yanked the first needle from Ioan's veins. "You can't rip them upward, it'll tear his skin even more badly, and he doesn't need the damage. Like this." He slipped a needle free with expert skill, shrugging as Kelly gaped in astonishment. "I had a century of lifetimes in your world, Miss Richards. I spent some time as a medic, among my many other professions. Aerin—yes, good," he said as she put pressure on another spot where she'd withdrawn a needle with the same confident motion Dafydd had used.

"No wonder he's remained unconscious." Lara pushed to her feet so she could see the sallow Unseelie more clearly. "They've been poisoning him. Not deliberately," she said as Aerin's expression darkened. "They just couldn't have known the needles would do him damage. They don't, usually. Not to humans."

"How could any fool think him human when they looked at him?"

Kelly, obviously understanding the sentiment if not the actual words, retorted, "Because there's no other option. We don't have humanoid alien species as far as anybody on Earth knows. Besides, they're probably dying for him to die so they can cut him up."

Aerin shot Lara a frustrated look. "When will your truthseeker's gifts burgeon enough to permit comprehension between worlds?"

"I don't know, Aerin. I don't know if it'll ever work that way. I think we're doing well in that you and I can communicate."

"Lara?" Ioan's voice scraped below theirs, rendering the bickering silent. "Truthseeker? Is it possible?"

"Tsha." Dafydd put a hand on his brother's forehead, no longer as distressed by Ioan's changes as he'd been. "We've come for you, Ioan. Aerin, Lara, myself. Even a mortal woman has ventured to your rescue."

Ioan opened his eyes, barely focused gaze lingering on each of them until he found Kelly, and chuckled roughly. "I remember you. You fought well. But you've sustained a wound. A shame, to scar that lovely face. Dafydd, we must..." His eyes rolled back, unconsciousness claiming him.

Kelly whispered "You weren't too shabby yourself," and pressed her knuckles against her mouth, eyes large as she looked to Lara.

"I think he's all right." The agonies of inaccuracy in that phrase almost made Lara laugh. Instead she clutched her head a moment, then made herself straighten and pay attention to Dafydd. "There must be back ways out of here, fire doors or something. If we take one of those and come in the front again to find Detective Washington, we can avoid trying to sneak past the contingent of government guards at the head of the ward."

"Do you really think they're government?"

"I think city or state police would be in blue uniforms, not black suits. If they're not government they're—"

"Something worse," Kelly supplied. "Corporations, maybe. Either way it's not good for the home team. Tell you what." She exhaled noisily, then glanced down at herself. "The big guy out there, the one who did the talking, is kind of my type, and I'm all Nurse Richards here. Should I go play distraction while you guys make a break for it?"

Dafydd lit up, but Lara shook her head. "If we were car shopping, I'd say yes, but it might backfire here. He might fall for it, or he might realize immediately it's a ruse. No matter how good the glamours are, I think if someone's really suspicious they might fail under scrutiny. We're better off being sneaky as a unit. The problem is, how are we going to get Ioan out of here? On the bed, like it's a gurney?"

"I'll carry him." Challenge sparked in Aerin's gaze as Lara blinked at her. "Do you think me too weak?"

Lara studied the slender Seelie woman, remembering more the ease and speed with which she wielded a sword than her apparently fragile form. "No. It just wouldn't have occurred to me to even try. The only way I could carry him at all would be in a fireman's carry, and that's probably bad for people with head injuries."

Aerin slipped her arms under Ioan's back and knees. Dafydd adjusted his brother's head so it lay against Aerin's shoulder, and Aerin straightened with apparent ease, a curious gaze on Lara. "What is a 'fireman's carry'?"

"God damn," Kelly said in admiration. "I want her personal trainer."

Lara, drily, said, "You really don't," and a moment later the gut-sickening magic of glamours enveloped them all.

A fingerful of Dafydd's lightning shorted out the emergency door's alarm system, and in moments they were free of the hospital building. Even with the jangling shards of misplaced light and shadow brought on by the glamours, Lara could see that Ioan's color improved beyond the hospital walls: the elfin races were simply not suited for the concrete and rebar buildings that so much of humanity hid within.

"Can the human be brought forth the same way?" Aerin stood with Ioan's weight in her arms as if it was nothing, unconcerned with what would be, to Lara, a staggering burden. Unconcerned for his weight, at least: her concern for the man himself was visible, which Lara found curious, given Aerin's enmity toward the Unseelie. "It would be best if he was not subjected again to your iron-filled walls."

"I know." Lara passed a guilty hand over her eyes, but shook her head. "I think he has to go back in, though. He only has a couple of injuries. They're bad, but a head wound and that cut he took to the thigh aren't on the same scale as what Detective Washington suffered. His torso was punctured repeatedly. Moving Ioan like this is a risk, but I think moving Washington the same way would be homicide. Dafydd's going to have to open the worldwalking spell right there in his hospital room and we're going to have to wheel him through, bed and all. Can you choose where we arrive? Could you bring us straight to the healers?"

"If I knew precisely where they would be, yes, but with a war going on, it's possible none of them remain within the citadel."

Dafydd looked apologetic. "It's less risky to bring him there, and ride for a healer, than to bring him onto the battlefield."

Lara whispered a curse, but nodded. "And the spell itself? Can you work it inside a human building?"

"I prepared it while you rented our costumes. It only needs to be triggered within the building, and that's easy enough. I did it at your apartment," he reminded her. "We only need be bold a little while longer, and then all will be well."

She scowled at him. "I don't believe there's any definition of 'well' that encompasses 'two men are in desperate need of healing, a traitor needs to be found in the midst of an army before he destroys two kings and claims their crowns, and ancient rivals have to be found, brought together, and made to remember a history neither of them wants to recall so that a truthseeker can find a way to mend the past.'"

"Mine does," he said irrepressibly, and to Lara's astonishment, stepped forward to pull her against himself and steal a lingering kiss. Astonishment, then a shy, foolish delight filled her, and in disregard of what they faced, Lara tangled her fingers in Dafydd's hair and held on.

"Ioan," Aerin said pointedly, "is not *that* light."

Dafydd broke free with a laugh, though he touched his forehead against Lara's and murmured "You're so terribly pragmatic I couldn't help myself," before turning a smile on Aerin. "I think this will be easiest if you remain hidden behind a glamour cloak while the rest of us strip away our costumes and come to the hospital as ourselves. All three of us know Detective Washington, and friends are expected to visit."

"That would be a better plan if I had real clothes with me." Kelly stood arms akimbo, making everyone else look at her. "Well, the rest of you are wearing real clothes under lab coats, but I went whole hog—all the way," she corrected herself with a half-serious glower in Lara's direction.

"I wouldn't have said a word," Lara promised.

Kelly snorted. "You always say something when I use vernacular."

"You can be the nurse bringing us up to Washington's room," Dafydd suggested, and Kelly, satisfied with that, relaxed out of her aggressive stance.

Aerin sighed. "Cast your change of glamour, then, Dafydd. I'm not sure I can hold a veil of unseeing within those walls."

Color and music became more bearable as the glamour fell away from Lara herself. In seconds, she and Dafydd were as they usually were in her world, and Kelly remained unchanged save the "hospital badge" swimming in Lara's vision when she glanced at it. Only Aerin was headache-inducing, a blur of not-quite-there that sat wrongly in the world. "All right. Let's get inside and up to Detective Washington's room quickly, then. The less time I have to see Aerin fading in and out like that, the better."

"I don't see her at all." Kelly sounded childishly delighted as she herded them into a tight group. Together they hurried through the parking lot to enter the hospital's front doors for the second time in less than an hour. Kelly went straight for the elevators, saying "He's on the third floor" over her shoulder.

The doors dinged open as they reached them, and Dickon Collins, Dafydd's cameraman and Kelly's ex-fiancé, stepped out. Shock jolted over Lara, stopping her where she stood, and similar surprise flashed over Dickon's face.

Then suspicion replaced it, and he lifted his voice to snap, "Security! The hospital needs security here *right now!*"

Twenty-four

Dafydd leapt forward, clapping a hand over Dickon's mouth and by sheer velocity knocking him back a step or two into the elevator. No more than that: Dickon was inches taller than the Seelie man, and broader in chest and shoulder than almost anyone Lara knew. He dug his weight in, stopping the backward stagger, and Lara rushed forward to clutch at Dafydd and Dickon's arms alike. "Dickon, we're not here to cause trouble. Dafydd, let him go. For heaven's sake, let him go or it'll look like security has a reason to be here!"

"Security does," Dickon barked as Dafydd released him. "You people are crazy. Dangerous. And if you're not here to cause trouble why is Kelly in hospital scrubs? Don't tell me," he said over Lara's head, voice sharp with mockery. "You've had enough of working at the bra shop and in the last four days you got a nursing degree?"

Kelly, usually quick with a comeback, only looked away, shoulders curved. Dickon made a sound of triumph and Lara balled a fist, taken with a rare urge to lash out physically. "Don't be cruel,

Dickon, we're here to try to help Detective Washington. Do you really want to stop us?"

Dickon spat, "Help him? After what you did? After how you abandon— Yes, right here! Security! This woman is impersonating a nurse!"

Two breathless security guards staggered up as Dickon shouted. One of them, red-faced, put a hand under his ribs and leaned on the open elevator doors while the other, fitter man gulped for air around a "What's going on here?"

"This is my ex-fiancé," Kelly said with immense bitter truth. "We're here to see a friend upstairs in intensive care, and he's decided we're dangerous criminals because I'm wearing scrubs."

"That's not tru—" Dickon broke off, scowling between Kelly and Lara. "I mean, it is true she's my ex—"

"I was at a costume party *with somebody else* last night," Kelly said, acidic tone changing not at all, though the untruth screeched over Lara's skin, "and he's crazy jealous is all, so he's trying to make my life hell. It's working," she snapped at Dickon. "Are you happy? Because I'm not."

She turned to the fitter of the security guards, folding her arms under her breasts as she did so. The guard's gaze dropped, his jaw clenched, and he made a visible effort to wrench his attention back to her face. Lara wanted to applaud his professionalism, but Kelly was in full theatrical mode, a tremble coming into her voice. Not enough to be overtly manipulative with a guard who wasn't allowing himself to be distracted by her assets, but if Lara hadn't known better, she'd have believed Kelly's emotional distress to be real. "A friend of mine just graduated medical school, so we all dressed up in scrubs and lab coats and threw a party to celebrate. If I was impersonating a nurse wouldn't I have tried to make a real-looking fake ID?" Kelly yanked her driver's license off the clip that held it to her shirt and handed it to the guard.

Its subtle glamour faded as he took it, and he cast a dubious glance at Dickon before asking, "Who're you here to see?"

"Detective Reginald Washington," Kelly said. "You want to know the truth, he's the reason Dickon and I broke up. I haven't even gotten to see Reg since he got hurt because Dickon's been vulturing around like it was just him and Reg who were friends, not me and Reg, too."

Dickon's jaw worked, splutters of sound emerging. Dafydd was carefully not looking at him, or at Kelly, for that matter, but Lara, close to his side, could feel laughter vibrating off him. Her own amusement was tempered with a combination of awe at Kelly's tale-spinning and the uncomfortable shivers the outright lies in her stories produced.

The second guard straightened up from the wall, still wheezing as he nodded a couple of times. "It's true this guy's been around all week. I thought maybe the guy up in ICU was his boyfriend."

"Oh my *God*." Kelly whirled on Dickon, her decibel level increasing with each word. "I *knew* the breakup had to do with Reg, but I had no idea you were playing both sides of the street! My God, how can you even be jealous if I went out with somebody else in that case? At least I'm a serial monogamist, not, not—" Words dissolved into a flood of tears and she buried her face in Lara's shoulder, howling, "I thought he *loved* me!"

"Jesus *Christ*, Kelly, I did love you! I do love you! I'm not dating Reg, for Christ's sake! We're just frie—" Dickon arrested the last phrase, recognizing it too late as one of the oldest, least believable things people said when they'd been caught in an affair. Kelly's tears redoubled and Lara patted her shoulder even as she felt overwhelming sympathy for Dickon. People were gathering at a safe distance to watch the drama unfold, and he'd done little, if anything, to deserve the scene Kelly was creating. He noticed onlookers, and, already frustrated, became grimmer yet. "To hell with you. To hell with all of you."

He shoved out of the elevator, the gathering crowd parting to let him pass. Kelly's sobs slid from dramatic hysterics to real tears. She dragged Lara down inside the elevator doors, shaking with misery. "I love him, Lara. I really, really do. What'm I gonna do? What am I going to do?"

Lara looked up at the guards, both of them looking increasingly dismayed. "There's a waiting room outside ICU, right? We'll bring her up there and I'll take her to a bathroom to get her calmed down before we try to visit Detective Washington. I'm really sorry for all of this."

"If there's another peep out of her, another outburst like this . . ." The fitter guard looked apologetic but resolute, and Lara nodded.

"There won't be. You'll be okay," she added into Kelly's hair. "You'll be okay, Kel. Come on. Let's go see Reginald."

Kelly snuffled and nodded, and Dafydd stepped all the way into the elevator, finally letting the doors close. As soon as they did, he grunted, and the glamour hiding Aerin faded to leave her staring incredulously among the three of them. "Humans are insane. What was that?"

"That was a distraction," Kelly said miserably. "I had to do something to keep Dickon from confessing we'd all been at the garage when Reg got hurt. It just worked better than I thought it would." The elevator dinged, warning they'd passed the second floor, and she whispered, "Better hide again. We're almost there."

Aerin disappeared, leaving nothing more than a shimmer in the mirrors. Lara stood and drew Kelly to her feet, all three of them briefly reflected before the doors opened. Kelly looked terrible, red nose and swollen eyes clashing with her green scrubs. Lara thought she herself looked a little shocked, but Dafydd was still clearly trying not to laugh. He went so far as to catch Kelly's hand and bow low over it when they stepped out of the elevator.

"I know I should offer my profound condolences and my sorrow for putting you through that, no matter how unintentionally, but I must instead admit to my deep admiration for your acting skills. I realize some of that was genuine emotion, but I have rarely, in a century of living among mortals, seen such quick-witted melodramatics. You are wasted fitting brassieres, Miss Richards. You should be on the stage."

The worst of Kelly's tears had stopped by the time he finished his extravagant compliments. She even managed a sloppy, tiny smile, though she shot a skeptical look at Lara. "Is he blarneying me?"

"He was sincere in every word," Lara assured her. Kelly laughed shakily and Lara pulled her into a hug, promising "You'll be all right" again before setting her back and grinning despite herself. "You really are an appallingly good liar, Kel."

"I've gotten much better at it since I met you." Kelly sniffled, then laughed more fully at Lara's expression. "I started really thinking about how to use most of the truth while telling lies, after I figured out nobody could lie to you. I mean, that doesn't work on you, you still know anyway, but it made me a much better liar. Okay. If I go wash my face will I be presentable enough to get into the ICU?"

"You had best be," Aerin said from nowhere, voice low and threatening. "Emyr's firstborn grows no less heavy as you stand and perform."

Kelly squeaked and ran for the bathroom as Lara studied Aerin, curiosity piqued. "Emyr's firstborn" was a far kinder way to refer to Ioan than the "traitor" Aerin had used earlier. She wondered if the Seelie warrior woman's thaw would last beyond returning to the Barrow-lands, or if her willingness to accept and help Ioan was merely an artifact of them being strangers together in a strange land.

A nurse came down the hall, wheeling a half-sleeping old woman toward the elevator. Lara scurried out of the way, but the woman reached out as they passed her, grabbing Lara's wrist and turning a vivid dark gaze on her. "Truth will seek the hardest path, measures that must mend the past."

Lara's heart caught in her chest, then hammered again too hard, making her dizzy. "Wo—"

The old woman's face brightened and she changed her grip, holding Lara's hand instead. "Breaker who restores the land, keeps the world gates well in hand."

"Mrs. Moloney, please don't do that," the nurse said wearily. She gently unwrapped the old woman's fingers from Lara's, offering an apologetic sigh as she did so. "She was a poet in her youth. I'm afraid she's in the early stages of Alzheimer's now and imagines her little rhymes to have some sort of deep meaning. She doesn't mean any harm."

"No," Lara whispered. "No, of course she doesn't. But you might want to listen to her, nurse. There might be something in what she says, even if it sounds like nonsense."

The nurse gave her a tired smile. "You're a good soul, miss. Most people find Mrs. Moloney disturbing. Maybe you should think about a career in nursing." She wheeled the old woman into the elevator, leaving Lara to massage her palm and stare after them.

"Poets and prophets." Dafydd took her hand, squeezing it gently as he, too, looked after the old woman. "What do you suppose she meant?"

"I don't think it'd be called prophecy if it wasn't cryptic," Lara said with a faint smile. "But that's three variants on it now. Oisín did tell me to ask any other prophets I met for a reading. Do you believe in fate, Dafydd?"

"More and more every day," he said in an odd tone. Lara glanced over to find him watching her intently. A self-deprecating smile played at his lips, but his gaze was serious. Breath rushed out of her and she turned toward him, an arm wrapped around his back and her face hidden in his shoulder.

"Thank you," she mumbled after a moment. "Thank you for that. My life has been turned upside down. You've turned it upside down. But somehow it just takes a look or a smile or a word from you and I find myself believing it's going to be all right. That all these choices and decisions are the right ones, somehow. And I don't know what Mrs. Moloney meant, but I think we needed to come here to hear what she had to say. Merrick might have done us more of a favor than he knew."

"I believe I love you, too," Dafydd murmured into her hair, and gave her a bright boyish smile as she pulled back, astonished, to gaze up at him. "I'm sorry," he said without a hint of sincerity. "I could have sworn that was what I just heard you say. Am I wrong?"

"No," Lara admitted. "No, I think you heard right. I just didn't know that was what I was saying."

"A truthseeker uncertain of her words. I have indeed shaken the foundations of the universe." Dafydd's smile lit up further as Lara blushed, but he stopped his teasing by kissing her. "Worlds come changed at end of day," he whispered. "And how they have, Lara. How they have. I had not anticipated this."

Kelly, brightly, said, "Well, I did. Boy, I leave you alone for two minutes and your whole relationship changes. You can get on with being kissy-faces later. Do I look okay now?"

Lara broke free of Dafydd with a laugh and gave Kelly a once-over before nodding in satisfaction. "You'll do for someone I haven't dressed."

"Lara, if you'd made my scrubs, we'd still be back at my apartment with you working on them. I'm sure they'd be beautiful, but all they needed to be was functional. All right." Kelly glanced from

Lara to Dafydd, then around like she sought the invisible Aerin before dusting her hands together. "Let's go save Reg."

By comparison to Reginald Washington, Ioan looked hale and hearty. The detective's dark skin was ashy blue, healthy color leeched away. An oxygen mask covered half his face, but his eyes were sunken with ill health, and though at least one of the IVs snaked into his veins was saline, he looked dehydrated. Dehydrated and bloated both, Lara thought; his hands were swollen, and his torso was patchy under the hospital gown, suggesting there was still material packed against puncture wounds. Small tubes drained the wounds, and the private room was filled with machinery beeping and the oxygen machine's rasp.

Kelly stopped inside the door, hands cupped over her mouth. "Oh my God. Can we even move him?"

Aerin set Ioan down in a chair, glamour disrupting as she did so. She rubbed her shoulders as she came to stand over the dying detective, a frown etched between her eyebrows. "He smells of infection. Will he live if we move him?"

"He'll die if we don't," Lara said to both of them, grateful she would be understood. Truth made her response sharp, and she wished it away, knowing it would do no good. "Aerin, I know you're not a healer, but is there any way you can use your magic to stabilize him a little? Stone is very stable . . ."

The Seelie woman pursed her lips, intrigued. "I would never have thought of such a use. But the earth here is very far away, Truthseeker, and iron spikes the space between us. I'm not sure if I can work a holding magic within these walls."

"Maybe set a spell to trigger when we enter the Barrow-lands, then. Something to link his strength to the land, the way you linked mine to it through the horse."

"The horses." Aerin focused on Lara abruptly. "Will we abandon them, then? We cannot bring this *de-tek-tiv* to the green place, nor bring them here."

Lara dropped her chin to her chest and swore. "We'll have to come back for them later."

"Will the time wrench us astray? Will the horses be lost to us, if we travel without them?" Aerin asked Dafydd.

He said "No" absently as he traced a door-sized rectangle in the air. "So long as I open the worldwalking spell on both sides myself, it should be fine. It's not meant to throw travelers out of time when properly worked."

"Lara? What're they talking about?" Kelly pushed away from the door and edged forward to grasp Lara's hand tightly.

"The balls we've dropped," Lara breathed, and Kelly gave her a sharp twisted smile.

"Look, you're Metaphor Girl again. How's that feel? What balls did you drop?"

Lara wrinkled her nose, letting the question of metaphors go in order to answer the more relevant one. "We came here on horseback and left the horses hidden on the Common. We'll have to come back for them."

"You'll have to come back to bring me home anyway," Kelly announced, then arched an eyebrow at Lara. "What, you thought I was going to stay here while you go traipsing off again? Not a chance. Besides, speaking of dropped balls, I don't want to be the one left holding the ball when Reg disappears out of the hospital room, so I have to go with you. How fast do we have to move once we've got all these beeping things unhooked?"

"Very," Lara guessed. "In fact, Dafydd, maybe you should go ahead and open the worldwalking door now."

"I am trying." Tension distorted Dafydd's voice. Lara turned in concern, finding him with his fingers clawed in the air, trembling with the strain of attempting a downward pull. Gold glimmered around his hand, but his entire body trembled, as though someone had struck him like a bell. "I'm trying, Lara, but the Barrow-lands are rejecting me."

Twenty-five

"What does that even *mean?*" Kelly asked the question, but it echoed Lara's stunned sentiment. She released Kelly's hand, taking a few quick, useless steps to Dafydd's side, but he warned her off with a sharp shake of his head.

"I'm not sure what will happen if more power is introduced to the magic," he said through his teeth. "And mortal magic—"

"—disrupts elfin. It must be Mrs. Moloney, Dafydd. She's still nearby, and Oisín and I didn't have to be especially close to Emyr to ruin his scrying spell." Lara backed away, though she couldn't retreat far enough to remove herself from Dafydd's space. "Is that it? Would the land itself reject you if it thought you were too influenced by mortal magic? Emyr said it was fond of Oisín."

"And if Oisín was here, we might face less difficulty." Dafydd ground his teeth. "Yes, it might well be unwilling to let the world-walking door be opened if it feared a mortal influx. The spell is of the land itself, Lara. It has that ability. What concerns me more is I cannot break *free.*"

"I can free you." Aerin sounded both certain and doubtful. "Reaching the earth here for you is unlike trying to stabilize the *de-tek-tiv*. He needs a light touch, and I am unsure if this world will allow me to connect with it so delicately. You need only be grounded. But it might—"

Dafydd gave a short hard laugh. "It might strip my power from me a second time. Better that than being caught with my hand in the cookie jar." He fell into English for the last few words, making Lara bite down on an equally sharp laugh and garnering Aerin's frown. She had understood the rest of what he'd said, though, and crossed to him, hands uplifted to call power.

"Wait." Lara's voice broke and she fumbled for the worldwalking staff strapped across her back. Dafydd's glamour still hid it, making her hands ache when she touched it, but its presence behind her had spared her the headache, and almost even the memory, of carrying a magicked weapon. "What would this do?"

"Oh, just *destroy the hospital*," Kelly half-shouted. "Are you crazy, Lara? You saw what that thing did up in the Catskills, and you want to unleash it in the middle of Boston?"

"Dafydd might be able to mitigate its effects. Emyr said it didn't like Seelie royalty, but Dafydd used it safely enough in the Catskills. It was only when I took it that things went wrong." It was pure guesswork, music lying flat and useless rather than making a promise or a lie of what she hypothesized. Lara shook the staff, frustrated by her own magic's tendency to cut in and out. A month earlier her inability to determine truth in conjecture would have only been normal; now it seemed a failure, and as if returning to her home world had reined in her talent's exponential growth. It was a gift born of the human world, but to reach its full potential, it seemed the magic-steeped Barrow-lands were necessary.

But that was perhaps no surprise. Truthseekers had been hunted out of existence, in Dafydd's world. The land, a living, active thing in its own right, had waited aeons for a magic like hers to come into it again. It wasn't impossible that it had poured itself into her power, encouraging it to heights she never would have imagined possible.

"Do not." Ioan's exhausted voice stopped Lara. He was sitting up, braced in the chair Aerin had put him in, and his color had improved in the little while since they'd taken him from the secure hospital wing. "The last royalty to use that weapon shattered Annwn with it. I would not see such a fate visited on your land, Truthseeker."

"It might not—"

"And it might." Ioan sagged as if the few words had spent all his reserves. "Aerin. Will you lend me your strength? Perhaps two royal scions can do what one cannot."

That, unexpectedly after the music's silence in her own guesses, rang false. Lara shook her head, alarm spiking through her. "It won't work, not as long as Mrs. Moloney and I are near each other, and I don't know where the nurse was taking her. Maybe she's gone, but— I don't *understand,*" she added more fiercely. "Inherent magics work fine. Dafydd's lightning wasn't compromised by being around me. Why doesn't spellcasting work?"

Dafydd lifted his free hand, the other still caught in the golden tear in space. "I haven't tried the lightning with more than one mortal talent nearby, Lara. It could fail. Shall I?"

"Don't you dare." It was true, though: he'd never called lightning when Oisín and she had been near to one another. Lara knotted her hands around the staff, frustration surging through her. "We're going to have to try Aerin's magic to get you free, then. What happens if a grounding spell goes wrong?"

"Earthquakes," Aerin said serenely. "But this is not a spell, Truthseeker, any more than that which makes you draw breath is a spell. It's part of me, and can be extended as I extended it to you while you rode."

"I thought that *was* a spell!"

"Your failure to understand doesn't change its inherent qualities." Aerin curled her arms around Dafydd, suddenly seeming more solid than ever before, as if becoming part of the earth in a way Seelie—and even humans—generally were not.

Lara's power had objected to the worldwalking spell, to the wrongness of tearing through time and space. But of the magics possessed by the Seelie, only the glamours had been disruptive to her magic. Nothing else had a component that lied to the eyes; as Aerin said, the gifts they possessed were no more striking to a people born of magic than the ability to breathe.

And to her astonishment, the truth of that rose up as Aerin gathered Dafydd close. Song washed out from the Seelie woman in long slow notes, the same kind of profound fathomless music Lara had once discovered buried within the earth. Similar, not identical: there were aspects to Aerin's magic that spoke of a connection to a land very far from Lara's own. But there was enough in common that when she reached deep, searching for a response from Lara's world, it was able to answer. Strength welled up, calm, steady, unhurried, and filled Aerin with the earth's living magic. She caught her breath, clearly sensing the same off notes that differentiated the Barrowlands from Earth, but she braced herself and the music changed ever so slightly, two disparate magics adapting to each other. "Mortal lands," Aerin whispered roughly. "Immortal magic is uncomfortable being worked here. Release him, and we'll disturb you no more."

Power surged out of her, connecting Dafydd to Lara's world in the same way Aerin herself was. No: the music changed instantly, not recognizing Dafydd and his lightning magics as it had recognized Aerin's bond with the earth. It seized him like a cat with a rodent, shaking and rattling ferociously.

He tore free of the worldwalking door, a shout of pain accompanying the ripped magic. But the earth had no intention of letting the invader go. Its slow music had the tonality of a threat, a recognition of a thing that didn't belong. Aerin's presence intensified, her own slightly alien song determined to show the similarities between what she was and what Dafydd was. "Different from mortal lands and mortal magics," she agreed, as though the earth itself could hear and respond to words. "But not dangerous."

A *lie*, whether she meant it as one or not. The earth far below bellowed, a roar that reminded Lara all too clearly of how the ground and sky had been rent asunder by the worldbreaking staff. She lurched forward, catching Aerin's arm, and thrust her own desperate reassurance into the growing earth storm: "I know you remember. I remember, too. But it wasn't *this* magic or this man who hurt you in the Catskills. Listen to my words, to my song. I'm a truthseeker, and you know what I say is true." She might have felt foolish, shouting at the world itself, except Aerin's approval was evident, and Lara clearly recalled the living earth responding when she had first wielded the worldbreaking weapon.

And the earth seemed to recall her, as well. A grumble rolled through its music, but it abruptly fell away, releasing Dafydd from its grip. He collapsed, Lara bearing his weight as Aerin released him and staggered the few steps back to Detective Washington's side. She fell against him heavily, hands planted on his shoulders, and for the second time, magic rushed from her, pouring into Washington. The music changed again, becoming truer than it had been when captured in either Aerin or Dafydd's frame. It *knew* Washington, knew him in a way the earth had known Lara as well, recognizing him as mortal-born and part of its domain. It embraced him more willingly—more willingly, even, than it had accepted Lara and her brand of mortal magic—and a note of sorrowing darkness came into the music.

"No." Aerin's voice was harsh but pleading. "Only hold him. Cradle him. Do not take him into your bosom. He is not yet meant for the barrows, not if the mortal healers are strong. Only lend him the stamina he lacks, so that time and determination might make him well. He will be yours in time, as all mortal things are, and he will come to you in body as all mortal things do. Let him live this little while yet, safe in your embrace."

Earth magic thrummed, deep song that vibrated the small bones of Lara's ears, then settled in contentment. Traces of its long slow notes lingered around Washington, an answer to Aerin's request. After long moments she released her hold on the magic, song falling away as she lifted her head, exhaustion evident in every movement. "He will live. If he is strong, he will live."

"That's fantastic." Pure truth made Kelly's voice a thing of uplifting music, but her tone was edged with panic. Lara, still supporting Dafydd, turned to find her friend pressed against the door, using her body weight to keep it closed. A resounding thump echoed from its far side, the door jumping, and she bared her teeth as she put her weight against it more heavily. "That's fricking fantastic, but we've got another problem. How the hell are we going to get out of here? There's a goddamned riot squad outside the door."

Lara flinched as the door thumped again, bewilderment coursing through her. "How do they even know something's wrong?"

"Oh, because everybody in here's been shouting for the past five minutes? Would somebody please *do* something?" Kelly shouted herself. Aerin took a handful of swift steps across the room, abandoning Washington to instead enfold Ioan in her arms. The look she gave Dafydd was as expectant as any Emyr had ever commanded, and Lara felt him draw himself up, preparing the glamour that would hide them from mortal eyes.

Felt, too, the line of tension that ran through him, and she spoke before he did: "The magic's gone, isn't it. You're cut off?"

"I am. Not so exhaustively as before, but—"

"We don't really have time to debate the details!" Kelly snapped. The door jolted again and she yelped. "Guys, I can't hold this. The only reason the door's not already open is they're probably trying not to kill me on their way in. You, Ioan, prince-guy. Can you do the big glamour magic and hide everybody? And I mean *everybody?*"

Ioan blinked at her fuzzily, then, much as Dafydd had, deliberately drew himself together, clearly searching for his own power. Lara took a breath to protest, then swallowed it on another realization: "You can understand her?"

Aerin shot Lara a brief uncomprehending glance before her gaze cleared. "Yes. What have you done?"

"I didn't do anything!" Out-of-tune music spun through the objection, searching for an aspect of truth. Lara pressed a hand against her temple, trying to push the automatic truthseeking away. "It doesn't matter right now. Ioan, can you—"

Like his brother, Ioan shook his head. "Annwn's magic hasn't deserted me, but I'm simply too weary, Truthseeker. A glamour to hide us all is beyond me."

Frustration rose up, though Lara kept sharp commentary behind her teeth. Dafydd had glamoured not only four people, but a vehicle, while so drained of magic he could barely maintain consciousness. Either his will or his inherent power was greater than Ioan's, though in Ioan's defense, he had sustained a head injury where Dafydd had not.

Aerin, cursing so vividly the meaning was lost to translation, dragged a glamour into place herself. "I will not be able to hold this as long as royalty might," she warned as she and Ioan faded away. "We have very little time."

"*Ow!*" Kelly ran forward, getting out of the way as the door flew open and security, including the fit older guard from before, burst through. Doctors, nurses, even Dickon Collins, flooded through after them, voices lifted in concern and outrage before one, then all, took notice of Dafydd, still standing in Lara's embrace.

He was radiant: she hardly had to look at him to know that. Radiant and utterly inhuman, with the fine chiseled features of the Seelie race no longer hidden by blunting glamours. Even human, he was beautiful, but his eyes were brown, not amber, and his slim form looked ordinary, not sculpted. Worse, with the glamour gone, the padded tunic and leggings that he'd worn under the discarded armor looked all the more out of place, enhancing every aspect of his inhumanity. Lara's heart lurched as she looked at him, taking in every aspect of his slender allure. Without fully meaning to, she stepped in front of him. He was the taller by several inches, impossible to hide, but a knot of determination unlike anything she'd ever known lodged itself inside her. The intruders might want to take Dafydd away, but they would go through her to do it. She wished she had a weapon and the knowledge of how to use it.

The worldbreaking staff came to life with the thought, humming urgently for her attention. Against all wisdom, Lara reached over her shoulder, drawing it from its bindings one fistful at a time, until she pulled it free and held it in front of herself at a crosswise angle. Power rushed through it, so eager to be used that the ivory vibrated in her hands. It could wreak havoc, it promised: it could make certain no one would take Dafydd from her. All it needed was her command. Less than that: tacit permission, almost granted by the act of drawing it, would unleash its magic. Nothing mortal would stand in its way.

Dickon, cautiously, said, "Lara, don't make this worse than it has to be."

"I don't want to." Truth shivered through the words, so cold she hardly recognized her own voice. "Believe me, I don't want to. But I won't let anybody take Dafydd."

"What *is* he?" One of the doctors spoke, less angry than baffled, despite the disruption in her hospital. She watched Dafydd as avidly as Lara ever had, though her interest seemed more scientific than romantic. "He's like the other one in the secure wing. What are they?"

"People," Lara whispered. "They're people, even if they don't look like us. They're not for experimenting on or dissecting or questioning. Please, just leave us alone. We'll go away and won't bother you again, but I will not let you take him from me."

The doctor flashed her a look of genuine sympathy, though it was riddled with less kind pity as well. "Do you really think that's your decision, miss? Do you even think it's mine?" She took a step forward and Lara lifted the staff.

Power crashed from the weapon, invisible but potent, a barely controlled wave that made all the equipment in the room surge and beep frantically. The doctor spun toward Detective Washington, concern for her patient slightly greater than fear or interest in Dafydd, and she shot Lara an accusing look as she checked the detective over.

Lara's knuckles went white around the staff, her whispered *"No"* directed at it alone. "No. Not unless there's no other way." She felt it struggling against her will, against the truth she invested in her words, and had an instant of wishing the weapon was slightly more alive than it was, so she could threaten it more effectively. The only thing she could potentially do was break it for disobeying, and that would have repercussions far beyond any she could anticipate.

"Nurse. Double-check this, please." The doctor's voice sharpened and two of the nurses broke away from staring at Dafydd to join her. The equipment had settled back down, beeping and thrumming regularly, but the doctor scrolled back through information on one of the machines, a nurse at her elbow.

"He stabilized," the other woman said after a moment. "A few minutes ago, his heartbeat stabilized from the arrhythmia we've been seeing the past four days . . ."

"An improvement that wouldn't have happened without Dafydd." The truth stretched but didn't break. Without Dafydd, Aerin never would have come to Boston; without Aerin, Washington's vitals wouldn't have stabilized, not as quickly as they had. Lara moved for the door, trusting boldness over rationality. "Call it a fair trade, Doctor. Let us go without a hassle."

"Wait!" Hope shot through the doctor's voice and she gestured around, obviously meaning to encompass the hospital as a whole. "Can he do this for everyone?"

Regret made a sharp place in Lara's heart. "Not any more than you could. I'm sorry."

Disappointment, but not surprise, etched itself across the woman's face. Lara could see conflict in her eyes, an uncertainty as to whether she should have them detained, and Lara gave a quick nod toward the door, hastening Kelly and Dafydd out before the doctor made a decision. The dreadful noise of a full glamour at work slid through her mind as Aerin slipped past as well, leaving Lara the last to abandon the room full of hesitant hospital staff. Dafydd scrubbed his hair forward, covering his ears, and hunched his shoulders, head down as they hurried for the elevators and for escape.

Seconds later, Dickon Collins's voice followed them: "Hang on. I'm coming with you."

Twenty-six

Hesitation ran through every visible member of their group, but Aerin, through what sounded like gritted teeth, said, "Let him. I cannot maintain this glamour long enough to argue, Truthseeker."

"I don't think I could stop him anyway," Lara muttered, and Dickon slipped through the elevator doors as they began closing. He folded his arms over his chest, making him more of a wall than usual, and turned a hard look on Dafydd.

"What'd you do in there?"

"I did nothing," Dafydd said with more light amusement in his voice than Lara thought warranted. "Dickon, my old friend, if you insist on accompanying us, perhaps I could walk in your shadow, as it were, while we escape this place." He lifted his eyes deliberately, showing Dickon his unglamoured countenance, and spread his hands in rueful admission. "Frankly, without your help, I'm uncertain we'll leave here unmolested."

Dickon's jaw clenched, face turning a fiery red brighter even than his hair. "You have a hell of a lot of nerve, Kirwen."

"I do, and yet you've chosen to join us, so I'm forced to determine my nerve will not go unanswered. Please, Dickon," he added more quietly, and for the first time Lara saw strain lining his ageless face and darkening his amber eyes. "I need your help."

"Reg is going to live?" Dickon's gaze went to Lara, who felt a pang of guilt as he ignored Kelly entirely. Not that Kelly had the truth-seeking skill that Lara possessed, but a handful of days ago they'd been a couple, planning to wed. To see Kelly so thoroughly dismissed hurt Lara, even if she understood.

And the only answer she had wasn't quite enough. "I think so. He made it this far, and he's stabilized now."

"You only think so?" The elevator doors dinged open behind Dickon, revealing three or four people who automatically moved forward, then startled and fell back again, exchanging glances with each other and at Dickon's broad back.

Lara shrugged. "I'd promise it was true if I knew it was, Dickon. If he's strong enough, he'll live." That had rung true when Aerin said it, but whether the detective had the strength to rally remained unknown.

Dickon scowled. "He's tough."

"Then he will live," Aerin snapped from nowhere. Dickon flinched, then grunted as Aerin shouldered past him as a blur of headache-inducing light and color in Lara's vision. She ran to catch up with the Seelie woman, making apologies to the people waiting outside the elevator as they were brushed aside by something they couldn't see.

Or could half-see, Lara feared, by the time she and Aerin reached the front doors. Aerin knelt off to one side, glamour flickering in and out around her like an ancient film as the others caught up to them.

"I'm sorry, Truthseeker. I lack the strength of Rhiannon that flows in Dafydd's blood. We must find shelter very soon."

"I'll get my car." Kelly ran for the parking lot, but Dickon's voice stopped her before she'd taken more than a few steps.

"My Bronco's right there." He strode toward an oversized vehicle in one of the nearest available parking spaces, Dafydd in his wake. Aerin surged to her feet again, hurrying after them. The vestiges of her glamour fell away entirely before they reached the Bronco, but not by much: Dafydd sprang into it and turned to catch Ioan as Aerin thrust him forward, then crawled into the SUV herself. Lara caught a glimpse of them all through the lightly tinted windows. At a glance they were unearthly in their beauty, but not quite inhuman, not with the windows just slightly marring their visibility. Her knees buckled, relief at the momentary reprieve, and within seconds she and Kelly joined the Seelie and Dickon in his vehicle, both human women crowding into the front seat. Lara put the staff behind her and said, "Don't touch that," to the three in back.

Dickon came around to the driver's side and climbed in, hands working against the steering wheel as he stared at the three alien beings arranging themselves in the Bronco's backseat. For a long time, no one spoke, until Dafydd finally asked, "What made you change your mind?"

"I'm not sure I have. You said you couldn't heal," Dickon said accusingly. "How'd you stabilize Reg?"

"It is not a healing, but a joining with the earth to offer him strength and stability. Lara, why do I understand this man? He speaks your language, not mine."

"Oh, sure, a joining with the earth," Dickon said under Lara's, "I don't know. Maybe our magics working together did something."

"Or perhaps your world, in accepting Aerin's magic, has also granted her the understanding of your tongues. If one of us spoke a third language, we could test the theory," Dafydd offered. Lara felt disbelief cross her face and bit back a protest as Dafydd grinned. "I know. It doesn't work that way."

His deprecation filled with sour tones and Lara shook her head, smiling, too. "Except magic might. I'm grateful for it, anyway."

"Tengo un poquito de espanol," Kelly said. *"Tu comprendes,* Aerin?"

"Of course I understa—" Aerin broke off, staring at Kelly before a smile flickered across her own features.

"Interestingly, so do I." Ioan opened his eyes again, though he looked as weary as before. "That would be more than the earth's gift. I think the Truthseeker has it right: mortal magic and immortal come together to clear away the difficulties of language. I gather I am in your debt," he added to Dickon. "I will in some way repay you."

Dickon muttered, "Great. Can you make me forget any of this ever happened? Kelly, what—" He thumped his head back against the Bronco's headrest, fingers still white around the steering wheel. Eventually he said, "What's going on," like he knew the question was inadequate, but couldn't come up with a better one.

"Reg is going to be all right," Kelly said in a low fierce voice. "I can't undo any of this, Dickon, but he'll be okay. I'm really sorry to have gotten you involved."

"You didn't. David did. He just didn't tell me."

"For which I, too, am sorry. Dickon, this is my brother Ioan and my friend Aerin."

"You've mentioned them. You forgot to say they were *elves!*"

"Actually, the brother I mentioned would have been Merrick. Ioan and I have been estranged, for lack of a better word. And I could hardly explain their heritage without explaining my own," Dafydd said apologetically.

Dickon glowered at him in the rearview mirror. "Which you could've done any old time."

"We should have this discussion somewhere else." Lara cast a nervous glance at the hospital. "They're going to notice sooner than later that Ioan's not in his room anymore."

"So you *were* up to no good." Dickon sounded vindicated.

Kelly gave a stiff shrug. "I'm not going to apologize for causing a scene, if that's what you're expecting. If you can just drive us over to my car we'll get out of your hair."

"Kelly, you've got a twelve-year-old two-door Nissan. They won't all fit."

"I'm hardly leaving them with you."

"For Christ's sake, I'm trying to help—"

Lara interrupted. "Will you take us to Kelly's apartment, Dickon?" and he shot her a scowl.

"Yes. Okay? Are you happy now, Kel? Your truth-hearing friend will tell you I'm not lying. Unlike some people I know. Where are you parked?"

Kelly tightened her jaw in a way Lara recognized as trying to prevent tears, and whispered directions to her Nissan. When they reached it, she jumped out of the Bronco and held up a hand to stop Lara. "I'd rather you went with them."

"You don't trust me?" Injury lashed through Dickon's voice, though Lara thought Kelly's distrust was at least a little justified.

Kelly obviously felt it was more than a little, her eyes flashing with anger as she looked past Lara toward her ex. "You're the one who couldn't handle any of this less than a week ago, Dickon. You're the one who walked out. So no, I really don't trust you even if Lara says you mean it. You might change your mind. Just drive them to my apartment, and then maybe we can talk."

"Whatever." Dickon flinched when Kelly slammed the door, looking like he wished *he* could have done that, rather than her. He slid a sharp glance at Lara. "Do *you* trust me?"

"Yes." It seemed like there should be something else to say, an explanation or a platitude, but her wit deserted her and Lara was left to wait silently on Dickon's response.

Surprise, then churlish gratitude coursed over his features, and without another word he drove them to Kelly's apartment.

"You first," Kelly said to him when they'd all reached that comparative safety. Ioan still faded in and out of consciousness, but he looked more comfortable sprawled on Kelly's couch than he had in either the hospital or the Bronco. Aerin stood in front of him, arms crossed over her chest and a scowl dark enough to be a credible threat on its own marring her flawless features. Lara perched on the edge of a straight-backed chair from the kitchen, while Dafydd, beside her in one of the armchairs, was the only one in the whole room with an air of relaxation. It was a lie: Lara could see that in the jump of small muscles around his eyes and the unconscious tapping of a fingertip, but the performance made some difference to the atmosphere, which was dominated by Kelly and Dickon facing off at the doorway.

"You came into Reg's hospital room like you were going to have us all arrested," Kelly went on, voice low with accusation. "Why'd you change your mind?"

"The doctor said Reg had stabilized. He was dying, Kelly. I've been there most of the last four days, listening to the doctors, and nobody ever said anything about stabilizing. That was what they said the first day, critical but stable. After that they dropped the stable part and kept trying not to look too worried when I was around. So I want to know what the hell happened back there, and if David had something to do with it, at least that's—"

"Wiping the slate clean?" Dafydd asked, just loudly enough to be heard across the room. "It might make some amends, but it doesn't forgive the sin of having lied to you about who and what I really am."

"Not that I would've believed you anyway," Dickon said bitterly. Kelly's chin came up in clear surprise at the admission, and Dickon left the door to sit across from Dafydd. *Well* across from him, Lara noted: the second armchair was on the long end of the coffee table, putting the two men as far apart as they could be within the confines of Kelly's living room. Still, it was a gesture of willingness to talk that Dickon sat down at all.

"There is that difficulty," Dafydd agreed. "One of several reasons to keep the truth hidden. I came to your world to find Lara, Dickon. Lara or someone like her. A truthseeker, to help my people find a murderer in their midst. I've been looking a very long time, and I swear to you, I meant for none of this to happen. Detective Washington never should have been injured, and I'm given to understand one other man died. That was never my intent. I would have protected them, and healed Reginald Washington when he fell protecting all of us, if I could have."

"But you couldn't because your fairy magic doesn't work that way, except she"—Dickon pointed accusingly at Aerin—"managed."

"It was not a healing," Aerin repeated impatiently. "That skill is not mine to own. I have a gift of earthspeaking, and even this iron-ridden world was willing to respond. Your *de-tek-tiv* shares the strength of the land he was born to for a little while, is all. It will lend him what he needs to recover, if he has the will for it."

"Yeah, well, what I get out of that is in the end Reg owes you his life, and regardless of how fucking weird this all is, he probably wouldn't like it if the babe who saved his ass ended up on a dissection table for her troubles."

Aerin flicked a glance at Lara, obviously wondering if the magic that allowed them to communicate had interpreted Dickon's words correctly. Lara wrinkled her nose, but nodded, and Aerin's eyebrows darted up in dismayed comprehension.

Dickon ignored the byplay, looking instead at Kelly. "And you.

You can just run with all of this? Just like that? I don't get it, Kelly. I just don't."

"I've known Lara since we were freshmen in college." Kelly sat down on the edge of the couch, trying not to disturb Ioan. "I thought she was kind of bonkers at first, because she was always so careful with what she said and always looked sort of pained when somebody said, like, 'Oh I'm fine' when you'd ask how they were. After a while I figured out she just always knew if somebody was telling her the truth, and that she never told lies herself. It's hard not to believe somebody like that when you've known them for years, even when they're telling you something preposterous. It's not really that I just ran with it. It's more that I've had a lot of time to get used to Lara, and *that's* what I ran with. That and I still think I was right. There was no happy way out of what happened at the garage and wasting any time at all would have cost David his life. It's what I tried telling you in the first place, and now even you came around to it." She made a gesture at Aerin, then fell silent, rubbing the ring finger of her left hand.

"Yeah, great, I'm the one who didn't want to run away from a crime scene and somehow I end up the asshole in this scenario."

"Oh, for God's sake, Dickon—"

Dafydd sat forward, interrupting Kelly with an uplifted palm. "We could spend hours throwing accusations and recriminations around, but I'm afraid we don't have the time. I very much doubt Merrick has been sitting idle in the hours we've been gone."

"Assuming it's only hours," Lara said. "Does the worldwalking spell automatically tie time together, or is that a separate component decided by the spellcaster, like deciding what buttons to use on a suit?"

Regret hit her unexpectedly. Less than a month ago in her personal timeline, she'd been given the opportunity to create a wardrobe for a client at her boss's tailoring shop, a chance that would have made her a master tailor in her own right. The client's suits had all been determined by the beautiful antique ivory buttons he'd brought in, salvaged from his own grandfather's suits a century earlier. Someone else would have completed Mr. Mugabwi's wardrobe, because the scant weeks of her own timeline had been well over a year in the mortal world. There were things she would never get back, no matter how the undertakings in the Barrow-lands played out.

Dafydd fluttered his fingers as if trying to pluck the answer out of the air. He looked exotic and prosaic all at once, an elfin prince sitting comfortably in Kelly's living room, and despite the flash of regret, Lara smiled. There were things she would never have discovered, either, had she not risked stepping between worlds.

"It doesn't bind the timelines together automatically, no. When I cast it to come here it was my will that let a decade pass for every day in the Barrow-lands. When I brought you there the first time, it was my intent to bind them more closely, so you would lose almost no time to the travel. But left on its own, without a deliberate concept of how much time should or might pass, it's desperately arbitrary, Lara. Oisín hadn't been in the Barrow-lands so very long when he first left us, but hundreds of years had passed in his native Ireland."

"Your idea of 'so very long' and mine might be very different," Lara pointed out. "Either way, I followed you back to Annwn less than half a day after Ioan brought you home. Whether Merrick meant for it to be or not, it was still six months there. We've spent most of a day here now. If it's been another six months..."

"Then it's possible the power balance has shifted entirely." Dafydd turned his hand up in a familiar gesture: Lara had seen him call sparks of lightning between his fingertips that way before. This time, though his brow furrowed with concentration, nothing happened, and he closed his fingers again, loosely. "And I now lack the power to open the worldwalking spell myself."

"It had to be done," Aerin protested roughly. "You would still be caught there, or—"

Dafydd shook his head, stilling her objections. "It's commentary, not accusation, Aerin. Lara's opened a worldwalking path once. Perhaps she can do it again."

"The Barrow-lands are a lot more receptive to magic than this world is, Dafydd. I don't know if I can breach the walls if I start on this side, not unless I use the staff."

For a moment everyone, even Dickon, looked toward the ivory staff propped in the corner of Kelly's living room. Out of Lara's hands, it was nothing more than an ornate and beautiful art piece, but the memory of its eagerness to be used sent a shiver over her skin. "There's Ioan," she said without much hope, and everyone looked from the staff back to the sleeping prince.

"Even if he were conscious, I think the magic would be his undoing," Dafydd said quietly. "The Barrow-lands are not forgiving, and I fear what they might take from him in return for the magics."

"There lies your problem, brother." Ioan spoke without opening his eyes, though his voice was stronger. "You, as always, seek the magic of the Barrow-lands, which by their very name we know to be the lands of the dead. *I* will call on the magic of Annwn."

Twenty-seven

Dafydd, after a moment's long silence, turned to Lara and with utmost sincerity gathered her hands, kissed her knuckles, and, dismayed, asked, "Do I sound that pretentious?"

A giggle erupted and Lara pulled her hands free to cover her mouth. "Once in a while, yes."

"Oh dear." He looked back at Ioan, whose offense was written plainly across his features. "Regardless of what you call it, brother, the land is one and the same. I—"

"But it's not." Lara straightened as Dafydd's words filled with an orchestra's worth of untuned instruments. "He's right, Dafydd. Annwn is what your world was when it was whole. The Barrowlands are dying. You're all dying. You must know that."

Not for the first time, Aerin spoke when it became clear royalty would not. "We see that we are stagnant, but it is something we . . . ignore," she finally chose. "Immortality grants that leisure. It's difficult to believe or accept that we are dying when so few of us ever do."

"Hell," Kelly muttered, "it's easy enough to ignore when you've only got threescore and ten. Nothing would convince humans they were a dying race if individually we lived for millennia."

"There are ways in which we are not so different," Aerin allowed, then transferred her attention back to Lara. "Dozens of us have died in this war already, Truthseeker. Perhaps hundreds, by now. No one imagines it to be a blow we can easily recover from, which is part of why we must win at any cost."

"You do see the inherent contradiction in that attitude," Lara half-asked, but she was watching Dafydd now, watching tension play in his shoulders and hands. "Annwn's magic might respond differently than the Barrow-lands', Dafydd. Ioan may be able to reach an aspect of your world that the Seelie have forgotten. And even if he can't, at least there's just one mortal magic user right now. Nothing should interfere with his attempt to build the spell."

"Nothing except his head injury," Dafydd snapped. Envy, Lara thought: Dafydd was envious of his older brother, the brother Emyr had always favored, for all that Ioan had been a child when he was made hostage to the Unseelie king. Maybe *because* he'd been made hostage: out of sight meant out of the possibility of wrongdoing, where any mistakes Dafydd made were in Emyr's eye. Envy could be born of that easily enough, and for the moment, Ioan had access to magics that Dafydd had been cut off from.

"Try to prepare the spell," she said abruptly, to Ioan. "We'll have to go back to the Common to get the horses before you cast it, but you should be able to tell if you can draw down the magic if you try preparing it now, right?"

Ioan nodded once and Lara got to her feet as brusquely as she'd spoken, offering Dafydd a hand as she did so. He looked askance at her, but took her hand and stood as she said, "I need to talk to you. Kel, can we use the bedroom you lent me?"

Kelly nodded, shooing them away with a gesture, then glanced at Ioan before saying to Dickon, "Maybe we should give him a little while to concentrate." She got up and went into the kitchen, which was only nominally a separate room, but offered the semblance of privacy without the intimacy of inviting Dickon into her own bedroom. Dickon hesitated a few seconds, then shrugged and followed her as Lara led Dafydd into the bedroom that had been hers for a few scant weeks.

"It's not so bad, you know," she said as the door closed. The room was as she'd left it only four days earlier, down to the pair of shoes she'd decided not to wear to court and had put on the bed with the intention of putting them away when she returned. She did that now, returning them to a box in the closet before she clarified, "I mean, being only mortal."

Almost gently enough to take the sting out, Dafydd asked, "How would you know?"

A knot in her belly forced a small breathless sound free as she looked back at him. There was a full-length mirror just beyond him, angled so she could glimpse herself as well as Dafydd. By human standards, Lara was delicate, small-boned, and fine-featured, but compared to the ethereal Seelie prince, she looked blunt and rough-cut. "Don't be cruel. Until the last few weeks my truth sense was never enough to make me more than quirky, not extraordinary. And even if it had been, you said yourself that there's no doubt it's a mortal magic. I'm only human, Dafydd. And I'm sure that having your magic stripped away makes you feel less than whole, but it's not that bad. Mortal existence isn't that bad."

"Would you have me stay here, then? Half of what I was, forever hiding my face?" Tunelessness ran through the questions, not because they were a lie, but because they were true. Because Dafydd had no wish to remain in Lara's world as any less than he had been for the century he'd spent searching for her. As any less than a chameleon, able to blend in; as a visitor, able to return to his immortal homeworld when the whim suited him.

"So instead I'd come to your world?" she wondered, though the question didn't really need asking. "Never see my mother or Kelly again, but knowing I'd outlive them? Becoming like Oisín, a single mortal among immortals?"

"You would be more, there, than you are here," Dafydd said softly. "The land would welcome and encourage your magic, Lara. You could become something great to my people, a long-lost arbiter of justice returned."

"I would be different," Lara corrected. "Not more. I make beautiful things here, Dafydd." She smoothed a dress in the closet, one of several Kelly had kept in the months Lara had been missing. It was handmade, as nearly all her clothes were, perfectly fitted and subtle with stitching. Even her experienced fingertips could hardly tease out the feeling of seams; that was the joy of tailoring, for her. All the pieces fit together flawlessly, her talent turned to a physical creation of a true thing. "I would be different. Maybe more powerful, and all for the cost of nothing more than a mortal life."

"I will bring you home again," Dafydd said in a low voice. "When this is over, if it's what you desire, Lara, I will bring you back to Boston and disturb you no more."

"I know you would." Lara released the dress and crossed to Dafydd, putting her arms around his waist and her head against his chest. His heartbeat was quicker than she expected, his distress echoing her own. "But would you stay? Such a short time for you, Dafydd. In less than the century you've already lived here, my life would be over. Would you stay?"

"If you would have me," he finally whispered, "yes."

Regret scored wounds through the music in his voice, but he spoke the truth. Lara laced her fingers behind his head and pulled his mouth to hers for a kiss that grew in urgency until Dafydd broke free with a laughing groan. "Our friends will be astonished by our lack of subtlety if we stay in here too long."

"How long does it take to set the worldwalking spell?"

Dafydd quirked an eyebrow. "An hour or two at the fastest, and Ioan is unlikely to be moving swiftly."

"Then they can be as astonished as they like." Lara flattened her hand against Dafydd's chest, surprised at her own determination. "We don't know what's waiting for us in the Barrow-lands, except war. We don't know *who's* waiting for us, and if it's Merrick having taken one or more crowns, the truth is we don't know if we're going to live through it. I'm not usually rash," she whispered, "but I don't want the last few minutes of my life to be filled with regretting lost opportunities. You, Dafydd ap Caerwyn, prince of Seelie, are not an opportunity to be lost."

Solemnity flashed into a brilliant smile that in turn faded to gentleness. "Nor am I one to argue with a truthseeker's verdict. I like this better, Lara. Solace sought after danger is heady in its own right, but I asked then if I deserved your attentions. I think this decision is a more thoughtful one."

"Dafydd," Lara said, suddenly cheerful, "shut up."

He laughed, murmured, "That I can do," and drew her toward the bed.

Sunset bled into Kelly's apartment, turning Aerin's short white hair to fiery gold as Lara and Dafydd emerged from the bedroom. Aerin gave them a look so neutral as to be hostile, but Kelly seized Lara's wrist. "Oh good, we were just talking about ordering dinner. Come tell me what you want."

Lara shot a bemused glance at Dafydd as she was hauled into the kitchen. Kelly lodged herself beside the refrigerator and whispered, "*Well?*" at such volume there could be no doubt everyone heard it. "Is elf sex better than human sex?"

Laughter burst free, accompanied by a ferocious blush, and Lara, much more quietly than Kelly had, asked, "If I say yes are you going to seduce Ioan?"

Kelly shot a look toward the living room, where the dark-haired Seelie prince sat in a meditative pose. Then her gaze strayed to Dickon, who had taken his seat in an armchair again and was trying hard not to stare curiously between Dafydd and Lara. "Maybe not. Dickon and I had a long talk," Kelly admitted in a more credible whisper, then gave Lara a significant look. "A *very* long talk. You two were in there three hours! And I don't think it's just because you were changing clothes."

Heat scalded Lara's cheeks again and she glanced at herself. She'd abandoned Unseelie clothes for jeans and a T-shirt, and changed her soft-soled boots for tennies. "These are more comfortable, even if I'll look strange in the Barrow-lands. And we fell asleep for a while, that's all. It happens."

"Uh-huh."

Lara elbowed her. "It *does*. What did you talk about?"

"Dafydd. Reg. Magic. Me being a criminal mastermind. The whole mess. He's not so angry anymore. Whatever Blondie there did to help Reg calmed him down a lot, so I don't know. Maybe we're working it out." Cautious hope lit Kelly's face.

"That's fantastic." Lara, smiling, caught Kelly in a hug. "I hope it works out, Kel. I really do. He's a good guy."

"He is. And I can't blame him for all of this being too much. I meant it, you know. If I hadn't known you for years . . ."

"Of course I know. Dafydd and I owe you more than I can say. We all do." Lara gestured to the other two Seelie, then wondered, "How's the spellcasting going?"

"I don't know. Ioan's been sitting like that since you went into the bedroom, and Blondie—"

"She's not really blond, you know."

"I know, but 'Whitey' sounds racist somehow." Kelly grinned at

Lara's expression. "Okay, fine, *Aerin* has been standing there glowering at the bedroom door like she could set it on fire. Once in a while she checks on Ioan, but I don't get the impression there's much she can do to help, and she was getting more mileage out of glaring at the door. *Is* elf sex better?"

Shy laughter caught Lara off guard as a vivid memory of Dafydd's featherlight touch came back to her. "Maybe a little."

"I knew it!" Kelly smacked Lara's shoulder in juvenile delight, then reached for the phone. "Do elves like pizza?"

"Dafydd does." Lara rubbed her shoulder and went back into the living room, leaving Kelly to place an order for half a dozen different kinds of pizza.

"I believe the spell is ready," Ioan said as she came into the room. He opened his eyes and gave Dafydd an apologetic glance. "You're right in that I'm not well-prepared to make this magic. Holding the place-images in mind long enough to construct a bridge has been more difficult than I expected, but I think I have it now. If, however, we're to wait a little longer before executing it . . . could someone please tell me how I *came* to this world?" The last words sounded plaintive and young.

"We were hoping you might tell us," Lara confessed.

Dismay rushed over Ioan's face. "I recall a skirmish in the hidden valley, and then very little until these past few hours. Glimpses, nothing more, as the worldwalking spell thrust me here. I saw your *cars*," he said to Lara. "I think that was how I knew I was in your world at all. My thoughts have been unclear. I remember . . . needles, and incessant sound, and exhaustion beyond any I've ever known. I couldn't so much as draw on my own magics to heal myself. Something prevented me, constantly."

"That was the hospital. The needles they used to keep your fluids up are made of what we call stainless steel. They're iron-based." Lara sat in the chair she'd abandoned earlier, and Dafydd offered a hand so she could lace her fingers with his. "They couldn't have known, but I'm sure that interfered with your magic, even if getting hit on the head didn't."

Dafydd said, "Even a head injury should have resolved itself by now. Our individual healing magics may be small, but they're determined. It would have been the iron, indeed. And we believe Merrick sent you here, Ioan, as he did us. I doubt very much he meant for us to find you, but the spell will lay its own paths if they're not firmly delineated in the caster's mind. Perhaps the Barrow-lands themselves are working against him."

"As they've chosen to work against you," Aerin muttered.

Injury splashed across Dafydd's face and Lara quelled the urge to kick the taller woman. "That wasn't his fault."

"Does it matter? He's now hardly more than mortal, and we're forced to rely on a traitor to bring us home."

Lara sighed. Aerin's forgiveness had extended only so far as Ioan's illness, it seemed. She hoped Dickon would be less fickle, and that his newfound inclination to forge past the events of the past few weeks would prove genuine.

When she spoke, she was surprised at the steel in her own voice. "I had a vision, Aerin, of how you might turn your back on Dafydd if he couldn't recover from fighting the nightwings in my world. If his gifts deserted him and left him mortal." She opened her eyes, meeting Aerin's gaze. "That vision was driven by jealousy. By the hope that I could somehow have him for myself. Maybe this attitude of yours right now is driven by the same thing, but I can promise you, it's no way to win his heart. I'm mortal. Even if I stay in the Barrow-lands and live for centuries, eventually I'm going to die. You don't have that certainty ahead of you. Ask yourself if petty envy and cruelty now is worth an eternity of enmity after I'm gone."

She wet her lips and looked away, unwilling to face any of the immortal trio just then. Instead she focused on Kelly, whose arms were wrapped tight around herself and whose face was marred by distress. "Maybe you'd better cancel that pizza order, Kel. I think we need to go to the Common and get the horses and leave now, before we fracture any more than we're already doing."

Kelly, wordlessly, went back to the phone, but Ioan got to his feet, relying entirely on himself for the first time. "No need. With a locus, I believe I can guide the spell to the horses and then into Annwn."

Dafydd shook his head. "That's not wise, Ioan. You aren't well, and there are four of us as well as the horses."

"Five," Kelly objected from the kitchen, and Dickon, half a breath later, said, "Six."

Ioan chuckled, making his way carefully around the room. "Hence the need for a locus, Dafydd. Regardless of how many travelers there are, the attempt would be foolish without a connective point to focus through. But I've been thinking about this for the last several hours, and I believe it's the surest way to succeed."

A heartbeat after Lara realized what he intended, Ioan laid hands on the worldbreaking staff.

Twenty-eight

Power roared from the staff, flaring through Ioan so brightly that, for an instant, Lara saw him as he'd been: a pale creature like Aerin and Dafydd, hair whitened by the magic coursing through him. It shot upward, ripping at the ceiling with a mind for destruction, and Lara could feel the weapon's unmitigated triumph at such an opportunity for release. The floor beneath them cracked, sending everyone but Ioan into a stagger: he was elevated just above the floor's surface, the staff's power wrapping him in a bubble of its own.

Wind and magic shrieked together, creating a song that whipped notes away too quickly for Lara to comprehend. Pictures flew off Kelly's walls and couch cushions rose up to be shredded. Within seconds the weightiest pieces of furniture were sliding, called by gravity toward the downward-slanting cracks in the floor and hurried along by howling wind. Dickon caught Kelly in his arms, but not even a man his size would stand long against the magic Ioan had set free.

"I can harness it!" Ioan bellowed over Kelly's screams, confidence and belief in his voice. A handful of weeks earlier, that would have been enough to make Lara believe he spoke the truth.

No longer. Now a greater truth crashed through her mind, drowning out Ioan's certainty with conviction of its own. The staff's power would overwhelm Ioan's, subsume him to its own ends as it had tried repeatedly to do with Lara. Her own magic, she suspected, was different enough—*mortal* enough—to make it harder for the staff's uncanny will to grasp and use it fully.

But Ioan, like the weapon, was born of Annwn, and all the more vulnerable for it.

For an instant her thoughts slipped sideways, leaping into conjecture: if Emyr or Hafgan had created the staff, built it out of the living land, then perhaps they, like Ioan, had underestimated what they were doing. It was just possible that the drowning of the land had been unintentional.

Music worsened, rejecting the hypothesis, and Lara had no more time to shake free ideas of what that rejection meant. She flung herself toward Ioan, clawing at the sliding couch and armchairs to give herself purchase against the shrill wind.

Abruptly, Aerin was beside her, standing easily, as if the wind that lashed and snapped at her short hair was nothing more than a mild breeze. She offered a hand and Lara grasped it, then gasped in astonishment as the shifting floor beneath her stabilized. A deep familiar song touched her, slow notes of the earth itself undisturbed as of yet by the magic Ioan had awakened but could not contain. Lara whispered, "Thank you," knowing the words would go unheard in the clamor made by magic.

Aerin nodded regardless, then leaned close to shout, "Can I stop him this way?" into Lara's ear.

"*No!*" It seemed like explanation should follow, but the effort necessary to be heard was daunting. Aerin, unconcerned, only nodded and let Lara go again, though the earthbound magic that gave her sure footing remained in place. The Seelie woman was full of contradictions, willing or unwilling to help on what seemed to be whim.

There would be time to wonder about Aerin's motivations later. Lara, teeth set together, ran forward as the floor collapsed into concrete rubble and rebar beneath her feet. Song surged, one part delight from the staff, one part a distrustful awakening from the earth below. "Aerin, soothe it!"

She caught a glimpse of Aerin dropping to her hands and knees, head lowered in concentration as she bent her magics toward a world only half willing to recognize her. Far below, the ground groaned with reluctance, then shuddered, sending a ripple through the building. Through the whole block, Lara feared, though the shake threw *her* over disintegrating floors and let her crash full-bodied into Ioan.

Panic made his youthful face age. "The spell isn't set! You can't take it from me!"

"You're going to destroy Boston!" Lara knotted her hands around the staff and felt its power lurch, suddenly torn between two users. Not masters: *she* could master it, if necessary; Ioan could only use it. The difference came clear in her mind with the sound of chimes, and again played up the possibility that the destruction of Unseelie lands had been accidental. Falsehood shot through the idea a second time and Lara struggled to shake it off, wondering abruptly if the thought came from the staff itself, its near-sentience trying to make it, in effect, a victim. Agreement ricocheted through her as the sound of deep brass horns, but her own exasperation flattened the staff's response. Being manipulated by living, breathing people was aggravating enough. To be the focus of trickery from an ivory staff was absurd, and she was in no mood for it.

A roar opened up inside her skull, a vast crash of magic that seized her own power and wedded it to Ioan's. Golden light flared everywhere, disguising the destruction around them, and exultation flared across Ioan's face. A familiar white streak bolted through the gold, not at all the simple doorway of the worldwalking spell, but Lara's magic creating a true pathway from one place to another.

To the horses, she realized with horror: a straight brilliant line smashing from Kelly's apartment all the way to the Common. Unified with the staff's wont for devastation, that path became a far more physical thing than she'd ever built before. It had been a guide in the past; now it lay down a presence of its own, ripping through streets, through homes, through buildings, which all began to fall in on themselves in the path's aftermath. Even over the sound of music and magic, Lara could hear cries of bewilderment and pain.

She released the staff, trying to claw back her magic, but it was already far too late. True vision showed her the havoc wreaked in mere seconds: a broad swath of the city was a disaster zone, as if struck by earthquakes. Girders jutted from ruined buildings, glass clattered and fell to the earth, bricks and steel creaked and collapsed for mile after mile. Cars lay askew in giant ruts that had torn open beneath them, astonished and frightened people climbing free all over the city. Everything was hazy with golden light that emanated not from the setting sun on the horizon, but from Ioan's magic, still pouring into the worldwalking spell. Half the city would be pulled with them into the Barrow-lands, if he didn't let go of the staff.

Kelly's apartment had become a quiet point, the eye of the storm. The floor stabilized under Lara's feet and she glanced down, dismayed but not surprised to see the hard white flare of her true path supporting her. Supporting all of them, as she'd once imagined it could do. That was still the staff's power, clinging to the magic she'd released, rather than her own active will. Hands clenched, she tried to quiet the music in her mind, searching for a static softness to drown it out and quell magic.

Instead, hoofbeats filled her ears as the horses burst down the road she and Ioan had laid. He yelled in delight, reaching for a mane to swing up by as one passed him, and letting the staff hang from only one hand as he did so.

Dafydd, wielding a broken chair leg like a baseball bat, smashed it into Ioan's forearm as he mounted. Ioan's arm spasmed with the strength of the blow, and he shot a look of astonished injury at Dafydd as his numb fingers dropped the staff.

Lara snatched it up, and the worldwalking door closed around them all, leaving Boston's destruction in their wake.

Rubble shattered against black mother-of-pearl flooring and splashed into Ioan's scrying pool at the heart of the Unseelie city. Lara ducked, arm folded over her head as iron bars clanged, bouncing down from above. Kelly let go short, repeated screams as more debris fell around them. Dickon hovered over her protectively, broad shoulders taking some of the scree that dropped, though he began to swear when a handful of larger pieces pelted him.

Lightning exploded everywhere, turning wreckage to dust. Lara lowered her arm to peer at Dafydd, a few feet away with his hands curved upward and satisfaction twisting his mouth. "I am accepted home again."

"And *you* are a raging fool!" Aerin strode past Dafydd to haul Ioan off his horse and smash a fist into his jaw all in one smooth motion. The two horses bolted away as Aerin stood over Ioan, fury making her voice harsh. "Did you not forbid the Truthseeker to use that weapon? What idiocy compelled you? How many mortals now lie dead because of you?"

Ioan sagged under the assault, though not, Lara thought, because he lacked the means to defend himself. She'd seen them both in battle, and Aerin's prowess, indubitably greater than Dafydd's, paled before Ioan's. But he made no attempt at defense, only gazed past her at where Lara crouched with the staff. "It seemed to be the only choice. The only chance. I could imagine so clearly how it would work..."

Lara, grudgingly, said, "It might not be his fault. The staff has a circle of influence. I thought it was just when it was close to me, but I'm not elfin. It might have been...encouraging him." She stood up, using the staff for leverage, and let herself forget about Ioan's travails for a few seconds.

Most of Kelly's apartment had come with them to the Barrowlands. Broken furniture, half-framed doors; even the bedrooms were spewed across the marble and metal garden. Everything was covered in dust, and bubbles of escaping air rose from rubble in the pool, sometimes hissing as a block of concrete fell in.

"My whole building's going to collapse," Kelly whispered in horror. "Oh my God. Jesus Chr—"

"Kelly. Don't use those words here." Lara kept her voice quiet, but it cut her friend off and earned Lara a look of bewilderment.

"Just because you don't swear doesn't mean the rest of us can't. What the hell, Lara, you never cared bef—"

"They're words of power here," Lara said just as quietly. "I destroyed nightwings with an exorcism. When I called on the holy trinity it made Dafydd flinch, and I almost burned Aerin from the inside out with a hymn. I don't think it matters if you believe, Kel. Just... watch your tongue, okay?"

Kelly put her hand over her mouth, eyes wide above it, then loosened it enough to whisper, "But my *apartment*, Lara..."

"I know. And it's worse, the destruction goes halfway across Boston." Lara swallowed, unable to look at Ioan. Unable to look anywhere but at Kelly and the increasing dismay on her friend's face. "Aerin's right. A lot of people are going to have died. Any later and I think we'd have been among them."

"Is that supposed to make it better?" Dickon asked hoarsely.

"That we got away and they didn't? Jesus *Christ,*" he said with obvious deliberation, and satisfaction lashed across his face when all three elves recoiled. "Does disaster just follow wherever you go?"

Dafydd, as softly as Lara'd spoken, said, "Not until very recently, I'm afraid. Worse, I fear there's very little we can do to salvage what remains of Boston. Even a whole host of our healers would be no more than a bandage to a gaping wound."

"What about her?" Dickon pointed an accusing finger at Aerin. "What about her earth thing? Can't she put it back together again?"

"All the king's horses and all the king's men," Kelly said in a high voice. "Lara, are we really in the Barrow-lands?"

"Your world responds to my magic only sluggishly," Aerin said to Dickon, more compassion in her voice than Lara had ever heard. "I might convince it to close where it's been torn asunder, but you riddle your earth with iron. No one among the Seelie could ever heal it the way you ask. No more than magicless mortals could."

"Then I want to go home so I can help clean up." Dickon got to his feet, face pale beneath dust-covered ruddy hair. "I can't just stay here and wonder what's going on. Send me back."

"Hang on." Kelly climbed to her feet as well, a hand on Dickon's wrist and conflicted hope in her eyes. "We're in a whole different world, Dickon. Don't you want to see some of it? It's not that I don't care what's happening in Boston. I do. You must know that. It's just . . . *fairyland.*"

The look Dickon settled on her was one Lara had encountered innumerable times in her childhood: puzzlement so profound it went beyond anger. When people turned it on her, it was usually because she'd pressed an insistence for the truth far past the point of reason. She'd learned, as she'd aged, not to push it, but it made Dickon's expression no less familiar. Kelly had once again moved so far outside his own boundaries that she'd become foreign to him, as alien in her own way as Dafydd or Aerin was. Lara had always loved her friend for that adventuresome streak, but Dickon, it seemed, was stymied by it.

"Okay," Kelly whispered after a long time. "Okay, Dickon. You go back. Good luck. Maybe I'll...call you when I get home." She turned to the others, lips compressed and her eyes bright as she asked, still in a whisper, "I mean, if it's okay that I stay? Because... because, I mean, I sell bras back at home. It's not like I'm going to be much help to a disaster relief effort, not unless there's a sudden need for well-fitted thirty-eight double-H's. So I know a war is going on here, but Lara's my best friend, and...it's fairyland. I'm never gonna get another chance. Am I?"

The last question was directed at Dafydd, who hesitated, but then shook his head. "Almost certainly not, I fear. Kelly, you're as welcome to stay as Dickon is to go, but I might ask of you one thing. Remain here, in the safety of Ioan's citadel, until we've resolved this dispute. There will be plenty to see and time to see it after, but until then, you would be—"

"A liability," Kelly said clearly enough, though she sniffled as soon as she'd spoken. "No, that's fair. I mean, no offense, Lara, but having to keep an eye on you in the middle of a war is probably enough work, without adding me to the mix."

"At least you can ride a horse without being magicked to it." Lara offered a fragile smile, and Kelly turned it into a shaky laugh of her own.

"Yeah, good point. Maybe I should be the truthseeker for the rest of this game." Consternation crossed her face. "Nevermind, I remember what that was like. It was horrible. Okay. I'll stay here awhile," she promised Dafydd, and he gave her a grateful smile before looking back at Dickon.

"The worldwalking spell will take some time to prepare."

"No. It won't." Another man interrupted, voice preceding him as he strode into the garden. Lara barely had time to recognize Hafgan, now resplendent in shimmering dark blue silks and black velvets, before he tore open a door between the worlds and unceremoniously dumped both Dickon and Kelly back through it.

"Where . . . when . . . did you send them?" Lara gaped at the fading door, certain the only reason she hadn't also been thrust through it was her distance from the other two mortals. "Why did you do that?"

Hafgan made a dismissive gesture. "Annwn's problems are not for mortals to interfere with, and from what I now see those problems run deep indeed. They are returned home, within a few minutes or hours of their departure. Nothing has changed for them. What are *they* doing here?" He thrust a finger toward Dafydd and Ioan.

Lara glanced at the brothers, but panic yanked her attention back to Hafgan. "You can't have sent them home. Not right where they came from. The building is collapsing. They'll *die*."

Dafydd put a hand on her shoulder. "The spell isn't that accurate. We never come and go from exactly the same place. That you hold Boston so close in your heart and mind as home is all that has kept us from arriving halfway across the country, or the world. It'll be the same for Dickon and Kelly. And at least they're alive, Lara. They'd have died when the building came down if the spell hadn't taken them with us."

Lara whispered "I hope you're right," then turned on Hafgan, anger rising. "That was completely unnecessary! Dickon was going home anyway and Kelly hasn't got any magic to interfere with yours. She just wanted to see your world!"

"A world riddled by chaos and war. It is not the face we put forward to the mortals we lure here, Truthseeker, and we have problems that run deeper than even I knew. These two cannot be here." Absolute conviction filled Hafgan's voice, so jarring in the face of truth that Lara shuddered with it.

She wrapped her arms around herself, as if it might prevent her from falling apart. "Why not?"

Hafgan ignored her, stalking instead to Ioan and Dafydd to inspect them as if they were sides of meat that lacked in quality. Even in clear fury, he was graceful, moving like a predator as he circled the princes twice. Only when he stopped before them did Lara recognize how high his shoulders rode, and how his jawline bunched with tension.

Neither Ioan nor Dafydd reacted. Ioan hadn't moved at all since Aerin's attack, still staring dully at the ground. He looked exhausted, like Dafydd had after drawing on all his own remaining power after fighting the nightwings. The staff had done that to him: had burned through more of his magic than he had probably imagined possible. Lara folded it closer to her chest, less possessive than determined not to let another elf lay hands on it and wreak further havoc.

A thread of coldness came into Hafgan, as icy as Lara had ever seen in Emyr. "You are meant to be in the Caerwyn citadel. How came you here? And *you*—" he said to Dafydd, but Ioan drew himself up until he was as aloof as Hafgan himself.

"I haven't been in the shining citadel since I was a child. These past several days I was the guest of mortal healers, whose best efforts were counterintuitive to my wellness."

Hafgan's attention lashed back to his adopted son. "Not three days ago I saw you crowned in Caerwyn."

"*Crowned?*" Four voices cracked the word together and rose toward the distant ceiling as an echo.

Hafgan looked from one to another of them, finally settling on Dafydd with a nasty crook to his smile. "Crowned, indeed. The war is over. Emyr ap Caerwyn is dead, and all of Annwn saw him fall at your hand."

Twenty-nine

"What?" Dafydd's faint question was all but lost under Ioan's urgent, "No. No, he can't be. Without him we have no *answers*, Father. No way of discovering history's truth."

"What does it matter? The Seelie king is dead and his son, my heir, sits on his thr..." Hafgan's smugness faded to a slow frown. He repeated, "I saw you crowned," then turned to Lara, angry incomprehension written on his features.

"Tell me what you saw." Lara heard cool command in her own voice, so remote she barely recognized it, and king or not, Hafgan acquiesced.

More than acquiesced: a twist of his wrist brought living flame up from the dust-covered floor, each lick dancing apart to become an image. Armies clashed together, flame rolling over itself as one side overwhelmed the other or fell back, very near to the edge of the chasm protecting the Unseelie city.

It was eerily silent; this was no scrying spell, no method of looking across or back or forward in time, but only the reconstruction of memory in an element that didn't carry voices. Water carried sound, if poorly; enhanced by magic it made a viable conductor, but flame had only its own snapping, crackling song as it ate away at the fuel provided. Without that fuel, all it provided was imagery, noiseless when it should have been ear-splitting.

The focus came closer, picking out individuals: Hafgan rode with his army, intent on reaching Emyr, whose icy pale countenance was somehow reflected in warm flame. But before Hafgan reached the Seelie king, Dafydd slammed through the Unseelie ranks, riding from behind them, his presence unseen by Hafgan until he was already past. Astounded Unseelie fell back; delighted Seelie made a path, silent faces lifted in cheers.

Dafydd ap Caerwyn rode straight for Emyr, and slammed a sword through the sovereign's chest when he reached him. Lara, knowing it wasn't true, knowing it to be impossible, still gasped at the impact, and Aerin let go a child's cry of horror.

On the battlefield, delight turned to dismay, cheers to howls, as Dafydd caught the falling king and tore the silver circlet from his brow. He jammed it onto his own head, triumphant in the midst of a mob that could no longer be called an army. Even Hafgan drew his horse up, too agape to ride on, and so no one was there to stop Ioan ap Annwn as he followed in Dafydd's wake, and slew his brother with the same efficient brutality Dafydd had shown Emyr.

This time the yelp of dismay was Lara's. She jerked forward, reaching for the fiery images against all sense, against everything she knew. Dafydd drew her back, his hands icy on her shoulders as they all gawked, horrified, at unfolding events.

There was no triumph on the flame-made Ioan's face, no joy as there'd been in Dafydd's. He slid from his horse, bearing Dafydd's body to the ground. It was too late by far to show Emyr such gentleness, but Ioan stood when both bodies lay at his feet, and lifted his silent voice to the stunned armies.

"The war is over," Hafgan echoed, putting words into the simulacrum's mouth. "Emyr and Dafydd are dead. I am Ioan ap Caerwyn, changed but still the last son of the shining citadel, and I will have no more of this war. We will bear these bodies back to Caerwyn and put them to rest, and there I will take the crown and embrace Seelie and Unseelie alike, so both my adopted people and my blood people might finally know peace. Do not defy me, my Seelie family. There are still far more Unseelie than there are of you, and I will have peace at any cost."

Flame melted away, leaving Hafgan staring at Lara with angry expectation. "Three days," he said, his voice his own again. "Three days later, three days ago, Ioan was crowned in Caerwyn, with Emyr and Dafydd buried in the barrows as they ought to have been. These two *cannot be here.*"

"All of that was Merrick." Even the attempt at further explanation defeated her. Lara took Dafydd's hand instead, trying to impart comfort. He flinched at her touch, then turned a suddenly haggard gaze on her.

"Is my father dead?"

Lara pressed one hand against her eyes, then shook her head. "I don't know. If I were Merrick, I'd have murdered Emyr in your guise, then built the illusion of Ioan coming for you, and switched from one role to the other when they came together. But I don't know. The way flame dances, Dafydd . . . it disguises any hope I might have of seeing through the illusions. If I'd *been* there, maybe . . ."

Hafgan waited a heartbeat, then two, before bursting out with, "*Merrick?* My own son sits on the Seelie throne, behind Ioan's face?"

"What bitter dregs those must be for Merrick," Dafydd said with a thin smile. "To plot and plan so long and be left wearing another man's mask when victory is in his hand. The war is not over, Hafgan. I will not allow Merrick to sit on my father's throne for long, no matter what the cost to myself or the Barrow-lands."

"You cannot be such a fool," Ioan protested. "Emyr is dead, our chances of learning the past's truth have slipped away, and you would still continue with these endless skirmishes, the eternal war? To what end, Dafydd? To what purpose?"

Dafydd whispered, "I might have let it go, if it were you. Changed or not, beholden to the Unseelie or not, beneath it all you are my brother and Rhiannon's son. Had you come to the throne of—"

"Of Annwn," Ioan put in strongly, and Dafydd broke off to stare at him a moment before continuing.

"Had you come to Emyr's throne I might have found my way past the differences between us. But Merrick has tricked and murdered his way there, and I will not let it stand. He was my brother, closer to me than you ever were, and this betrayal runs too deep. My father is *dead*."

"Is he?" Aerin asked the question this time, with more grief than either Dafydd or Ioan had shown. Her green eyes were red-rimmed, a show of emotion that seemed tragically mortal to Lara, and the hope in her face was more desperate yet.

Lara, for the second time, whispered, "I don't know. It feels like all of Annwn believes it, and I can't tell if it's the land or the truth whose music I'm hearing."

Hafgan sneered. "Perhaps you do not wish to know. A truth-seeker is of no use if she refuses to accept her power."

A sharp laugh broke from Lara's throat. "It really has been a long time since you've dealt with a truthseeker, if you can make yourself believe that. I've spent a lifetime wondering why people don't just accept the truth. I don't think there's any comfort in not knowing. But it doesn't matter how I twist it in my head, 'Emyr is alive, Emyr is dead,' neither one sings clear. So neither is true or they both are." She sharpened her gaze on the Unseelie king. "The sleepers under the sea. Are they alive?"

"Yes."

Discord crashed through his answer and Lara released another sharp laugh. "But do they live?"

"No."

The same wrenching music played, and Lara dropped her forehead against the staff, hanging on for a few long seconds. "So they're dead."

This time Hafgan gave no answer at all, and when she looked up again, irritated confusion had settled across his face. The others were so silent as to be statues, not even their breath stirring the air as she turned to them. "There's a chance, then. If I can't tell, then maybe he's somewhere between dead and alive. That means there's a chance he's alive, maybe in the Drowned Lands, maybe . . . you said there was a place of remembrance in the citadel, Aerin. Does it share any of the drowned city's aspects? Could there be a stasis hall beneath it?"

"We never found one, playing as children." Aerin sounded as if the lack of discovery implied it was impossible one should be there.

"It took me to find the way in the drowned city," Lara reminded her. Aerin shrugged an eyebrow in cranky assent and tension-ridden amusement sparked in Lara. Whether it was her mortality or her magic, the idea that she could find what Aerin couldn't visibly annoyed the Seelie warrior, and Lara didn't quite blame her. She was the outsider, usurping far too many things, but momentum had her in its grasp. Dafydd and then Ioan had asked for her help, setting her on this path, but now she wanted the answers for her own sake. Nothing would stop her, though the thought brought a shiver of alarm.

"You cannot imagine I will allow you to seek out my old enemy if there's a chance he still lives," Hafgan said in soft astonishment. "To see Ioan, Seelie by birth but Unseelie by choice, take Emyr's throne would have been triumph enough. But my son by blood and birth has ascended through wit alone, and you think I will let you go?"

"I was your son." Each word scraped from Ioan's throat like a wound, his gaze on Hafgan bleak and betrayed.

"And I loved you. But I love my own flesh more. How could I do less, when he's devised and won such a game? I will embrace him, so he might cast aside the false face he wears and the Seelie people will know we're united in ruling them."

"He said four," Lara said, quiet and mellow in the face of Hafgan's delight. He scowled and she turned a palm up, explaining, "He said there were four people between himself and sovereignty in the Barrow-lands. Emyr, Ioan, and Dafydd are three. That leaves you, the last king. Do you really think Merrick has any plans to power-share, Hafgan? You gave him up as a child. Why would he want to give you your due as his father?"

Uncertainty, then anger, flashed in Hafgan's eyes. "If he's so callow as that, then he can be replaced. Emyr is dead or lost to the Barrow-lands, and I have his heirs here before me. Like Merrick, there is now only one person standing between myself and kingship over all the land."

Fire gouted up as he spoke, dancing over rubble-coated surfaces and melting the black opalescent stone that made up the Unseelie citadel's floor. Metal-laden trees buckled, then disintegrated as flame exploded over them. The surface of Ioan's pool hissed and bubbled, brought to boiling in an instant as the fire rushed Lara's group. She clenched her mouth shut, appalled at the air's searing heat. It would take accelerants to make a fire explode so dangerously in her world, but here it took nothing more than the will of an angry man. She moved backward, heat at her back telling her there was already nowhere to go: the center of the Unseelie palace was entirely alight, raging flame consuming all it touched. There wasn't even the blessing of billowing smoke to grant them a chance at easy passage. Hafgan's magic burned clean, so greedy it left nothing at all behind.

A true path might save them, if she could find one that led out of the inferno. The staff might save them, if she was willing to pit one unearthly magic against another. Its enthusiasm for the prospect made her grab it harder, uncertain if her grip was meant to quell or encourage. *Truthseeking magic,* she reminded herself: that was her strength, and that was their chance. The staff would only wreak more havoc, and the image of Boston's ruins already left a mark in her mind. She would not release that power within the Barrowlands, not if she could help it. Even if it meant leaving the lands drowned, if she could find no way to control the staff's devastating magic, she would not again call on its power. Her own would have to be enough. Resolute, she whispered the phrase that had helped her open a true path the first time: "Follow the yellow brick road."

The familiar bouncing tune cut across the fire's roar, helping her to focus, though it did nothing at all to alleviate the air's scalding heat. She coughed on it, trying to draw her next breath through her nostrils, but their moisture was already gone. She had to do more, had to do better, and had to do it quickly. Another breath or two and her lungs would burn trying to draw air that fire already consumed.

Beneath the flame's noise, at Lara's side, Ioan whispered, "Oh no, Father," and water began to fall from a rocky sky.

She had forgotten. Had forgotten the waterfall and river that fed the cavern, if they were even necessary to Ioan's power. Had forgotten Ioan's element entirely, anathema to Hafgan's fire. And, truth be told, had hardly realized the sheer potential of released power, when two such elements were flung against one another in battle.

The first drops hissed to steam so quickly they might not have fallen at all, save for Hafgan's squall of outrage. The deluge came after that, bucketsful of water pouring down. Steam billowed every-where, as dangerous in its own way as the fire. Lara screamed, cow-ering from clouds of superheated water as they rolled toward them. There was no true path opening up to save them: terror stymied her magic thoroughly, and if there was a song to be heard, it was that of elemental destruction. It was wilder than the earth songs she'd heard, full of crackling enthusiasm and the clash of water's rush against fire's snap.

Earth song erupted around them, mother-of-pearl flooring shat-tering upward as the granite beneath rose in a shield that steam couldn't penetrate. Lara shrieked again, too-hot air still ripping at her lungs, and Aerin, red-faced with heat and concentration, gave her a withering look as more rock shot up, protecting them from the worst of the colliding elemental excesses.

Ioan barked a rough sound of approval and new water formed on the inside curve of their protective wall, dripping down on them to mitigate the heat. Within seconds they were safe—comparatively safe—in a pocket of cooler air. Lara whimpered and smoothed her hand over the condensing water, then rubbed it over her face, more grateful for its presence than she could vocalize. She wanted to lick the wall just to replace a little of the water she'd lost, but urgency pressed at her: Ioan and Hafgan's battle was only in its infancy, and the city could still trap them. The respite had to be enough. She bent her attention a second time to building a true path, and instead was swept away by the raging song of combat.

Hafgan stood encircled by flame, power and heat blazing off him. Nothing Lara could think of stood against water, not in the long term. Even fire so hot it boiled the bottom of the ocean ultimately conceded its battle, stone cooling and rising under water's implaca-ble pressure. But that was at home, where magic didn't hold sway. In the Barrow-lands, it was possible a king's will and power might de-feat even the most relentless element that Lara's world knew.

Even as she thought it, the strength in Ioan's calling changed. Its music softened, drawing back, and the heat beneath Aerin's stone shield intensified again. Dafydd let go a curse, fingers curled uselessly: *he* might survive throwing lightning into the raging fight between fire and water, but Lara would be electrocuted, and even Aerin, literally grounded, was unlikely to live through the attempt. The fight was Ioan's alone.

Ioan's draw of power faded, sending a spasm of despair through Lara. A true path still refused to respond, and with Ioan's magic faltering they had no more than minutes, perhaps seconds, to live.

Falsehood sang through the thought, and Lara, abruptly, thought of tsunamis.

An instant later a wall of water crashed into the city's heart.

Fire guttered inside a breath, drowned by the mass of water rolling over it. Shocked relief ricocheted through Lara as the tidal wave rolled harmlessly around them, guided in its entirety by Ioan's will. Hafgan's howl crashed through the water. There was no sense, though, of his life being quenched, only the inferno that had eaten at the garden. Within seconds, even that was struggling to rebirth itself, though the stunning amount of water pouring through the city gave fire little purchase. But it only needed a little, when powered by magic instead of conventional fuels.

Lara drew in a breath of wonderfully cool air and knotted her hands around the worldbreaking staff. "Your power, bent to my will," she whispered to it. "I can open the path out of here, and you can make it solid so we can run on it, or we can burn and drown at the bottom of this cavern. Those are the choices. Take your pick."

Anticipation stretched from the staff, its semi-sentience searching for the flaws in Lara's offer. There were none: she'd spoken with a truthseeker's conviction, certain that they—and the staff; most importantly, in its view, the staff—would lie cracked and lost beneath the boiling inferno if it didn't choose to bend to her will. It pushed at her resolve, which, a little to her own surprise, held firm: she would rather die there than release the staff's power into the world unmentored.

Pure petty resentment flared from the staff, but it acquiesced, and the silly, catchy song sprang into Lara's mind again: *Follow the yellow brick road!*

White light, not yellow brick, exploded over the city, pathways parting water as they plunged low, and making brilliant streaks as they shot across the granite sky. Even guided by her desire, the staff had a mind of its own, but it wasn't reaching for destruction. After an eternity of seconds, one of the pathways crashed into being around them, turning the gloom inside of Aerin's stone shell to a spotlight-brilliant glare.

All four of them grabbed each other's arms and scrambled up the escape route they were offered, leaving the conflicted city behind.

Thirty

Only the fear of falling back into the city took Lara to the path's end. It angled too steeply upward, and at any other time the incline would have defeated her. Her legs alternated between stabbing pain and rubberiness as they reached the far side of the chasm that protected the Unseelie city, where she and the others simply dropped to the ground, gasping sickly for air. A new sense of determination rolled from the staff and Lara let go a frustrated yell, casting it away so it couldn't take advantage of her weakness. Contact with the land wasn't enough: it needed a cognizant wielder in order to parlay its power, and she was determined not to become that conduit when physically and mentally exhausted.

She became aware, slowly, that there were others around them. The city, quiet as it had been, had not been abandoned: dozens of Unseelie lay scattered around them, men and women who had taken the paths that appeared through the dying city and who had run to safety along a road of magic. Like her little group, they were too sickened by the escape to react for a long while, but an explosion within the city jolted everyone out of their collapse to stare slack-jawed as the granite shell began to fall.

Voices slowly lifted in bewilderment, fear, and growing despair as flame engulfed their home. Their gratitude for surviving was so far beyond them that it was as yet unimaginable. It would come in time, along with guilt if anyone had been left behind, and with anger for what had been visited upon them. Lara, numb beyond comprehension, spared a prayer of thanks that they had survived, but like them, she had nothing in her but blank shock at what was unfolding.

Dafydd, dully, said, "Worldbreaker," to Lara. The word held no accusation; it was just an exhausted and apt descriptor.

Aerin, beneath that, said, "Lara's home, now Ioan's. All that is left, Dafydd, is our own. 'Worlds come changed at end of day.' What will you leave us with, Truthseeker?"

"I don't know." Lara stared bleakly at the fire. She had in her life never visited destruction on anything more than a pillow, and now she had overseen the ruin of two cities in barely as many hours.

No wonder Hafgan had hunted down and eradicated the truth-seekers.

"The city's fall was my decision, not your failure. I could have drowned him, and chose not to. The survivors will know who destroyed their home. Perhaps it's a way to mend the schism between Seelie and Unseelie. Especially, perhaps, if Emyr is indeed dead, and the crowns must fall to a different generation." Ioan put a hand on Lara's shoulder, then let it fall, as if afraid physical contact would make the uncertainty in his voice easier for her to read.

"What about Hafgan? Is he dead?" Looking at the blaze, it seemed impossible the Unseelie king could live, but Ioan shook his head.

"He'll be in a fit of ecstasy, bathed in his element that way. It will fade, and he'll come to the Seelie citadel in search of either Merrick's capitulation or his own retaliation, but we have a little time. Time enough, perhaps, to learn if Emyr of the Seelie lives."

"Time enough to depose a pretender and make a united stand against the Unseelie," Dafydd growled.

Lara put her hand on his thigh, the gesture weary. "Don't. Don't you start hating the Unseelie as a whole, Dafydd. You defended Merrick when the rest of your people dismissed him because of his heritage. Don't follow them down that path. I couldn't bear it."

"I defended an unworthy man."

"Yes, but that doesn't mean the rest of them deserve to be painted with that brush." Lara's shoulders dropped, weariness rolling over her again as she thought of how much Kelly would like hearing her use the vernacular phrase.

Dafydd crouched to put his arms around her shoulders and pull her close, murmuring a promise into her hair. "You're right. I shouldn't. I'm just tired of this game, Lara. I've never particularly liked politics, and now it seems they're costing me the lives and love of people around me."

"At least you were born to it. A month ago I was just a tailor."

"Tailors," Dafydd said solemnly, "are meant for great things. Someday I'll have to tell you all the fairy tales that say so."

Lara groaned, glad for a jolt of humor even as she said, sincerely, "Don't. If I'd known that I might never have become a tailor." The blatant untruth made her laugh, and she rocked in Dafydd's arms, face buried against his chest. He smelled of fire and water, though none of them were as wet as she thought they should be after the deluge. Ioan's doing, probably; there was no reason for anyone to stand around dripping when a master of the element was on hand. She finally exhaled heavily and sat back, though remaining coiled in Dafydd's arms for hours was by far the most pleasant prospect she could think of. "Okay. Whether we're finding Emyr or deposing

Merrick, that means we have to get to the Seelie citadel. We don't have any horses. How far is it to walk?"

Dafydd looked at the tennies she'd traded her soft Unseelie boots out for, then crooked a wry smile at her. "Far enough that you'll be glad of those."

"Can we get there before Hafgan does?"

"I may be able to help." Aerin lifted her head. "The magic the horses use is a gift to them from the Barrow-lands, but it's not far removed from my earth magics. With time—which we'll have a-plenty, walking from here to there—I should be able to convince the land that we take seven steps for our every one."

"Aerin, that will leave you exhausted. You've already used more magics today than anyone normally would in years. Decades," Dafydd amended.

Aerin's expression turned so sour it bordered on funny. The look she gave Dafydd said far more than words could, and he ducked his head in apology. "Forgive me. I didn't mean to state the obvious, but I fear for you. You could find yourself—"

"I know. What choice do we have?"

"Find herself what?" Lara straightened, concern washing through her. "Not mortal?"

"Just useless for a very long time," Aerin growled. "Useless, most particularly, in battle. My prowess is learned, but the strength that lets me fight inexhaustibly is the land's. Without it, I'm no more than any other Seelie warrior, and if things go badly, we will need far more than ordinary fighters."

"I do not believe," Lara said with unusual clarity, "that anything could make you less than extraordinary on the battlefield. I've watched a lot of you fight now, Aerin. Ioan's better than you are. I haven't seen anyone else who even holds a candle to you."

Surprise, then chagrined pleasure slid over Aerin's face and she looked away. Lara wrinkled her eyebrows in confusion at Dafydd, and was only further confused at his quick smile. He leaned forward to kiss her and murmured, "You couldn't have said anything better," against her mouth, then lifted his voice to say, "Then we'll rely on you, Aerin. Thank you."

Aerin grunted, and in a little while they gathered themselves, preparing to begin their journey. Lara took up the staff again, about to slid it crosswise over her back when a thought struck her. It responded to emotion and need, and emitted emotions and desires of its own. She said, "Thank you," aloud, if quietly, and after a few long seconds felt a sullen sort of pleasure from the weapon. Grinning, she tucked it away and fell in with the others as they struck out toward the distant Seelie citadel.

The Unseelie joined them, not so much willingly as with the air of people who had no other option. Ioan walked among them as they set out, offering what reassurances he could. They were scant, but Lara admired that he tried. Hafgan's return had reminded them, sharply, that the man they'd called king for centuries was no more than heir to the throne. There seemed little resentment among them for the deception: as Ioan had suggested, they appeared more content with continuity than strict truth. Their distress now was for the betrayal laid upon them by the king who had returned; for the man who commanded fire, and who had burned their home to molten rock. A few came forward to walk with Lara, to verify she was a truthseeker, and that it was through her magic and Ioan's that anyone had survived immolation in the fire. When those few fell back, satisfied, Lara thought Ioan had earned himself a small personal guard, men and women whose loyalty was to Ioan himself, not to the Unseelie crown. It could mean nothing or everything in the reshaping of Annwn that they intended, but either way, she was glad of it.

It had been midday when they abandoned the citadel, but night came on more quickly than Lara expected. There was no chill in the air to suggest short winter days, and not until the moon's light hopped unexpectedly high in the sky did she jog forward to catch up with Aerin. "Is this you?"

"I'm already doing all I can. I had hoped I could move us as quickly as the horses would go, but two legs aren't as quick as four, even magicked. The best I can manage is three steps for every one." Aerin looked tired and alien, the long contours of her skull more easily visible with sweat matting short hair against it. "The horses would have us there by morning. The best I can do is three days, perhaps."

"The best you can do," Lara echoed in astonishment. "I've read people can walk twenty or thirty miles in a day. You're moving us sixty or ninety? How far do we have to go, Aerin? How long do you have to keep this up?"

"Unassisted, it would take a sennight or more to walk this distance." Aerin cast a glance back at the Unseelie, among whom were children. "Probably more."

The corner of Lara's mouth turned up. "Thanks for looking at them, and not at me."

Aerin quirked an acknowledging eyebrow, then exhaled noisily. "This requires concentration, Truthseeker."

"Right. Just don't . . . burn yourself out, if that's what can happen. Be careful, Aerin."

"The time for care is long past." Aerin quickened her pace by a step or two and Lara took the hint, falling back again. Night grew deeper in quick lurches, until she was certain midnight had come and gone. Only then did Aerin stop abruptly, and the travelers slept where they fell, only to rise and walk again not long after sunrise.

Lara awakened to muscles and feet so sore that every step was a challenge. No one else complained, and she wondered if mortal weight connected with the land harder, or if she was simply outrageously unconditioned compared to everyone else. They all shared a certain drudgery of intent, but she caught no one else wincing with each footfall. That evening Dafydd silently stripped her shoes from her feet and massaged the tender flesh.

The second day was worse, grime and hunger building up. Ioan, Dafydd, and a few of the others broke away to hunt. There were always streams for water, but Lara could hardly feel her body, numbed from repeated impacts against the earth. Even Kelly's relentless good nature and enjoyment of adventure vacations would be hard-pressed to find much fun in the trek. Lara was torn between worry about when and where she and Dickon had landed back on Earth, and weary envy that they probably had access to showers.

Aerin stopped them earlier that evening, not long after sunset. She was slender to begin with, as all the Seelie were, but she looked as though she'd been eaten from the inside out, her muscles thin and ropey and her eyes sunken with fatigue. "We should arrive by midday," she told Dafydd. "If we hunt and eat well tonight, and sleep well, we may be in some condition to face whatever awaits us. Ioan might scry to see what lies ahead."

"It could alert Merrick to our presence." Ioan had recovered from his injuries as they walked, though like everyone else his shoulders slumped with weariness. "We might be better unannounced. The surprise would be as much theirs as ours."

"Can you cast a glamour to get us inside unseen?" Lara asked Dafydd. A darker thought spun out of that: if he could get them inside the citadel unseen, there was no reason they couldn't assassinate Merrick under that same cloak of invisibility. She met Dafydd's eyes, and saw the same idea flash through his mind before he shook his head.

"Glamours are much more successful against mortals. The constant use of power gains notice among our own kind. Call it what you will, paranoia or curiosity, but there's always someone looking for it, and a glamour large enough to hide even a handful of us would be observed long before we found Merrick."

"Then isn't what Aerin's doing going to draw attention, too? She must be using huge amounts of power."

"But the horses use a version of this magic all the time," Aerin reminded Lara. "It's a constant draw, so typical as to go unnoticed. Far more likely that the destruction of the Unseelie citadel has been noticed than my call on the earth's magic."

"There was an army of Unseelie out here," Lara said in dismay. "If they know their city was destroyed are there going to be any Seelie left alive by now?"

A little silence met her question, and Dafydd finally sighed. "They'll have fled, Lara. Even with Merrick's fine speech, the truth is that with Emyr's death, most of the army will have taken to the forests. If they even believe he's Ioan, they won't trust him, not with the change he wrought upon himself. They would have fallen with Emyr, and their first instinct will be to preserve those who are left. The citadel is a symbol, but not enough to rally them without—"

"You," Lara finished. "Without Emyr's heir, particularly when his other son apparently sits on the throne already, as one of the Unseelie."

"Assuming I'm enough. First they saw me murder Merrick, and then they watched me kill Emyr, both in cold blood. Even having a truthseeker substantiate my story may not be enough."

Cold dismay filled Lara's chest. "You knew this all along, didn't you? When we decided we were going to the citadel, you knew it wasn't going to be full of Seelie ready to fight the good fight. And you didn't tell me."

"I told you exactly what we're going to do." Dafydd fixed his gaze forward, quiet determination in his posture and voice. "We're going to depose a pretender and make a united stand against the Unseelie."

"The four of us? You made it sound like—" Lara bit the words back. Dafydd had told the truth. Her way of interpreting that truth had been glossy, perhaps. Fanciful, full of hope, and none of them had seen fit to disillusion her during the exhaustive journey. Subdued, she asked, "How are we going to win this?"

"We may not." Dafydd gave her a wan smile. "But that's a problem for the morning."

Thirty-one

Are you sure *this is going to work?* wasn't a question Lara was given to asking. She had always known whether someone was sure, and both Ioan and Dafydd were certain of their plan.

But surety wasn't interchangeable with being right, and the problem with plans was she had no way of determining whether they would succeed. She'd laid down law with her voice once or twice, but the wholesale demand that events go her way lay beyond her. Perhaps only because she thought it did, but that was enough: the limitations she argued were her own.

The glamours disguising them were subtle enough to hardly bother even her. Aerin's burned hair had been darkened to buttery yellow, and her eyes made blue, but her appearance was so altered from extended use of earth magic that little else needed to be done. Dafydd's golden tones had been bleached, leaving him wraithlike, and he had taken on fuller-featured aspects: a lusher mouth, cheekbones less angled, and the sweep of his hair longer to help change

the line of his jaw. Lara had observed once how alarmingly similar
the Seelie looked to one another, and now the understated changes
in Aerin and Dafydd reminded her of that. They weren't themselves,
but they could have been any of their people: a police witness would
be hard-pressed to single them out of a Seelie lineup.

Lara's glamour was little more than a change in her height, and
the shape of her ears had been altered. She was pale enough already,
and her features delicate, so stretching what she had over a frame
seven inches taller did most of the disguise work by itself. Even with
the headache it induced, she wanted to stare at herself in reflec-
tive water a long time, struggling to fully see and appreciate what
she looked like as a Seelie woman. Alien and beautiful, but all the
more extraordinary for knowing a human lay beneath the imagery.

Ioan stalked along behind them, darker of countenance and nar-
rower in his features than normal. Of all of them, he was the only
one armed: Lara and the others dragged along in ropes, Seelie prisoners to an Unseelie guard. None of them had needed begriming or
theatrics to play the role of downcast prisoners, not after days of
forced marching. Ioan had the hardest part, Lara thought: he was
meant to be fresh and triumphant at having captured a handful of
runaway Seelie.

"Why wouldn't he just kill us?" Lara had wondered as the plan
was laid out.

Aerin and Dafydd had exchanged glances, and once more Aerin
answered when Dafydd clearly didn't want to. "Merrick always re-
sented being an outcast within the Seelie court. Rightfully, and I did
less to mitigate that than I might have," she admitted grudgingly.
"But I think while he would have every Seelie in the Barrow-lands
put to the sword, he would first want to have them captured and pa-
raded before him."

"So they could see his ascension," Lara guessed.

Aerin nodded. "And so he could perhaps give them false hope of survival, and then enjoy their execution all the more. I'm sorry, Dafydd, but Merrick has always been petty."

"Maybe he'd have risen above that if he'd been better-treated," Dafydd said without heat. "It no longer matters. What's important is I suspect Aerin's right, and that will give us our best way into the citadel. The glamours will be too subtle to draw attention—we use such minor ones all the time, to straighten disheveled hair or smooth wrinkled clothes. It's not like entirely hiding four people from sight, or changing our looks completely so we all appear Unseelie."

"There are more Unseelie than Seelie," Lara said. "Will the citadel be too full for us to get to the remembrance gardens without being noticed? Or would they expect us to go straight to the throne room?"

"Unlike you," Ioan pointed out, "I can lie, Truthseeker. If necessary I can tell any curious passersby that you three are being taken to the gardens to meet and appreciate the Seelie dead before joining them yourselves."

A sour twitch crossed Dafydd's face, though he said nothing. He had been overruled: he'd wanted to go directly for Merrick, only acquiescing to searching for Emyr first when it was pointed out that the reappearance of two apparently dead Seelie royals would do more to dishearten the Unseelie than just he could.

"And if we find out Emyr really is dead," Lara had said with more bloodthirsty pragmatism than she'd realized she possessed, "then no one, present or future, will blame you for taking action against Merrick. Not once the illusion is exposed."

Dafydd had looked at her a long time, then nodded, and a few hours later they'd infiltrated the citadel that was his home. It remained unaltered, pearlescent stone bright with light of its own and hallways suddenly giving way to gardens large enough to be called parks. Only its people were different, making splashes of color against the white city walls where the Seelie had nearly blended in. Like the Seelie, they shared a greater homogeneity of features than any ethnic group Lara had ever encountered at home, but the range of hair colors—from coppery red through shades of brown and into shining black—gave them more distinction than the uniformly pale Seelie. Many scowled or sneered as Ioan herded his trio of captives by, but none of them questioned him. Authority, Lara supposed, was authority, regardless of what world it was in. Ioan acted as if he had every right to be there, and no one suggested otherwise.

Aerin, however, actually led the little band of outlaws, guiding them through the citadel through the quietest corridors. She finally veered under an ivy-coated archway and into sunlight. Sunlight, not the opalescent light of the citadel's floating orbs. Lara squinted up through tall winding trees to see the garden was open to the sky. Shining towers made a sculpted framework above the garden, and light glittered down as if poured like water, soft and soothing. Lara exhaled so deeply her shoulders rolled inward. It took all her concentration to not simply fold up and rest on the mossy garden floor.

Of the others, Aerin had no compunctions against doing exactly that. She caught herself on a bench that looked grown, not carved, for all that parts of it appeared to be marble. There were others like it scattered along green pathways and under the twisting trees, some few of them backing up against latticework fences riddled with ivy. Water burbled over a short wall, though once it must have been as tall as the stonework surrounding it: its edges were worn down and smoothed by centuries, perhaps aeons, of water drifting over it. The little waterfall's music was soothing, as was the breeze that drifted through the gardens, carrying a sweet scent too subtle to be cloying. The entire space had the aura of holy ground, unspoiled by divisiveness or conflict.

Dafydd crouched by Aerin, brushing a thumb over her temple as she coiled on the bench. "Rest awhile," he whispered. "You've done more than your part. The gardens will revitalize you."

"Wake me when you leave. I would see this through."

Dafydd nodded, but Aerin came awake enough to give him a sharp look, and Lara a sharper one. Bemused, Lara promised, "We will," and only then did Aerin settle again, trusting the truthseeker's word. She was asleep within a breath or two, and even in that little time looked healthier, as though the garden had revitalized her already.

"It would have been better to refuse her," Dafydd said quietly as he came back to Lara and Ioan. "She's exhausted and probably needs the rest more than we need her blade. Metaphorically," he added, glancing at his own weaponless hands.

"Probably, but she'd never forgive you."

Dafydd quirked a smile. "I seem to recall someone saying forever is a very long time, to immortals."

"And it appears we can hold a grudge that long," Ioan said drily. "Truthseeker, can you find a way?"

Lara nodded, glad she hadn't sat for fear she would never have gotten back up. Even so, her eyes fluttered shut in the garden's quiet. The music in her mind was soft, unhurried, as if the garden itself affected it, and Lara shook off its effects with an effort. "Do Seelie ever just give up on living and come here to fade away?"

A startled silence met her and she blinked her eyes open again to find Dafydd examining her with consternation. "Occasionally. How did you know?"

"It's just that peaceful here. A little like a hospice, as much as holy ground. It seems like the kind of place people might come to die." Unexpected truth sang through the last words, finally wakening her thoroughly. "Where would they go?" she asked, but not of the men.

Of the music, which flared in trumpets, then lay down a path through the garden, zipping forward. Suddenly reinvigorated, she ran after it, chasing it through doorways and down paths that extended through a far greater area than she'd imagined possible. Ioan and Dafydd came after her, catching up as her bright truthseeking path plunged into the earth and Lara stopped, frowning at it.

"No one said we'd need a shovel. The remembrance gardens in the Drowned Lands had a door, not a . . ."

"Barrow," Dafydd said softly.

Lara covered her mouth with one hand, cool shock splashing over her. It stood to reason, and yet she hadn't expected it. "Is digging the only way into a barrow?"

"There are often cairns atop them, which might be moved to reveal a door, but here . . ." Ioan trailed off, shaking his head, and Lara turned in a full circle, examining the garden segment for anything that might be a door.

"Truth will find the hardest path. Well, going through the dirt is hardest, all right. I should have been looking for . . . the key?" Warbling music played, the concept neither wrong nor right. Lara kept it in mind, sour notes dancing as she studied the garden a second time. "There must be something."

"Must there be?" Dafydd sounded interested and amused. "Why?"

"Because I have a hard time imagining any Seelie digging up six feet of dirt to get into a stasis chamber, and if you were hiding people there, you wouldn't want to call in servants to do the job. Secrets only stay secret if you keep them."

An amused voice said, "A truth very few people ever fully appreciate," as an old man tottered into the garden, a wry smile on his aged features.

"Oisín!" Lara ran to hug him, unsurprised that he caught her confidently for all that his eyes were filmed over, signal to the world that he couldn't see. She had never made friends quickly or easily, but the ancient poet had found a place in her heart the first and only time they'd met. "You're still here!"

"I'm too old and fragile to run, even from a war that comes within the citadel walls. The lands have watched over me," he said genially.

Lara released him and stepped back, smiling. "Emyr said the Barrow-lands liked you."

"Only he sounded it a curse when he said it," Oisín guessed. "My long years here have never enamored him of me."

"Unlikely," Dafydd murmured, "when my mother was so fond of you. I'm glad to see you're well, Oisín. Do you remember my brother Ioan?"

"Better than he remembers me, I dare say." Oisín turned an un-erring blind gaze on Ioan. "Changed in body but not in heart, I think. Welcome home, Ioan ap Caerwyn."

"Ap Annwn," Ioan murmured. "My dreams are for this land as a whole, not the white citadel alone."

"As you will." Oisín looked back at Lara, putting a hand out for her to take. "And you have grown greatly in power since we first spoke. Have you met another prophet?"

Lara breathed a laugh. "A human one. It started out the same way, 'truth will seek the hardest path, measures that must mend the past,' but then she said 'breaker who restores the land, keeps the world gates well in hand.' I don't know what it means. I don't like prophe-cies, Oisín."

"Nor fairy tales," he agreed, and Lara ducked her head to mutter the already-familiar refrain: "And yet here I am, in one." More clearly, she said, "This was always going to happen, wasn't it? You sent Dafydd to Earth looking for a truthseeker who would break the world. If he found me, or any truthseeker, I was always going to be a catalyst for change here. Oisín, my power is strengthening, but I just don't know if it's going to mature fast enough for me to do what's necessary."

Oisín, serenely confident, said, "It will. Begin by locating the key for the door, Wayfinder. I'm far too old to be digging in the dirt, and these two, as you surmised, are far too elfin."

Vague insult crossed Dafydd's face, though not Ioan's. Lara laughed as she closed her eyes again, this time trusting her power over the garden's lullaby. "Truthseeker, wayfinder, worldbreaker. I don't think I like titles very much either, but since I don't even know if we can get in there without the right key, I think this *is* the only way. Maybe it just takes a little more delicacy than laying down a true path."

A memory of the lights she'd followed in the Drowned Lands came back to her, fireflies rather than beacons. They were more inquisitive than the truthseeking paths, which bolted hither and yon with great integrity but no subtlety. In some cases that was perfect, but in the green-growing gardens, more gentle means seem called for. Dozens of tiny bells rang with delighted tones as firefly lights scattered behind her eyelids, flitting from one spot to another around the gardens.

More than once, urgency came into their chimes, then faded, as if they found things of interest but not exactly what they sought. The garden seemed littered with those things, and Lara's heart hopped with interest, wondering what treasures might lie forgotten in a place so old as this one. If all went well, she would have time to discover them later.

And if all didn't, the Barrow-lands themselves might be lost to eternity. Lara shivered at the thought and her seeking magic redoubled its efforts, sparks of light clearly agitated at the idea of such loss. Reflecting Lara's own emotions, she realized, which could become dangerous if not controlled. Bad enough a truthseeker could make a thing true by commanding it, but if her magic rolled over into making things true because she *felt* them, she could wreak havoc without ever meaning to.

The staff, largely quiet over the past few days, thumped with appreciation for the idea. Lara bared her teeth and it went silent again as glints of truthseeking magic discovered and hovered over Aerin a little while, considering her as the answer to their search. Ultimately they slipped away again, but with more purpose, as if something about the sleeping woman triggered recognition. Within a few more minutes, the dancing lights swarmed into another segment of the garden, and music fell into place in Lara's mind, creating a symphony.

The remembrance garden was laid out in a mirror-image to itself, with the entrance at the center. Lara saw it from above, as if the sparks of her magic flew upward to show it to her. She stood with Dafydd and the others inside the whorl of one elegant pattern, and across the garden, in its opposite place, stood a small stone cairn, no more than a dozen rocks piled neatly atop one another. Lara squeaked, "Ioan!" and thrust a finger after her magic, sending him into a run led by firefly lights. Lara spun to watch the grass where her truthseeking path had ended, but even expecting it, she let go a yelp of surprise when, after a few minutes, it crumbled to reveal an earthen pathway.

Propelled by her own yell, she leapt down the path, leaving impressions in dirt as she ran into a chamber darker, earthier, and emptier than the sanctuary within the Drowned Lands.

Emptier, but not empty.

Hafgan stood over Emyr, an uplifted blade in his hand.

Thirty-two

Later she realized that her truthseeker's voice, the one that could command things to be true, would have been the safest and most effective way to prevent regicide. But she was already in motion, rushing down the pathway like a child at play, and in the moment, it didn't occur to her to stop.

Lara flung herself at Hafgan's midriff, momentum carrying an impact that her slight weight otherwise could not. She hit hard enough to earn a grunt from both of them, and caught a glimpse of metal as Hafgan's blade fell away. They crashed into the wall, soft earth indenting with the impact. Lara staggered back, astonished at herself, and spun with the brunt of a blow she never saw coming.

Breath was knocked from her lungs as she hit the earth. The left side of her face bloomed with pain, new bursts building on the last. She couldn't see, tears spilling from wide-open eyes to dampen the earth beneath her face. She'd thought migraines had accustomed her to head pain, but the tight bands and bright lights of those headaches were nothing like the deep throbbing ache in her cheekbone. Still blind with tears, she worked her fingers toward her face, searching for evidence that the bone was shattered. Nothing gave way, not in a manner that suggested ruined bone, though the flesh was already swelling.

Hafgan, wheezing with outrage, grabbed her hair and hauled her head back, dagger flashing in her vision as he brought it to her throat. Lara gurgled and vicious pleasure twisted the Unseelie king's voice as he spat, "*Truthseekers.* Blights on the land, meant to be eradicated."

The dagger jerked, and bewilderingly, Hafgan was abruptly no longer above her. New pain ripped over Lara's scalp. She howled and curled herself in a ball, fingers exploring her head and coming away bloody.

Dafydd crashed to his knees and lifted her against his chest. "I'm sorry, I'm so terribly sorry, you're all right now, you're safe. You're safe, Lara. I have you now. It's all right."

Astonishingly, impossibly, every word sang with truth, their music quiet but determined, like the opening strains to a marching song. Nothing would stand in their way, as if Dafydd were determined to make them true if they weren't already. As if he commanded her power, which he had named a curse as much as a gift. "Your poor hair. I'm so sorry, Lara. I'm so sorry."

The apology made sense of her bloody fingers, of her skull's thick raging pain. A handful of hair had been pulled out, leaving a messy oozing patch of skin and broken roots. Lara blinked again, trying to clear tears away, and raised her head to see Hafgan slumped against Emyr's bier, a shining sword jammed through his shoulder.

Lara's sword, the one she'd been given to ride into battle with, and had inadvertently brought to her own world weeks ago. She gaped at it, comprehension beyond her, and finally transferred the stare to Dafydd, who smiled fragilely. "It was at Kelly's apartment. I

took it when we left the bedroom. It needed only a very light glamour to hide it, when no one expected me to have it at all, and I
thought we might be well-off with a hidden weapon. I'm so sorry I
wasn't quicker, Lara. I'm so very sorry."

"You were quick enough." Her voice sounded like someone
else's, strained with pain and tears. "I don't like this, Dafydd. I *hate*
this. I'm a tailor. I'm not supposed to get beaten up and almost killed
and..." Lara strangled the protest before it turned to convulsive
sobs, but Dafydd gathered her close, mouth careful against her hair,
and pain-laden fear drove her to tears after all.

"I wouldn't have asked you to join me if I'd known it would come
to this." Weary regret, but no lies, were in the confession. "Before
we went to war, before Ioan asked you to find the truth of a long-
dead land, yes, I would have still asked, but not this, Lara. This is
more than I would ever have asked, even if it meant my eternal exile
in your world."

Lara gulped air, trying to steady herself. "Somehow that makes
me feel better. And makes me more determined to see this all
through."

The words were stronger than she was: Lara remained curled
against Dafydd's side. Most of her head throbbed, the stickiness in
her hair increasing with each pulse, and her cheek felt like it had
doubled in size while she wept. There were other biers scattered
around the small earthen room, and for a few long moments she
considered simply climbing onto one of them and sleeping until she
was well again. That was nominally the chamber's purpose, though
Hafgan had been uninjured when he entered the similar room in the
Drowned Lands. It seemed they could simply be used for rest and
stasis as well.

"Is he dead?" Ioan's voice interrupted her musings before she
mustered the energy to approach the biers.

"Hafgan?" Dafydd shook his head above Lara's. "No. After all this trouble, it seemed foolish to strike him down, though the temptation still remains. If he's conscious, he may even have cauterized the wound by now, and be waiting on us to make some small error upon which he can capitalize."

"How did he even get in here? The cairn wasn't opened, or knocked over, or whatever you had to do to trigger the chamber opening." Lara craned her head toward Ioan, surprised she could move that much.

"There's a magic built into the cairn, something old and strong. Rhiannon's, maybe. I stood and watched as, once taken apart, the stones rolled together again and rebuilt themselves."

Lara put her forehead against Dafydd's chest carefully and mumbled, "That sounds like something out of a fairy tale. Oh, my head hurts. You know, we're lucky he tried to kill me instead of just grabbing the staff. It might be all over now if he'd done that."

"An oversight I will not make again." Hafgan, pale with pain, lifted his head and reached for the hilt of the sword pinning him to Emyr's bier.

His features contorted as he tried to free the blade, but he lacked the leverage and the strength to pull it out. Lara almost admired that he even tried. She hurt badly enough herself that moving much was still nearly inconceivable, without having a length of metal still jammed through her body.

Dafydd, less admiring, rose and crossed to crouch before the Unseelie king, his hand just above Hafgan's on the short hilt. "An oversight you won't have the opportunity to make again. Don't be a fool, Hafgan. Try to escape and I may not be inclined to let you wake a second time. I have the Truthseeker here, and I doubt your state of consciousness will matter to her ability to gather answers from you. Ioan, help me."

Ioan took a handful of quick steps across the room before fully realizing he'd obeyed without question. He slowed, obviously annoyed, then hunched his shoulders and went to Dafydd's side. Lara laughed, sparking a new wash of dull pain through her, but humor gave her the strength to stand. She would do no one any good huddled on the floor, and had an idea of what Dafydd intended.

He nodded once as if in warning, then withdrew the blade from Hafgan's shoulder and dropped it on the floor. The Unseelie king went white, making a sound so sharp it couldn't reach the volume of a roar. He retained a hold on consciousness, but barely, and when the princes heaved together to lift him from the earth, his head fell back, somnolence claiming him again.

They put him on the bier closest to Emyr's, dark king and fair lying head to head. Lara took a few unsteady steps toward the unconscious kings, digging into herself for resolve and for magic.

"A step closer," Merrick ap Annwn murmured, "and she dies."

She dies seemed an unlikely way to phrase it, though the Unseelie prince's voice was silken with truth. *You* die, Lara thought; that would make more sense, and that was what made her turn toward Merrick in puzzlement, despite the threat to her life.

Not hers, she understood an instant later. Not hers at all.

Merrick stood on the earthen rampway with Aerin wedged in his arms. Her eyes were glazed, more than just the exhaustion of extended magic use. Merrick had one arm around her throat and the other under one of her arms so he could grasp his own wrist, giving her no room to maneuver. The muscle playing in his arms said he put pressure on her throat, rendering her into a state of semiconsciousness.

She didn't so much as claw at him, suggesting he'd caught her entirely by surprise. Had caught her sleeping, no doubt, and recognized her as the valuable hostage she was. Lara took a breath to whisper "Let her go," and Merrick's grip on the Seelie woman tightened. Lara raised her hands, placating, and pressed her lips together to seal off any threat of using her voice against him.

"Of all of us in this room," Dafydd murmured, "Aerin is the one you least want dead, Merrick. My brother," he said even more softly, an ache in the words. "Merrick, how can this have come to be?"

"How else could it have come to be? Sons are nothing to immortal fathers. What power is there but that which we seize ourselves? Step away from them," Merrick ordered. "I thought keeping Emyr alive would draw my father here, but I had no idea I would find all the royal blood of Annwn gathered in one room. I was meant to be long-since rid of you. The human world should have destroyed all of you by now."

"And it might well have, had we not had a truthseeker at our side." Dafydd took a few steps forward, his hands spread wide and empty. "Let Aerin go. Pitch your battle with me instead. I think you owe me that much, for having me branded a murderer and traitor among my own people."

"I owe you nothing. I owe *none* of you anything at all." Merrick's grip on Aerin's throat tightened and what little support she'd been able to offer herself slipped away as she went boneless.

Lara whispered, "May I speak?"

Merrick's gaze sharpened on her. "If you watch your words."

Lara nodded once, a promise as binding as language, and breathed a silent prayer that her conjecture would prove right. "You have almost everything you want. You kept Emyr alive to draw Hafgan here, maybe, but there's more to it, isn't there? Emyr was Rhiannon's husband and that might make him first heir to this land. You can't be sure what happens if he dies, so he has to be kept alive, here in a stasis room. You must have known it was here from stories of the Drowned Lands, and knowing how closely twinned they were with the Barrow-lands. That was clever. More clever than anyone else has been."

A flash of smug pride lit Merrick's face, and for a moment she could see his father in his narrow features. He was handsome, as they all were, though anger and pride marred the lines of his face, and the breadth of shoulder that so suited Ioan and Hafgan was less filled out in the Unseelie prince. He wore that like a wound itself, his physicality a little less than those around him, and therefore, she suspected, his need to be praised all the greater.

It seemed a lifetime ago that Lara had made suits and coats for similar men in her own world; arrogant with wealth but always hungry for compliments. It helped that Merrick *had* been clever, that his plans were well-laid and his deceptions layered, so that truth could align with what she needed to say. "And now you have Emyr and Hafgan both where you need them to be. Resting here, where they'll lie undisturbed and unawakening while you rule. It's only Rhiannon's sons in the way now."

"I was her son, too," Merrick insisted, full of childish defiance. "She died saving me. Who would do that for another than her own son?"

There was enough conviction, enough truth, in his voice to draw Lara up. She cast a glance at the supine Hafgan, wondering: no one had mentioned *his* wife, or Merrick's mother. "Níamh died birthing him," Ioan murmured on cue.

The name struck Lara like a gong, music reverberating through her. A professor of Irish studies had mentioned her as another queen of fairyland, a thing Lara had never thought to pursue. "Who was she?"

"Rhiannon's sister. Another of Llyr's daughters, but not the goddess of Annwn. She came to us after Rhiannon made this world, and lived in it as her sister did."

Lara, unwisely, said, "No wonder they hated you," to Merrick. "To cost them Níamh and Rhiannon both, no wonder they hated you. And no wonder you're looking to make your own mark," she added hastily as his expression blackened. "You have nothing else, do you? Only your own worth, which needs to be proved to fathers and cousins who see you as nothing more than the vessel which took their wives and mothers."

Clanging objection slammed through the words, making her head hurt more, though the truth she spoke was, Lara thought, very close to the one Merrick believed. The rage and hurt on his face spoke to that.

She stepped aside with as careless a gesture as she could make. "They tell me truthseekers were the arbiters of justice in Annwn, once upon a time. This is my arbitration, then: defeat Emyr's heir in single combat, and I will name you king over all these lands."

Dafydd gave her one shocked look, and then Merrick cast Aerin away and came toward him in a swarm of swords.

Thirty-three

Lara shrieked a useless protest as two blades glittered in Merrick's hands. She'd seen the sword at his hip, but not the long dagger on the other, where Aerin's slumped form had hidden it. Bad enough that she'd thrown Dafydd into combat against one blade when he didn't have one in hand himself, but two seemed egregiously unfair.

Dafydd flung himself to the side, rolling through soft dirt to come up with the blade he'd discarded. Merrick was there in an instant, raining downward blows as Dafydd struggled to regain his feet. Merrick scored a glancing scrape against Dafydd's forearm and he swore, giving up trying to rise and instead hatchet-kicking the side of Merrick's knee. It popped and he gave a shriek as loud as Lara's, dropping his weight to the other knee. Dafydd rolled up, and for the space of a breath they fought on their knees, too close to do much more than batter one another with their sword hilts. Dafydd punched Merrick in the diaphragm with his free hand, then skittered back, regaining his feet as Merrick wheezed.

Lara slipped around the outer edge of the chamber, kneeling at Aerin's side to check her breathing. She did, shallowly, and her color was returning. Ioan shot Lara a sharp look from beyond the contestants, and she nodded, earning mixed relief and chagrin from the elder Seelie prince. He worked his way around the room from the other direction, moving slowly so he would distract the combatants as little as possible.

Merrick surged to his feet again, though he limped on the left side now. That was the side he carried the dagger on, too: less reach and more vulnerability, Lara thought. Dafydd saw it as well, and feinted, but no more than that. Merrick brought the dagger up in an effective block, and Dafydd fell back again, nodding as though the entire action had been a test. He dropped his guard as he did so and Merrick lurched forward, driving his sword toward Dafydd in a desperate thrust.

Dafydd leapt aside, nimble enough to remind Lara that Dickon had once commented on his unearthly grace. With a sweeping step, Dafydd rebounded off the side of Emyr's bier. He crashed on top of Merrick, body weight bearing the other man to the ground, then slammed an elbow against the back of Merrick's neck. Merrick roared, driving himself upward, but Dafydd was gone again, this time running for the chamber's far side. He vaulted Emyr's bier and disappeared, then came up again armed as Merrick was: a short sword in one hand and a long dagger in the other.

Merrick's gaze, comical with offense, snapped to Lara for an instant before he turned his attention back to Dafydd. Lara pressed her hands against her mouth, fighting down a frantic laugh. She'd forgotten the blade Hafgan had almost killed her with. The battle suddenly was matched, neither scion having the weaponry advantage.

"What were you *thinking?*" Ioan hissed at Lara's elbow.

She startled, having almost forgotten him, too. "I couldn't think of any other way to get him to let go of Aerin without killing her. I thought if I gave him a chance to get what he really wanted—"

"Did it occur to you Dafydd might *lose?*"

"Obviously not!"

They both fell silent, Ioan dragging Aerin closer to the back wall. The Seelie took a deeper breath, beginning to wake as Dafydd and Merrick met again. Lara knew too little about swordplay to follow their fight clearly: to her it was a rush of sound, full of its own music, and of brilliant flares as weapons scraped off one another and flashed again in fresh attacks. Neither of them scored marks against the other. The scrape on Dafydd's arm was the only drawn blood.

Sudden quiet exploded through the chamber as the combatants dropped back, the only sound their harsh breathing. Frustration twisted Merrick's face, and after a moment of panting he muttered, "We were always well-matched."

"In arms skill. Not in duplicity. I could capitulate and you could fight Ioan instead."

Hope leapt in Lara's heart, not for Dafydd's safety, but because Ioan was the superior swordsman. Merrick sneered. "The Truthseeker said to defeat Emyr's heir. We both know Ioan forsook that role when he embraced the Unseelie path."

"And yet you wore his guise to take the Seelie throne. I look forward to that unmasking, *brother.*"

Merrick's lip curled again, and the respite was over, both princes coming at one another in a blur of motion that made the same kind of song that Lara had heard upon riding to battle with the Seelie army. There was a purity in combat, a focus that stripped everything else away. Kill or be killed; survive or die. It wasn't beautiful, but it was honest, and a part of her wanted to rest inside that music, confident that its truth would hold her until the song's violent end.

Closing her eyes to the battle, though, would make it no less real.

Lara huddled uncomfortably against the chamber wall, the staff pressing into her spine, and stifled a cry when one of Merrick's blades came alarmingly close to Dafydd's throat.

Even watching intently, she almost didn't see the blow that ended the fight, and even in reconstruction, she hardly knew how it had been done. Dafydd lost his footing on the soft floor, and in the same instant Merrick disarmed him, knocking the sword out of his hand. His remaining dagger simply lacked the reach: Lara could see that, and the gasp she drew in was cold with horror.

Merrick lunged, thrusting downward with his sword, and Dafydd twitched his dagger upward.

It slid easily into Merrick's belly, just beneath the breastbone. Momentum kept him falling forward, but his grip went boneless and he dropped his own dagger, clutching his stomach instead.

Dafydd rolled to the side, avoiding Merrick's collapse, and came to his feet with an expression of ancient sorrow.

Merrick, on his knees, said, "You've killed me," in pure astonishment, and Dafydd watched him fall before murmuring, "In all likelihood, yes."

Ioan, voice strange, said, "That was well done. I think I could not have done it myself."

"We were too well-matched." Dafydd stepped on Merrick's blade, then bent to pick it up, turning it this way and that to see where blood made dirt stick to the metal. "We've fought practice bouts our entire lives. It was necessary to do something he wouldn't expect."

"What do you mean?" Lara's hands were ice cold, so numb she could barely turn them into fists. "What did you do?"

"The slip was deliberate," Ioan said, still with the note of strain. "It's difficult to take a fall like that without making it obvious it's a feint. Especially if you know your fight partner well."

Sickness boiled up in Lara's stomach, washing away the cold in a burst of heat. *"Deliberate?* I thought you were—!" She couldn't say the word, not even after the fact, too afraid that speaking it aloud would somehow make it real.

Dafydd, less concerned with the power of words, said, "Dead? Yes. That was the idea," as if it were all a remote theoretical exercise. Then his eyes pressed shut and he took a shuddering breath before throwing Merrick's sword away. Lara lurched to her feet, crossing the small chamber in a matter of steps so she could crash into Dafydd's arms and hold him.

He staggered with the impact, but caught her and lowered his head over her ruined hair. "I'm all right. I believe you may have lost your mind, but I'm all right despite that. Mortal combat, Lara? What happened to my gentle tailor? I thought you would talk him out of his madness."

Lara laughed against his chest, a shaky sound. "He would have killed Aerin if I'd tried. I could hear it in his voice. Aerin." She looked toward Ioan and the Seelie woman, and Ioan gave her a brief, encouraging smile as Aerin took another sharp breath. Lara exhaled until her lungs were empty, then inhaled again to speak with relief. "There was only one thing he wanted badly enough to not kill her, and that was the crown. Dafydd, I'm so sorry. I know he was your—"

"Brother," Dafydd finished. "In all ways that mattered. At least his death is a matter of clear battle now, rather than foul murder. Though I'm not certain simply producing a body will endear me to my people. They already think he's dead by my hand."

"Not dead." Ioan had moved while they spoke, rolling Merrick's unmoving form over. Red bubbles formed at the Unseelie prince's mouth, and once silence fell, Lara could hear his short, wet gasps as Ioan said, grimly, "He lives, if barely. Dafydd?"

Dafydd looked to Lara, whose heart thudded heavily. "Why me?"

"Truthseeker, wayfinder, worldbreaker. Arbiter of justice. You said defeat me, and he has failed in that. You didn't say kill or be killed, and so his fate must lie in the decision you now make."

"Kill him." Aerin spoke hoarsely, but without remorse. She pushed herself upright against the wall, feeling cautiously at her throat even as she threw a hateful look at Merrick. "He'll never be anything but trouble."

Truth, almost unquestionable, swept through her accusation. Only a note or two sounded off, one instrument among many in an orchestra, but it was enough to give Lara pause.

Not Dafydd, though; untouched by music, his shoulders dropped with weary acknowledgment "I'm afraid Aerin's right. The ambitious rarely let failure stop them. His next game might be worse still."

"Worse than attempted regicide, homicide, fratricide?" Lara ticked the crimes off on her fingers. "Worse than throwing the Seelie and Unseelie nations into war that could still wipe out both sides? The only thing worse would be if he succeeded. Right now there's no chance of that, not with the condition he's in. Put him on a bier."

The elves exchanged nonplussed glances, Aerin's expression bitterest of all. It was she who put the obvious into words, voice flat with disbelieving anger: "What?"

Lara shook her head, determination rising in the face of Aerin's disapproval. "If I'm going to break a world and rebuild it, I'm not starting out with blood on my hands, not if I can help it. I don't care how wrong he's been. Maybe it's not any better to put someone in a stasis chamber forever than it is to kill them, but maybe this place can heal his . . . soul," she finished awkwardly. It was the wrong word for a people whose immortality was physical, not spiritual, but she didn't have a better one.

Dafydd and Ioan looked at one another again, and Ioan turned a palm up, gesturing to Merrick's body. "You asked the truthseeker for her justice. Will you now ignore it?"

Bemused, Dafydd said, "No," and crouched to help Ioan lift Merrick onto one of the biers.

Lara's shoulders unknotted as he came to rest. "Maybe it can heal the broken places inside him as well as his body. If not, at least here he can't hurt anyone."

"A gentler prison than your world offers," Dafydd said. "I think we have very little time to seal this room again, else he'll die despite our noblest efforts."

"Great." Magic objected to sarcasm. Lara winced an apology as she went to help Aerin up and nodded toward Emyr and Hafgan. "All right. Neither of them are dying. Let's bring them up into the garden, and then we'll break the world."

Oisín awaited them in the garden, his genial presence so unexpected that Lara stumbled on seeing him. Humor flashed over Oisín's wrinkled face. "I may be nimble for a blind man, but exploring caves and earthen chambers is more daring than I'm inclined to at my age."

Dafydd laid Emyr out on the grass with a grunt, then looked up at Oisín with good-natured suspicion. "Are you sure you're blind, Oisín? No one said anything."

"People say as much with their breath and their feet as they do with their lips and faces," the old poet replied. "I've had a long time to learn those languages. You've found the sleeping king?"

Lara gave him a questioning look. "Emyr, not Arthur. Even I know that mythology."

"And I do not. Your sleeping Arthur must be a story from after my time, Truthseeker. Perhaps one day you'll share it with me. For now, who else do we have here?"

"My father Hafgan." Ioan put Hafgan on the grass beside Emyr, earning a groan for his efforts: Emyr slept, but Hafgan had only been injured, not sealed away in the chamber for healing.

Lara glanced toward the pathway they'd taken below the earth, unsurprised to see it filling itself in again, grass growing back over the door leading downward. Rhiannon's magic, Ioan had said, and if so, it was more consistent, stronger even millennia after her death, than any other magic Lara had seen worked. It left behind no broken afterimages, no headache-inducing wrongnesses. Her will was made manifest, and Lara, disconcertingly, found herself accepting that the legendary Seelie woman was a goddess indeed.

"Ah." Oisín stood and went to the two kings, kneeling between them. "Both halves of the whole. There is a story here, Truthseeker, if you wish to seek it out."

Lara smiled, though it made the swollen bruise on her cheek hurt. "Storytelling's your business."

"And truthseeking is yours. Together we might tell a tale such as man has never known, and elfkind has long since forgotten."

"I am desperate to hear that tale," Ioan said in a low voice. "I've waited for it more years than I know how to recall."

Oisín, with the grandiosity of a conductor, gestured to Hafgan. "Take his hand, then, and Dafydd, you take Emyr's. Aerin, will you join us?"

Aerin crawled toward them and sat hard at Dafydd's side, losing every evidence of grace as she did so. "I would be loathe to miss it."

"Truthseeker?"

Lara joined them, sitting cross-legged like a tailor at Hafgan and Emyr's heads. Oisín gave her a beatific smile that faded into sorrowful caution. "Now is the time to wield that staff, Lara."

Heart pounding, Lara loosened the staff from its bindings. Its anticipation outweighed hers, churning her stomach until she was ill, but she held it out parallel to the ground, focusing on the blind man beyond its intricate carvings. "What now?"

Oisín wrapped his ancient fists around the ivory. Recognition leapt in the weapon, a thrill of delight utterly at odds with anything else Lara had felt from it. Oisín smiled and whispered something too soft for Lara to hear, though the sense of it was a greeting, and then lifted his unseeing gaze to hers. "Place it across Emyr and Hafgan's chests, Truthseeker, and do your calling. Seek answers from millennia past, and if you three would see and hear the story told, grasp the staff as well, when she puts it to them. Do not let go." Urgency colored the old man's voice. "Whatever happens, *do not let go.*"

Murmurs of assent met his demand. Lara held the worldbreaking staff aloft, waiting for the subtle change in Oisín's grip that would say he was prepared to begin. After long seconds she felt a fractional relaxation of his muscles, and brought the staff down across Hafgan and Emyr's chests in a smooth motion. Ivory warmed with excitement as the three Seelie laid hands on it. Lara seized that enthusiasm and gave it a focus, mutating the words of the prophecies she'd heard: "Truth has sought the hardest path for measures that will mend the past. If finders know the only way, tell me how worlds came changed at end of day."

Gold ripped across the citadel, like the worldwalking spell turned the size of the land. The Barrow-lands folded around them, inverted, and spat them out its other side.

Thirty-four

"You are not here," Oisín whispered in Lara's ear, but he wasn't there when she looked for him. She retained a reassuring grip on the staff, but she was otherwise alone under a healing sky. Gold leached away, leaving a growing streak of blue behind, as if someone wove fabric together at an impossible speed to create a picture and hide what had been there before.

There was a wrongness about the streak across the sky; a wrongness that she'd felt time and again with the worldwalking spell, only much greater. The worldwalking spell was a tiny breach, a tear that even she could put to rights if she wanted to. The magic stitching itself together above her was primeval in its strength.

And its music was relentless. Like the earth's song, it rang in deep tones that stretched so far that Lara couldn't hear a beginning or an end to even one note, much less the entire symphony. Only divinity could sing that song. Lara shivered, pulling her gaze from the sky to study the world around her.

Familiarity struck a hard chord of surprise within her. She stood on an ocean shore, silver-gray water idling in an elegant cove. Behind her, green mountains rose. There were no roads, no signs of farmers or civilization, but the valley was unquestionably the hidden home of the remaining Unseelie people.

A woman walked out of the sea, water streaming down her shoulders and turning to soft flowing robes of shimmering blue. Slicked-back hair dried with each step, until it crackled full and white and fell well past her hips. Aerin's hair had been like that, only somehow *less* so, as if this woman's were the ideal, and everyone else's a modest shadow.

This woman. As if there was any doubt that she was Rhiannon, Llyr's daughter and goddess of Annwn. She was slightly less alien than her father, but by comparison to her, the elfin races' exotic features seemed as blunt and thick as humans. She was porcelain to their stoneware, so beautiful that Lara's heart ached to look at her.

"None of us are here," Oisín's disembodied voice whispered, rich with sorrow. "We can only observe, and change nothing. Remember that, even when you would act."

Time sped forward, Rhiannon exploring Annwn. At first she was clearly pleased, but as she explored, loneliness came over her. She returned to stand at the ocean's shore like the little mermaid forbidden her home. In time she picked up a white sliver of shell from the beaches and split her palm open.

Where drops of blood fell, Annwn's people sprang up. From sea-pale to earth-dark, they grew fast and tall and strong, denizens of the earth and of Rhiannon's blood. Two among them were easily recognizable: Hafgan and Emyr, who laid eyes first on Rhiannon, and then on each other. Ice and fire snapped through the salt-laden air, and a rivalry was born that had not yet found its end.

Rhiannon cast aside her slivered shell, and took no notice when

Emyr and Hafgan both stooped for it, nor when they broke it apart
and each secreted a piece safely away, physical symbols of the day of
their creation.

Time rushed forward again. Rhiannon's children multiplied and
spread across the land. Rhiannon's mother Caillech sent rain and
warmth to soften the land as Kerne, god of the earth, taught them
the ways of agriculture and of shaping stone and wood to build their
homes. Others of the old gods passed through Annwn as teachers,
then faded away.

Rhiannon herself worked among the Seelie and flitted between
Emyr and Hafgan like a butterfly from flower to flower. She saw
nothing of the dark looks they exchanged, though many of the
Seelie over whom she ruled did.

One by one, over centuries, over millennia, the elders, the first of
Rhiannon's blood, died. There were accidents, there was weariness,
there were fights between individuals that turned to doom, until
almost none of them were left. Emyr and Hafgan survived it all,
growing in power, growing in loathing. Rhiannon wandered to the
mortal world and back again, bringing dalliances and lovers with her
as she came and went.

Through it all, their jealousy grew. So did the citadels that were
their individual homes: Emyr's in the forests, and Hafgan's at the
sea, each of them like a peacock preening its feathers to attract
the mate they both wanted. They were all still Seelie, vibrant and
healthy as they lived and loved among each other, no one trend of
coloration setting them apart.

Rhiannon opened a worldwalking spell and was gone; gone long
enough that it became a lapse, then a gap, in the fast-forward history
of the world. Hafgan and Emyr each blamed the other for her disappearance, though she'd been inconstant ever. For the first time a
schism was born between forest and shore-dwellers. Emyr's forest-
folk claimed the name "Seelie" for themselves, degrading Hafgan's

faction to the "Unseelie," the unreal people. Individual dislikes became periodic skirmishes between groups. The land responded, encouraging one or the other. Lara heard confusion in its music, its uncertainty as it looked for a master with the strength and gentle confidence shown by Rhiannon.

By the time Rhiannon returned with a handsome mortal poet at her side, the rival kings had developed a taste for power.

It was in their eyes—in the way they watched her—and in the way the deference they'd once shown was now frayed. They were the last of the old ones, the last born direct of Rhiannon's blood, and there was no one but their queen and goddess to hold their ambitions in check. But her attention was all for the blue-eyed mortal who told tales of love and rue.

Bit by bit, Hafgan and Emyr slipped away from her.

Time slowed suddenly, events now unfolding at a pace that made words and motivations comprehensible. Hafgan and Emyr stood at a forest's edge, green growing up behind Emyr, the distant sea cool and protective behind Hafgan.

"She is lost to us," Hafgan said.

"She has never been ours. The *land* is lost to us while she remains. Which do you want more, Hafgan? The woman or the crown?"

There was no need to respond: the answer was in Hafgan's eyes. "Then she must be contained," Emyr said. "She has no children birthed of her own body, and only we two left born of her blood. Together we can control her. Forget the poet. She will marry us, one or the other, and the other will ask for another wife of Llyr's blood. For the good of the land, which is weaker than it was when Rhiannon's children walked it with her."

Hafgan looked thoughtful. "The truthseekers will never allow it."

"The truthseekers," Emyr said, "can be removed. A little time, a little patience, and I see no reason why they should stymie us. Rhiannon will be too charmed with the idea of birthing a child of her own to notice. One of us will be its father, and with the union we'll bind her power to ourselves."

"No. Not ourselves. I won't give you that advantage, if she should choose you." Hafgan palmed the sliver of shell from so long ago, blood still red and visible on its edge. "From the sea as she is, and wetted by her blood. Bind her to this, and we have a bargain."

Emyr reluctantly drew his own bit of shell and laid it alongside Hafgan's. For the first time in millennia, they sealed together again, a single white shard streaked with ancient blood. "It's not enough to contain her."

"It will be."

Once more, time leapt forward, hissing through decades as the rival brothers secretly, subtly, hunted down the truthseekers who were their world's arbiters of justice. Their deaths were violent; the abrupt end to their songs shocking Lara each time, though she couldn't look away.

At the same time, elsewhere, Rhiannon dallied with Oisín and flirted with the brother kings, until she was drawn away from the mortal poet by the enticing prospect of a child of her body. It was Emyr's bed she came to, perhaps inevitably; he had more of Llyr's pale look of the sea than Hafgan did, for all that he had made his realm the forests. Wedded, blissful, in love, Rhiannon gave herself up to the idea of bearing children, and Lara had a startling, piercing understanding of the elfin goddess's innocence. She had created a world capriciously, peopled it out of loneliness, left it time and again in search of new amusements. Through none of it had she become other than what she was: a child of the sea and earth, dedicated wholly to the moment, never thinking beyond the now.

Hafgan and Emyr were not so limited, and with each year that passed, they made her a little more their queen, and a little less their goddess.

It took the hindsight of centuries passing in moments to see it happen. To see how Rhiannon's radiance faded until she looked like one of the Seelie: exceptionally beautiful, but not heartbreakingly so. To see how her concern for the land became ever-more entwined with concern for the child growing within her, until that son was born and her attachment to Annwn became an attachment to him. With each small change, a little of what she was slipped away.

And Emyr gathered it, weaving it, commanding it, holding it in his palm. Shared it, year in and year out, with Hafgan. The shard passed from one brother to the other, and Rhiannon faltered and shrank and became less than she had been. Lara's heart pounded like a racehorse's as she leaned against time's constraints, desperate to warn Rhiannon of her fate.

Oisín did, even at the time. Still young, still handsome, but importantly, mortal and able to see treachery in a way that the stagnant Seelie could not. Rhiannon's fondness for him never faltered, but neither would she hear the prophecies he made, and he was helpless then as Lara was now, watching a goddess crumble.

Níamh came from the sea early in the brothers' plot, wedding Hafgan as Rhiannon married Emyr. She was fair and bright, like sunrise on the sea, and there was less of her to begin with than there had ever been to Rhiannon. Merrick's birth was her ending, and had perhaps been so since the moment she left the waters.

For the briefest moment, in the scant handful of years after Níamh's death, Rhiannon recovered some of what she had been, as if her sister's loss awakened the goddess within her. For a little while she was vivacious and full of laughter, fascinated by the boy she'd given birth to, doting on Oisín once more, and freshly delighted to find herself with child again.

Emyr, though, was displeased, and Hafgan furious. That sparked the exchange of firstborn children, the exchange that led, on all paths, to Lara entering the Barrow-lands herself.

In the distant past, Dafydd was born. Rhiannon faded again,

Emyr working hard to strip away the energies she expended in giving birth so they could never return to her. The magics reminded Lara of the worldwalking spell, setting in motion things that were never meant to be, but which were made possible by the very godhead whose power they stole. The shell was as long as his arm now, Rhiannon's bloodstain upon it still an indelible link between goddess and land.

The ending came in a rush, for all that Lara knew Rhiannon had only scant years to live once Dafydd was born; that she would drown in the sea saving Merrick, and everything would change for Annwn.

And it did, but not in the way Lara had imagined.

Rhiannon rushed into the water she'd come from, determined to save her sister's child. The sea was her birthplace, her home, and sudden raw strength roared through her, a reminder of what she'd been. Tumultuous song filled Lara until she felt like she might fly apart with it, but Rhiannon had no such fears. She gathered that power, remembering what it had been to be Annwn's goddess, and still within the sea, she pushed Merrick to shore on a wave of compassion and rage.

And there on the shore, at the edge of sea and sky and earth, Emyr drove the bloodied shell shard into sand; into the sea-laden earth at water's edge, and worked a magic to put all history to shame.

The pieces to make the spell were Rhiannon's, not his. The sea her father, the sky her mother, the blood her own, and so it was the magic of Annwn itself that Emyr commanded. But Annwn had no will of its own, and could only be directed.

Directed by a king, himself made of Rhiannon's blood, who was the closest thing to the goddess herself the land recognized.

Everything Rhiannon threw at the shore, her impotent anger, her desire to save Merrick, her memories of what she had been and what she might yet again be, came together at a single focal point. Emyr took them all in, draining Rhiannon of all the strength she might ever wield, and bound it in an item of power.

Lara opened her eyes, finally recognizing the rage within the staff as the terrible fury of a goddess confined.

Thirty-five

The others awakened more slowly. Dafydd and the other Seelie had unforgiving eyes for the sleeping kings, but Oisín, like Lara, gazed at the staff, grief aging his lined face even more deeply.

"You knew." Accusation was beyond Lara. The best she could manage was soft horror, and that was enough.

Pain spasmed across Oisín's features, but he nodded. "I suspected. The staff would not—will still not—abide the touch of royal hands. That, I think, was what drowned the lands, far more than any intent on their part." He made a small gesture toward the kings, and Dafydd stirred.

"Then you didn't see?"

Lara's stomach twisted. "See what?"

"How Emyr raised the staff and unleashed its magic on the valley. He meant to destroy Hafgan's court so Rhiannon's power was his alone. No wonder we think of the seas as killing. They took Rhiannon and the valley all in the same day."

"No." Lara shivered, looking around the gathering. "I didn't see that. I woke up when I realized what they'd done to Rhiannon. I thought the lands had drowned before she died. I thought..." She trailed off, not really doubting the truth in Dafydd's voice. History so old it became legend was hardly reliable, even for those who had lived it. Not even her magic could winnow falsehood from truth at such a remove. She was reminded of her world's stories of Robin Hood, none of which had ever satisfied her. Neither could this world's tales of drownings and retributions, not until now, with the story played out for all of them.

"I almost remember." Aerin's eyes were closed, her voice faint and distant. "I do remember she went into the water after Merrick. I remember that the sea rose up and cast him out. I do not... quite... remember that it kept coming, only that we took to the horses quickly, and rode hard. Dafydd had seen only a handful of summers. He rode with me. That, I remember. How can I forget that which I was witness to?"

"You were young," Oisín answered. "Young, and lied to, and memories slip into fog as time passes by. You're not to blame for forgetting, Aerin, though I, perhaps, am."

He took the staff from Lara, resting it across his lap, fingers light on its carved surface. "I wasn't at the ocean that day, but I recall that tremors shook the whole of the land until Emyr cast this away. My eyesight was failing by then, and I took it up, never certain of why its presence felt so familiar. I imagined it to be my Rhiannon, returned from the sea, but I am a poet. Pretty stories are my trade."

"I must have known Emyr had it when we left the shore that day. It always reminded me of my mother. Why did you refuse to give it to me?" Dafydd asked.

"Because you were too young to stand against Emyr, and the staff would have asked it of you."

Lara gave Oisín a bemused look. "It doesn't *ask* for anything."

"It would have, of Dafydd. Of her son."

"Ioan's her son, too, and it was ready to burn through him and obliterate Boston!"

"But we were right." Ioan spoke for the first time, interrupting Oisín's drawn breath. He gestured at the staff, though he made no effort to actually touch it. "Emyr drowned the Unseelie lands. My people have been done wrong by, Truthseeker. Will you help us now?"

Lara, sourly, said, "Hafgan isn't exactly innocent of wrongdoing himself," but wiped her words and tone away with a movement of her hand. "It's not your peoples' fault, though. It's these two. The kings who are the last of Rhiannon's blood."

"Not the last. Ioan and Dafydd are as much her blood as any of the firstborns," Aerin objected. "Give them their fathers' crowns, if the Barrow-lands need kings."

Lara breathed a laugh. "Just like that? Depose Emyr, to whom you've been unswervingly loyal?"

Aerin shrugged, obviously untroubled by the notion. "He has never deserved it. The dishonor is not mine, nor any of those who served him. No one will doubt the truth when you tell it to them, and minds will be changed. We don't cling to the past. If we did, someone would have clear memories about Rhiannon's fate."

"Is it that simple?" Lara asked with real curiosity. "Humans would complicate it. We'd question their loyalty, question the ambition of the sons who will become kings. We'd wonder if we'd been tricked. Somebody would form resistance cells, even if most believed the right thing had happened."

"There will be resistance and anger. We've fought for . . . ever." Aerin smiled and Lara smiled back, hearing no mistruth in the phrase. "But no one will disbelieve you. Not with Dafydd's return from the dead and with Emyr's sleeping but living body here, and not with Merrick unmasked and alive. The evidence is in truth's favor, even if we lacked a truthseeker to speak it, but we're a people of magics, Truthseeker. With you to bear the news, there may be opposition, but there will be no doubt. Perhaps it's an advantage we have over humans."

"Maybe it is. I'll try," Lara said to Ioan. "Of course I'll try to raise the lands. I've said that all along. But what are we going to do with these two?"

"Put them with Merrick in the chamber below. It'll keep them out of trouble until we have a better idea." Dafydd stood, gaze still grim as he studied the sleeping kings. Then he left the garden nook abruptly, and a few minutes later the entrance to the chamber cave open again. Ioan waved off Aerin's help, carrying first Hafgan, then Emyr, to the biers below, and the four of them remaining walked together to meet Dafydd at the remembrance gardens' entrance.

"The citadel is still filled with Unseelie. Shall we play at prisoners again to make our escape?" Aerin sounded resigned, but Oisín made a dismissive noise.

"The Truthseeker can open a way to the stables for us. No one will see us coming or going."

"The Truthseeker will what?" Lara's eyebrows shot up, despite the serene confidence in Oisín's voice. "Oisín, I only made a walkable pathway with the staff's help!"

"You made a very fine path out of the forest the very night I met you," Oisín disagreed. "You need not cross chasms, Lara, only make a road from here to there visible to your companions alone. Or did you think following truth's path would mean leaving us all behind? That would be lonely indeed."

Lara put both hands to her head, as if the act could physically hold in her feelings of astonishment. "I can make roads the people with me can see but no one else can?"

Oisín pursed his lips. "A wayfinder would be of little use if she could not. I wonder at times if that's how the very first roads between our world and Annwn were created, by wayfinders in search of new roads."

"I thought that was a magic of the land. That only royalty could . . ." Lara trailed off, putting her hands over her face. "Except I did open a way between worlds. Maybe other wayfinders always could, but only the blood of the land has been able to since they were massacred. Assuming wayfinders and truthseekers are always the same. Are they?"

"It has been far too many millennia since either have walked this world for us to know. Now," Oisín said gently, "open a pathway, Lara. Bring us to the stables, so we might go to the shore where this story began, and bring it to an end."

They were a motley enough group, Lara thought, all of them wind-whipped and weary from a ride that had taken more hours, even on distance-eating horseback, than she could count. Aerin had frowned at the earth time and again, muttering about its discomfort, and when Lara reached for its rich music, she found shards and tones of dissonance, its song gone wrong.

"No one is guiding it," she'd finally realized aloud. "It's been listening to Emyr and Hafgan for aeons, and now they're both asleep. The magic isn't working as well as it should."

"I've been Annwn's king for centuries," Ioan protested. "Shouldn't it hear me?"

"Emyr and Hafgan stole the power to make it hear them, and they literally rose from the earth and from Rhiannon's blood. I don't think just being her son and wearing a crown will do the job, Ioan."

They rode in silence after that, Lara searching out glimmers of true paths to help the horses cross the land, but even so, the journey was exhausting. Aerin, already worn to the bone, looked emaciated by the time she slid from her horse and leaned heavily against its side on the unwelcoming shore.

The seas were heavy, rolling slate gray and foamy white against shifting sands. The sky spat cold rain as if trying to drive Lara and the others back into the valley. Song turned against itself, disharmony in the clash of thunder and lightning. Lara bent beneath its clamor, trying to find the soothing slow notes that were a land at peace, and finding herself pummeled and headachy instead.

"Shh, shh. I can't think, I can't make sense of anything with all the noise." The complaint was whispered into uncaring wind, words snatched away. Lara pressed her fingertips against her temples, struggling to concentrate. There was a truth buried deep in the land, the truth of Rhiannon's deposal and of the slow corruption that had changed Annwn to the Barrow-lands. Rhiannon's truth, her story, had been drowned, but it could be lifted again and Annwn set right, if Lara could only hear its song through the storm.

"You'll need this." Oisín offered her the staff, warmth from his hands still marking the ivory as she took it. "Not even a truthseeker can raise the lands without Rhiannon's help."

"I can't." She had learned so much, come so far, but this truth was a stark and simple one. "I can only just manage to control it when things are stable, and this is chaos. I've used the staff here before and nearly destroyed everything. I don't know how to master it in the middle of a storm."

"Dafydd will help you." Oisín fell back a few steps, gesturing to the blond Seelie prince.

He looked, Lara thought, very much as he had the day she'd met him. His clothes were different, no more slim-cut suit and long raincoat, but the Unseelie garb he wore added enough breadth to his shoulders to remind her of his more-human form. His hair was dark with rain and plastered around his temples, as it had been that day a few weeks and many months earlier. She could see the upward drift of his ears, pointed elfin tips something he would never allow to be visible in her world, but there was enough humanity in him that she smiled.

Smiled, then laughed with dismay as Oisín's words settled in. "You didn't see what happened last time one of Emyr's sons held the staff, Oisín. Dafydd can't do anything to help."

"He could not," the old man agreed serenely, "if he was Emyr's son."

Gongs crashed through the storm's cacophony, dismissing everything else from Lara's hearing. Images, the memory of time gone by, rose in her vision and replayed themselves, making clear things that had gone unnoticed before. Days played out with impossible rapidity, but not so fast that Lara couldn't separate them, couldn't mark details of what happened, and when.

Rhiannon rallied after Níamh's death, after Ioan's birth. Became a little of what she had been before, a bright and beautiful goddess, in love with her son and doting once more on Oisín, the mortal poet who had been her companion for so long. Delighted to find herself with child again, so soon after birthing Ioan.

With child, when Lara was certain that she had not gone again to Emyr's bed. Only her mortal lover had come into Rhiannon's arms, and in all the world, only three of them knew it.

Confrontation, so quick it had slipped by unseen in the greater view of history: Emyr, outraged, threatening Rhiannon; threatening the unborn child. Rhiannon, cool-eyed and not so capricious after all, warning that Annwn itself would come unleashed should she die or should the coming infant be harmed. She already lacked the power to stop his thievery, but she knew of it. She knew of it, and had made her single move against him.

And Oisín, watching, knew that Annwn's footing changed, but not how or why. He would have stayed anyway, even beyond Rhiannon's death, because the land was now his home, and like Rhiannon, it was fond of him. But he stayed for the child, as well, even knowing that Rhiannon's blood would breed true, that there would be no mark of mortality on the bright-haired boy born to a fairy queen and a mortal poet.

Not until the day Dafydd asked if he might have the staff that so reminded Oisín of his mother. Not until the ivory stave had reacted eagerly, images of destruction sluicing through Oisín. Destruction and then temperance, even against the weapon's own desires: the very land whispered a promise that it would not be ruined, not if Rhiannon's younger son wielded the staff against his nominal father. Annwn might be restored, if that battle came to pass.

But not when Dafydd was still little more than a boy, uncertain of his own elfin powers, much less the mortal blood that connected him to a cycle of life in a way no Seelie could ever quite echo. He was ephemeral, capable of choosing a mortal existence, and in that way, didn't belong to Annwn at all. And only those who were *other*, whose magic the staff couldn't subsume, could master.

Dafydd was a dying goddess's last stand against the kings who had taken her power.

Lara shook herself, throwing visions off to gawk at Dafydd, whose expression mirrored her own. When he finally spoke, it was with a child's incomprehension, picking one irrelevant detail out of the mass of information he'd come into: "But Emyr's already dead. Or out for the count, at least."

"Not even a goddess can plan for everything." Oisín gestured to

Lara and the staff. "She awaits you, Dafydd. Together you will master the magic and raise the lands, and Annwn will be restored."

Dafydd looked from Oisín to Lara and back again, then swore. Clearly refusing to give himself time to think, he stalked forward and caught the staff on either side of Lara's hands.

Magic and music erupted around them.

Thirty-six

Lightning spattered, Dafydd's elemental gift seized by the storm. It arced toward the water and the sky, reached for Oisín and the others, and the staff shrieked anger when Dafydd's wordless howl called it back and refused its unleashing upon his friends.

It tried again, throwing forth an impulse to drive ivory into the sand, so it might ground itself and break the world apart. Lara shouted that time, familiar with the desire, and called on a strength she didn't know she had to keep Dafydd from upending the weapon and doing as it asked. "Stop it, stop it, don't listen to it!"

Dafydd bellowed, "I'm not!" but the lie of it was in his voice, and he knew it as well as she did. Lightning flared again, making a cage around them. Triumph surged through the staff and the electrical cage collapsed, dropping close enough to singe Lara's arms before it dissipated under Dafydd's frantic control. "It wants, it wants—"

"It wants to command your magic and destroy the Barrow-lands!" Lara shouted. "Like it did with Ioan's in Boston! But it's *your* magic, Dafydd! Yours, and if you're part mortal, then it can't just take over the way it did with Ioan! You have to let it and so help me God, if you let it, I'll...I'll..."

A completely boyish grin broke through his panic, disarming not only Lara's warning but also the staff's strength, as though it relied on terror to overwhelm him. "You'll what, Miss Jansen?" Dafydd asked with cheery confidentiality. "What threat does a tailor make? Seven at one blow? Will you slay me a giant, then?"

"I'll kick you in the shins." Wet hair was in her mouth, across her face, and the storm screamed around them just as the staff roared impotence in their hands, but Lara laughed as Dafydd looked disappointed. "I'm sorry. It's the best I've got. Now, listen—"

"I am." The laughter was gone from his face, wonder replacing it. "Lara, there's song in the storm. Kettlehead drums and rainsticks and cymbals and—"

"That's its power," she whispered beneath all those instruments and more besides. "You'll be here forever, naming them. But I was talking to the staff. *Listen,*" she said to it again. "You recognize Dafydd's power, don't you? You can't make it do what you want, but it connects you to this world in a way I can't, so if he *lets* you use it, if you let him and me direct you, then you'll have your chance. You want to wreak havoc, we can do it. We can uplift the land and send the ocean back. Changes that will break the world. Those are your choices. Take it or leave it."

Resentment churned through the weapon, but its acquiescence was never in question. Not to Lara, at least; she had carried it long enough now to understand its rage wanted release in whatever manner it could get it. Dafydd, though, raised a startled gaze to her as the staff quieted, readying itself to be used. "How do we direct it?"

"Listen to the song." Lara closed her eyes, reaching for the land's song, so long drowned by the sea and corrupt kings. It lay below the surface fury, below the thrashing music of the storm, below the stirring earth that responded to the lashing waves. Those were mutable, and had been in so many ways mutated, with Emyr and Hafgan remaking the world in their own image.

But beneath that lay the music of the sea and of the sky; of Llyr and Caillech, who had come together to make the child who became Annwn's goddess. That song remembered everything, its notes stretching so far back through time that even now the reverberations were from a tune plucked aeons in the past. That music knew how the land and sea had once been, and how it might yet be again, if the crushing weight of Seelie magic was lifted.

Lara whispered, "Sing to me. Show me the way," and light flew apart from every aspect of the universe.

It was almost like the true path she'd laid down to escape the burning Unseelie city. Almost like the great golden tear through time that had shown them the story of Rhiannon's fall. Almost, and yet entirely unlike either.

Ancient land formations rose as crescendos of music, fixed in place by light that pinned them to the sky. Orchestras drove the waters back, chased by pathways of light and held where they belonged by an archaic sense of rightness. This, Llyr's voice sang to her, this was how the valley once was; this was the land she had walked beneath the waters, gifted with his ability to survive there. This was an image of how it was, a true vision, but not even a truthseeker's magic could unmake the past.

Lara hung on to the staff, hands aching with effort as she held in mind the true landscape, long since drowned. Time fought her, demanding its due: it shot piercing notes through the brilliance holding magic in place. Here and there it won, shattering the way it had been into something new and different. No one and nothing could stop time forever; its ravages would have left their mark whether

Emyr drowned the lands or not. Lara held against it as best she could, clinging with all her failing strength.

And then joy ripped from the staff, pure, undiluted madness, held in check by nothing more than Dafydd's will. The land responded to an influx of familiar power, of Rhiannon's power guided by Rhiannon's blood. Where Lara clung to images of what a drowned land had looked like, the world surged up to fill those memories and gaps with earth, and to drive back the seas. Astonishment rippled through Annwn's song, a sigh of relief that went to the backbone of the world.

Once begun, it went on forever. Rich soil spewed forth, sucking down the salt-laden sand to disperse it deep in the earth, so greenery could grow at the surface. Mountains tore upward, young forests aging rapidly on their slopes. Clouds boiled across the sky and faded, then came again as the atmosphere grew less humid, then more so, then found a balance it was content with. Nothing remained untouched: Lara felt the Unseelie citadel's granite cavern collapse into the earth, and knew meadows stretched to cover the land it had once claimed. Devastation wracked its way across the countryside, reshaping, remaking, rebirthing a world murdered thousands of years in the past. Time was given its free hand to shape Annwn, but all at once, changes coming in a rush instead of gradually.

Lives would be lost to it, Lara thought, and then felt Dafydd's determination that it would not be so. The earth changed beneath their feet; beneath the feet of thousands across the countryside, but never heaved them upward nor clawed them down: that was the limitation Dafydd put on the staff's desires. The land was its to change; the people were his to protect.

The sun was red and raw on the horizon when Annwn's song finally settled again, content with the new shape it had been given. The wrong horizon: it should have set over the water, and instead rose bloody on fresh mountains. Lara dropped to her knees, releasing the staff and staring without comprehension at the sky. Time had passed, but how much she had no idea. Days, months, even years seemed possible, though a wavering hand passed over her clothes suggested they hadn't disintegrated so far as months or years might encourage. That was good. There was some hope, then, that she might return home within her friends' and family's lifetimes, at least to say good-bye. To make certain, if nothing else, that Kelly and Dickon had returned safely, and to see Boston's reconstruction in the wake of the staff's rampage.

"This is more than I might have dreamed." Ioan's whisper wasn't so much unwelcome as jarring, pulling Lara back into the world when she'd hardly been aware of leaving it. The elfin prince had wandered a few feet away and turned slowly, gazing over land that had risen and renewed itself. "I had thought ... the Drowned Lands uplifted, nothing more. I had thought of decades working the soil, returning it to health. I never imagined this kind of gift. Truth-seeker, we owe you everything."

"You owe Dafydd and Rhiannon just as much. Dafydd, the staff ...?" Lara put one hand in the dirt, bracing herself, and heard a quiet upswell of music, contented earth welcoming her. It wouldn't last: she was mortal, but for these few moments, the land itself felt she belonged. Muscles watery with exhaustion, she put her other hand out for the staff.

"It's as tired as we are, I think. That surge of sentience, its de-sires ..." Dafydd shook his head. "It's quiet now. Almost satisfied. Its work is done."

"No. There's one more thing."

"Can't it wait?" Dafydd asked, voice low with concern as he knelt before her. "Merrick is punished for his misdeeds, two conniving kings are put to rest, and the Barr— *Annwn*. Annwn is whole once more. You have done everything, and more, that was asked of you. Can it not wait?"

"No." For all the uplifting song in Dafydd's voice, there was even more resolute truth in Lara's. "I might not ever be connected to my power and this world like this again. It has to be now."

"You're not Seelie," Dafydd whispered. "Mortals who burn themselves out in youth rarely recover, Lara."

Lara took her fingers from the dirt to slide them along his jaw, drawing him close for a kiss. "Some things are worth the risk."

She grasped the staff with her free hand, and went searching for the song she knew lay within it.

Dafydd was right: the staff's magic was as exhausted as they were, lying quiescent even when she brought her power to bear. There was no struggle, no eager leap for domination, only the faintest spark of awareness that said a goddess still lived within the ivory.

True song whispered that she would recover, in time. That the staff would eventually become as dangerous and destructive as it had always been, bent on a revenge it might never have.

Lara, in the depths of that song, whispered, "No."

It was nothing, that denial. In the face of everything she'd tried, everything she'd learned, the one small word was impossibly soft and almost meaningless. There was no pain of harsh truth written in it, hurting her very being in the way forcing others to hear true things had done in the past.

And it was all the more powerful for its gentleness. It lay down a single line of melody, thin and true, which became a thread of light winding its way into the heart of the ivory staff. It picked up notes as it coiled deeper: single instruments taking up the song of Annwn as it had been and as it should be. Sun, earth, sea; together they were the land, and that, too, was Rhiannon's music, reflected here and there within the staff's intricate carvings. Lara sought those similar places, binding notes together to bolster their sound. The pathway she created ran a little ahead of her, intensified enough to shake away calcification and find new elements of music to respond to and grow with.

It went slowly, so slowly. Lara's weariness was mirrored in the staff's passiveness, and the terrible amount of time since Rhiannon's binding handicapped them both even when eagerness might have hastened the journey. But finally the ivory began to shift, carvings growing indistinct, then fading entirely. The staff lost length, turning from a rod to a long shard, then bit by bit shrank to a stained bit of shell stolen from the beach.

Lara smeared her thumb across still-red blood, wiping most of it away, and in the distance, a woman walked free of the sea.

Thirty-seven

Dafydd and Ioan went still as stone. Aerin fell to her knees, and Lara sagged, eyes closed against the astonishing song that accompanied the woman. Viewing Annwn's history hadn't warned her of a music so deep and strong that it connected Rhiannon to all the myriad aspects of the world and universe. Lara had barely touched those herself, and already knew she could never stand against them. Looking at Rhiannon was looking into those secret symphonies, and she lacked the strength to even try just then. Someday, perhaps, but not today. A headache tightened a band around her skull, so mundane that Lara laughed wearily and put her hand over her eyes.

The song lessened abruptly and two fingers touched her under the chin, tilting her head up. Lara frowned upward and met Rhiannon's equally frowning gaze, then climbed to her feet as the white-haired goddess's fingers remained beneath her chin. Sympathy tempered Rhiannon's voice as she said, "Truthseeker and mortal. I can change neither, but let me banish the pain in thanks for your services." She trailed her finger from Lara's chin to her forehead, tapping the latter, then turned away, utterly unconcerned as Lara's headache vanished and she slumped in astonished relief.

Looking at Rhiannon was possible now, the connection she had with Annwn less visible, less loud, though the woman herself was no less stunning. She was much taller than Lara had imagined, towering over the gathered elves. Aerin was closest to her in height, but still dwarfed by a palm's length as Rhiannon, looking youthfully delighted, drew the Seelie woman to her feet.

"Granddaughter," she said with obvious pleasure. "Many-times granddaughter, but I see my look in your bones and feel Annwn's pulse in your blood. This land has not been so badly served, if those such as you still walk it. Who is your master?"

A shiver rose up from Aerin's core, her green eyes wide. "Emyr ap Caerwyn was, lady. He was king over all of us who called ourselves Seelie, but he has proven himself unworthy. The people don't yet know, but I do. Let me be the first to lay my sword at your feet, and the first to bow my head to our goddess returned. Welcome back, my lady. Welcome home."

Rhiannon smiled, so brilliant it could be a blessing in itself, but then her expression fell into such solemnity it suggested a child's transition between joy and abject disappointment. "But you're not carrying a sword."

Aerin knotted fists at her hips, disappointment flashing across her own face. "Then let me be the first when we've returned to the citadel and I'm garbed as a warrior should be."

"Ap Caerwyn. The citadel of white stone," Rhiannon murmured, as if she'd needed more pieces for even Emyr's name to fall into place. Then recognition turned her voice hard: "I remember now."

She turned toward the mountains, lashing a hand out. Space foreshortened, bringing the citadel impossibly near in vision if not in fact. Lara winced, expecting her headache to return, but her vision remained clear as Rhiannon's voice filled the air, musical thunder: "Empty these walls. The city falls."

Towers that had remained standing through the land's upheaval crumbled as she spoke. Within seconds, people fled from the shaking city, rushing out by dozens and hundreds, then trickling away to a handful, and then to none. Rhiannon clenched her fist and pearlescent walls shattered, collapsing in on themselves and turning to dust. It continued for a long time, and when she finally released her fist, all that remained of Emyr's city was a sheen in the air, settling across oak forests already growing up anew.

She turned her palm up, capricious, demanding, and not one among them doubted what she asked for. Lara dropped the shell shards into her hand, and for the second time Rhiannon made a fist, delicate calcium falling between her fingers. "Flame, anathema to my birthplace, come."

Fire burst upward in her hand, searing the disintegrating shells before heat erupted in a contained explosion, utterly destroying the fragile pieces. It spewed from within the ruined citadel as well, a brief flare that sent land flying upward and falling back down in a rain of dirt and roots. Lara gasped, a hand clapped over her mouth, and even the elves surrounding her flinched. Rhiannon, satisfied, flicked the image of the citadel's ruins away and turned a wholly guileless smile on the little group who had unbound her.

"You . . ." Lara swallowed, then tried again. "Was that Emyr and Hafgan?"

"Born of my blood, destroyed as my blood. Never again can it be used against me," Rhiannon said blithely, then tipped her head, once more childlike with curiosity as she examined Ioan and Dafydd. "Born of my body. Must you be destroyed as well?"

"No!" Lara jolted in front of Dafydd, hearing as much panic as truth in her own voice. "None of us knew where we'd end up when this started, but they're mostly responsible for you being free at all. Don't you dare take revenge out on them."

Rhiannon's eyes widened with laughably pure astonishment. "You tell me what I may and may not *dare*?"

"Remember, Rhiannon, that mortals are impetuous. It was what you liked about them. They reminded you of yourself, once upon a time." Oisín stepped forward, gentle humor deepening the lines of his face.

Rhiannon, uncertain, said, "Oh," and then "*Oh*," and put a hand to Oisín's cheek. "My poet. I remember you. You've changed."

Oisín put his hand over hers, smiling. "Time, kind as it may be in Annwn, takes its toll on all mortals. I'm satisfied to stand in your presence once again."

"For a little while." Rhiannon looked crestfallen. "Only for a little while, my poet. I can see the end of your song as I can see the end of our son's."

"What?" Dafydd's voice broke, startled human sound in the one word, and Rhiannon turned to him with compassion tempered by a remoteness not present when she looked at Oisín.

"My blood runs true in you, Dafydd ap Annwn, but Oisín's leaves its mark as well. You cannot be king over this land. That is the price of your blood. But its gift," she said more softly, "is that unlike any other born to Annwn, you may choose a mortal existence, if you so desire. And I think that unlike any other, it may be a choice you are glad of."

She dismissed him that easily, bringing her attention to Ioan. Lara fumbled for Dafydd's hand and found it cool with shock. She drew breath to speak and he shook his head, then glanced toward Rhiannon and Ioan.

Ioan knelt as Lara looked their way, Rhiannon's fingertips light against his forehead. "You might be king in Annwn," she said to him. "Blood of my blood, blood of the land. Do you wish a crown?"

"I've worn one half my life, whether I wished it or not. Annwn doesn't need a king, Mother. It needs its goddess, the life and light of the land. That's what gives us our strength."

Darkness came into Rhiannon's voice: "And, it seems, your ambition."

"I have very few ambitions that are not already met. A family, perhaps." Ioan lifted his eyes to smile briefly at Dafydd and Lara, then returned his attention to Rhiannon. "I would gladly be your steward, if you have no wish to rule Annwn yourself, but I will not wear a crown."

Rhiannon, with more clarity of mind than Lara expected from such an elemental creature, admitted, "I am not meant to rule. To create, to love, to destroy, perhaps, but had I the desire or talent for holding a crown, none should ever have taken it from me. You will do, my son. You will do well in making Annwn what it should be, and should you ever need my guidance, your white-haired witch there can call me through her bond with the land."

She bestowed a smile on Aerin, then offered a hand to Oisín. He took it unerringly, but drew Rhiannon to a stop as they passed Dafydd and Lara. "Worlds come changed at end of day, Truthseeker. You've done well."

"For Annwn, maybe. My world didn't come out of it so well. Rhiannon, your ... majesty? Your ..."

Amusement rushed across Rhiannon's face. "My people call me 'lady,' mortal child."

"Lady," Lara echoed with relief. "My lady, is there anything you can do for my world? For Oisín's world? The staff was used there— you must know that, you were the—" She broke off, unnerved by Rhiannon's wide-eyed gaze. The goddess either had no sense of or no emotional connection to the destruction she had wrought from within her ivory prison, and after a few seconds Lara swallowed and offered the explanation Rhiannon seemed to have no awareness of. "The staff was used there and part of a city was destroyed. I know our world is iron-laden and unfriendly to the Seelie, but..."

Surprise, then slight regret sluiced over Rhiannon's features. "Seelie magic isn't meant to be worked in the mortal world, Truthseeker. Annwn takes from, but never gives to your world. Not willingly." She glanced at Oisín predatorily, then considered the newly risen land, breathing deeply of its rich fresh scent. "But Annwn is renewed, and I am in your debt. Truthseeker, wayfinder, worldbreaker, gatekeeper. For a little while, mortal child, you may stand between this world and yours. Through you, perhaps some of Annwn's health will flow to your broken citadel. It is the best I can do." More, her voice warned: it was *all* she would do. "Do not let the gate be passed through too often, lest the payment be stripped from your bones."

"I won't. Thank you." Lara knuckled her hands against her mouth, swallowing down the feeling of her heart trying to escape a sudden influx of fear and hope, then turned to Oisín. "Come back for a little while, if you can. I have the stories of the Drowned Lands to tell you. I promised them I'd have you write them down."

Fascination lit the old poet's face, and he nodded. "We'll cross paths again, Truthseeker. Stay away from prophets in the meanwhile, if you can."

"I'll try. Take care of yourself, Oisín."

Insult came into Rhiannon's voice. "*I* will take care of him."

Lara grinned, stepping back. "I meant no disrespect."

Rhiannon huffed, a soft offended sound that reminded Lara of Aerin. She smiled as the two ancients, one immortal and the other not, walked past her to fade into the landscape without a whisper of glamour to set Lara's senses awry.

Ioan got to his feet, diffident as he half-looked Dafydd's way. "We have much to do here. Homes to rebuild, old wounds to heal. You will...join us when you're ready?"

"I will." Dafydd put his hand in Lara's again. Aerin watched them a moment before she nodded and walked with Ioan, leaving Lara and Dafydd behind.

"A mortal lifespan," Dafydd said when they were well out of earshot. Like Ioan had with him, he didn't quite look at Lara, nervousness betrayed in the angled glance.

Hope and humor clenched Lara's heart. "That's not really the kind of thing you should decide quickly."

"No. But here, even a mortal life span can be..." Dafydd smiled carefully. "Forever."

"Nearly forever." Lara bit her lower lip, then squeezed Dafydd's hand and faced him, words tumbling in her haste to have them spoken: "I want to go home, Dafydd. She said gatekeeper, and not to abuse it, so I could. We could. For a little while. To see what's happened to Boston and to make sure Kelly and Dickon are all right and to repay that newspaper vendor and maybe to let my mother get to know you. And I'd like to go back to the tailor shop and finish my apprenticeship even if it won't mean anything here, but it's only another year and it'd make me happy and the worldwalking spell could make it so almost no time passes here—"

Dafydd laughed, stopping her rushed speech. "Yes and yes and yes. We have time, Lara. We have so much time. Even in mortal years spent in the mortal world, we have so much time, and if we choose mortal years spent here, we have forever." His grin broadened. "And you know what that means."

A certainty of what he would say burst through Lara and turned to a broad smile of her own. "Don't say it."

"I have to."

"You don't *have* to. I don't like fairy tales."

Dafydd grinned, pulling Lara close. "And yet here you are, participating in one. I believe that means, Truthseeker—"

"Shh. Stop it." Lara put a finger over his lips, though she couldn't stop her burgeoning laughter.

"And it should be you saying it, with the power of prophecy in your voice—"

"I'm not *going* to say it. And if I were even a little bit superstitious, I would say you saying it will jinx it."

"But you are not," Dafydd whispered, and lifted a hand to cup her jaw, to trace her mouth with his thumb before kissing her again, this time soft and lingering and slow. "And so I'll risk it, and you'll hear the truth in my voice, Truthseeker, when I say you and I will live happily," a kiss, "ever," another kiss, and Lara, smiling, whispered the last word with him:

"After."

ABOUT THE AUTHOR

C. E. (Catie) MURPHY is the author of two urban fantasy series (The Walker Papers and The Negotiator Trilogy); The Inheritors' Cycle, which includes *The Queen's Bastard* and *The Pretender's Crown*; and *Truthseeker*. Her hobbies include photography and travel, though she rarely pursues enough of either. She was born and raised in Alaska, and now lives in her ancestral home of Ireland with her family and cats.